"Rice's trademarks are fine writing, a good eye for small detail, and an uncanny way of conveying the mysterious glue that holds families together."—*Kirkus Reviews* (starred review)

PRAISE FOR THE TRANSCENDENT NOVELS OF LUANNE RICE

SILVER BELLS

"Lost souls, found again...Lyrical and lovely: a standout Christmas story."—*Kirkus Reviews*

"Rice's romanticized vision of Manhattan is sharpened by local detail, and her heartwarming Christmas story will please readers who like a nice dose of pathos with their holiday fare."—*Publishers Weekly*

"Book after book, Rice never fails to deliver a beautiful tale full of emotion. This book is destined to become an enchanting Christmas classic for future generations to enjoy for years to come. Stirring and poignant, it is full of hope and love both lost and found. It speaks to the reader of magic, miracles and pursuing your dreams, no matter what the cost. When the hustle and bustle of the holiday season start to get you down, pick up this book and let its magic work wonders as it enlivens your soul."—*The Best Reviews*

DANCE WITH ME

"A return to what the author does best: heartfelt family drama, gracefully written and poignant."—*Kirkus Reviews*

"Once again, Rice captures the wonder of life, warts and all, and puts in a bid for hope. *Dance With Me* is a stellar example of why Rice continues to gain popularity."—*Booklist*

"In *Dance With Me*, Luanne Rice once again shows her ability to craft characters readers can relate to, both in their good and bad times."—*Orlando Sentinel*

"Luanne Rice pens another novel sure to please legions of fans. *Dance With Me* is a good read that sensitively deals with issues like secrets and their impact, aging and loss."
—*Chattanooga Times Free Press*

"Rice, always skilled at drafting complex stories, again reveals her special strength in character development—including all the ancillary personae who round out this tale of love, loss and hope."—*Newark Sunday Star Ledger*

"Readers should...appreciate the strong message about families working earnestly to heal past wounds."—*BookPage*

"I remember Luanne Rice's first novel, *Crazy in Love*, and how struck I was by its honesty; I see that same honesty in *Dance With Me*."—Bookreporter.com

BEACH GIRLS

"Like a milder Northern cousin of *Secrets of the Ya Ya Sisterhood*, Rice's latest celebrates the near mystical persistence of female bonds....Gorgeous descriptions and sensitive characterizations...Few writers evoke summer's translucent days so effortlessly, or better capture the bittersweet ties of family love. Those who can't get to the beach will feel transported there upon opening this book, which will likely be a seaside essential for many readers."
—*Publishers Weekly*

"[A] beautiful and tender love story set against an idyllic backdrop of sand and surf and dealing with many facets of love. Another winner for Rice, who breathes life into poignant tales not only about love but also about forgiveness."—*Booklist*

THE PERFECT SUMMER

"A beautifully crafted novel...Rice's ability to evoke the lyricism of the seaside lifestyle without over-sentimentalizing contemporary issues like adultery, anorexia or white-collar crime is just one of the many gifts that make this a perfect summer read."—*Publishers Weekly* (starred review)

"A loving look at family and the issues that must be faced when a crisis threatens its cohesion."—*Booklist*

"Rice has done it again. *The Perfect Summer* is hard to put down until the last page is turned."—*Sunday Oklahoman*

"If you're into stories that explore human emotions, that delve into different psyches and extol those who manage to triumph over some of life's tragedies, then you'll enjoy *The Perfect Summer*."—*Detroit News & Free Press*

THE SECRET HOUR

"Familiar Rice themes of sisterhood, loss and the healing power of love are spotlighted, but Rice's interest in the human psyche has its dark side as well....The shore scenes, including a cinematic climax...[are] among the novel's strongest. Rice's heartfelt personal tone and the novel's cunningly deranged villain make this a smooth-flowing and fast-paced effort, with justice served all around at the satisfying...conclusion."—*Publishers Weekly*

SAFE HARBOR

"Luanne Rice has a talent for navigating the emotions that range through familial bonds, from love and respect to anger.... A beautiful blend of love and humor, with a little bit of magic thrown in, *Safe Harbor* is Rice's best work to date."
—*Denver Post*

"Irresistible...fast-paced...moving...Through Rice's vivid storytelling, readers can almost smell the sea air. Rice has a gift for creating realistic characters, and the pages fly by as those characters explore the bonds of family while unraveling the mystery."—*Orlando Sentinel*

"Heartwarming and convincing...a meditation on the importance of family ties...buoyed by Rice's evocative prose and her ability to craft intelligent, three-dimensional characters."—*Publishers Weekly*

"Luanne Rice's exploration of the difficult emotional balance between professional success, personal fulfillment and family ties is pure gold. Evocative descriptions add interest to an already compelling tale. Equal parts romance, mystery, and character study...Readers beware: don't start this book at bedtime; you may not sleep at all!" —*Library Journal*

"A story for romantics who have never forgotten their first love."—*Columbia (SC) State*

FIREFLY BEACH

"A beautifully textured summertime read."
—*Publishers Weekly* (starred review)

"Rice does a masterful job of telling this powerful story of love and reconciliation."—*Booklist*

SUMMER LIGHT

"Few...authors are able to portray the complex and contradictory emotions that bind family members as effortlessly as Rice....This poignant tale of love, loss and reconciliation will have readers hitting the bookstores."
—*Publishers Weekly*

"The prolific Rice skillfully blends romance with magic."
—*Booklist*

"Luanne Rice awakens in the reader the excitement of summer and love at first sight in this enjoyable novel."
—*Abilene Reporter-News*

DREAM COUNTRY

"A moving story of love and reunion...an absolute joy to read...I finally put *Dream Country* down at 2 a.m. and almost called in sick the next day to finish it."—*Denver Post*

"Superb...stunning."—*Houston Chronicle*

"Captivating...*Dream Country* will cast a spell on readers."
—*Orlando Sentinel*

"A transcendent story about the power of hope and family love...A compelling plot and nuanced character portrayals contribute to the emotional impact....Rice creates believable dramatic tension."—*Publishers Weekly*

"Engaging...a taut thriller...Rice's descriptive gifts are impressive."—*Minneapolis Star Tribune*

"Highly readable...moving...a well-paced plot...Rice pulls off some clever surprises."—*Pittsburgh Post-Gazette*

FOLLOW THE STARS HOME

"Addictive . . . irresistible."—*People*

"Involving, moving . . . stays with the reader long after the last page is turned."—*Denver Post*

"Uplifting . . . The novel's theme—love's miraculous ability to heal—has the ingredients to warm readers' hearts."
—*Publishers Weekly*

"A moving romance that also illuminates the tangled resentments, ties and allegiances of family life . . . Rice spins a web of three families intertwined by affection and conflict. . . . [She] is a gifted storyteller with a keen sense of both the possibilities and contingencies of life."
—*Brunswick (ME) Times Record*

"Powerhouse author Luanne Rice returns with a novel guaranteed to wrench your emotional heartstrings. Deeply moving and rich with emotion, *Follow the Stars Home* is another of Ms. Rice's classics."—*Romantic Times*

CLOUD NINE

"A tightly paced story that is hard to put down . . . Rice's message remains a powerful one: the strength of precious family ties can ultimately set things right."—*Publishers Weekly*

"One of those rare reading experiences that we always hope for when cracking the cover of a book . . . A joy."
—*Library Journal*

"Elegant . . . Rice hooks the reader on the first page."
—*Hartford Courant*

"A celebration of family and the healing power of love. Poignant and powerful... One of those rare books that refresh and renew the landscape of women's fiction for a new generation of readers."—Jayne Ann Krentz, author of *Sharp Edges*

HOME FIRES

"Exciting, emotional, terrific. What more could you want from a late-summer read?"—*New York Times Book Review*

"Compelling... poignant... riveting."
　　　　　　—*Hartford Advocate*

"Rice makes us believe that healing is possible."
　　　　　　—*Chicago Tribune*

"Good domestic drama is Rice's chosen field, and she knows every acre of it. . . . Rice's home fires burn brighter than most, and leave more than a few smoldering moments to remember."—*Kirkus Reviews*

BLUE MOON

"Brilliant."—*Entertainment Weekly*

"A rare combination of realism and romance."
　　　　　　—*New York Times Book Review*

"Eloquent... A moving and complete tale of the complicated phenomenon we call family."—*People*

STONE HEART

"A highly suspenseful, multilayered [novel] about the complex subtleties that lie beneath the surface of a family."
—*San Francisco Chronicle*

"A joy to read. Luanne Rice has hit her stride as a novelist. The sense of foreboding is almost overpowering."
—*Atlanta Journal-Constitution*

"Deserves a place among the best fiction of its kind, alongside Judith Guest's *Ordinary People* and Sue Miller's *The Good Mother*."—Eileen Goudge

"Powerful ... electrifying ... The contrast between romance and reality is what gives this novel its wonderful, terrifying, always compelling tension."—*Kirkus Reviews*

"Engaging."—*Publishers Weekly*

More Critical Acclaim for
LUANNE RICE

"What a lovely writer Luanne Rice is."—Dominick Dunne

"Ms. Rice shares Anne Tyler's ability to portray offbeat, fey characters winningly."—*Atlanta Journal-Constitution*

"Luanne Rice handles with marvelous insight and sensitivity the complex chemistry of a family that might be the one next door."—Eileen Goudge

"Miss Rice writes as naturally as she breathes."—Brendan Gill

LUANNE RICE

Summer's Child

BANTAM BOOKS

SUMMER'S CHILD
A Bantam Book / June 2005

Published by Bantam Dell
A Division of Random House, Inc.
New York, New York

ISBN 0-553-58762-5

Printed in the United States of America
Published simultaneously in Canada

www.bantamdell.com

OPM   10 9 8 7 6 5 4 3 2 1

To Amelia Onorato

Acknowledgments

Thank you to Irwyn Applebaum, Nita Taublib, Tracy Devine, Betsy Hulsebosch, Cynthia Lasky, Barb Burg, Susan Corcoran, Carolyn Schwartz, Jim Plumeri, Kerri Buckley, and everyone at Bantam Dell for celebrating summer with me; Mia and the BDG; Sarah Walker; Paula Breger; Kim Dorfman and Mika and Alek Glogowski; everyone from the SoundHound sessions: Jeff Berman, Tom Spackman, Frank Cabanach, James von Buelow, Melissa Lord, Teresa Wakabayashi, Lori McCarthy, Melissa Rivera, Michelle Lewy; and the friends I saw in Phoenix: Jocelyn Schmidt, Mary McGrath, George Fisher, Lane Rider, Phil Canterbury, Greg Bresson, and Steve Maddock.

Summer's Child

Prologue

At the time, it was the biggest story in the state. Every newspaper covered it on the front page. Her face was as well known as the governor's—and much more beloved. The excitement in her blue eyes, the enormous smile, the shimmer—yes, that's what it was—the way she positively shimmered with life, radiated goodness. She looked like everyone's favorite sister, best friend, and girl next door, all rolled into one.

The fact that she was pregnant when she disappeared gave the story an extra, terrible jolt. When you looked at her photo, now you saw her joy—as if you were right there with her. You imagined how thrilled she was to be having a baby, and you knew that she would be a wonderful mother. Some people hide their feelings, keep them inside for no one to see—not Mara. She'd never hidden anything. You just looked at her picture and knew—that smile and the brightness in her eyes left no doubt at all.

She was right there, smiling into the camera with the

same degree of love and presence that she brought to everything in her life. *I love you—you know that, don't you? Take the picture so we can save it forever, put it into the baby book and prove how excited we were to know our child was on the way....* Did Mara actually say those words, or were they just a trick of memory?

Being so open requires a sort of innocence. A hope—no, more than a hope...a conviction that the world was safe, that people were good. That life was a gift, and nothing moved except as a positive power. Bad things happened—attacks, violence, crimes—yes, unfortunately they did. But they could always be explained and therefore, eventually, understood—so they wouldn't have to happen again. So the people who did them could be helped, and could change.

Those were Mara's beliefs. Or they had been, back in the days just before her picture appeared on the front page of every paper in Connecticut. She had been an only child; her parents were dead. Perhaps that was why the whole country adopted her, searched for her, and grieved for her as they would have their own daughter, sister, or friend.

The anniversary of her disappearance always brought a new flurry of stories. TV stations ran recaps of old video shots, endless loops of her smiling, waving, holding the yellow watering can and wearing a pair of matching buttercup-yellow rubber rain boots in the garden. Newspapers reran the story every June 21, the anniversary of her disappearance and the longest day of the year, to remind readers of what had captivated the country so many years ago....

On the first night of summer, adorable five-foot-nothing, pregnant-as-could-be Mara Jameson went out to water the garden. Whether she hitched a ride and changed her identity, walked into the hands of a brutal stranger, or was already dead at the hands of her husband has never been known. Her body was never recovered; she was never seen again. No baby was ever born—or at least not with a mother named Mara Jameson listed on the birth certificate. The only clues were the yellow rain boots, left neatly standing next to the trickling hose.

The articles were grave, somber, but oddly wistful. They added up to a life never lived—a mystery never solved. What could have happened that would make her stop watering the garden and walk away? Who could ever forget that smile?

That smile that would never be smiled again....

Chapter 1

Being retired had its pluses. For one thing, it was good to be ruled by the tide tables instead of department shifts and schedules. Patrick Murphy kept the small *Hartford Courant* tide card tacked up by the chart table, but he barely needed it anymore. He swore his body was in sync with the ebb and flow of Silver Bay—he'd be pulled out of bed at the craziest hours, in the middle of the night, at slack tides, prime times to fish the reefs and shoals around the Stone Mill power plant.

Stripers up and down the Connecticut shoreline didn't stand a chance. They hadn't for the two years, seven months, three weeks, and fourteen days since Patrick had retired at the age of forty-three. This was the life. This was *really* the life, he told himself. He had lost the house, but he had the boat, the truck. This was what people worked their whole lives for: to retire to the beach and fish the days away.

He thought of Sandra, what she was missing. They had had a list of dreams they would share after he left the Connecticut State Police: walk the beaches, try every new restaurant in the area, go to the movies, hit the casinos, take the boat out to Block Island and Martha's Vineyard. They were still young—they could have a blast.

A blast, he thought. Now—instead of the fun he had thought they would have together—"blast" made him think of the divorce, with its many shocks and devastations, the terrible ways both lawyers had found to make a shambles of the couple they had once been.

Fishing helped. So did the Yankees—they had snapped their losing streak and just kept on winning. Many the night Patrick combined the two—casting and drifting, listening to John Sterling and Charlie Steiner call the game, cheering for the Yanks to win another as he trolled for stripers, as his boat slipped east on the current.

Other things pulled him out of his bunk too. Dreams with dark tentacles; bad men still on the run after Patrick's best waking efforts to catch them; a lost girl; shocks and attacks and bone-rattling fears that gave new meaning to Things That Go Bump in the Night. Patrick would wake up with a pounding heart, thinking of how terrified she must have been.

Whether she was murdered, dead and buried all these years, or whether something had happened to drive her from her house, her grandmother's rose garden, to someplace so far away she had never been seen again, her fear must have been terrible.

That's the thing he could never get out of his mind.

What fears had Mara Jameson felt? Even now, his imagination grabbed hold of that question and went wild. The case was nine years old, right at the top of his unsolved pile. The paperwork had been his albatross, his constant companion. The case was the rock to Patrick's Sisyphus, and he had never—not even after it promised to ruin his marriage, not even after it made good on that promise, not even now, after retirement—never stopped pushing it up the hill.

Mara's picture. It sat on his desk. He used to keep it right beside his bed—to remind him of what he had to do when he got up. Look for the sweet girl with the heartbreak smile and the laughing eyes. Now he didn't really need the picture. Her face was ingrained into his soul. He knew her expressions by heart, the way other men knew their wives, girlfriends, lovers. . . .

She'd be with him forever, he thought, climbing out of bed at five-thirty A.M. He had only the vaguest idea of what his dream had been—something about blood spatter on the kitchen floor, the spidery neon-blue patterns revealed by the blood-detecting luminol, trickles and drops. . . spelling, in Patrick's dream, the killer's name. But it was in Latin, and Patrick couldn't understand; besides, who could prove she'd been killed when her body had never been found?

He rubbed his eyes, started the coffee, then pulled on shorts and sweatshirt. The morning air felt chilly; a front had passed through last night, violent thunderstorms shaking the rafters, making Flora hide under the bed. The black Lab rubbed up against him now, friendly bright eyes flashing, knowing a boat ride was in their future.

Heading up on deck, he breathed in the salt air. The morning star blazed in the eastern sky, where the just-about-rising sun painted the dark horizon with an orange glow. His thirty-two-foot fishing boat, the *Probable Cause*, rocked in the current. After the divorce, he'd moved on board. Sandra had kept the house on Mill Lane. It had all worked out fine, except now the boatyard was going to be turned into condos. Pretty soon all of New England would be one big townhouse village, complete with dockominiums . . . and Patrick would have to shove off and find a new port.

Hearing footsteps on the gravel, he peered into the boatyard. A shadow was coming across the sandy parking lot; Flora growled. Patrick patted her head, then went down below to get two mugs of coffee. By the time he was back on deck, he saw Flora wagging her tail, eyes on the man standing on the dock. Angelo Nazarena.

"Don't tell me," Patrick said. "You smelled the coffee."

"Nah," Angelo said. "I got up early and saw the paper; I figured you needed company so you wouldn't get drunk or do something really stupid. Longest day of the year's to-morrow, and the articles are starting already. . . ." He held the *Hartford Courant* in one hand, but accepted the heavy blue mug in the other as he stepped aboard.

"I don't drink anymore," Patrick said. He wanted to read the story but didn't—at the same time. "As you well know. Besides, I'm not speaking to you. You're selling my dock."

"Making millions in the bargain," Angelo chuckled. "When my grandfather bought this land, it was considered crap. The wrong side of the railroad bridge, next to a swamp, stinking like clam flats. But he was smart enough to know waterfront is solid gold, and I'm cashing in. Good coffee."

Patrick didn't reply. He was staring at Mara's picture on the front page. It had been taken in her grandmother's rose garden—ten miles from here, at her pretty silver-shingled cottage at Hubbard's Point. The camera had caught the light in her eyes—the thrill, the joy, that secret she always seemed to be holding back. Patrick had the feeling he so often had—that if he leaned close enough, she'd whisper to him, tell him what he so desperately wanted to know....

"These papers really get a lot of mileage out of nothing," Angelo said, shaking his head. "The poor girl's been gone nine years now. She's fish food, we all know that."

"Your Sicilian lineage is showing."

"She's gone, Patrick. She's dead," Angelo said, sharply now. He and Patrick had gone to school together, been altar boys at St. Agnes's together, been best man at each other's wedding. He and Patsy had introduced him to Sandra.

"The husband did it, right?"

"I thought so, for a long time," Patrick said.

"What was his name, though...he had a different last name from Mara...."

"His name is Edward Hunter. Mara had her own career. She kept her own name when she married him."

And now Patrick saw Edward Hunter's handsome charm-boy face, his stockbroker's quick, sharp smile—as wide and bright as Mara's, but without one ounce of her heart, soul, depth, integrity, authenticity, spark.... As a state cop, Patrick had encountered smiles like Edward Hunter's thousands of times. The smiles of men pulled over for speeding on their way home from places they shouldn't have been, the smiles of men at the other end of a domestic violence call—smiling men trying to convince the world they were better than the circumstances made them seem and reminding Patrick that "smile" was really just "slime" spelled sideways.

"Everyone thought so—not just you. But the bastard didn't leave a body behind. So you can't try him, and it's time for you—"

"We could have tried to pull a Richard Crafts," Patrick said, naming Connecticut's infamous killer convicted of murdering his wife, whose body was never found, on the basis of a few fragments of hair and bone discovered in a rented wood chipper. "But we didn't even have enough for that. I couldn't even find enough evidence for that."

"Like I was saying, it's time you moved on."

"Okay, thanks," Patrick said, his expression saying *why didn't I think of that?*, his Irish rising as he faced his friend Angelo—who had brought over the morning paper with Mara's face on the front page, who was about to sell his boat slip right out from under him. Flora had gone for a run around the still-deserted parking lot, and now she leapt back aboard the boat.

"What I mean is..." Angelo said, trying to find the words to fill the hole he'd opened up.

"What you mean is, it's time I got a life, I know," Patrick said, giving his old friend an old-friends glance—the kind of look that tells them they know you better than anyone, that you take their point, that they were right all along, when what you really want is to just shut them up and get them off your case.

"Yeah. To be honest, that's what I mean," Angelo said, chuckling with relief even as Patrick was folding up the newspaper and tossing it through the hatch—purportedly for disposal but actually to save forever.

As he saved all of Mara's pictures.

Because, he thought as he started up the engine and Angelo cast off the lines, as they headed out to the fishing grounds, it was one of the ways he had found to keep her alive. That, and one other way...

The whole world assumed that Mara Jameson and her unborn baby had died all those nine years ago, and they still did. Patrick thought back to his Catholic childhood, that phrase in the Creed: *We believe... in all that is seen and unseen.* It was pretty much impossible to have faith in what you couldn't see. And the world hadn't seen Mara in over nine years.

Backing out of the slip, hitting the bow thrusters, he eased into the channel. The boat chuffed through the deepening water as gray herons watched silently from shadows along the green marshy shore. The rising sun shone through scrub oaks and white pines. Bursts of gold glittered on the water ahead.

The dead never stayed hidden. The earth gave them up, one way or another. Patrick knew they were relentless in their need to be found. The Tibetan Book of the Dead described the hungry ghosts, tormented by unbearable heat, thirst, hunger, weariness, and fear. Their realm seemed familiar to Patrick; having spent his career investigating homicides, he believed that the dead had their own emotions, that they haunted the living until they were found.

And Mara had never been found.

After all the work he'd done on her case, Patrick believed he would know—deep inside his own body—if she were dead. He felt Mara Jameson in his mind, his skin, his heart. He carried her with him every day, and he knew he'd never be able to put her down until he knew for sure what had happened to her. Where she was...

The birds were working up ahead, marking a school of blues just before the red nun buoy. Angelo got the rods ready. Flora stood at Patrick's side, her body pressed against his leg as he hit the throttle and sped toward the fish and tried in vain to escape the thoughts that haunted him wherever he went.

And he knew that when he got back, he'd be ready to write her this year's letter.

Ah, it was about to start again. As it did every year at this time. Just as the last traces of New England's long chill were gone from the air, just as the birds had returned north from their winter's journeys, just as the roses were coming into bloom and the gardens were awash with color, just as summer solstice was upon them, with its gift of the longest day . . . the time had come around again.

Maeve Jameson stood in her garden, pruning. She wore a wide straw hat, white linen shirt, and hot-pink garden gloves. In spite of all the cover-ups, she also wore sunscreen. They hadn't known about sun damage when she was a girl—they had all thought the sun was the great healing force—the more of it the better.

But she'd had a small skin cancer removed from her cheek last year, and was determined to do her best to keep it from happening again, to stay as healthy as she could, to stay alive until she knew the entire truth.

She had always been fastidious about putting lotion on her granddaughter. Mara had had such fair skin—so typically Irish, pale and freckled. Her parents—Mara's, that is—had been killed in a freak ferry accident on a trip to Mara's mother's hometown in the west of Ireland.

Maeve had taken over raising their daughter, their only child; every time she'd ever looked at Mara, she'd seen her son, Billy, and she'd loved her so much, more than the stars in the sky, more than anything—because she was a direct link to her darling boy, and she'd dutifully put sunscreen all over her freckled skin before letting her go down to the beach.

"You have the soul of your father in your blue eyes," Maeve would say, spreading the lotion.

"And my mother?"

"Yes, Anna too," Maeve would say, because she had loved her Irish daughter-in-law almost as if she'd been her own child. But the truth was, Mara had been all-Billy to Maeve. Maeve couldn't help herself.

So now she just stood in her garden, clipping the dead heads from the rosebushes. She tried to concentrate on finding the three-leaf sets, but she was distracted by the two newspeople standing out by the road. They had their cameras out, clicking away. Tomorrow—the anniversary of Mara's disappearance—the headlines would no doubt read, "Grandmother Still Waiting after All These Years" or "Roses for Mara's Remembrance" or some other malarkey.

The local newspeople had always made a cartoon of the situation—tried to boil everything down into an easily palatable story for their readers to understand. When no one knew the whole truth—except Mara. Edward had played his part in the terrible drama, and Maeve knew some segments, but only Mara knew it all.

Only Mara had endured it.

The state police detective had learned some of it. Patrick Murphy, another Hibernian, although not in the tradition of Irish cops that Maeve remembered from growing up in the South End of Hartford. Those fellows had been tough, all steel, no nonsense, and they'd seen the world in black and white. Everything was one way or another. Not Patrick.

Patrick was different. Maeve had taught school for fifty years, and if she had ever had Patrick Murphy in her class, she knew that she would never have pegged him to be a police officer. Not that he hadn't done a thorough investigation—if anyone could find Mara, Maeve knew it would be Patrick. But there was something in his makeup that reminded Maeve of Johnny Moore, an Irish poet she had once known.

She had seen it the day he had come here to Maeve's house, held her hand as they sat in rockers on the porch, and told her about the blood they had found on Mara's kitchen floor. Maeve's heart had frozen. It really had. She had felt her heart freeze and constrict, felt the muscle shrink, pulling all her blood back from her face and hands, so that her head had dropped down on her chest.

And when she'd come to, just a second or two later, Patrick was kneeling in front of her, with tears in his eyes because he was thinking the same thing she had so often feared would happen—that Mara was dead, the baby was dead, that Edward had killed them both.

Maeve had only to think of the tears in Patrick Murphy's blue eyes to feel her heart twist now, again, as she snipped away at the tangled rosebushes. She knew that he would come by—sometime in the next week or so—to check on her.

Maeve held the green plastic-handled garden shears in her pink-gloved hand, clipping her rosebushes. Cutting far enough down, right to the place where new life in the form of tiny green leaves emerged from the stem. Her arthritis was acting up.

She could almost feel the photographers wanting to ask

her to go get the yellow boots and watering can, stage the yard as it had been that day nine years ago tomorrow.

"Hello, Maeve."

Looking up, she saw her neighbor and lifelong best friend, Clara Littlefield, coming through the side yard. Clara carried a wicker picnic basket overflowing with French bread, grapes, Brie, saucisson, and a bottle of wine.

"Hi, Clara," Maeve said. The two women bumped straw hats as they kissed.

"The roses look so beautiful this year," Clara said.

"Thank you ... look at Mara's beach roses—they've really come into their own, haven't they?"

"They have," Clara said, and the two women admired the full bushes, lush with pink blooms, planted by Mara the year her parents drowned. So many years ago, meant to cherish her parents' memory, and now they were all Maeve had of Mara herself. Maeve's eyes filled with tears, and she felt Clara's arm slip around her.

"You brought us a picnic?" Maeve asked.

"Of course. I can't come to stay at your house without bringing food. It's like those sleepovers we had sixty years ago, when we'd take turns providing the s'mores."

"The sleepovers continue," Maeve said, smiling. "No matter how old we are ... "

Clara laughed, hugging her again, almost making Maeve forget the reason for this particular sleepover, this picnic. Every June for the last eight years, Maeve's best friend had come over to stay, to spend the night before that day when Mara put down the green garden hose and yellow watering can, slipped off her yellow boots, and walked out of her grandmother's yard forever.

Forever was such a long time.

But, Maeve thought, holding Clara's hand as they walked into the kitchen to delve into the picnic basket, it went by just a little easier when you had a best friend by your side.

Chapter 2

The two girls had missed the bus, so they walked home from school, kicking a pebble ahead of them on the bumpy road high above the Gulf of St. Lawrence. They took turns. First Jessica would give it a good smack with her sneaker, send it bouncing along. When they caught up to the stone, Rose would take her shot. In between kicks, they walked and talked.

"Favorite color," Rose said.

"Blue. Favorite animal," Jessica said.

"Cats. Favorite book."

"*The Lion, the Witch, and the Wardrobe.*"

"Mine too." Rose laughed as she kicked the pebble and got air, sending it in a long arc down the middle of the road. "Did you see that?"

"Okay, you get the gold medal," Jessica said. "Back to Question Time."

"We've played this before," Rose said. "We already know the answers to all the questions."

"Not *all* the questions," Jessica said mysteriously. "We've only been friends since I moved here in April. I'll bet you don't even know where I'm from."

"Boston," Rose said.

"That's just what we tell people," Jessica said. She had a pretend-scary look on her freckled face. "But there are secrets that even my best friend won't know—*until she asks me...*"

Rose giggled. She and Jessica were almost nine, and it felt delicious to imagine that her new friend had deep dark secrets—and to know that to find out about them, all she had to do was ask. Mulling that over, she walked in silence. Off to the left, the Gulf of St. Lawrence stretched on forever. It was very calm and bright blue, with just the finest of haze spread like a silk scarf over its surface. Rose knew, when she saw haze like that, summer was almost here. She scanned the bay, in search of Nanny...when summer came, so did Nanny.

Jessica mis-kicked the pebble into the weeds, so she started over with a new one. Rose inched a little way down the bank to find the old stone; something made her want to keep it, so she put it in her pocket. By the time she looked up, Jessica had disappeared around the bend. Rose skipped a few steps. When she broke into a run, her heart fluttered like a trapped bird.

"Don't you want to know?" Jessica asked, dribbling the pebble the way she did a soccer ball on the field.

"Sure," Rose said.

"Then ask," Jessica teased. "Go on—I'll give you a clue. Ask me my real name."

"I know it—it's Jessica Taylor."

"Maybe it is, maybe it isn't. Maybe Taylor is my stepfather's name, or maybe we decided to name ourselves after James Taylor. We love his music."

"So do my mother and I!"

"My real father saw him in a concert once. At Tanglewood."

"Your real father?" Rose asked. She wanted to ask more, but something about the look on Jessica's face made her hold back. Stress pulled her eyes tight and made her jaw square. It only lasted a moment, was gone in a flash, but Rose had seen. The words "your real father" slashed between them; Rose felt them in her heart, like another trapped bird.

"The air sure is clean up here," Jessica said, changing the subject as they started walking again. "It's the reason we moved to Cape Hawk, so far from pollution and junk in the air. Or, at least, that's what my mother tells everyone. But maybe..."

"Maybe what?" Rose asked.

"Maybe the real reason we moved here is another scary secret!" Jessica said. She tugged on one of Rose's braids, then pointed up at the mansion on the hill. Deer tracks led through the thick brush, into the pine forest surrounding the great big stone house where the oceanographer lived. "Let's go up there and spy on Captain Hook."

"I don't think that's such a good idea," Rose said, feeling

the strange flutter again. "Considering he's our friend and my mother has her store right next to his office."

"Yes, but that's way down at the dock," Jessica said. "She probably has no idea what goes on inside his big, crazy house. What if he's a mad scientist and we have to save her? What if he's a real pirate, with a name like Captain Hook?"

"His name is Dr. Neill," Rose said. She knew the kids called him Captain Hook, but she never did. Rose knew that people were different, in all sorts of ways. She loved the things she and Dr. Neill had in common, and it made her sad when kids made fun of him. He was so tall and quiet, with that dark hair and deep-set eyes, and a thin mouth that never smiled. Except when he was near Rose and her mother.

"I feel bad that your mother's beautiful shop has to be right next door to him," Jessica said. "Any one-arm guy who spends his life chasing *sharks*..." She shivered. "When the rest of his family is so nice, with their whale-watch boats."

"My birthday party's going to be a whale watch," Rose said.

"I know, I can't wait. Because it's my birthday too."

"No! You're kidding!"

"Maybe I am...and maybe I'm not."

Rose pictured their classroom, with one bulletin board decorated with colorful squares, showing all her classmates' birthdays. Jessica's was in August.

"You *are* kidding," Rose said. "Because it's August 4—right up there on the board."

Jessica smiled. "You caught me. Well, only one of us gets to celebrate on Saturday. You, lucky girl!"

"I just hope Nanny's back by then. She's always here for my birthday."

"Who's Nanny?"

"You'll meet her."

"Will we really see whales?"

"Yes," Rose said. "They come back here every summer. This is their home, just like it's ours."

"Is that why the Neill family is so rich? Because they have all those whale-watching boats?"

"I guess so." Rose's fingers began to feel numb. She felt prickles race across her lips. The road inched upward, toward the eastern curve. Once they got to the top, they could start down. They were almost to the pinnacle.

"My stepfather says whales are just overgrown fish and people who pay good money to see them are suckers. He had an ancestor who got rich from whaling."

"Whales are mammals," Rose said, concentrating on every step. "They breathe air, just like us."

Tall rock cliffs ringed the town—from behind the big white hotel out to headlands jutting into the protected bay, which led into the Gulf of St. Lawrence. The icy Lyndhurst River flowed down, cutting a jagged path through the steep rock and forming a fjord. Rose had learned in school that this whole area had been formed by the Ice Age—that the rocks were from the glacier, and that the river flowing into the bay attracted fish and was the reason this spot was so popular with whales and seals.

"Come on," Jessica said suddenly, grabbing Rose's hand, tugging her toward a deer track leading up to Dr. Neill's house. Rose lifted her eyes. The sturdy Nova Scotia pines seemed to somehow elevate the stone house, hold it up above their branches toward the sky—sunshine glanced off the vast slate roof. She heard songbirds—just back from their long migration to the south—singing in the trees. Even with the glinting sunlight and the birdsong, and the hope of seeing Dr. Neill, the path was just too steep.

"Are you coming?" Jessica prodded.

Rose leaned forward, hands on her knees, resting a little. "Let's go down to my mother's shop instead, okay? She'll give us a snack, and maybe she'll teach you how to needlepoint your initials."

"You're just chicken!" Jessica said. But Rose noticed that Jessica actually looked relieved that they didn't have to go up the dark and spooky hillside. Rose shrugged, pretending to agree. She stayed there, leaning on her knees, conserving her strength.

"Okay, then," Jessica said. "We're soccer players. I'll pass you the ball, and let's see you take it down the field."

Jessica kicked the pebble her way, expecting her to dribble it the way she had. Rose started, but the walk home had been so long, and the trapped-bird feeling was getting worse. She glanced down at her hands, and saw Jessica follow her gaze. Her fingers were blue, and the expression on Jessica's face was pure shock.

"Rose!"

"I'm just cold," Rose said. "That's all."

"But it's hot out!"

Feeling panicked, Rose kicked the stone into the bushes—as if by accident. Jessica whooped with disbelief, then began to run down the hill toward the harbor.

"Come on," she called.

Rose wanted to sit down, but she couldn't bear for Jessica to see. Jessica was her new friend, and she didn't know. . . . *It's all downhill,* she told herself. *I can do it.* . . . She scanned the harbor town, fixed her eyes on her mother's store. Then she took a deep breath and began to walk.

Cape Hawk was not the sort of fishing town lined with elegant houses once occupied by sea captains. Its sidewalks were not of brick and they were not shaded by graceful elms. These wharves were not magnets for long white yachts and the people who sailed them. There was one beautiful hotel and a small campground for travelers. The nicest houses in town were owned by one family, the same people who ran the hotel and owned all the whale-watching boats.

This small northern outpost of Nova Scotia's herring fleet had four roads, called Church Street, School Street, Water Street, and Front Street. Frost heaves kept buckling the sidewalks, and the sea winds were so constant and relentless that only the sturdiest pines and scrub oaks could withstand the battering. No sea captain but one had ever made enough real money from the hard life in these waters to build houses worth commenting on, and he had built three—for himself and his children. That man was Tecumseh Neill.

This particular house, down by the quai, had been built in 1842, after Captain Neill's third voyage around the Horn aboard his ship, the *Pinnacle*. Town legend had it that he had been in pursuit of a single whale during the last years of his life, but three trips previously he had successfully caught whales and sold their oil in New Bedford and Halifax before building his house in Cape Hawk.

Glistening white clapboard with black shutters and a red door, his "downtown" house rose three stories to a widow's walk overlooking the Gulf of St. Lawrence. This structure, like the others he had built, had never left Captain Neill's family, having been passed down through the generations. For two centuries it had been occupied by his descendants, but this generation had split it up and rented it out—the top two floors being apartments, and the ground floor divided in half for commercial space. The house had wide granite steps, a wide front porch with white railings, and a red door.

Once inside the door, visitors stood in a small common space, the front hall. Captain Neill's original chandelier hung over the staircase. Lily Malone, the woman who rented one of the two first-floor stores, had tried to make the center hallway welcoming by hanging needlework done by herself and other women from the town. She had also hung some of her daughter Rose's paintings.

Lily Malone sat in the back of her shop, finishing up the party favors. She had sixteen pink paper bags lined up under her worktable, hidden from view, in case one of the intended recipients happened to wander in. So far today she had had five customers, three of them Nanouk Girls— members of Lily's needlepointing, hanging-out, and support club. She had also received two deliveries of thread and yarn, including the much-sought-after French-Persian wool-silk blend that everyone had to have, in rich, wonderful colors ranging from morning clover to sunset mesa.

Her store, In Stitches, had two big windows overlooking the dock, the whale-watch boats, and Cape Hawk harbor. Needlework was her shop's focus, and she carried threads for embroidery, cross-stitch, and needlepoint, a garden of colors in cotton, silk, wool-silk, French wool, Persian wool, and metallic fibers. The colors were varied and gorgeous— she had twenty-two shades of pink alone: shell pink, sand pink, lollipop pink, dawn pink, geranium pink, old rose pink, sweet-william pink, and many more.

On a symbolic level, she liked the idea of stitching things together, making something beautiful one tiny stitch at a time. On a practical level, it put food on the table. This gorgeous place happened to be about a million miles from absolutely anywhere. The women of the region flocked to her door. Some spent money they didn't even have. Lily let them buy yarn and canvas on credit; she collected big-time in terms of free babysitting and casseroles.

The hotel was also a great boon for business—at least in the summer months. Lily glanced out the window, up the hill. The sprawling, elegant, three-story white building sparkled in the sun, like a citadel of the northlands. The roof was bright red, topped by an ornate cupola emblazed with the name CAPE HAWK INN. Two rambling wings curved outward around perfectly manicured gardens of roses, zinnias, marigolds, larkspur, and hollyhocks. Camille Neill knew how to grow flowers—Lily gave her that.

Just then the school bus rumbled down the wharf. Lily pulled back the lace curtain to watch the last kids get off. She felt a small, almost imperceptible, wash of relief: if the bus was here, it meant Rose was home. It was silly, and she knew it. Rose was almost nine years old, so bright and self-sufficient and constantly reminding Lily that she could take care of herself.

Suddenly the door opened, and two women walked in. They were regular customers, Nanouk Girls. Marlena was local, but Cindy was from Bristol, forty miles away. Lily smiled and waved.

"Hi, Cindy, hi, Marlena," she said. "How are you?"

"Great, Lily," Cindy said. "I finished needlepointing my last dining room chair seat, and I'm finally ready to move on!"

"She's been at this project now for, what—three years?" Marlena asked.

"Did you bring one for me to see?" Lily asked. She kept her ears tuned for the phone to ring—either she or Rose always picked up the phone to call each other after school. Cindy dug into her satchel, pulled out two needlepoint squares—elegant bargello patterns, fine flame stitches done in autumn shades of deep red and gold.

"They match her dining room perfectly," Marlena said.

"They're wonderful," Lily said, examining the perfect stitches. "I remember when you started the first one, in the club. And you did six of them?"

"Eight," Cindy said proudly.

Lily laid the squares out on the desk. They were skewed slightly out of shape, like all needlepoint worked in hand. The canvas was fine, ten-mesh; the very edges, once white, were slightly gray from months of being handled. No matter how carefully a person washed her hands, skin oils transferred to the work and pulled dirt into the yarn.

"I know it's time to wash and block them," Cindy said. "What do you recommend?"

"Horse soap," Lily said, placing a pint jug of equine wash on the desk. "It's gentle and cheap, and it will do the trick. I'm undercutting the tack and feed store."

The women chuckled, and Lily glanced at the telephone—it still hadn't rung. She heard herself explaining how to block the work—get it back into a perfect square after all the pulling exerted on the canvas. Wash it, roll it in a towel to absorb the excess water, work it into shape using a T square, and pin it to the ironing board using stainless steel pins.

Cindy paid for the equine soap, while Marlena browsed through Lily's hand-painted needlework canvases. Lily picked up the phone; she'd make a quick call, just to make sure Rose was okay. But then Marlena leaned over.

"This is wonderful," Marlena said, holding up a canvas depicting a house by the sea, with window boxes cascading with petunias and ivy, and a sailboat in the distance. "Are there more of this series?"

"I sold out," Lily said.

"You do land-office business," Cindy said. "And well deserved. You're the only real needlework place within fifty miles of this godforsaken place, and you do the circle besides.... I swear I'd have left my husband three times over if I didn't have the Nanouk Girls to talk to."

"And I got over mine leaving me for the same reason, talking to all of you," Marlena said, placing the last of Lily's "Home Sweet Home" needlepoint canvases on the counter.

"Are you coming on the cruise?" Lily asked, laughing as she rang up the purchase.

"For Rose? And with everything we have to celebrate? You betcha!"

"We wouldn't miss it," Cindy said.

"See you Saturday, then," Lily said. "At the dock. We've chartered the *Tecumseh II*—the best boat in the fleet."

"Nothing but the best for us Nanouks! See you then!"

The minute they left, Lily reached for the phone and dialed. She got the machine. Rose's recorded voice came on: *Hello, we're not home right now....* As soon as she heard the beep, Lily said, "Rose, are you there? Pick up?" But no one replied.

Footsteps creaked on the front porch. Lily pulled back the white lace curtain expecting to see Dr. Liam Neill, the oceanographer who kept his office across the hall. He was descended from the sea captain, Tecumseh Neill, the house's original owner. Instead of fishing or whaling like the rest of his family, he spent his life researching fish—sharks, specifically. Moody, elusive, the man spent more time with sharks than people—what more needed to be said?

But it was just the FedEx man, dropping something off at Liam's office.

Lily hung up the phone. She sat and picked up her own needlework—the habit had always soothed her—and took a few stitches. Rose might not have heard the phone. She could be outside, feeding her ducks. Or possibly she had gone to someone's house and forgotten to call. There were so many normal explanations....

When the door to her store opened, she turned with a start. It was Jessica. Rose's age but so much taller, standing in the doorway in her blue plaid pants and yellow shirt, her mouth just slightly open, beckoning to Lily.

"What is it, Jessica?" Lily asked, already on her feet. "What's wrong?"

"It's Rose, something's wrong with Rose, she can't walk, her fingers are blue, and she had to sit down!"

"Where is she?"

"She's in the square, by the stone fisherman," Jessica said, and she started to cry, but Lily couldn't stay to comfort her as she ran out of her store as fast as she could.

Rose sat on the wall, leaning against the fisherman statue. The effort to hold her head up was too much, so she rested her forehead on her knees. Her chest felt tight, and every breath made her lungs burn, as if she were drawing air through a straw. Even before Jessica's footsteps faded, Rose heard someone big running over, and staring down at the ground, she could tell by the big heavy boots that it wasn't her mother.

"Rose, your mother's on the way. Your friend just ran to get her."

It was the oceanographer, Dr. Neill; his boots were glittery with fish scales. The sunlight made them look like bits of broken crystal, all bright fire and rainbows. He crouched down, and Rose felt his hand on the back of her head. "You're safe, your mother's on the way. Just relax and try to breathe, okay, sweetheart?"

Rose nodded and opened her mouth, taking in air. She knew the moment would pass, and she would be fine; she always was, but it was alarming when it happened. Her mind raced ahead to what would happen next. She pictured doctors, Boston, the ER. Yes, her day in the ER was coming again, it was. She wasn't even nine yet, but she could almost write her own medical chart.

Dr. Neill touched her forehead. She closed her eyes. His hand felt cool. Now she felt his hand move down to her wrist; she knew he was taking her pulse. Maybe he was scared by what he felt. Rose knew that some people were. She looked up at him. People were scared of him too. They had that in common. He wasn't smiling, but then, this wasn't something to smile about.

Once a teacher had pushed her down so hard, making her lie down even though all Rose needed to do was wait where she was. Another time a girl's mother had panicked and driven her all the way to the clinic in Telford, no matter that Rose told her she shouldn't go there. The oceanographer didn't do any of those things. He seemed very calm, as if he knew that some things couldn't be fixed so easily.

He sat on his heels and held her hand.

She stayed calm. Their eyes stared into each other as she breathed. She didn't even want to blink, but just keep looking into his deep blue eyes. Sharks swam in water as dark as his eyes, but she wasn't scared. He blinked once, twice, but he didn't smile.

"Don't go away," she said.

"I never would," he said.

"I want my mommy."

"She's on the way. Just another minute..."

"I want Nanny."

"We all love Nanny," Liam said. "And she's coming. She gave me a ring this morning, to let me know she's on the way."

"For my birthday?"

Dr. Neill gave a start, and his eyes flashed at the mention of her birthday. His family owned the boats, and in spite of the fact that the party was going to be all girls, Rose wanted him to be aboard. She knew that he didn't usually run the whale-watch boats, but maybe he could make an exception. She wanted to ask him, but she felt too weak.

"Yes, Rose. For your birthday. Just keep your head down. That's my girl. Just breathe."

There were so many things Rose wanted to say; she

wanted to invite him to her party, wanted to ask him if it hurt when he lost his arm, wanted to tell him she was sorry he had had to go to the hospital and have surgeries, the way she did. But she couldn't do it. . . .

Now her mother came—Rose could feel her presence even before she heard or saw her. Her mother came across the square and suddenly was right there—Rose knew before she said a word. The oceanographer kept holding her hand. When he let go, he gave a slight squeeze. Rose squeezed back.

"I'm here, Rose," her mother said.

Rose felt her arms around her shoulders and knew, in a different way, that everything was going to be fine.

"We walked home," Rose said. Her mother held her so lightly, not wanting to press against her heart or lungs. Rose concentrated on breathing, getting oxygen. She stared at Dr. Neill's prosthetic arm, his hand—when he was young, he had had a hook, and the town kids had called him Captain Hook. The mean nickname had stuck. Now she looked down at her own hands. Her slightly clubbed fingertips were still blue, but less so than they had been a few minutes earlier. She was breathing better now and started to push herself up.

"Why don't you stay there for another minute?" Dr. Neill suggested.

"Thank you for helping her," Rose's mother said.

"No problem. I'm glad I was here."

"You knew what to do. . . ."

He didn't reply. Rose glanced up and saw him looking at

her mother—their eyes met for a second, and she saw her mother blush. Maybe because she thought she'd said something stupid. Of course he knew what to do; he'd known Rose all her life. Rose stood up and saw tiny stars.

"I'm better now," Rose said, ignoring the pricks of light.

"Give it another minute," her mother said, but Rose shook her head vehemently.

"I'm fine—and we *don't* need to go to Boston today. We can wait till we're supposed to."

"You missed the bus?" her mother asked, ignoring Rose's mention of Boston.

Rose didn't even have to nod. Her mother knew her so well.

"You could have called me."

Closing her eyes, Rose thought of Jessica. Her new friend didn't know everything, hadn't watched Rose miss every tryout, every team meet, every soccer game. She didn't know that Rose got driven door-to-door—unlike the other kids, who were dropped off at convenient intersections or waypoints.

"You walked the whole way here? From school?"

"Yes," Rose said. Her breath was coming back. Dr. Neill had been standing right there, but suddenly he backed away—as if he didn't want to embarrass Rose further by hearing her mother scold her. Rose looked up, but he had already turned his back. "Mom," she said.

"It's okay, Rose."

"I can still have my party, right?"

"Rose's birthday," Dr. Neill said. "That's a red-letter day if ever there was one."

"Thank you, Liam," her mother murmured, with a funny, bright look in her eyes.

"No problem. Take care, Rose."

"You too," she said, and watched him go. White clouds moved across the blue summer sky, and seagulls circled above the docks. When she looked down, she saw some rainbow fish scales lying on the ground. Very carefully, she put them in her pocket with the first stone she and Jessica had been kicking. He had called her birthday "a red-letter day."

"A man of few words," her mother said, the way she made comments about people she didn't like much or didn't understand.

Rose's shoulder leaned firmly against the stone fisherman. While her mother stared after the oceanographer, Rose lifted her head and looked straight up at the statue's face. He wore a sou'wester and held a lantern aloft, seeming to peer out to sea. Engraved into the base were the names of all the town fishermen lost at sea—this was their monument.

The stone fisherman looked over all the missing, no matter where they were now. He was cut from granite, just like the blue rock cliffs above the town. Rose looked down at her blue fingertips; what if she turned blue all over, cold as stone? What would happen to her mother if she did?

"It's nearly the end of the day," her mother said. "I'll close up early."

Rose nodded. She watched as the oceanographer walked over to his office. He had a few words with Jessica, who was standing on the steps. Then he went inside. Rose's stomach flipped as Jessica came toward her. Their friendship had just changed; no matter what, once someone saw, everything was different.

"Are you okay?" Jessica asked.

"I'm fine," Rose said. "It was no big deal."

"You looked a little like a ghost—pure white."

"I'm better now."

"That's good," Jessica said.

"Would you like a ride home, Jessica?" Rose's mother asked.

Jessica hesitated, seeming to think about it. Rose felt her color rise—was their friendship over before it really started? Was Jessica embarrassed to be with her? Or did it have something to do with Jessica's secrets, the fact that her real name might not really be Jessica Taylor? Could she really be named after that singer, James Taylor? Maybe Jessica's mother liked love songs, like Rose.

"Well, I'm not really supposed to get into cars without asking my mother, but in this case I think it would be okay."

"We'll call your mother first—how's that?" Rose's mother asked.

And they did.

Chapter 3

Driving Jessica home, Lily was actually doing several things at once. Keeping her eye on the narrow road, keeping her eye on Rose, and trying to assess how upset Jessica was by what had happened. Lily glanced in the rearview mirror and smiled.

"Thank you for coming to get me," Lily said. "For thinking so fast."

"She didn't seem to be feeling too good," Jessica said.

"Well, she wasn't. But she's fine now."

"What happened?"

Lily glanced down at Rose. This was the moment Rose always dreaded. Because the town was so small, most people had known her for her whole life. They knew and loved her—and, the thing Rose disliked the most, compensated for her. Lily knew she could answer right now—say something vague and dismissive. Or she could take the direct approach and tell Jessica the truth. But she had learned over time to leave it to Rose. What Rose wanted her friend to know, she would tell.

"I had a spell," Rose said.

"You're under a spell?" Jessica asked, not understanding.

They drove past a few summer cottages and the old mill. The road was shadowed by steeply rising cliffs and tall spruce trees. Lily glanced down at her daughter—her wavy brown hair and gold-flecked green eyes. Lily had to hold herself back from explaining. She watched Rose formulate the words, knowing that once she said them, her friendship with Jessica would change, however slightly.

"Yes," Rose said. "An evil wizard put it on me."

Lily glanced down, taken by surprise.

"He turned your hands blue?"

"Yes. And sometimes makes me dizzy and weak. He attacked my heart."

"Rose..." Lily began.

"Is he real?" Jessica asked, sounding nervous. "Will he put a spell on me? It's Captain Hook, isn't it? I saw him standing there, just before you had to sit down!"

"No, it's not him. He's good," Rose said. "It's someone else. He lives far up the fjord, in a cave in the tallest cliffs, surrounded by straggly old pine trees. Sometimes he turns into a fish hawk. You hear him cawing in the early morning, gliding over the bay in search of sweet little things to eat."

"Rose Malone," Lily said. Her daughter looked up defiantly. She knew that Lily wasn't about to call her a liar in front of her friend; on the other hand, she had to know that Lily couldn't allow Jessica, newly moved to this remote and foreboding part of Canada, to think that there was an evil wizard attacking little girls. The road twisted up the crevasse behind the village, onto a flat stretch overlooking the bay's wide blue expanse.

"I live here," Jessica announced as they pulled up in front of a small white house.

"Jessica, there's not really an evil wizard," Lily said.

"There is," Rose insisted. "And he puts slivers in people's hearts so no one will ever love them. The heart is where love lives."

"Rose, everyone loves you," Lily said, smiling in spite of herself. "So you'd better make up a better story than that."

"Okay, then. He put a spell on my heart that makes all kinds of crazy things happen. He gave me a heart condition."

"But," Jessica said, frowning, "my grandmother has a heart condition—you're too young for that!"

"Even babies can have them. I did as soon as I was born."

"Will I get it?" Jessica asked, the frown deepening.

Now Lily knew she had to step in. "No, you won't," she said. "Rose was born with a heart defect—you can't catch it or anything. She's had all the best treatment, and she's doing great."

"I'm just not supposed to walk home from school," Rose said. "Or do things like that, till I have the last surgery. I'm having it this summer, and afterwards I'm going to be really fine. I'll be able to run and everything."

Just then the front door of her house opened, and a woman stepped onto the porch. She hung back, watching for Jessica to get out of the car. Lily waved. The woman seemed to hesitate—not sure whether to walk over and say hello or not. Lily saw her marshal herself—literally draw herself up taller—and she came toward the car.

Jessica opened the door to get out. Lily felt Rose's anxiety as she watched her friend go. This was the big moment, Lily knew. What would Jessica make of what had happened? Lily wished she could soothe her daughter, assure her that it didn't matter, that Jessica would like her no matter what.

"Thanks for giving Jess a ride home," the woman said.

"It's our pleasure," Lily said. "I'm Lily Malone, by the way—Rose's mom."

"I'm Marisa Taylor—Jessica's mom."

The women smiled, acknowledging that they knew there was much more to both their stories. Something mischievous flashed in Marisa's eyes, and Lily thought she saw a Nanouk Girl in the making. Jessica stood very close to her mother's side, staring through the car window at Rose.

"You like to garden," Lily said. "Your window boxes are beautiful." She gestured at them—pink, white, blue—geraniums, petunias, blue moon verbena, and cascading tendrils of ivy—stark against the whitewashed cottage. Some old, thick-stemmed red roses, carefully pruned and tied to a trellis by the door, were just starting to bloom, tongues of fire in the afternoon sun.

"Thanks," Marisa said. "Yes, I do enjoy it."

"I like your roses," Rose said from the back seat.

"They're my favorite flower," Marisa said. "They have been, ever since I was a little girl. I love your name."

"Thank you." Rose smiled.

"I thought this would be a different growing season from what I'm used to. But seriously, my flowers are blooming as if we were in New England—or even farther south."

"You'll find that we're on an earlier schedule than the rest of Nova Scotia," Lily said. "The Annapolis Current runs just offshore, keeping us much warmer. It's amazing, but that's why your roses are already in bloom. We're at least three weeks ahead of Ingonish, and even Halifax."

"That explains it," Marisa said. Then, crouching down to look through the window, she added, "When Jessica called to say you'd be giving her a ride home, she said that something had happened to Rose. Is everything okay?"

"Rose has a bad heart—like Grandma," Jessica said. Her voice sounded thin, as if she'd been holding it in, and suddenly she started to cry.

"No, honey," Lily said. "What Rose has is different—she was born with heart defects. She's got the best doctors, and in July, right after her birthday, they'll be replacing an old VSD patch." Marisa nodded, as if she knew what Lily was talking about. Lily just kept talking: "We expect it to be her last surgery. Just wait—she'll be running races. . . ."

"Winning them," Rose said.

Jessica shuddered and cried harder. Marisa hugged her, and Lily looked on, feeling helpless. She could feel Rose's friendship dissolving right then and there.

"What happened to your grandma?" Rose asked.

"She … she …" Jessica said.

"She had a heart attack," Marisa said.

"Well, I won't have one," Rose said.

Once again Lily and Marisa's eyes met. The air was full of mothers and grandmothers and sisters who weren't there, yet somehow were. Lily felt the spirit of her own mother, coming to give her strength—she felt it all the time. Overhead, the tall pines rustled in the warm summer wind.

"You know we're counting on you," Lily said, glancing back at her daughter. "To help us celebrate Rose's birthday and give her a good send-off for her surgery. I hope you're both planning to come."

"It's a whale-watch cruise!" Rose said. "It's going to be my friends and the Nanouk Girls."

"The what?" Marisa asked.

"The Nanouk Girls of the Frozen North," Lily said. "After one winter here, you'll understand. We meet to needlepoint, eat, and gripe."

"Sounds divine," Marisa said.

"So you'll come on the cruise?"

"We're in," Marisa said. "Right, Jess?"

Jessica was still crying a little. She was an almost-nine-year-old who had seen a little too much hard truth about what can happen—to her father, to her new best friend. Lily felt a pang in her own heart. She'd been wanting to protect Rose from the hard truths as long as she'd been alive.

"It won't be the same without you," Rose said. "Please

say you'll come, Jessica? Please? I swear, I'm almost normal!"

Almost normal. The words sliced Lily in half, and Marisa saw.

"We'll be there," Marisa said.

Jessica nodded, giving a real smile. She asked her mother if Rose and Lily could come in for a snack, but Marisa acted as if she hadn't heard. Instead she waved, walking Jessica toward the house. Rose pivoted in her seat as they pulled away, watching her friend and Marisa as long as possible, until Lily turned the corner beneath the granite cliffs, driving down the long, steep coast road toward home.

Marisa closed the door behind her, the palm of her hand slick, slipping on the brass knob. She wiped her hands on her jeans, walked into the kitchen to get Jessica her snack. "Can we invite them in?" Jess had asked. Lily had heard, had seen Marisa ignore the question. Staring at the sky, at the hawk flying overhead—an osprey, silver fish in its talons. Looking anywhere but into Lily's eyes. Mother to mother—the unspoken language of life. Lily had seen, and now she would wonder.

"Mom, we're really going to the party?" Jessica asked.

"Yes, you can go." Marisa heard her own voice speaking to Lily: the quick, enthusiastic *We're in*. So when she backed out, her regret would seem sincere.

"So I can pretend it's mine?"

"Honey—"

"I can't even tell my best friend that we have the same birthday!"

"Jess, you know why. People use last names and birthdays and social security numbers to search for other people."

"You mean Ted. Why don't you just say that, instead of pretending that everything is nice and normal? We're hiding from him, not 'people'!"

Marisa took a deep breath. Jessica had been handling the move, and everything associated with it, so well. At first she had been so relieved to get away, she would have gone along with anything. She had taken to their new identities almost as if it were a game. With the help of Susan Cuccio at the Center, they had made up new names, birthdays, and family histories. Jessica had been so helpful with the history part, helping to weave in the real and beloved—her aunt, her first cat, their love of music—with the fictional.

But now, especially as her real birthday drew near, everything changed. Marisa had been fighting depression—finding it hard to stay the course, get up in the morning, do everything she had to do. She had been wavering, wondering whether they had done the right thing, coming up here. No wonder Jessica was upset and confused.

"You're letting me go to Rose's party, but I couldn't go to Paula's back home."

"That was different."

"Because *he's* not here?"

"Sweetheart..."

"Will he ever find us?"

"Let's not worry about Ted," Marisa said. "We've got plenty to do, just taking care of ourselves. Now—peanut butter and jelly, or oatmeal cookies?"

"Cookies and milk. I don't like it here that much, Mom. Except for Rose. She makes being in this cold, rocky place almost okay. Rose is the best, best friend I've ever had. Mom, is she really going to be okay?"

Marisa walked over to the refrigerator and opened the door, so Jessica couldn't see her face, or see her hands shaking. Mystification, it was called...not being straight with your own child, keeping them in the fog.

"Mom, is she?"

Marisa thought of what Lily had said—that Rose had been born with heart defects. That meant multiple. VSD, so that meant ventricular. Aortal as well? She still had her textbooks from nursing school—where were they? If she could put her hands on them, maybe she could learn more about what was happening with Rose. Pediatric cardiac care wasn't her specialty, but at least she could help Jessica understand.

"I want her to be okay," Jessica said, looking up as Marisa set down the milk and cookies.

"I know you do."

"Maybe we could use our secret savings, to pay for an operation and save her life. We have the money, right? Or one of our friends could do it for free?"

Marisa picked up the remote, turned on the TV. They had a satellite—up here, so far from civilization, it was the only game in town. Hundreds of channels, with endless choices. A person could grow old just clicking the remote. She found an Adam Sandler movie she thought Jessica would like and stopped there.

"Mom?"

"Jess, why are you saying that? Rose's mother is taking care of her."

"Okay. Fine. But you didn't see her down by the dock. She practically turned blue, and she couldn't breathe, and I didn't know what to do, and that horrible scary man with the fake hand had to help her!"

"But you did know what to do—you went to get her mother. You stayed calm."

"I did," Jessica agreed, munching her cookie in thoughtful agreement. Then she stopped and looked up. "Like I did when Ted hurt my puppy."

On the screen, Adam Sandler was being hilarious. All over the world, people were watching this movie and laughing. But not this mother and daughter. Marisa was too busy staring at Jessica, noticing the way she said "hurt"—when Ted had killed Tally, not just hurt her.

"I really don't mind that we're hiding. As long as he never finds us, and you never take him back. You know that, right?" Jessica asked.

"I know that," Marisa said.

Jessica nodded, accepting, good daughter that she was. She stared at the TV screen; Marisa felt a slide of guilt for parking her daughter in front of Adam Sandler, wanting to distract her from all the questions. She went to the window and looked out, and as she did she remembered where her textbooks were: boxed up and stashed in the storage unit, along with almost everything else.

Through the trees, down the hill, she saw the wide blue sparkling bay embraced by craggy cliffs and granite headlands. The big white hotel with its long red roof lorded it over the small town—Lily's shop, the whale-watch boats. Marisa knew that although she'd let Jessica go on the birthday cruise, she herself would have to cancel. A woman's club might be a little too dangerous. She blinked into the bright early summer sun, and her eyes stung. In Boston, she knew this would be considered a house with a "million-dollar view." To Marisa, it just felt like somewhere far, far from home.

Because she didn't like feeling that way, and because she knew a way to feel closer to home, she went online. E-mails, her favorite message boards, and a secret chat room—better than cocktails in the afternoon for making everything nice and numb. Intimacy and friendship without the dangers of being found out. Instead though, bypassing her favorites, she went straight to the website for Johns Hopkins, the nursing school she had attended. She typed in her username and password, went straight to cardiac care, and started to read.

Chapter 4

"Sharks, overfishing, and biodiversity," Gerard Lafarge said from the deck of the *Mar IV* as she came toward the pilings.

"Yeah, what about it?" Liam Neill replied, walking along the dock.

"We got a freaking genius in our midst."

"Something tells me you don't mean that in a good way," Liam said with a grin, using his right hand—his good hand—to catch the bow line Gerard threw, looping it around the cleat on the dock, then walking aft to do the same with the stern line.

"Seriously," Gerard said, jumping off his fishing boat to set the spring lines. He was grimy and unshaven from days at sea. The boat rocked in the gentle harbor swells. The smell of fish was strong, and flocks of seagulls swooped down, screaming. "You think articles like that are good for us? We make our living doing the stuff you write about. Mako brings big money at the market. Tastes like swordfish, only sweeter, and without the mercury. You're giving us a bad name."

"First of all, I'm impressed you saw the paper. I didn't know you read oceanographic journals." He might just as well have stopped with "I didn't know you *read*."

"Believe me, this one's making its way around the guys. Let's just say, you caught our attention."

"Second of all, mako sharks aren't endangered, so you're within your legal rights. But it's more a matter of thinking about the future. You overfish now, the species dwindles, and what'll your kids do?"

"You think I want my kids fishing? Shit, I don't want them working this hard, maybe buying it in a winter storm—I'm making all I can now, getting rich off the sea, to send the brats to McGill or Harvard, so they can stay on dry land and support me and Marguerite in our old age."

"Is that why you're going after dolphins now?"

The banter stopped, the look on Gerard's grizzled face turning ice cold. His glance slid to the deck, where his crew was icing the catch. Liam stared at the hacked-off dorsal fin lying in a pile of debris.

"What do you know, Neill?" Gerard barked. "The rest of your family does an honest day's work on the water—while you sit in judgment of us all. I heard what you said to your uncle. You want to stop him from whale-watching, just like you want to stop me from fishing."

"I don't want to stop anyone," Liam said. He continued out the dock, where he met his cousin Jude Neill. Jude had been hosing down the flat-bottom Zodiac, one of the smaller boats in the family's whale-watching fleet. He'd stopped, obviously to listen to Liam and Gerard.

"But you do," Jude said, smiling.

"I do—what?" Liam asked.

"Want to stop us from whale-watching."

"You going to start in on me too?" Liam asked.

"Someone's got to keep you in line," Jude said.

The cousins glared at each other, then broke into grins. Jude stood aside so Liam could climb aboard. Water from the hose splashed his boots. The day was sunny, but in the distance a dark wall of fog was approaching fast.

"See anything today?"

"Five fin whales, a few minkes, a whole lot of dolphins. The crowd was happy."

"That idiot Lafarge had a dolphin dorsal fin right there in the bottom of his boat. He didn't even try to hide it when I walked by."

"Look, I'm sure he didn't catch it on purpose. He long-lines, and there's no helping what you catch that way. What should he do, let the meat go to waste?"

"He shouldn't long-line."

"Truce, okay, cuz? I'm on your side with this one. All the tourists love dolphins—they're good for family business. So you're preaching to the converted. Just don't lecture me on the Marine Mammal Act, and on getting too close to the sweet, cuddly air-breathers. I got you and the patrol boats giving me grief on one side, and on the other I got my customers wanting to get the whales up close and personal on camera, pointing at my less conscientious competitors who practically let them pet the freaking things."

"Yeah, well . . ."

"Remember when you, me, and Connor used to go out, see how close we could get? Connor used to like to put his hand right over the blowhole. . . ."

"He'd say he could feel the warm air."

"No one could get close like Connor," Jude said.

"Nope. No one could," Liam said. The blue bay sparkled; as he squinted into the sun he thought he saw the back of a white whale, a beluga, surface about fifty yards out. Suddenly he remembered being twelve, when Jude was eleven and Connor was nine. Three boys with the whole summer ahead of them . . .

"The kid spoke their language. He spoke whale, that's just a fact. And when I—"

Liam interrupted him. "No human speaks whale. Look, the reason I came down here was to ask you about a charter."

"You want to charter a whale watch? *That's* a first," Jude said, trying to hide his hurt feelings with sarcasm. Liam just let it pass; he wanted to get off the dock, back to his dark office, away from any sightings of the white whale.

"Not me. A birthday charter—for Rose Malone's birthday party."

"Ah, yeah. This Saturday. Lily booked the big boat for the morning. Nine to eleven. Why? What about it?"

"Who's going to be captain?"

"Captain? I don't know. Let's see—sixteen giggling, screaming girls and their mothers? Whoever picks the short straw, I guess. Why?"

"I want you to do me a favor. I want you to captain."

Jude stared at him. One eyebrow dramatically raised, then lowered. He seemed to be waiting for the punch line. When none came, he said, "I never work Saturdays. It's the only single perk I get, owning the fleet, top of the food chain. You know?"

"I'm asking you a favor, Jude," Liam said. "It's important."

"Why?"

"Because you're the best, and because you never flinch, and because you know what to do in a crisis. Rose is going in for surgery soon. I don't think there's going to be a problem—"

"Her mother already told me there's nothing to worry about."

"Good. But still."

Jude squinted. "What are you trying to tell me? Is Rose Malone your secret love child? You did it with Lily? You and Miss Unapproachable 2005 got it on ten years ago and you're suddenly feeling protective?"

Liam shook his head, smiling. If it made Jude feel more like captaining the cruise, he'd let him think what he wanted. People had always speculated about Lily Malone, and because of his history with her, people always wondered.

"Will you do it?"

"Am I looking at liability here? The girl has a problem on board..."

"She won't, I'm sure. The surgery has been planned— it's routine, for her condition. Besides, if you're using the big boat, there's no faster way to get her to the heliport if it's necessary."

"Great. You're making me nervous. Maybe I should cancel."

"You won't. You're not going to ruin Rose's birthday."

"You're an arm-twister, you know that? Some cousin..."

Liam knew then that Jude would captain Rose's birthday party. He waved, walking back down the long dock, toward the town square and its statue of the fisherman— right where he had stood with Rose earlier. He felt a long shiver go down his spine.

The air was getting warmer, making you almost believe you could go swimming. These northern waters were still cold from the winter snows melting up north, filling the rivers, entering the Gulf. But on an early summer day like this, he traveled back in time. He was twelve, and Jude was eleven, and Connor was nine. He could almost believe they were all together. Liam could feel the way they all used to be, back when he still had both arms, back before Connor.

But he had trained himself not to think such thoughts—summer day or not—and he walked past the stone fisherman without even a sideways glance, up the stairs of his office, where he slammed the door shut behind him.

At home, Lily Malone sat on the porch, needlepointing while Rose knelt in the garden. She wore the half-glasses she'd recently started needing—bright pink rims to make the whole idea seem somehow festive instead of quite depressing. Peering over them, she kept one eye on her daughter while trying to be surreptitious about her project. Every year for her daughter's birthday, she had done a needlework square. Of course Rose knew she'd be getting one again this year, but it was part of the fun for Lily to hide it and for Rose to pretend to be surprised.

"Mom, look," Rose said. "The morning glories are coming up. And here—some zinnias. At least, I think that's what they are. The leaves are so tiny."

"Check your map," Lily suggested.

Rose pushed herself up and walked over to the garden shed. Lily watched how slowly she moved. She watched Rose's chest rise and fall, counting her breaths. She checked her color, which was pale, but not too pale—her lips weren't at all blue. Her balance seemed steady—she wasn't dizzy. Over the years, Lily had developed the ability to assess Rose's minute-to-minute health. She wasn't foolproof, but by tuning in to the small things, she felt she had a good sense of what was happening.

"Mom, they *are* the zinnias and morning glories we planted!" Rose said, emerging from the shed with the map they had drawn last month, after tilling the garden's hard earth, mixing it with potting soil, pressing in the tiny seeds.

"That's great, Rose!"

"I'm going to be a horti—how do you say it again?"

"'Horticulturist,'" Lily said, smiling.

"Horticulturist," Rose repeated. "A plant scientist. A morning glory doctor!"

Lily glanced up. So much with Rose harkened back to medicine—because that was what she knew. Doctors, hospitals, tests, procedures, operations...Lily swallowed down the wish that her daughter could have an unfettered experience in the garden—without thinking about doctors.

"The morning glories are going to grow tall," Rose said, kneeling down again, brushing dirt away from their delicate stems, fragile green leaves. "They're going to climb up the trellis, all the way to the sky."

"With bright blue flowers," Lily said.

"I'm just so glad they're up already," Rose said.

"Already?"

Rose nodded. "So I don't have to worry about them, while we're gone. If I hadn't seen them, I might think the seeds hadn't worked. I'll be glad to picture them growing and blooming while I'm in the hospital."

"They grow like crazy," Lily said, smiling, hiding how fierce she felt at that moment. "They go wild all summer, right into September. They'll bloom, all right."

"Will I be home before September?"

"You will, sweetheart. You'll be in the hospital for one, maybe two weeks. You'll have plenty of summer left after we get back."

"Will it be my last surgery?"

"Yes," Lily said. She tried never to lie to Rose about her medical care; not because she wouldn't have done anything to protect her, shield her from the realities of being a cardiac patient, but because Rose always knew... she always knew when her mother was telling a lie, and that just made her worry more. But Lily was almost certain about this—the doctors had assured her that replacing the old patch should be *it*.

Rose crouched down, hands in the earth, pulling out weeds. She had an instinct, knowing what should stay, what should go. She had the innate ability to nurture a flower bed, just like her ancestors. Lily remembered childhood days in the garden, when her mother had told her that gardening was the same as prayer: being quiet, present, and appreciative of nature. The gardening gene was alive and well in Rose.

"How come Jessica's mother didn't want us to go inside, after we dropped her off?"

"Maybe she was busy."

"Jessie says her family has a mystery."

"All families do," Lily said, stitching slowly.

"Does Dr. Neill's?"

"Mmm," Lily said. One mystery was why he hadn't gotten married. Lily had watched him dating a little—a female ichthyologist from Halifax, a divorcée from Sydney. But Liam stayed unattached.

"I like him."

"Hmm."

"You don't, do you?"

"He's my landlord," Lily said. "I like him fine."

"But you don't act as if you like him. And he's our friend!"

"I'll try harder," she said, and her heart caught just slightly.

"I want him to come to my party."

Lily lifted her eyes over the rims of her fuchsia half-glasses. Rose was gazing back gravely—challenge in her green eyes.

"It's *my* party," Rose reminded her.

"I know, but we asked the Nanouk Girls too. We have that no-men rule, you know? We wrote up that charter, and we all signed it—you too, remember? Our gatherings are women only."

"Can't we make an exception? A birthday party exception?"

Lily's lips tightened. She really hated saying no to Rose. Her daughter was the least manipulative child on earth—when she wanted something, she came right out and asked for it. The unspoken words between them had to do with the upcoming surgery. Every request from Rose had a shimmer and a poignancy to it: what if Lily said no, and it was Rose's last request? She shook her head, reminding herself to be a mother—not a doomsday prophet.

"No, Rose. It wouldn't be fair to the other Nanouks. We can save him a slice of birthday cake. Okay?"

"Not okay," Rose said. She kept digging for a while. Then, leaving her pile of weeds on the grass, she walked up the porch stairs. Lily shielded her needlepoint so Rose wouldn't see, but she needn't have bothered. Her daughter walked straight by without even a glance, into the house, screen door banging behind her.

Lily took a deep breath. She thought of her no-lie policy and wondered whether Rose sensed that it had just gone flying out the proverbial window. Because her reasons for not wanting to invite Liam Neill to the party had nothing—or at least very little—to do with the Nanouk Girls' charter.

Nothing, in fact. Lily steadied her hands and just kept stitching. The wide needle slid in and out of the small white squares, one after another, as she tried not to think. There was so much not to think about: her daughter's surgery next week, whether she'd finish her needlepoint before the party, Liam Neill. The warm breeze blew, and the sun beat down on Rose's garden. Lily kept moving the needle, trying to finish the picture.

Rose went to her room. At the back of their one-story house, her window overlooked their yard, the heathery hillside, and the outer curve of the bay. Standing in her doorway, she took a deep breath. She began to move. She was walking, yes, using her feet, but in her mind, she was flying, held aloft by invisible wings, as hard and clear and indestructible as the cicada's wing she'd found in the garden last summer. Circling her room, she touched things—her maple bedpost; the bureau painted by her mother with fish, shells, whales, and dolphins; the books on her shelf; her collection of carved whales. Here she paused, making sure her fingertips brushed each one—whales carved from wood, soapstone, bone.

She felt the whales' power. They were mammals, just like her. They breathed air and raised their children. Now her wings turned into fins. Rose dived under the surface, swimming easily with the whales. She felt the water rush over her body as she swam deeper, deeper . . . she continued to touch everything in her room, all the precious things that reminded her of her life, of her mother.

By the time she reached the wall beside her bed, her eyes were full of salt water. She blinked the tears away, gazing at the eight framed birthday squares. Her mother had made her one for every year of her life. Rose stared at them now:

The first was a country cottage with a black door and pink shutters with four cutout hearts, a garden filled with lilies and roses.

The second was a white baby basket carried over the green countryside by a red-and-yellow hot-air balloon.

The third was a blue station wagon parked among snow-laden pine trees, with four golden-eyed owls hidden in the dark branches.

The fourth was a carousel with whales instead of horses.

The fifth was fish flying through the sky and birds swimming underwater.

The sixth was nighttime, with the spruce tree in their backyard decorated for Christmas, with hearts instead of bulbs, and real stars instead of lights.

The seventh was the same cottage as the first square, but shrunken down to the size of a doll's house ... with a blue door instead of a black door ... and with a hot-air balloon lifting it up, carrying it out to sea.

The eighth showed a group of girls and women, all wearing hats and heavy coats, warming their hands by a fire on the snowy, rocky shoreline while a white whale frolicked in the foreground; there were Rose and her mother, Cindy, Marlena, Nanny, and all the Nanouk Girls of the Frozen North. Rose recognized all the figures except two women off to the side ... her mother had told her that they were her grandmother and great-grandmother.

The ninth ... well, Rose knew that her mother was busy stitching the ninth one right now. Rose closed her eyes, wishing. . . . She knew how terribly much her mother loved her. Even though she was only almost nine, she knew that her mother sometimes hurt with loving her so much. Having such a fragile heart made Rose feel certain things more than normal. Her skin would tingle, as if a cool breeze were starting to blow, and she'd be filled with other people's dreams and words, as if their hearts were talking directly to hers.

Not everyone, but some. Nanny, for instance. Rose had always been able to read Nanny's mind. She could feel her joy and curiosity, her power and strength. And Rose's mother; Rose always knew when her mother was happy or sad, tired or, especially, worried—worried about Rose. Like now, waiting for her surgery, planning the trip to Boston— it was almost all her mother could think about, even with the birthday square to finish and the party to get ready for. But Rose wasn't tuned in to either of them, or even to Jessica, another kindred heart spirit.

Dr. Neill. She couldn't stop thinking of him. It was funny. At bad times, whenever she needed him, there he was. He had knelt with her down by the stone fisherman, holding her hand and letting her know she wasn't alone. Rose knew that if she had a father, that's what he would have done. He would have stayed with her and held her. He would take care of her.

Dr. Neill was so big. He had put his arm around her for a minute, when she was the most scared, when she felt the most unable to breathe. Rose closed her eyes and almost swooned. She wanted a father to hold and love her. All her friends had fathers—even Jessica, whose father was a step-father; it didn't matter.

Rose felt her heart beating through her green T-shirt. She wished and wished for her heart to be whole again. She had a mother who loved her; if only she had a father too. All the birthday squares, all the parties, all the surgeries in the world couldn't do for her what that would do.

Why wouldn't her mother let Dr. Neill come to her party? Even if she didn't like him—and Rose wasn't dumb, she knew that her mother *did* like him, deep down—shouldn't Rose be allowed to invite him anyway? Even though the other kids were scared of his artificial arm, even though they called him Captain Hook, Rose loved him. She knew that if she had a father, he would be just like Dr. Neill.

He would love whales, dolphins, and even sharks. He

would not give up, just because one part of his body didn't work right. And he would always stop, no matter what he was doing, to help a little girl having heart pains at the foot of the stone fisherman.

He would, he would . . .

Chapter 5

Secret Agent's desk was his flying machine. When he sat in his Aeron chair and hunkered down at his Dell laptop, he could be in Anywhere, USA. He could be on the wireless network, sailing on a cruise ship in the Caribbean or the Atlantic or the Indian Ocean for that matter. He could be in Paris, France. Or Akron, Ohio; Hartford, Connecticut; Phoenix, Arizona; or Walla Walla, Washington. He could be in Vancouver or Toronto. He could be at the South Pole. In reality, he was located in Boston's North End, above a café that smelled like espresso all day.

The apartment was small, but no one need know. It could be a penthouse on Park Avenue in Manhattan, a ranch in Montana, a beach house at the Jersey Shore with the Atlantic out one window and Barnegat Bay out another—or maybe a place near South Beach, not far from where that psycho had killed Gianni Versace a few years back. Or it could just be the house-next-door, where he was just a regular guy trying to bring home the bacon and keep everyone happy.

He was hungry. Before getting started, he grabbed a root beer and microwaved two beef burritos. Set the plate down on his desk, booted up, got ready to take off. Really hungry—ate one burrito in three bites. Waited for the machine to stop clicking, logged on. Where to go today? Where should the flying machine touch down this evening? It was Friday night....

His favorite sites: scrolled down the list, looking. He had his ladies' sites, his playtime sites, his sports sites, his business sites. First and foremost in his mind was always the search: he was looking for someone, and he knew the kinds of Internet sites she liked to go. It was a full-time job, trying to find her. But he had other irons in the fire as well; might as well make some money while looking for his girl—the bitch formally known as his wife. Today, looking at the list, he focused on his "doing business" sites. The bank account was getting a little dry. One of his most fruitful and profitable Internet destinations had lately been SpiritTown.com. A fan site for the followers of the band Spirit.

The band was decent musically and popular enough to still be selling out stadiums and arenas twenty years after its first album. It could always be counted on to join all those group lovefests, raising money for good causes. Save the Rainforest, Free the Unjustly Accused, Women's Rights, Peace, all that bleeding-heart liberal stuff. His wife had loved Spirit. Little Miss Save-the-World...

Secret Agent trolled the SpiritTown message boards. The members liked to take their names from Spirit's song titles—so typical, and so easy for him to spot the soft touches. The names practically ensured that they'd give him the money he asked for—PeaceBabe,OneThinDime, Wish23, Love_or_die, LonesomeDaughter...His wife used to occasionally post here as "Aurora," but he had a feeling she'd changed her screen name after their breakup. He hadn't seen Aurora here in a long time....

He took a glance at the list of recent topics—about half the threads were discussions of Spirit music, lyrics, shows, and bootlegs. The rest concerned politics and events of major interest to Spirit fans. This was sad—he actually chuckled as he prepared to start typing. These people were practically begging to be taken—they cared about everyone and everything. "Breast Cancer Awareness," "World Hunger," "Can We Help Kids Who Don't Have Enough?"

He had registered as a member of the site six months earlier, and during that time had posted six thousand times. He had established himself as a huge Spirit fan (not true), a collector of their CDs (not true), a left-leaning Democrat (totally not true), a divorced father of two (partly true). His log-on name, Secret Agent, was taken from one of Spirit's biggest hits, "Spy on You": "I look through your windows, I come through your door / I know why you're hiding, I know what it's for / You're afraid of the world, afraid of its pain / I'm your Secret Agent, I'll make you brave again...."

He wolfed down his second burrito and got ready to

make some money. He clicked the "New Topic" button and typed in the heading "Lost in the Hurricane." His name, Secret Agent, popped up. Then, in the body of the message, he started: "Hey everyone—did you read about that big storm, the first hurricane of the year? Hit South Florida pretty hard. My sister's family lost everything. Everything. Their roof blew off. Jake, my nephew, got hit with window glass—it's a nightmare."

Then he hit "Send." "Your message has been posted" appeared on his screen. He clicked "Return to Forum," then sat back to wait for replies.

Secret Agent was still hungry. He walked into the kitchen, threw two more burritos into the microwave. He predicted that by the time he got back to his desk, he'd have what he wanted. It was the dinner hour, prime time for all the losers—home from work, either single or not in the mood to talk to their loving husbands and wives—to log on and meet up with their friends.

The bell chimed, and he ate standing up at the counter. This way he could stare at his refrigerator door: pictures of his wife and Ellie covered every inch. Individual shots, the two of them, even some with him in the frame—rare, because he didn't like having his picture taken. He wiped the burrito grease from his lips and leaned forward to kiss his wife. The closeness made him mad—he started to feel the heat rise. How dare she leave him—how the hell dare she?

He rinsed his plate and cracked another root beer, cooling off a little. At least he didn't have to worry anymore about wiping out the cookies—the temporary Internet files stored in computers. His nosy wife had figured out how to check up on him. She'd get in there, snoop around, see what he'd been doing online for fun and work.... By the time he headed back to his desk, he had what he needed: five quick responses to Lost in the Hurricane. Secret Agent scrolled down, reading them quickly:

"Secret—that sucks!"

"Hey, man—is your nephew gonna be okay?"

"The roof blew off? Literally?"

"Where's the family going to stay? I read about that hurricane—it's super-bad. Lots of people evacuated, and the ones who didn't go got trapped. Is your nephew badly hurt?"

And then—paydirt:

"Secret Agent—what're friends for? Let's set up a fund on the board. I know everyone will want to help out. You've got a PayRight account—I know, cuz you sent me money for those boots last month. We'll send the contributions to you, you'll give it to your sister."

Secret Agent couldn't help smiling: what a kind bunch of people. His wife had very good taste in bands and message boards. She'd be proud of her online friends, to know they'd risen to this occasion. For that matter, she'd probably be proud of her husband—to think of him caring so much about the people harmed by the hurricane.

"Thanks, man," he typed. "My sister will be really thankful. You guys are great ... let me check with her, to make sure. (She wouldn't want charity.) But I'll try to talk her into it—gotta think of my nephew's medical bills and all...."

Even as he typed, more responses poured in:

"Any sister of Secret Agent is a sister of ours!"

"Your sister has one great brother, you know? I'll be the first—here's $100. Wish it could be more...."

So do I, Secret Agent thought. He scanned the member names popping up on the message board. Looking for Aurora... Where are you? Where did you go? Do you think you can hide forever?

That would be his *real* payoff: finding what was his and bringing it home.

It was Friday evening, and Liam was working late. He spent too much time at the office, he knew. Right now, nearly nine P.M., the sky was still light—summer in the northern latitudes. His mind told him to keep working, but his body was telling him other things. He was hungry and tired, and he felt an old yearning that he'd thought was long dead.

He had piles of data to go through; sharks had been active in local waters this week. Liam logged onto the "Predator Report," a website originally designed to track near-shore sightings or attacks by sharks. Normally it dealt with seals, schools of bluefish and herring, the occasional dolphin or whale. But yesterday a man surfing the break just east of Halifax had reported a great white attacking his board.

Liam read the account—of course the board was yellow.

Shark people referred to yellow surfboards as "yum-yums." Sharks would spot them from below, confusing their oblong shape and pale color with their favorite food—seals. Based on the fourteen-inch radius of the bloody bite mark, Liam figured the shark to be a juvenile great white. He read the account:

"I didn't see anything before the shark hit. He zoomed straight up and hit my board so hard, it sent me into space. I looked down from the air and saw a shark with his head out of the water, my board in his teeth. I landed on his back—smacked into his dorsal fin—at least eighteen inches high. I rolled off, and he turned and bumped me—right in the armpit. The impact tore my wetsuit, and I thought it was all over—but then the shark just went under and disappeared into the waves."

The words had a force all their own: Liam felt he was right there, seeing the shark break the surface, watching that huge dorsal fin rise out of the sea. He closed his eyes; he remembered the first and worst time he'd seen it in person, how the fin had looked like a black sail on the devil's boat. With his eyes shut, the water turned red in his mind . . . and when he opened them, he looked out at Cape Hawk harbor to see the darkness finally falling on the water, spreading over the still surface, making the blood disappear.

Liam took notes, writing down the guy's name and address. He checked his clock—maybe he'd call him, finish his report right now. But it was ten after nine on a Friday, and he decided against it. Not just out of courtesy, but also because he was sick of being the geek who worked all the time, sick of being someone so obsessed with sharks and shark attacks and people who survived predators and people who didn't.

He shut off his computer, stood, and stretched. Turned off the lights, locked the door, walked out of his office into old Tecumseh Neill's grand entry hall. The original chandelier gave off a soft, welcoming light. It bathed the wall hangings—most of them made by Lily, but a couple of paintings done by Rose. Liam stood quietly in the light, staring at the needlework. He felt as if this center hall was the warmest place he knew. *Home is where the heart is*. He read the words on Lily's sampler. How strange it was, to leave work to go home...yet to feel that this hallway—empty except for the few hangings—really *was* where the heart was.

As he stepped outside into the dim twilight, he headed toward his car. Strains of music, haunting and romantic, issued from the family inn. He hesitated, but the band was playing, calling him up there. The kitchen would be closing soon, but he knew he could get something to eat anyway. Besides, he could check up on his cousin, make sure everything was set for Rose's party tomorrow....

He crossed the quiet street, followed the music up the stone steps to the walk that curved across the long, sloping lawn. White Adirondack chairs, arranged in pairs, faced the harbor; people sat in them, enjoying the sunset and the last light, watching the stars come out. An owl streaked across the sky, into the pine forest that rose behind the inn, that sheltered Lily's house above the town.

The inn seemed fairly full for a weekend this early in the summer. A placard advertised Boru, a Celtic band brought in from Prince Edward Island. Standing in the doorway, he listened to the guitar, fiddle, and pipes. His elderly aunt, Camille, swept by on her way into dinner. He faded back, not up for a third degree from the family grande dame.

"What brings you up here? I can't remember the last time I saw you out on a Friday night...."

Liam wheeled around, came face-to-face with Jude's wife, Anne. While Jude oversaw the boats and whale-watch part of the family business, Anne managed the inn. She was equally excellent with people and with numbers, and she kept everything running well in the black. Liam knew their parents and grandparents would be proud. Camille had to grudgingly admit her talents. Camille had never been the same since her husband's death—on a trip to visit a shipbuilder in Ireland for their whale-watch fleet.

"Good band, Anne," he said.

"I've auditioned everyone from here to Quebec," she said. "So many good musicians out there, but there was something about these guys—I hear them play, and I want to fall in love."

Liam laughed. "You and Jude are coming up on your—what is it—twentieth anniversary?"

"And what's wrong with falling in love with my own husband?" she asked. Then, gently punching him in the arm, she added, "I understand that you are responsible for making him work tomorrow—this will be his first Saturday at the helm in I don't know how many years!"

"Well, I just thought someone really experienced should—"

"Captain the birthday cruise?" Anne teased. "You think the nine-year-old girls will mutiny? Or perhaps their mothers..."

Liam pictured Rose sitting in the town square, her head down, trying to get a good breath. His own heart squeezed as he remembered how cold her hand felt in his, the pleading in her eyes. "It's good for him to take the Saturday duty," Liam teased back. "Instead of getting too important for his own good."

"Well, he'd better find plenty of whales for the birthday girl," Anne said. "Or he'll have to answer to me."

"You?"

Anne nodded. "I'll be aboard. I'm a Nanouk Girl, you know."

"Lily's club, right?"

"Oh, we're just a bunch of friends. We all met through Lily and started a sewing circle. But we're all going aboard to celebrate Rose's birthday." At that, Anne's expression grew serious. "We're all worried that it could be—"

"Anne, no—it won't be," Liam said. He heard the echo of her unspoken words: *her last birthday.* Even with the doctors' optimism, laypeople were intimidated by Rose's condition.

"Lily has been so manic lately," Anne said. "Planning the party, making Rose's present, getting Rose ready for the surgery. I'm so glad you thought to ask Jude to captain. Honestly, if it weren't Lily, I wouldn't book the charter at all. The potential for liability, but that's not the main thing. It's just, well, you're a scientist, Liam. Not a doctor, a medical doctor, anyway. But you're a biologist—you must know—what are the chances Rose will survive? Not just this operation—but into adolescence, adulthood?"

"Like you said, I'm not a doctor," he said, his stomach flipping. "But Lily tells me Rose will be fine, so I believe her."

"I know it's serious," Anne said. "Lily tries to accent the positive, whenever possible. She's done such a good job of mainstreaming Rose. But even the name of her condition..."

"Tetralogy of Fallot," Liam said.

"It scares the heck out of me. Sounds like a monster."

"In a way, it is," he said. "Rose was born with a heart with four defects. From the Latin, *tetragonum*—quadrangle. Four."

"God," Anne said, shivering. "Lily is always so matter-of-fact about it. She talks about Rose so openly. Rose's illness is just a part of her life. She wants Rose to have all the fun and opportunities of any other nine-year-old."

"And she should."

"I worry about her, Liam. What would happen if... well, if something happened to Rose. I always remember your mother, after Connor..."

"It's not the same," Liam said sharply.

"No, it's not. At least she still had your father, and you. Lily has no one."

Liam just stood there, listening to the band play. His arm began to tingle—not his right arm, his good limb, but his left, the one that wasn't there anymore. He felt the skin prickling—pins and needles, as if he had just lain on it for too long, as if the feeling were just starting to come back. The band slid into a sweet waltz, and people at the tables got up to dance.

"Lily," Anne began, but Liam interrupted. He turned to face his cousin-in-law, ice in his eyes.

"Lily won't have to face what my mother went through," he said. "I let Connor die, but I won't let Rose."

"Liam! It's not the same! You couldn't have saved Connor—no one could have. That shark really *was* a monster—and you were just a boy, hardly older than your brother."

"Sharks aren't monsters," Liam said. "They're just fish. My brother shouldn't have been in that water. None of us should. . . . Look—I have to go now. Have a good cruise tomorrow. Watch out for Rose, will you?"

"We all will," Anne said, her blue eyes troubled.

Liam turned to walk out. As he strode through the lobby—filled with weekenders in town to enjoy the scenery, the peace, the band—he sensed people giving him a wide berth. He was tall and dark, and he felt the scowl radiating out. People always noticed his prosthesis. He was different, *other*.

"Hook," some kids had called him in high school. "Scar,"

others had whispered, those who'd seen him with his shirt off in gym class, who'd seen the jagged tears. Reconstructive surgery wasn't what it was now, and the fourteen-inch bite radius—the shark had been a juvenile great white, just like the one he'd read about earlier that evening, attacking the surfer east of Halifax—looked like a crater in his flesh. The bite had been so deep, the serrated teeth had nicked three of his ribs.

The funny thing was, as he exited the lobby of the Cape Hawk Hotel, he realized that although he still felt different, it wasn't for the same old reason. It wasn't so much his arm or his scars anymore. They were part of him. No, he felt different because he was so alone. With all this family around him, all he could see were couples, families, here in Cape Hawk for the weekend. Spending time together...

When Anne had said Lily had no one, Liam had felt a stab in his heart. He felt that way himself.

And it was worse than anything.

Chapter 6

The day was brilliant, clear and fine, perfect for the cruise. Rose woke up with the sun. She lay in her bed, watching orange rays come through the pines. They roused every bird in the forest, and suddenly the air was alive with song. She lay still, listening, wondering whether Nanny could hear the birds and know they were singing "Happy Birthday" to Rose. Would Nanny show up for her party? Almost nothing mattered to Rose more. Except for wishing that Dr. Neill would be allowed to join them...

As Rose began to sit up, she felt a tug in her chest. It took her breath away. She lay back down for a few minutes, on her side with knees drawn up, closing her eyes tight. Outside, the birds grew louder, as if more were arriving by the minute. They were migrating north after the long winter. Rose imagined how tired they must be, how fast their tiny hearts were beating.

Once Dr. Neill told her that pine siskins migrated all the way down to South America—birds no bigger than a pinecone! And he said that whales and dolphins migrated down to the Caribbean Sea. If they could do it—fly and swim all that way—then Rose could do it too. All she had to do was stay well enough to have her surgery. One more surgery, and she would be fine.

Sometimes thinking made her feel better—dreams of birds, or of Nanny, or of her birthday. Her best friend Jessica . . . she thought of Jess, joking that they had almost the same birthday. Only why didn't it feel like a joke? To Rose, it had seemed true—and how wonderful that would be, if it was. Very slowly she sat up again, swung her legs over the side of the bed. She looked down at her hand, gripping the mattress. Her condition had left her with slightly clubbed fingers—another way she was different. Today they didn't bother her—it was her birthday, she thought, getting out of bed. The spell had passed. Padding barefoot down the hall, she smelled fresh orange juice.

"Good morning, sweetheart," her mother said. "Happy birthday . . ."

"Thank you. I'm nine now," Rose said, smiling.

Her mother smiled back. She tried not to show that she was checking Rose for symptoms, and Rose, for her part, tried hard not to exhibit any. She knew she should tell her mother that she'd just had a blue spell, but she also knew that might make her mother cancel the party.

But she made it through the once-over, drank her orange juice and ate her cereal, took her vitamin and antibiotic—counting down to the surgery, preventing any possible heart infections that would delay things. Her mother was playing music on the CD player: one of Rose's favorites—"Aurora," by Spirit. It made her happy just to hear the song, and she knew her mother had put it on because she loved it so much.

"Should we save these for the boat?" her mother asked, standing there with several wrapped packages.

Rose rubbed her hands together and bounced in her seat. Her mother's smile widened, as if she were happy just to see Rose so excited. "Do we have to?" Rose asked.

Her mother shook her head. "Not at all, honey. It's your birthday—you can open them all right now."

So Rose did. Her mother had wrapped every package differently—with beautiful papers of pink roses and blue ribbons, of birds flying in formations shaped like hearts. Rose undid the bows, pulled off the paper, and found four new books, a telescope, a diary with a lock and key, and the new needlepoint square.

"Mama," she said, unrolling the canvas. It wasn't framed yet, like the others. Rose felt the square in her hands—the fine meshwork around the edges, the soft field of yarn creating a picture straight from her mother's heart—the latest in the story of Rose's life, to hang on her bedroom wall. "It's beautiful."

"Do you like it?" her mother asked, leaning over, arm across Rose's shoulders.

"I love it," Rose said, gazing at the images of Cape Hawk: the great sweeping bay backed by the tall cliffs and pines, the grand white hotel . . . and in the foreground, two girls—unmistakably Rose and Jessica—riding on the back of a white whale. "Me and my best friend," Rose said.

"Everyone needs a best friend, sweetheart," her mother said.

"Will she come today?"

"Jessica? Her mother said she would. Now, let's get ready. The boat leaves at nine sharp, and we don't want it to leave without the birthday girl."

Rose nodded. While her mother quickly did the dishes, she walked down the hall to her room, to change into her party clothes. She placed the canvas on her bed, staring down at the smiling faces—Rose and her two best friends: one old, one new. Closing her eyes, she stood by the window and wished, wished . . .

Her birthday had always brought many different wishes, most of them secret. In past years she had wished for her father to magically appear in her life, to love her, to want her, to want to be part of their family. She had wished for a grandmother to appear in the garden and make the flowers grow. She had wished for a healthy heart . . . not just so she could run and play, but also so her mother wouldn't have to be so scared, so worried about losing her.

But this year, Rose wished for just two things. They were so, so small—not so very much to ask, considering all the gigantic wishes she had made over the years. Two small, secret wishes . . .

At eight-thirty, Marisa and Jessica drove past the sign NEILL FAMILY WHALE-WATCH CRUISES and into the gravel parking lot. Marisa still hadn't completely stopped looking in her rearview mirror, checking to see that she wasn't being followed. She had chosen this location because it was so remote—the likelihood of Ted stumbling upon them—if he was searching at all—was so very small. But at the same time, she had a secret reason for coming here that would shock him if he ever figured it out.

Her husband's great-grandfather had been a whaler from Canada. And in one of his old photo albums, there had been a picture of the whaling ship—right here at this same dock, in winter—with the snowy cliffs of the fjord rising majestically behind the ice-coated spars. Marisa remembered staring at that picture, thinking it looked like a port at the end of the world. Beautiful, austere, and mysterious.

Now, parking the car, she backed into the spot—so she could see what was coming. She didn't like anyone coming up from behind her.

She had left a man so brutal, he had killed her daughter's puppy—just because she barked at night. Marisa had had to uproot her child, run away from their home, make up pretend birthdays to throw him off the track. She had learned to be careful, always.

Opening her purse, she pulled out a small box.

"Honey, I know we said we would stay completely true to our story, and our new lives, but I couldn't resist this. Happy birthday to you…"

"Mommy!" Jessica said. "It's for me? Can I open it?"

"Yes. Your real birthday is in just a few days. I thought

we would use Rose's party for a secret celebration of our own."

Jessica pulled off the ribbon, tore the paper, and opened the little velvet box. The look in her eyes was worth every minute of trouble they'd been through: sheer and total happiness.

"It's Grammie's ring!"

"That's right, honey. Her nursing school ring..."

"She wore it when she was a Navy nurse, and a pediatric nurse, and a private nurse, right?"

"Yes. You know all the stories. She loved helping people so much, and that's what inspired me to become a nurse too. Maybe it will inspire you."

"So I can help Rose?"

Marisa nodded. She had been up late last night, reading as much as she could about pediatric cardiac care. She didn't know Rose's diagnosis, but from the symptoms she had exhibited and the fact she was scheduled for surgery, she knew that it was serious. Maybe having Marisa's mother's ring would give Jessica a feeling of some control, in the face of her friend's serious illness.

"Mommy, will we get seasick on the boat?"

"No. That's why I got you this bracelet," Marisa said, slipping the elastic circlet over Jess's thin wrist. "The little bead rests against your pulse, and it keeps you from feeling motion sick."

"What about you? Will you wear one?"

Marisa didn't reply, concentrating on getting the bracelet into position.

"Mom, you're coming, aren't you?"

"Honey, I have things to do at home."

"Like what? Sleeping?" The words snapped out before Jessica could call them back—Marisa saw the regret in her eyes.

"Don't say that," Marisa said, but Jess was right; since moving to Cape Hawk, Marisa had spent most of her time lying down. Depression did that to a person: sapped her strength, stole her hopes, made her feel like hiding in the darkness. And when she thought about the causes of her depression—the same reasons that had driven her to uproot herself and Jess, move hundreds of miles away—well, it made her feel so exhausted and helpless, sleep seemed all the more alluring.

"If you're not going, I'm not going," Jess said.

"Jess, it's not the same thing. Rose is your best friend, and she wants you at her party. You've got a nice gift for her, and you made her a beautiful card. Her mother has all her friends, and I don't know anyone . . . besides, I need to clean. You know I've let it get away from me. . . ."

Just then another car drove into the parking lot, horn tooting. It was Lily and Rose, with huge, bright smiles on their faces, hands waving, Rose bouncing in her seat with obvious joy. Marisa's heart skipped a beat, and she felt herself smile—a true smile, from inside. In that very same instant, tears popped into her eyes. She couldn't remember the last time anyone other than Jess had looked genuinely happy to see her.

Lily and Rose got out of their car and came over. Marisa rolled down her window.

"You don't have to wait in the car," Rose said. "We can go on the boat right now!" She grinned through the open window at Jess, who glanced at her mother.

"Please?" Jess whispered.

"You're coming, right?" Rose asked, now looking at Marisa.

"Oh, you have to," Lily said. "We made party favors for everyone—one has your name on it!"

"Mom?" Jessica asked.

Marisa felt the smile—not the one on her face, but the one inside—get bigger. Lily's eyes were bright and shining, staring into hers. Marisa had the strangest feeling—that Lily understood the hesitation she was feeling. For an instant, she wondered whether Lily could read her mind, know what was really going on; she'd been feeling so raw and transparent for so long.

"I can't," Marisa heard herself say, and suddenly tears began to flow as if someone had turned on a water faucet.

Lily reached into the open window and put her hand over Marisa's. Marisa felt electricity flowing right into her skin, and the look in Lily's eyes was sharp and understanding. At that moment, Jessica got out of the car and she and Rose backed away, to look into the souvenir shop windows.

"I'm only guessing," Lily said. "But I think I know."

"I never tell anyone," Marisa said.

"We need to talk," Lily said. "Not now, because of the party. But soon. Look, come on the boat with us. It's just women. Come, for Jessica's sake. She needs to see you strong, enjoying yourself."

"I just don't feel like seeing people...."

Lily smiled. "Is that why you chose this place at the end of the world?"

"How did you guess?"

"I'll tell you another time...right now I have to get on-board the boat, for Rose. Will you come with us?"

Marisa's palms were sweating, but she felt herself nod. Funny, her years of working as a nurse had taught her plenty about dissociation—how people who'd been traumatized could go through the motions of life and barely notice what they were doing. As she gathered her purse, Jessica's present for Rose, and her car keys, she knew that she had been sleepwalking for most of the time they had been in Cape Hawk.

But as she locked the car, and felt Lily take her hand, squeeze it, she knew she was waking up. She wasn't sure she wanted to, but Lily's smile was so bright and real, she thought maybe she'd give it a try.

So together, two mothers and two daughters walked up the gangplank to the *Tecumseh II* and got down to the business of a birthday party.

At eight forty-five sharp, Liam sat in his office, watching Jude check the birthday party aboard the *Tecumseh II*. The dock parking lot filled up with cars, and girls and their mothers walked up the gangway, loaded with wrapped boxes, warm jackets and fleeces, and binoculars—Lily and Rose among them, climbing aboard with another woman and Jessica, the little girl who had come to find him when Rose needed help. Anne Neill ran down the long green hill from the inn, kissing Jude as she climbed on deck.

Liam's stomach jumped. Was it from thinking of the birthday party? Seeing Rose looking so happy? He held in his mind's eye the picture of her yesterday—crouching by the statue, such fear and exhaustion in her big green eyes.

He tried to look away from the whale boat, but found he couldn't. There was Anne standing with Jude, talking, seeming to cajole him, arm around his waist—Liam nearly smiled in spite of himself; his cousin's MO was to take weekends off, no matter what. Anne was just trying to smooth the fact that he was on duty on a Saturday. Liam could see the affection between them, and for some reason that gave his stomach another lurch.

Liam had spent the morning so far tracking various sharks, whales, and dolphins via transmitters attached during catch-and-release programs or ongoing tracking projects. He had lots more data to record, but now that it was nearly nine, he switched his program from the desk computer to his laptop. He could do the work later, from home. Grabbing his sweater and duffel bag, he shut the door behind him.

The crew cast off lines, Jude sounded a long blast from the wheelhouse, and as the *Tecumseh II* pulled away from the dock, the whale-watch cruise got under way. The whole party had gathered on the upper deck, facing seaward. All except Rose. Liam saw her standing in the aft section of the deck, smiling back—at him.

Liam gave her a big wave. He made his way down the pier, past the few fishing boats that hadn't left on the dawn tide. Gerard stood on deck, glaring as Liam walked past. They ignored each other—the battle lines had been drawn the minute Liam had spotted that dolphin fin, sliced off and lying among garbage in the bottom of Gerard's boat.

Climbing into his flat-bottomed Zodiac, Liam started up the Yamaha 150 and backed into the harbor. The *Tecumseh II* had a good head start, but Liam followed in its wake—a pale green swath of foam cutting a trail through the calm blue bay—just like kids in the fairy tale, tracking dropped bread crumbs. The thing was, he could find his way blindfolded. He knew that the whale boat was making for the feeding grounds—the best place to find whales.

Liam told himself he was on a research mission. He had positive transmission from at least seven migrating marine mammals, all scheduled to arrive in Cape Hawk waters sometime today. He had data coming in from a whale shark as well as a great white, not to mention the whales and dolphins that had already arrived from southern waters. He had himself practically convinced that his trip to the feeding grounds had nothing—or at least, very little—to do with Rose Malone's ninth birthday party.

The day was clear and beautiful. He told himself that he could follow the signal for MM122 (marine mammal 122, a nineteen-year-old Beluga whale) and greet her as she returned to her spawning grounds. MM122 was a local favorite, and summer wasn't summer until she arrived. Unlike other whales, she was coming from the north—she migrated in the opposite direction, loving and craving winters of ice and snow and northern lights. He knew by the beeps of her transmitter that she would appear on the scene today; whether it would happen during Rose's birthday cruise, he wasn't positive.

But *if* she showed up, and *if* he picked her up on his laptop, maybe he could radio Jude to send him in the right direction.

He pounded across the water, following the boat. Off in the distance were seven fine spouts—a pod of fin whales, reliably feeding on krill and small fry, detritus churned up by the flume coming down the fjord and upwelling caused by the wave action on the peninsula's west coast. As the *Tecumseh II* neared the whales, a great cry went up on deck—all the girls pointing, sighting the whales, laughing with excitement.

Liam pulled out his laptop, tapped in a password, pulled up the transmission screen. Okay, there it was—MM122. According to his data, she should be in the bay now—out by the headlands, swimming fast toward the feeding grounds. Liam flipped on his radio, called his cousin.

"T-Two, this is your Marine Bio Cuz—do you copy?"

"That's a roger. What are you doing out here?

"Tracking belugas. If you steer due west one hundred meters, you should meet up with MM122 when she comes up for air."

"You're kidding me. You're deigning to share real-live scientific data with us money-grubbing whale watchers?"

"It's a one-shot deal. What are you waiting for? Change course now."

"You got it—and hey, thanks. I think."

Liam didn't even reply. As the big whale boat turned west, Liam gunned the engine, slicing over the *Tecumseh II*'s wake and around her starboard side in a big S. He drove alongside, guiding his cousin to the spot where MM122 was most likely to surface. One eye on the water ahead, one on his laptop, Liam slowed down. He heard the waves lapping the sides of his inflatable, as well as the disappointed voices of the girls and their mothers. They had seen the whales feeding—now about two hundred yards behind— and couldn't understand why the boat was turning away.

As the boats slapped over the small waves, Liam glanced up on deck. Rose and her mother were standing at the rail with several others. Lily had her arm around Rose's shoulders. She stared straight ahead—not back at the whales— as if she was ready for whatever would surface in her path. The morning sun hit her dark hair, making it look as sleek and glossy as a seal. Liam nearly couldn't look away, but he had to glance at his computer screen.

He saw that the depth of MM122 had changed; the whale was coming up for air.

"Rose," he called.

She looked down from the deck, shielding her eyes against the sun. She waved, seeming excited to see him. Lily looked down now, not even taking her arm off Rose's shoulders to wave or block the sun from her eyes. She just squinted hard, looking straight at Liam and sending a depth charge into his heart.

"Dead ahead," he said, letting go of the steering wheel to point with his good arm. Lily didn't ask questions, and if she had any doubts, they didn't show. For some reason she just trusted what he was saying to her—without even knowing why, and it was that fact more than anything that moved Liam to the core. He watched Lily shepherd Rose toward the bow, away from the other mothers and daughters. The *Tecumseh II* was fitted specially for observation, with a bow pulpit that extended ten feet over the open water. Lily held tight to the stainless steel rail and guided Rose straight out.

Liam gave Jude the signal, and he throttled back. The two boats waited, their engines idling in near silence. Liam's heart pounded with anticipation, scanning the open water. He imagined Jude doing the same thing. They had whale-watching in their blood; back when they were Rose's age, they would do this for fun, every day, every year, competing for who would see the whale first. Connor always won.

This time, Liam felt her before he saw her. Maybe it was the tension coming from Lily and Rose—he saw them gazing intently, their muscles tight, their eyes alert. Liam felt their energy—or was it that of the old whale, having made her mystical journey home, south from the frozen sea at the very top of the world, yet again?

What had she encountered along the way? What sharks

had she dodged? What ice had she broken with her dorsal ridge, needing to breathe just as vitally as Liam himself? What fishing nets had she avoided? She was old now, and Liam had the passionate wish that he could understand her will to keep living, her desire to return again and again to this bay where she had been born. She was here—he felt it.

"Nanny!" Rose cried out.

And there she was: the white whale, the St. Lawrence beluga. She surfaced glinting brilliantly in the sun, white as ice, lifting her head as if to survey her surroundings. Four meters long, pure white, with no dorsal fin, but a thick dorsal ridge, running the length of her back. Her spout shot three feet in the air—hardly visible, compared to other whales. Liam heard her breathe once, twice. He wondered whether Rose and Lily could hear, all the way up on the big boat; he wished they were in his Zodiac; he wanted Rose to feel Nanny's great life force.

Just then he caught Lily's eye. Rose was still staring down at Nanny, reaching both her arms out, as if she could somehow embrace the old whale, take hold of her and go for a ride. But Lily stared at Liam. Her eyes were so big and round, wide with both wonder and something hidden, a shock of pain, he'd always thought, that she carried with her all the time. It was Rose, he thought . . . loving her girl so much. Living with all that worry.

"She's going to be fine," Liam said out loud, looking straight at her.

Lily cocked her head. Of course she couldn't hear over

the low engine noise, or the excitement of everyone at Rose's party. He saw her mouth the word "What?"

The wind blew his hair into his eyes, and he had to let go of the wheel to brush it back. He didn't want to break eye contact with Lily. But in the instant he looked away, he heard Nanny take one deep breath and then sound. After up to ten breaths at the surface, she'd be down below for about fifteen minutes. Lily and Rose had turned away, inching down the bow pulpit, joining the others on deck.

Liam had done what he'd set out to do. He knew the party would go on without him. Revving his engine to return to the dock, he heard voices rising.

"Thank you, Dr. Neill!" Rose called. "For taking us to Nanny!"

"Happy birthday, Rose," he called back.

Lily didn't say anything, but she was staring at him again, those huge eyes so full of questions. He knew they had nothing to do with him, but he wanted to answer them anyway. He gazed back at her, letting certain realities shimmer between them. Rose had a big surgery ahead of her next week. This was her ninth birthday. Lily was as fierce as a mama bear, and she'd do anything to make sure her daughter stayed safe.

Liam and she were cut from the same cloth—he knew it. He had taken them to Nanny because it was Rose's heart's desire, and because he wanted Nanny's power to flow into her, take hold of her, fix her heart so she would live long. He was a scientist—he had gone to McGill University, and then to graduate school at the Marine Biological Lab in Woods

Hole, Massachusetts. But he was also born by this northern bay and knew the force and magic that came from nature, from things unknown and unseen.

Just then another boat steamed away from the dock—it was Gerard Lafarge, coming closer to see what everyone was looking at. Liam's blood felt cold in his veins. He felt danger coming from the man—he knew that anyone who would do what he'd done to the dolphin would hurt other unprotected creatures. Liam kept the Zodiac between Lafarge's boat and Nanny; but even more so, between Lafarge and Lily and Rose. He saw Lafarge pick up his binoculars and train them on the white whale. Then he put them down and looked over at Lily—just stared at her for a long time.

Turning his boat around, Liam made a wide circle around the *Tecumseh II*, not unlike the way a male osprey will circle the nest, keeping an eye on things before flying off to fish. Liam's laptop was blinking with all the marine mammals returning from their long migration home, but for the moment Liam ignored them, driving his boat in wide, slow circles, just doing his job while his heart beat faster and faster.

Chapter 7

They had come from all over, some driving a hundred miles, to gather together, to celebrate Rose Malone's ninth birthday. There were mothers and daughters, sisters, aunts, grandmothers, old friends, and new friends. Over the years, they had met in some pretty odd places—starting with In Stitches, Lily's needlework shop on the harbor, where their club had been born. They had met at the inn, people's homes, the visitors' lounge at the hospital, and, one summer evening, in a sunken garden. But this was the first time the Nanouk Girls of the Frozen North had ever met at a birthday party on a boat.

Rose sat right in the middle of the circle, Jessica by her side. The other young girls pushed in close, to watch her open her presents, and the older women stood back slightly, watching and talking. Lily felt her own heart beating, steady, steady. . . . She gazed at the daughter she loved so much and thought of every single birthday she'd ever had. They had streaked by, faster than a comet.

It touched Lily to see Rose surrounded by so much love. Every single person in the room cared about her and would be rooting for her when they went to Boston. The sound of Liam's engine came through the open windows; it kicked Lily's heartbeat up a beat, but she stayed focused on the girls and women inside the cabin: the Nanouks. Glancing around the circle, Lily knew every woman but Marisa so well. She knew all—or almost all—the thrills, joys, heartaches, sorrows that had made her friends the amazing women they were. This moment of celebration belied so much; life went on, it always would, but Lily knew how important it was to stop for moments like this.

Rose opened her packages—she got books, a watercolor set, modeling clay, a silver bracelet, a wallet, two CDs, and a sweatshirt with a beluga whale on the front. Lily could almost feel her daughter's delight. Sometimes it was as if they had one skin; was it because Rose had been sick for so long, or were all mothers wired into their children? But Lily just felt the joy pouring through her, straight from Rose.

Just then, the loudspeaker crackled, and Jude's voice filled the room: "Calling the birthday girl...you and your friends are wanted on deck. We have a few lessons for you, regarding *les baleines*...."

"That means 'whales'!" Rose translated for Jessica.

But several of her friends were French Canadian, and Lily knew Jude had said it for them. She loved the Neill men's kindness, and she was grateful her daughter—who had never even known her father—could experience it.

As the girls went out on deck, Lily glanced at Marisa. Lily had started the Nanouk Girls out of a very personal, secret need; she recognized the exact same thing in Marisa.

"Fine party, Lil," Anne said, coming over to where Lily stood by the window.

"She's having a great time," Lily said, watching Rose laugh with her friends as Jude gathered them on deck.

"It didn't hurt that Nanny showed up."

"How did that happen? It was almost as if Jude and Liam got together and planned it."

"It wasn't Jude," Anne said.

"Well, Liam then. He's always tracking something on his computer. I walk past his office and see it blinking, hear it beeping...."

"He spends too much time with sea creatures," Anne said. "And not enough with humans."

"I'd spend time with him," Marlena said, walking over with a glass of punch. "If I hadn't sworn off men forever."

"Oh, c'mon now," Anne said. "You don't mean that. Just because Arthur was a louse doesn't mean all men are."

"Hey, I know you're married to a great guy, but when my Barbara was just five, her father up and left, moved in with a whole other family, forgot all about us. So I don't know about all men, but I do know about one bad one...."

Marisa stood off to the side, as if wondering whether she should join in. Lily smiled, drawing her closer, knowing that this was what Marisa had come for, whether she knew it or not.

"She missed her father so much," Marlena continued. "She'd work herself into a fever, crying every night. I'd read her a bedtime story, and any time there was a daddy in it, she'd be just inconsolable. She'd fall asleep and dream about her father, and then wake up crying so hard she couldn't get back to sleep. I had to keep her home from school a couple of days, because she was so tired."

"Do you think children can literally get sick from missing their fathers?" Cindy asked.

"Depends on the children," Jodie said.

"No, depends on the fathers," Marlena said. "When they don't care enough to be a part of the kids' lives..."

"Come on," Suzanne said, smiling. "You're not still that bitter, are you?"

"Trying not to be," Marlena said. "I'm working through it, as they say."

"Just don't let it eat you up, honey," Doreen said.

Lily listened with interest, but more for Marisa's sake than anything else. She had spent long hours with her own demons, many years ago. The Nanouk Girls had helped her exorcise them for good.

"I'd like it to eat him up," Marlena said. "Maybe a nice big shark. If Dr. Neill could find a white whale for Rosie, maybe he could find a nice big great white for Arthur."

"Don't joke about sharks with Liam," Anne said quietly. Even as she spoke, Lily turned slowly, to look out the window. She saw the Zodiac moving in wide, slow circles ound the whale boat. Liam was tall and rangy, and at the wheel of his boat he hunched his shoulders. His hair was dark brown, but where it waved slightly, it glinted silver.

Lily stared out the window, watching Liam. There was another boat out there too. She squinted to see—Gerard Lafarge's. There was something in his manner—his cockiness, the entitled way he walked around—that Lily didn't like. Gerard was watching Nanny with binoculars, and the sight gave Lily a chill.

"No," Lily echoed. "Don't mention sharks in front of Liam—after what happened to him and his brother."

"And Jude," Anne said. "My husband was there too. They've never gotten over it, and I'm sure they never will."

"Some things are too terrible to get over," Marisa said.

Everyone turned and looked at her. Lily had introduced her when they first came aboard, and she knew they were all curious. But Marisa, as if she already regretted her words, was backing off, turning away. Lily glanced casually back at Gerard, and was relieved to see him turn around, driving the boat out to sea.

"Marisa, wait," Anne said. "Come talk with us."

"Yes—while the girls are on deck, tell us a little about yourself," Cindy said. "What brings you to Cape Hawk? Is your husband a fisherman? Or oceanographer?"

"I'm . . . um, I'm divorced," Marisa said. Lily's full attention was on her now, and she seemed very uncomfortable—not quite embarrassed, but more as if she were safeguarding a secret and didn't want to let any details out. Lily knew the dynamic so well.

"Only three things would bring a person way up here," Alison said. "Family in the area, an insane love of nature, or escape from a bad marriage."

From the way Marisa reddened, Lily thought Alison had guessed one of the reasons.

"When you said 'some things are too terrible to get over,'" Marlena said, "I thought—yep. Betrayal, beatings, and behaving like a four-year-old. The big three."

"I can't," Marisa began.

"The girls are outside," Anne said. "They won't hear."

Lily edged closer to Marisa. She wanted to explain—or at least to give her the sense—that the group wasn't about gossip. They didn't need to know the gory details of each other's lives.

"We're far from home, some of us," Lily said. "We've become each other's sisters."

"I have a sister," Marisa said, her eyes starting to glitter. "Who I haven't talked to in so long..."

"Do you miss her?" Lily asked.

"More than you can imagine."

"Why can't you call her?"

"Because he might have her phones tapped. He said he'd never—never—let us go."

"But you got away."

"We did," Marisa stammered. "But instead, we feel trapped."

"Because you're afraid?"

"That, and other things . . . we can't move freely. Can't be ourselves . . ."

"It passes," Lily said.

"I feel so lonely up here sometimes."

"You have us now," Cindy said. "We just met you, but we're your friends. We're glad you're here, Marisa."

Marisa tried to smile, but she couldn't quite. Sensing that it was all too much for her, Lily took her elbow. "Let's get some punch, okay?" she said, leading Marisa toward the buffet table.

It seemed so casual, two women pouring paper cups of pink punch, taking small plates of cut-up cheese and fruit. Jude's voice drifted in the open window, explaining to the girls about how baleen whales were filter feeders, eating four to five metric tons of krill a day, the weight of an adult elephant. The Nanouks were still talking, some of them embroidering or needlepointing as the stories poured out.

"When you said you were lonely," Lily said, "you meant for him, didn't you?"

"Him?" Marisa asked, looking shocked.

"Your husband. Or ex-husband—that's right, you said you were divorced. Is he Jessica's father?"

"He's her stepfather," Marisa said, the glass of pink punch halfway to her lips.

"You finally left him . . . it took so much courage. You're lonely for the dreams you had. The love you believed, right down till the last day, that was in him."

"How do you know?" Marisa whispered.

"I could be a fortune teller," Lily said quietly. "When it

comes to this. Let me see. You loved him—more than you ever imagined possible. He swept you off your feet, right? He made you believe in love at first sight. You let him into your life. There were things, though."

"Things," Marisa said. Outside, on deck, Jude was saying that a blue whale's tongue weighed as much as a young elephant, its heart as much as a small car.

"The lies. How you never knew quite whether you could believe what he told you. And the way you were always wrong and he was always right. Scary things too."

"Yes," Marisa said. "Very scary . . ."

"You had doubts. You wondered sometimes, but you told yourself you were wrong. You loved him so much. Your poor wounded man . . ."

"How do you know he's wounded?"

"They all are," Lily said, smiling. "Terribly, terribly so. And it's always someone else's fault."

"It always is," Marisa said, starting to smile for the first time.

"Beginning with their parents. They always have the absolute worst childhoods. Straight out of Dickens, complete with utter poverty and someone who was horribly cruel and beat them black and blue. . . ."

"Which justifies them being cruel to us."

"Of course," Lily said.

"Do you think they actually have awful childhoods? Or is that just another lie?"

Lily took a slow, careful sip of punch. She closed her eyes and thought of all the very many times she had asked herself that same question, how many long-ago sleepless nights she had stared up at the moon and stars, asking them how such terrible things could be visited on human beings.

"I grieve for any child who is hit," she said. "Or hurt in any way. But you know, to grow up and use that as an excuse to hurt us—uh-uh. I don't buy it. So, in that way, whether it's true or not is beside the point."

"I never thought of it that way," Marisa said.

"Is that one of the things that makes you lonely for him?" Lily asked. "Remembering how you used to hold him and comfort him? Are you wondering how he's surviving without you?"

Marisa nodded, and the smile was gone. "I'm a nurse," she said. "He told me I was healing him."

"While he was destroying you?"

"He never actually hit me."

"No, neither did mine," Lily said. "There are worse ways to destroy a person. I'm glad you got away. It had to be bad, for you to have come so far away. Away from your friend. I think what you're actually missing is not him."

"But there's such a hole in my life," Marisa whispered, her voice so hoarse, it sounded like bark being torn from a tree.

"You miss love," Lily said. "You miss the dream. You miss the dream of love you thought you had with him. That's why I started the Nanouk Girls of the Frozen North."

"The Frozen North. Canada," Marisa said.

"Oh," Lily said. "Did you think the name refers to

geography? It doesn't. It's here—" She touched her own heart. "The Frozen North is where we lived, loving them, for so long. You're free now, Marisa. Welcome to the thaw."

On deck, Rose believed she had never felt so happy. Her birthday party was a crazy wonderful success—all her friends were having the time of their lives. Captain Neill had showed them fin whales, humpbacks, minkes, one blue whale, and of course, Nanny. He had told them how Nanny and other belugas are born light brown, but molt every year, until turning white at age six.

He brought all the girls into the wheelhouse and let them take turns holding the wheel, reading the compass, watching the radar, and tuning in to Dr. Neill's reports on where Nanny and the other whales were.

"Would you like to talk on the radio, birthday girl?" Captain Neill asked.

"Me?" Jessica asked.

Rose laughed at her friend's joke, watching Jessica blush.

"I'm just kidding," Jessica said.

"You're a regular comedian," the captain said. "My wife runs the inn, and we could use you on Friday nights. We're always looking for a good act. What's your name?"

"Jessica Taylor."

"Ah. 'Jessica Taylor, the Birthday Girl,' " he said. "Not!"

All the girls laughed, as if he was the comedian. He was tall and ruddy, with dark brown hair like his cousin, Dr. Neill. He had lots of lines in his sun- and wind-weathered face, and a wide grin, as if he enjoyed joking and making people laugh. He drove the boat over the waves here at the mouth of the bay, with a sort of gentleness that Rose appreciated. Her chest hurt today. She felt breakable—as if the impact of going over the open water could crack her open, so everything inside would spill out. But somehow the salty air felt so fresh and cool going into her lungs, it soothed her into forgetting.

"What is your birthday, Jessica?" Allie asked. "Your real one, I mean."

"Today," Jessica said, laughing. "And tomorrow. Oh—and the next day too!"

"Come on, real birthday girl," the captain said over the giggling, tapping Rose on the shoulder. "Get on the radio and ask my cousin where the whales have gone."

"I don't know how," Rose said.

"You go like this—" the captain said, showing her how to lift the mouthpiece and push the button on the side. "Push to talk, and then say 'over,' and listen. All twelve-year-olds should know how to talk on the radio."

"But I'm only nine!" she said.

"You're kidding."

She shook her head.

He rolled his eyes and shook his head, as if he couldn't believe it. "Well, you had me fooled. I could have sworn you were twelve. You're such a big kid."

Rose liked the way he made a half-circle with one arm, for her to stand in. She also felt proud, listening to what he'd said about her age. She was so much smaller than her friends—with her heart condition, she had never really grown right. Some boys at school called her "midget" when she walked by. Captain Neill had just made her feel both normal and special at the same time. And now she was getting to use the radio.

"Dr. Neill," she said, pushing the button. "Over."

"Rose, is that you? Over."

"It's me. Thank you," she said.

Now, looking out the wheelhouse window as she held the mike, she saw him in the orange Zodiac, making wide circles.

"You saw Nanny on your birthday," he said. "How about that? She knew, and came back just in time."

"Do you think she really knew? Over."

"I do. I think she sensed that we wanted her here. Whales are very intelligent, Rose. Especially Nanny. She's been around a long time, and I think she knows the people who watch out for her."

The people who watch out for her . . . Rose heard him say those words, and she saw him in the Zodiac, and then turned to look at her mother in the main cabin, just through the wheelhouse door. The people who watch out for her . . .

"I want Nanny to watch out," Rose said in the lowest voice imaginable, without pushing the button, "for my mother."

"What's that you say, sweetheart?" the captain asked. "You've got to speak up—and don't forget to press that little button there. That's it. Talk into the mike—there you go."

"Thank you again, Dr. Neill," Rose said.

"Ask him where the whales are now," Captain Neill reminded her. "He's the expert."

"Where are the whales now?" Rose asked.

"Just east, a few hundred yards," Dr. Neill said. He was holding the mike in his good hand, so he pointed with his prosthesis. Rose followed with her eyes. She saw spouts, the vapor iridescent in the sunlight.

Behind her, Britney and Allie giggled and whispered; Rose felt a pang when she heard someone squeal, "Captain Hook!"

It felt like a punch in the chest.

She turned around, saw Britney imitating a person with a hook for a hand. Her hand bent sharply at the wrist, fingers extended and held tightly together, stiff as a paddle. Their eyes met, but instead of stopping, Britney waved with her claw-hand. That made Allie shriek with laughter. Rose felt Captain Neill's eyes on her and her friends, and her shoulders pulled together in front, with shame. She handed him the microphone, sure he wouldn't want her to use it anymore—not with friends who made fun of his cousin.

But the captain just patted her head, told her she was doing a great job. He was saying something about asking Liam where Nanny was, but just then Rose felt the leak get bigger. It was like a bicycle tire that has a tiny pinprick...

the air just hisses out a little at a time, till the little hole be-comes a tear, and then it starts to rush.

Rose swayed—bumping against the hard steel wheel, and then against the captain's arms. She heard Dr. Neill's engine idling—such a comforting sound, to know he was right there. She had to turn around, had to see Britney. Jessica stood between them.

"What's wrong, Rose?" Jessica asked.

Rose opened her mouth. She knew she didn't have much time.

"Rose—it's like what happened on the way home from school, right?" Jessica asked, but she didn't even wait for Rose to answer. Rose knew she was running for her mother.

"Britney," Rose said, staring into her friend's brown eyes. "Don't call him that...please? He's my friend. He wanted me to see Nanny for my birthday."

"I know, I'm sorry," Britney said, looking stricken—was it because of what Rose had said, or the fact that she was turning blue? Rose had seen that look in the eyes of so many of her friends when she started having a spell.

The dizziness flooded up, surrounding her like waves, pulling her under the sea. Her thoughts were crazy. She re-membered her two wishes: one of them had come true. Nanny was back, and Rose had seen her. But her other wish—even greater, more urgent—came upon her now. She wanted it with such passion, she thought she would die of it, and she knew she might. Rose had never been intimidated by that thought—her heart was working so hard to keep her alive, but Rose knew it might not forever.

"I want my father to be," Rose mumbled, her legs giving out. "I want him to be, I want him to be..."

"What, sweetheart?" Captain Neill asked, grabbing her hard, lifting her up in his arms.

"I want my father to be a good man," Rose said. "A good daddy who loves me..."

And then she went away.

Chapter 8

The first Liam noticed that there was some kind of problem was when he saw that the *Tecumseh II* had stopped and was drifting.

He had been heading east, following the undersea ridge—he could see it on the sonar, the geological phenomenon that created upwelling, attracting the whales with a rich food source. He had several screens going at once—sonar, radar, and tracking. There was MM122, dead ahead—right at the blue surface, glistening bright white in the sun. That's when Liam turned, to make sure Jude was steering in the right direction.

But Jude wasn't steering at all. The *Tecumseh II* was definitely not under command. Drifting slowly, sideways, miles from any land, but alarming nonetheless. Liam clicked on the radio. He made a quick call.

"Calling *Tecumseh II*—Jude, you there?"

The speaker was silent. One hundred yards away, the seventy-four-foot whale boat rode the current. Broadside to Liam, it reflected sunlight back at him. Squinting, he lifted the binoculars to his eyes and saw everyone on deck rushing to the wheelhouse. Without waiting for a reply, he pushed the throttle down and sped across the water.

Liam's heart was pounding faster the closer he got. He knew it was something bad, something terrible. From his own history, he knew that the worst cries for help were the silent ones. *Rose's birthday,* he thought. It was so sunny for her special day, her whale-watch cruise, and Nanny had come back. Weren't those signs? Didn't they count?

Then he thought of Connor. The warm water, the best swimming they'd had all summer... the amazing number of whales, all swimming so close to the harbor... the fact that Liam and Jude had counted twenty-five shooting stars the night before. How could something go wrong on the day after two boys had seen twenty-five shooting stars? Or on a little girl's ninth birthday?

Now he was close, circling the bigger boat in his Zodiac, calling on the radio again. "Pick up, Jude, someone, tell me what's going on. Tell me, someone. Who's with Lily and Rose? Is someone with them?" He wasn't getting an answer, and he wasn't waiting. He backtracked in a half-circle to the stern, and he looked up and wondered how he was going to climb aboard with one arm and no ladder.

Lily knew there was no time to blame herself, but that's the first thing she did: *You shouldn't have waited so long for the surgery, you should have overridden the surgeon's*

recommendations, you knew she was having more blue spells, you knew a whale-watch boat trip was risky....

Everything seemed to happen so fast.

Jude yelled her name, and she knew. She had been drinking pink punch with Marisa—festive bubbly punch, ginger ale mixed with raspberry juice, Rose's favorite birthday drink, dark pink like her favorite rambling roses— when she heard her name.

The look on Anne's face: *oh my God.*

Jude's voice—it was the panic in his voice that got them both. Lily dropped the punch. The glass tumbled from her hand, as if her bones had just turned to jelly, couldn't hold on for anything. But her legs worked. Her front covered with Rose's birthday punch, she ran through the main salon. The Nanouk Girls lined her way—she had the fleeting impression of mouths open. Spectators on the marathon route, cheering their friend to the finish line. Only this wasn't cheering.

Rose was in Jude's arms, against his chest. He was trying to lay her on the chart table, but she was so blue and delicate, he hesitated, as if he was afraid that the hard Plexiglas surface would bruise her or hurt her, as if he just didn't know what to do, where to go with her.

"Is she breathing?" Anne asked, because Lily couldn't. Lily was already with Rose, nearly crawling into Jude's arms herself, climbing aboard with her daughter, ear to her small mouth, the blue lips, darker than the rest of her skin. Lily prayed to feel the tiniest breath—just the small moist warmth of one breath. Her very skin was attuned to Rose's life—the hairs on her cheek were alive, alert for the exhalation.

"She's not," Lily heard herself say, her voice high and raw.

"What do we do?" Jude said.

"You're the captain, you know first aid," Anne said. "Calm down, Jude."

First aid? Lily thought. She nearly fell apart at the words. After all her baby had been through. First aid had been given before the end of her first week of life. And so many times since. Rose had fought and fought...

"She has a pulse," Jude said, frowning as he felt Rose's wrist.

"Okay, that's what we need to hear," Anne said.

In the background, from the main salon, Lily heard a ruckus. The girls were screaming, and one of them cried, "It's a pirate!"

The girls felt Rose's trauma, Lily knew—it was radiating through the party, and they all picked up on it, and suddenly everyone was sobbing. Lily clung to her daughter, grabbing her out of Jude's arms. If he didn't know first aid, well, Lily did, and she'd do it herself. She was already breathing into Rose's mouth, trying to remember how to count, one, two, one, no... Tasting the salt of her own tears, the sweetness of punch from Rose's lips, hearing the girls cry, and scream the name Captain Hook.

Oh, and that name made Lily start to cry herself. The first tears had been nothing, but now they turned into sobs. Liam was here, of course he was. She felt his good hand on her shoulder. Jude was explaining, talking fast and sharply, describing how Rose was steering the boat and then suddenly how she just collapsed. And Anne was shushing him, saying the details didn't matter but acting fast did.

Liam said, "Drive, Jude."

"But where?"

"Get us to Port Blaise."

"No!" Lily said. "That's too far! She won't make it. Take us to the dock, call the ambulance, we'll go to the medical center—Dr. Mead knows her, that's the best thing—"

"Port Blaise has a heliport, Lily. We can call the rescue helicopter right now."

"The Coast Guard," Anne said. "I'm calling right now."

Lily felt the push of the engines, throwing her off-balance as the *Tecumseh II* picked up speed. She was the "fast cat" in the Neill family fleet, and she was flying now, up on her plane, hydroplaning across the bay.

"But in the meantime," Lily tried to say. These people loved her and Rose, she had no doubt of that. But they hadn't spent nine years raising a child with cardiac defects. They didn't understand that *now* was what mattered—not getting to the heliport, flying to the medical center. Rose was still and cold. Lily wept with panic.

Liam's arm was prying them apart.

"No!" Lily shrieked.

"Come here," he said roughly. "Anne," he said, asking for help.

Now Anne was in on it—all the Nanouk Girls, pulling

Lily away from Rose. Lily stretched like elastic—her hands wouldn't let go, her fingertips stuck to Rose's skin like the pads of a tree frog, suction cups holding tight with a death grip. She heard Marlena's voice, and Cindy's, Doreen's. . . .

"Come on, love," Marlena said. "She's in the best hands now—"

"She is, sweetheart," Anne said. "Let it happen."

And that made Lily look up and see—that Rose *was* in the best hands. . . .

Marisa had stepped forward. The pain in her eyes was gone. Her posture and attitude as a wounded bird, abused woman, had disappeared. She stood tall and confident, one hand resting gently on Rose's chest, the other sliding down her frail left arm, fingers finding the pulse. She nodded.

Beside Marisa, Liam fumbled with the first-aid bag, the emergency oxygen tank, using his one good hand to slide the green strap around Rose's head, the clear plastic mask over her mouth.

Held up by the Nanouk Girls, Lily almost felt the oxygen flowing directly into her own mouth and nose, into her bloodstream. Her lungs filled—the air was so clear and clean, and it was bringing life back to all the dead parts. Lily felt Marlena rubbing her back, Cindy holding her left hand, Anne clasping her right hand. The other girls were there, fanned out like a team, like Lily and Rose's team. Mothers and daughters; while Marisa treated Rose, Jessica stood glued to Lily's right leg. All the Nanouk Girls were here, silently watching. They were witnesses to this birthday, and this lifesaving. Lily shuddered with the terror that comes with a certain kind of joy, too primal to name.

"She's been through so much already," Lily cried.

"And she'll just keep going," Anne said, almost sternly.

"What if..."

No one even replied to the question Lily couldn't bring herself to ask. Instead they all just stood together as the boat went faster and faster. All these mothers and daughters, best friends in this cold climate, pulling together for Lily and Rose.

"May the sea cradle you, the angels protect you," Jessica whispered.

"What's that?" Allie asked.

"My father's Irish prayer," Jessica replied.

Marisa ministered to the patient, gently and with strength. Like a seasoned pediatric cardiac nurse, she turned her onto her side, helping her into the knees-to-chest position. Bending over, whispering in Rose's ear, counting the beats of her heart as she took her pulse, eyes on her watch.

Now she put her ear to Rose's chest, and when she stood up, she was frowning. She palpated Rose's side, spending time. Liam held the oxygen mask, adjusting the flow. Jude was talking on the SSB to the Coast Guard, but when he hit the big questions he couldn't answer, he handed the mike to Marisa, who said, "The patient is nine years old, female... Tetralogy of Fallot... scheduled for reparative surgery, but... yes... pulmonary stenosis... enlarged liver. Kidneys. The surgery was scheduled for Boston, but I don't think..."

Lily heard Marisa's words, but suddenly they were lost to her, a blur. Because Liam had turned—halfway around, to meet Lily's eyes with a great big smile, nodding, there at Rose, who had opened her eyes, her bright-green, alive, birthday-girl eyes. And Rose was looking around, and because Liam knew there was only one person Rose wanted to see, he stepped aside—still holding the mask—so Rose could look straight at her mother.

Chapter 9

Maeve Jameson sat in her garden, on the ancient wrought-iron bench, under the shade of the sea oaks. The smell of roses filled the salt air, and the warmth of summer lifted from the rocky earth. A soft breeze blew, rustling the leaves overhead. Her eyes were closed, and to anyone who might happen to pass by, she looked as if she were resting, at peace. That was far from the truth.

Down by the rocks, the tide was rising. She heard the waves splashing higher and higher. It was impossible to not think back, see that young girl playing in the water, swimming like a seal with her brown hair so sleek and smooth. She loved to dive, as deep as she could go, and come up with handfuls of shells and seaweed. Maeve had sat on this very bench, watching her dive and swim for hours on end.

When she heard the car door slam, she felt she could take a breath. She'd been waiting for this visit. It had to happen—it did every year. But this year, it felt different.

Maeve's heart felt heavy, as if another layer of hope had been torn off.

"Top of the morning, Maeve," came the voice. She could barely open her eyes to look at him. But when she did, she smiled. Couldn't help herself. He still looked as young and handsome and eager as the young cop who had stood on her doorstep so many years ago. His dog, a black Lab, ran straight past Maeve, down to the water's edge.

"It's not morning," she said. "It's three in the afternoon."

"You going to start busting me before I even walk through your garden gates?"

"Darling, those garden gates were taken down years ago. Come on, enter the hallowed ground." She watched him walk past the wishing well—with its curved, wrought-iron arch, emblazoned with *Sea Garden*—the name Mara had given the house when she was just a little girl. Patrick stole a glance at the letters—spidery now, after all these years of salt air wearing away the iron.

"Hallowed ground," he said, standing before her.

"Sea Garden," she said. "Still waiting for the young maid to return."

"Maeve . . ."

"Darling—you're going to tell me to be realistic, aren't you? I can hear it in your tone. Nine years have passed. . . ."

"It does no good to hold out hope when we both know . . ."

"Both know what, dear? What do we actually know? That she lived here, that she disappeared, that her baby would be nine years old today—or yesterday, or tomorrow...I don't know her exact birthday."

"We don't know that she had a birthday," Patrick said. "It's most likely she didn't."

"Then why do you come to see me every year? Why do you keep asking questions, as if you still expect to find her?"

Patrick blushed, his freckled skin turning as red as sunburn. His blue eyes glinted in the sun. Sometimes Maeve thought he regretted telling her about aspects of his investigation, his sleepless nights, the way his marriage had broken up over his obsession with the case. Maeve had tried, as gently as possible, to impress upon him the craziness—there was no other word for it—of trying, even though he was now retired, to solve the case of a missing woman he honestly, deep in his heart, believed to be dead.

Maeve just didn't find it credible.

"What does Angelo have to say about this?" she asked.

He let out a low whistle, shaking his head till the red hair fell right into his blue eyes. "Low blow, Maeve," he said.

"Didn't you tell me that Angelo was your friend, the one who tries to convince you you're chasing rainbows, still looking for my granddaughter?"

"First of all, I'm not looking for her. The case is closed, and besides—I'm retired. Second of all, Angelo is an asshole."

"Really? I thought he was your best friend."

Patrick nodded. He was standing directly in front of

Maeve, and she angled her position so his head would block the sun from shining in her eyes.

"Yeah, he is," he said. "But when it comes to solving cases, he doesn't know shit. Flora! Get away from that goddamned seaweed! You know she's going to have my car smelling like low tide, don't you?"

Maeve beamed. She didn't know why it tickled her so much, to have Patrick Murphy swear like this. Normally she didn't go in much for profanity. She supposed she liked it because it seemed to reflect the passion he felt for keeping the dream of Mara alive—in spite of what he was telling her out of one side of his mouth.

"Dogs love my rocks. Now, back to Angelo."

"He doesn't know squat about my cases."

"Well, he's not in law enforcement, is he? What would he know, when you get right down to it?"

"Not much," Patrick said. "What've you got there?"

"These?" she asked, holding up her hot-pink garden gloves. But he was shaking his head, pointing.

"That," he said.

"Oh," Maeve said. "I was just watering the roses."

"That's one old watering can," Patrick said. "Yellow. Kind of unusual."

"Hmm," Maeve said, pushing her dark glasses down from the top of her head, where they had been resting. She thought now would be a good time. The last thing she wanted was for this young man to see any eyes filling up with tears. She coughed, for good measure, kicking the yellow boots under the bench. Choosing her moments, Flora abandoned the tidal pools and sea wrack to come over for a pat. She nosed the boots while she was at it.

"What are those?" he asked, watching his dog lick the rubber boots.

"Enough," she said—to Patrick, not Flora.

"Maeve."

"Does the expression 'keep the home fires burning' mean nothing to you? What kind of sentimental Irishman are you, anyway?"

"A realistic one."

"Ah, yes. You gritty Irish cops would never understand anything like hoping a long-lost granddaughter and great-grandchild would come home again. You're too busy chasing after ghosts."

"She was wearing those boots and using that watering can the day she disappeared," he said, and he'd lost every speck of color from his face.

"She was."

"I should never have brought them back to you from the evidence room. Get rid of them, Maeve, for your own sake."

"Never."

"Maeve, we found flecks of blood on the toe. You want to live with those boots, and what happened to make Mara walk away from them?"

"Mara pricked her thumb on a thorn," Maeve said sharply. She couldn't stand to think about blood and Mara—or any hurt, any pain, any of the terrible scenarios imagined by the police at the time. She couldn't bear it. She set her jaw, letting Patrick know the subject was closed.

"Any word from what's-his-face?" Patrick asked.

"Mr. Wonderful," Maeve said.

"Why is it neither of us can stand to say his name?"

Maeve just gave Patrick her best deadpan gaze. Words couldn't express the depth of hatred she harbored for Edward Hunter; even thinking his name caused her stomach to tighten and her face to wizen. She let her left hand trail down beneath the seat, her fingers closing around the top of one of the yellow boots. It comforted her, to hold on to something Mara had once worn. Made Mara feel real and alive.

"He writes or calls on the big occasions. Holidays, her birthday..."

"What do you say to him?"

"I act, darling. I thank him and ask about his career, his 'family.'" She had to put the word—such a precious word at that, "family," in invisible quotation marks when using it in conjunction with Edward and his latest victims—he had had Mara declared dead, so that he could marry one of his brokerage clients. "I've learned to keep my enemy close. One never knows what he might reveal. He's living in..."

"Boston."

Maeve blinked with surprise. "No—he's been living in Weston, with his new wife."

"She left him last spring," Patrick said, enjoying giving her the news. "They had their house on the market, and as soon as it sold, she took off on him. Didn't get much of the money, from what I hear. Most of it was in escrow, but she just cut her losses, took her kid, and went away. He'll end up with all her money—what he hasn't already taken from her. Women do that with Edward. They give up everything they have to escape him."

Maeve had no retort to that. She just let her fingers trail around and around the rim of the boot. Oh, if only Mara would choose today as the day ... to return from wherever she was hiding, just walk through the garden gate that Maeve had torn down so many years ago now ... just walk in, carrying her baby.

The reality shocked her—the child wouldn't be a baby now, but a nine-year-old child.

"So much lost time," Maeve said. "When I think about the years I've spent without her. I raised her, you know."

"I know, Maeve. After her parents died in the ferry accident."

"In Ireland. Such a poetic place and poetic way to die. That's what I told myself at the time. But then I'd hold Mara, crying herself to sleep every night, and I realized— there's no poetic way to die."

"Nope."

"That's right. I'm talking to an old homicide cop, aren't I?"

"Major Crime Squad," he said.

"Did I ever tell you that you remind me of a darling old friend of mine, an Irish poet, Johnny Moore?"

"Every time I see you. I still can't figure out why."

"Because you write letters to a girl you believe to be

dead," Maeve said. "That's why. Come on. Come inside, and I'll pour us some iced tea. Clara might stop by with some of her sugar cookies, if I tell her you're here."

"Sugar cookies," Patrick said, holding out his hand to pull Maeve up. As he did, his eyes fell upon the old bench. Made of wrought iron by the same person who'd done the wishing-well arch, it was weathering only slightly better—it was forged of thicker iron, and Maeve had been more fastidious, painting it every year with Rustoleum. She followed Patrick's gaze, looking at the bench.

There was room for four people to sit on it. The slatted seat sagged slightly in the middle; the arms and legs were ornate, decorated with Victorian curlicues. But it was the back that was the great work of art. There were four scenes depicted—of a boy and girl sitting beneath the same tree.

"Your four-seasons bench," he said. "Winter, spring, summer, and fall."

"Yes," Maeve said, lifting the yellow boots even as he took hold of the watering can, then linking her arm with his and walking down the narrow stone path that led to her front door. "My father had it made for my mother, by the same ironworker who made the *Sea Garden* arch. It symbolizes the passage of time."

The passage of time: since Mara's disappearance, since Patrick had started looking for her. Young people these days were always amazed by things that lasted. And she certainly included Patrick—who was probably about forty-five—in the category of "young." This was a throwaway society; Maeve and Clara said it to each other all the time.

They were both dismayed by all the plastic wrapping everything came in. Not to mention the way rich young people would buy up lovely, gracious cottages, tear them down, and build the most unspeakable monstrosities. Even here in Hubbard's Point, the practice was rampant.

"Do you want to hear my theory?" Maeve asked.

"Of course," he said as she opened the front door and led him inside. The kitchen was cooled by shade and the sea breeze blowing through all the open windows.

"In the future, and not so far in the future, the properties that will be worth the most are cottages like this one. Lovely, small houses, built to nestle into the land. People with money are ruining everything—cutting down all the old trees, knocking down the small houses, and building their stupid showplaces."

"They think they're increasing the value of their real estate."

"Darling, I've heard about what's happened to the boatyard. I'm so sorry. But yes, it's the exact same phenomenon. After a while, when people tire of their big air-conditioned, fancy-hot-tubbed houses, they'll all yearn for places like this. That fit the shoreline so beautifully. I think of Mara coming home and not even recognizing the place, with all the ugly houses going up."

"She'd recognize the place," he said. "She'd know it anywhere."

"It was in her heart," Maeve said, opening the refrigerator, taking out the big pitcher of iced tea. Sprigs of mint from the garden floated on top, and she strained the tea into tall Kentucky Derby glasses. Then she poured a bowl of water for Flora, and the dog slurped thirstily.

"Tell me about her," Patrick said.

"You know everything there is to know about my granddaughter," Maeve said. "Probably as much as I do."

"No one knows as much as you, not when it comes to Mara," Patrick said. "Come on—tell me something I don't know about her."

Maeve frowned. What could, or should, she tell him? Leading him from the gray and yellow kitchen, past the old table with one end built into the wall, with the bright flowers and figures painted on the wood by Maeve herself long before such things were in decorating fashion—around the corner into the living room, with its sweeping views of Long Island Sound, Maeve's mind was racing with thoughts and memories.

Mara as a baby, as a three-year-old learning to swim, as a six-year-old constantly reading, as a teenager resisting the boys who fell in love with her as often as the east wind blew, as a successful needlework designer, as a young woman married to Edward Hunter.

"Which story should I tell you?" she asked. "From which part of her life?"

"Tell me the one that will help me find her," he said.

"Don't you think that if I could have, I already would have?" she asked, smiling sadly as he admitted—without coming right out and saying it—that he didn't really believe she was dead. Or didn't want to . . .

"I know I ask you this every time. But have you ever

gotten anything that might be a sign from her?" he asked, trying a different tack. "A phone call, where the person hung up? Or a postcard without a signature? Or ..."

"No."

"Anything odd, out of the ordinary, that gave you pause?"

"They undercharged me at the Shell station," she said.

Patrick rolled his eyes. Flora trotted over to lie panting at his feet. "Anything else? Along the lines of mistaken identity?"

"Mistaken identity?"

"Well, where something really unexpected occurred, and you thought there had to be some mistake. As if maybe it was meant for someone else."

"Well, last fall," Maeve said, her heart flipping as his words opened a door—an opportunity. She spoke slowly, to not betray emotions. "Late fall, I think. Just before the holidays."

"What was it?" Patrick asked.

"I got a phone call from the membership department at the Mystic Aquarium. The woman was so lovely and kind. She told me that she had been given my name by someone who thought I might be interested in joining, and wanted to offer me a membership."

From Patrick's expression, Maeve knew that this was not the sort of thing he'd been hoping for. But Maeve's pulse was racing—she felt a thread of electricity running up her spine, as if a ghost or angel had just flown into the room.

"Well, they know you live on the water," Patrick said. "They probably thought you'd like to go see the fish, or whatever they have there."

"Maybe," Maeve said. "I asked the woman who had given her my name, and she said the person wanted to be anonymous."

"Maybe she was just trying to sell you a membership."

"No. It was a gift. The person had bought it for me."

Now she had his attention. He raised his eyebrows, thinking. "A gift?"

"I thought it might have been Clara—she loves museums, and Mystic Seaport, and the aquarium. But it wasn't her. Then I thought it had to be one of my old students. I was always making them observe nature."

"Huh. Have you enjoyed the membership?"

"I've never gone," Maeve said. "Why go to an aquarium, when I have all this right out my window?" She gazed out at the blue Sound, waves pushing in from the east. The two granite islands, North and South Brother, lay half a mile offshore; she remembered the time Mara had wanted to swim to them, and Maeve had rowed alongside, to keep her safe.

"Right," Patrick said. "Why would you?"

Maeve stared at him.

They heard the kitchen door open—the screen door needed oil. She knew that it was Clara. She lived right next door, and she had probably spotted Patrick in the garden. Maeve could almost smell the sugar cookies.

"It's me," Clara called.

"We're in here," Maeve called back.

"But hey," Patrick said. "Humor me, will you? Do you have that woman's name? The one who called?"

"Somewhere, probably," Maeve said, sliding over on the sofa to make room for Clara. Flora stood at attention, tongue lolling out, and focused on the plate of cookies. Everyone said hello; Patrick stood to shake Clara's hand, and Maeve lifted her face to kiss her best friend. Of course she remembered the woman's name; she knew exactly where she had put the paper where she'd written it down.

"I brought some cookies, as this lovely dog can see," Clara said. "To go with Maeve's mint tea."

"I'm a lucky guy," Patrick said. "You behave yourself, Flora."

"It almost feels like a party," Clara said, slipping Flora a piece of cookie.

"A birthday party," Maeve said, feeling that electric shiver again as she went to get the name—it was on the membership materials that she had shoved into a middle shelf on her bookcase, right between *Islands in the Stream* and *Yeats's Collected Poems*.

Two of her favorite books.

Again, electricity zinged up her spine. She almost wondered whether a thunderstorm was on the way.

Chapter 10

The helicopter had so little room inside, Rose had to go without her mother. By the time the boat reached the dock at Port Blaise, and the helicopter landed to pick her up, Rose felt so much better. Not perfect, not even just okay, but no longer fainting and blue. She was awake, and she could hear, and she didn't like hearing that she had to fly alone to the hospital in Melbourne.

"Mommy," she said, lifting the oxygen mask so she could talk. "Come with me."

"There's no space, honey," her mother said, crouching right beside the gurney, where Rose lay flat, ready to be loaded onto the waiting helicopter. "But don't worry—I'll get in a car right now and drive down to Melbourne. I'll be there in an hour. Two at the most."

"Don't speed," Rose warned her.

"No," her mother said, and Rose was so relieved to see her smile.

"We'll take good care of her," the helicopter nurse said to

her mother. They began to lift Rose, but her mother wouldn't let go of her hand. Jessica's mother, who had helped Rose on the boat, stood right there, waving at Rose. Rose's mother still clutched her hand. Finally, Dr. Neill stepped forward and gently put his good hand on Rose's mother's, pulling it away from Rose's.

"Let her get going," he said. "The sooner she does, the sooner you can see her in Melbourne." He was staring straight at Rose as he spoke; she saw the spark in his eyes, and it made her smile, even though she was a little scared of the roaring helicopter blades. Dr. Neill knew what Rose was thinking—she was positive of it.

"Don't be worried, Rose," her mother said. "These people will take care of you, and I'll be there as soon as I can."

Rose nodded and smiled wide. She held her lips in place, her teeth showing, so her mother would remember the smile. Then she gave her mother the thumbs-up she always gave when she was being wheeled into surgery. Her mother gave it back, with an equally brave grin on her face.

"Bye, Rosie! We love you, Rose!" called Jessica and her mother and all the Nanouk Girls. The oxygen mask was back over Rose's face, so she couldn't shout back. Dr. Neill was standing right by her mother, towering over her because he was so tall, and Rose had one fleeting impression of him as a mountain. Sturdy, steady, rock-fast. She liked thinking of him that way, and it brought the smile back to her face.

Things began to happen fast.

The EMTs made sure she was strapped in; the nurse hooked her up to the blood pressure cuff and began listening with her stethoscope. The pilot was talking on the radio. Now an EMT was on another radio, calling to the hospital. Rose had been through it all before. The ground crew slammed the helicopter door, and when she couldn't see her mother anymore, Rose closed her eyes.

Her mother had looked so worried, and Rose knew it was because she thought Rose was scared. But Rose wasn't. She had had a wonderful birthday, but now she was tired.

The fear her mother had seen in her eyes had actually been worry for her—her mother. Her mother always did so much. She worked so hard at the shop, and she tried to always make Rose happy and more healthy. As the helicopter began to lift—straight up, making Rose's heart drop, as if it could stay on the ground forever, with her mother and Dr. Neill and all the people she loved—Rose clenched her fists and thought of her mother.

She knew that as much as her own heart wanted to stay on the ground, her mother's heart was rising like the helicopter, flying right here with Rose. Rose could feel it, as if she held her mother's heart in her own hands. She worried about her mother's worry. When Rose thought about her illness, it wasn't herself that she felt bad for—it was her mother.

Jessica's mother had a healthy daughter; why couldn't Rose's? Rose thought back a few days, to when she had been teasing Jessica about the evil wizard that lived in the hills. Just thinking of him made the splinter in her heart hurt. It was ice, sharp as a needle.

She thought of the fairy tales her mother had read when she was little. Evil wizards put spells on people. But Rose didn't think that was what had happened. She thought that she must have done something bad. When she was a baby, or a very little girl. Her mother had never told her, but something to drive her father away forever. It left her with a broken heart, and an evil wizard instead of a father.

Her thoughts spun. She breathed in the oxygen, staring into the strange nurse's eyes. When she went through blue spells, she wasn't always sure what was real and what wasn't, what was a dream and what was awake.

There was no evil wizard—her mother had chided her for teasing Jessica. But, then, why did Rose feel that there was? Instead of a good father?

She forced herself to breathe, and to think of her mother. She wished that she would get well, so her mother wouldn't have to worry. They could do normal things to-gether—running and playing, planning for next Christmas without wondering whether she would have to go back into the hospital, might need more surgery. Rose's condi-tion made everything so up-in-the-air.

Just like flying in a helicopter.

This was real. It wasn't a dream. She wasn't being flown on devil wings to the mountain wizard's demon cave. She wasn't being kidnapped by anyone. Her father hadn't sent people to find her. No, no. She made herself stay awake and know where she was. The beat of the helicopter engine felt strong and comforting.

Real, real, she told herself. *Going to the hospital to get better. But still, up in the air.*

One minute she was at her birthday party, seeing Nanny, laughing with her friends, and the next she was in a helicopter, with a stranger listening to her heart and trying to smile, being flown to the hospital in Melbourne.

Up in the air. Rose was up in the air, but her heart was down on the ground, with her mother. It was all true, and all real.

Lily was numb, moving by rote. Anne and Marlena gathered up Rose's presents, boxed up the cake—and the candles, not yet lit and blown out—and promised to get them to Lily's house. Lily had only the vaguest sense of hearing Anne say she'd keep the cake in the inn's freezer till Rose came home.

She knew she should go home and pack a bag. From experience, she knew that trips to the hospital were usually longer than not, and once there she would need her toothbrush and the book she was reading and a few changes of clothes. But she couldn't take the time to drive all the way back home. She had to rent a car, right here in Port Blaise, and drive straight to the hospital.

"Would you like me to come with you?" Marisa asked.

"No, but you were wonderful on the boat. Thank you so much," Lily said.

They held hands, looking into each other's eyes. Lily saw something more awake than she had previously—as if by helping Rose, Marisa had connected with the deepest part of herself, long ignored in the heat of escape.

"I don't know much about Melbourne Hospital," Marisa said, "being so new here. But the chopper staff seemed really competent and attentive."

"They are, and the hospital's good. For palliative care, anyway," Lily said. "Rose has been there often. Marisa—I saw you listening to her belly. What did you hear?"

"Fluid," Marisa said hesitantly. "And Lily, her liver and kidneys felt enlarged."

Lily heard the information and stored it instantly in the part of her brain that wouldn't touch or talk to her heart—not, at least, while she was making the long drive from here to Melbourne. She couldn't let herself start crying now, or she might drive off the road, and that wouldn't do. Rose needed her too much.

She and Marisa hugged, and she felt surprised by how tight her new friend held on—as if she didn't want to let her go.

"What is it?" Lily asked.

"Just—thank you. For getting it."

"I get it because I've been there myself," Lily said softly. "The world is divided into two kinds of people. Those who have loved men like your husband and mine, and those who haven't. Ending a relationship is one thing. But recovering from a marriage to a sociopath is another. I'll see you when we get back, okay? I want to hear more of your story, and tell you mine."

"Thank you—give our love to Rose."

"I will," Lily said.

Lily was gearing up for the drive—she'd have to ask one of the Coast Guard guys for a ride to the mall, a few miles away, where she was 90 percent sure she had seen a car rental place—patting her pockets to make sure she had her house keys for when she got back, and checking her shoulder bag, over and over, just reassuring herself that she had it with her, hadn't left it on the boat. She knew she was in a familiar sort of shock—the one she entered every time Rose went to the hospital.

The Nanouk Girls had disembarked, trying to convince her to let them go with her. The *Tecumseh II* sat at the strange dock, with Jude and his crew on deck, gravely gazing up at the sky, where the helicopter was now no more than a dot.

"I have to get a car," Lily said to Anne.

"Liam's on it," she said. "He knows the Coast Guard commander, from sharing technology or some crap like that, and he's arranging for someone to take you to Hertz. Want me to drive with you?"

Lily shook her head. "I'll be fine." She just wanted to get on the road now. Every second was a second she wasn't with Rose.

The Nanouks huddled around her in one huge hug— as if they knew she didn't have time for individual good-byes or kisses. But she felt the weight of her best friends and their daughters crushing against her, as if they could carry her themselves, on their shoulders, down to Melbourne.

"We love you, Lil."

"We'll be with you both."

"Call us, sweetheart."

"We'll send you anything you need."

"Let us know the minute you hear anything."

"I will," she promised, dry-eyed and resolute, fortified by their strength and love. Pulling away, she walked to the top of the dock. The Coast Guard station, white with its red roof, attached to the conical white brick lighthouse, stood nestled in short, wind-scrubbed pines at the top of a small hill.

Lily felt almost breathless, climbing the stairs. She had a long journey ahead of her—the drive would be the easy part. There was Liam, talking to the commander, in his white uniform. A younger Coast Guard member had been dispatched to get a car, and he was pulling it round, into the semicircular gravel drive.

Now Lily began to run—the car was here—all she had to do was jump in, and the young man would drive her to Hertz. She passed Liam, knowing she owed him thanks, but not able to take the time right now. Hand on the passenger door, she was dismayed to see the young Coast Guard man turn off the ignition and get out of the driver's side.

"No," she said, the panic rising. "Please—we have to go *now*. Get in, drive me, please—"

The young man looked sheepish, a little embarrassed. "Ma'am," he began.

"Now, oh, please—you're kind to drive me, but I'm late, I have to get to my daughter!"

"Get in, Lily," Liam said, opening the door for her.

"Oh, thank you, Liam," she said, all in a rush. Wow, she'd really owe him some thanks. "Tell them he has to take me right now, fast, okay?"

Liam didn't reply. He closed the door behind her. Now he was talking to the two Coast Guard men, just standing there—taking up the driver's time with who knows what. Lily watched the three of them talking, keys being handed off, words exchanged—for the love of *God*! She wanted to scream.

When Liam opened the driver's door, the look in her eyes was daggers and solid ice. Tears had formed—angry, furious, rageful tears—for the three men whose chatting meant she'd be that much later to the Hertz office, and for the fact Rose's birthday had been ruined, and for the fact that Rose's heart was giving out.

"Jesus, Liam," she said. "I've got to go!"

"I know, Lily," he said, climbing into the car, reaching across his body to close the door behind him with his good arm. Now he turned the key, starting the car.

"*You're* taking me to the car place?" she asked, not understanding.

"To the hospital," he said.

"But it's in Melbourne," she said, still not getting it, still envisioning the time it would take to rent a car, wondering why Liam didn't understand that she had one more step in the process of driving south to Rose.

"I know."

"Liam—"

"The commander is a friend of mine," Liam said. "This is his personal car—he's loaning it to us so I can drive you to the hospital."

Lily was too numb to argue, but it did begin to sink in as he pulled out onto the lighthouse road, accelerated as soon as he could, sped to the main highway that led south to Melbourne. The car was sporty, with four-wheel drive and roof racks, and the back seat was filled with buoys, nylon line encrusted with dried seaweed and mussel colonies, and an enormous flashlight.

"What will the commander do without his car?" Lily asked.

"He said he'll use the truck."

"Why are you doing this?" Lily asked.

"Because you need to get to Melbourne."

"I know, but I could have driven myself."

"You need to get to Melbourne fast. And honestly—I wasn't sure you were in any shape to drive."

"It's not your responsibility," Lily said.

Liam was quiet, pushing the pedal down. She cringed, hoping that she hadn't just sounded as ungrateful as she felt. Miles sped by—roadway lined with pines and oaks on one side, open water on the other. Even from shore, whale spouts were visible in the bay. Lily thought of Rose's face, the look in her green eyes when she had first spotted

Nanny. Lily squeezed her eyes shut to preserve the moment of amazement.

When she opened them again, she glanced across the seat at Liam.

"I'm sorry," she said.

"You're forgiven," he said. He looked intent on the road, as if he barely cared about conversation at all. His eyes were totally focused, dark gray-blue. Patches of sunlight came through boughs overhanging the road, flashes of light making his eyes look bright, then dark, then bright again.

"Seriously," she said. "I was wrong to say it. I didn't mean to be mean."

"Haven't we been down this road before?" he asked.

She knew he didn't mean the highway.

"Yes," she said. "And I've been sorry ever since."

He threw her a look across the seat.

"Not for the reasons you think," she said. "But because I don't like to be beholden to you. Or anyone."

"You're not beholden to me," he said. "In any way."

Lily stared out at the bay as they flew down the coast road. She knew he was telling her the truth. He had never expected anything from her—never, not once. But after what Lily had been through, before Rose was born, before arriving in Cape Hawk, she had lost the power to trust. She had once believed that people were good at heart, that they meant to help each other. That was how she had been raised.

But by the time she arrived in Cape Hawk, those beliefs had been shattered. It was Liam's misfortune, she thought, that he had been one of the first people she'd encountered after arriving in the small fishing village at the back-of-beyond on Nova Scotia's northernmost coastline.

She closed her eyes, went inward, back nine years. So pregnant she could hardly move. Just out to *there*—in a new place, in a house she was sure she couldn't afford, with a rattletrap car that needed a tune-up and four new tires after her long drive north, with not even enough money for an oil change. As she sat beside Liam in the commander's car now, she let her hands drift to her belly. She could remember carrying Rose as if it were yesterday.

"There's another reason, okay?" she asked, opening her eyes to look at him.

"Another reason for what?"

"That I've felt sorry ever since." She stopped herself, to think of how to phrase it. "Ever since we first met, and you did what you did."

"And why would that be? You feeling sorry?"

"It's just that I don't..." she said, no longer looking at him, but out the window instead—at the wide expanse of blue ocean, and the wheeling and circling white seabirds, and the occasional ripple that might or might not be the back of a whale. "I don't treat you very well. Not well enough, anyway."

"You treat me fine," he said.

"No," she said. "I know I don't."

They rode in silence for a few minutes. She was glad that he didn't try to contradict her. One thing she could count on about Liam was that he was very true to situations. He didn't sugarcoat things. He wouldn't try to make her feel better about something if it meant telling her a lie.

She glanced over at him. Why was she so tongue-tied today? What she wanted to say was, *I might treat you "fine," but it's not what you deserve. You've been nothing but wonderful since the day you met me, met us. Rose loves you.* She couldn't, and wouldn't, say such things.

So instead, she said, "Thanks for driving me, Liam."

And he didn't reply, but she saw him smile.

As he drove ever faster.

Chapter 11

The old brick hospital was on the crest of a hill overlooking Melbourne Harbor. The World War I memorial rose beside it, a single block of granite, quarried from Queensport. Liam and his brother had both been born here; so had most of their cousins. Liam remembered coming here to pick up Connor when he was three days old, the day they brought him home.

While waiting for his mother and the baby to be ready, his father had taken him to the reflecting pool, under the tall monument, and told him that his great-grandfather had fought in World War I. Liam still remembered holding his father's hand, listening to the story. His great-grandfather had been badly wounded in battle, and seen many soldiers killed.

The idea of his great-grandfather being so injured in a war made the three-year-old Liam cry—in spite of the happy fact that he had a new brother and his mother was coming home.

"Some things are worth fighting for," his father had told him, picking him up.

Liam remembered that now, parking the car and walking with Lily into the building. He had been here for many other reasons over the years. The first surgery on his arm had been done here; this was where they had brought Connor's body. He had also been here to visit Rose more than once. Both he and Lily were old hands at Melbourne General, so they bypassed the front desk and went straight up to the third-floor Pediatric ICU.

Lily seemed to be tightly wound, in control. He watched as she pushed the elevator button—purposeful yet calm. Doctors and visitors came on, pushing Lily and Liam to the back. She was just about five foot one. Maybe five one and a half in her sneakers. She wore jeans, a yellow T-shirt, and a dark blue Cape Hawk Elementary sweatshirt that zipped up the front and had a hood in back. Liam towered over her. He tried not to look down at her silky dark hair.

When the doors opened, she jostled through the crowd, with Liam right behind her. He registered people on the elevator looking at them with pity—getting off at Pediatric ICU. Lily didn't even notice. She went straight to the speaker box, mounted on the wall beside the locked ICU doors, and announced herself.

"I'm here to see my daughter, Rose Malone," she said.

"Someone will be right out to get you," the disembodied voice crackled.

The waiting room had one single window, facing the monument and reflecting pool. Several green chairs facing a television set, tuned to a talk show. Whatever was happening must have been hilarious, because the laugh track was deafening. Liam turned it down.

Lily remained standing right in front of the ICU doors, waiting for them to swing open.

"Why don't you sit down?" he asked.

"That's okay," she said, glancing over her shoulder. "Do you think she's up here yet? I just realized, they probably brought her in through the ER. Maybe we should have stopped there first."

"The nurse probably would have told you when you buzzed just now," Liam said. She was still looking at him— hadn't turned back to the door yet. Her eyes were somewhere between gray-green and gray-blue. Their color made him think of the great blue heron that lived in his pond. He watched the bird every morning, from the minute the sun rose. Lily's eyes were as still and grave and calm as the blue heron, and as beautiful, and he tried to smile with confident reassurance because they also looked so worried.

"You don't have to wait," she said. "I mean, I know you want to make sure she's okay. But after that. You have to get the commander's car back to him."

"I know," he said. "I do. But I'll wait for now. Just to see how she is."

"Okay. Right," Lily said. "Why aren't they coming to the door?"

"It's just been a minute."

"A minute's too long!"

It was the first sign that she wasn't as calm as she looked. Her voice rose, and she grimaced.

Liam went to the wall and pressed the buzzer.

"Yes?" came the voice.

"We're here to see Rose Malone."

"Yes, I know. Someone will be right—"

"Look," he said, using his shark researcher voice, the one that scared people, the one he used to get classified data out of Ottawa and Washington, and to get Harvard and Woods Hole to give him access to their mainframes. "We need someone right now. Rose's mother is out here, and Rose was airlifted out of her ninth birthday party, and her mother needs to see her *now*—okay?"

When he turned to Lily, he saw her chin wobbling, and her blue-heron eyes were creased with even more worry, and he just stood there instead of pulling her against his chest, the way he wanted to.

"They're coming," he said.

"Thank you."

Two seconds later the door opened. A tall, young nurse stood there with a clipboard. She smiled gently, as if completely unperturbed by Liam's shark voice.

"Mrs. Malone?" she asked.

"I have to see Rose," Lily said.

"Come with me," the nurse said.

Lily rushed past her, through the doors, which closed behind them. Liam stood in the green waiting room, his heart in his throat. He hadn't actually expected to go inside. That's what he told himself.

He went to stand by the window, gazing out at the monument. It was tall and narrow, elliptical, carved with deep grooves and topped with a peak. When he was three, it had seemed massive and austere. It still did. A monument to those who had served and those who had died. He could almost see himself and his father standing in its shadow; he could almost feel his three-year-old sorrow, for a great-grandfather he'd never known.

Two doctors stepped out of the elevator, both wearing white coats over green scrubs. They pressed the buzzer and were admitted to the ICU. Liam's stomach flipped, wondering whether they were here to see Rose, to talk to Lily.

When he turned back to the window, he noticed leaves on the trees, a bed of marigolds planted at the base of the monument. It was summertime. The monument's shadow was lengthening, like the day. He checked his watch—it was already seven o'clock—and as he did, he remembered another part of his great-grandfather's story, the part that involved the family left at home. The part about them waiting, about his great-grandmother not knowing whether he would ever come home again.

He thought of Lily inside the Pediatric ICU, waiting to learn what would come next for Rose. Sometimes waiting was the hardest thing of all.

The nurse, whose name was Bonnie McBeth, led Lily through the unit. There were infants and children hooked up to all kinds of machines, but Lily had eyes for no one but the girl in the second bed on the left: Rose.

The sight of her caught Lily's heart like a fishhook. Before she even saw her face, she knew it was Rose in that bed: the size of her body under the white honeycomb blanket, the funny way she always liked to hold on to the guardrail with her right hand. There were her small fingers now, holding the stainless steel rail. Lily came around the curtain and held that hand and leaned down to kiss Rose's face.

"Mommy," Rose said.

"Hi, sweetheart."

Her green eyes looked sharp at first as they looked Lily up and down, drinking her in, making sure she was really there. But then the lids flickered, up-down, and her eyes rolled back, and then focused again, and then closed. Lily knew then they were giving her morphine. She held Rose's hand a little tighter.

The machines clicked reassuringly. The IV was set. Lily examined Rose's arm, to make sure they hadn't bruised her inserting the needle. Her veins were sometimes thin and brittle, but since it had been a long time since her last IV, they were quite healthy. There were no bruises, no signs of false insertions. Lily had once gone nuts, truly insane, watching an IV technician stick Rose four times in a row without getting a vein.

While Rose slept and Lily held her hand, Bonnie McBeth stood close by. Lily glanced over at her. She had seen Bonnie on other visits, but she'd never been Rose's nurse before. Rose's main cardiologist was in Boston, so Melbourne was really only for emergencies—which, thankfully, Rose hadn't had many of recently.

"She's resting comfortably," Bonnie said in a low voice. "We gave her morphine to keep her calm. She was very agitated when she first arrived."

"Thank you," Lily said. "She had to fly by helicopter."

"That would agitate anyone," Bonnie said, smiling.

Lily nodded, still holding Rose's hand.

"Would you like to step over here, to the desk, where we can talk? I know she seems to be asleep, but..."

Lily hesitated. She didn't want to let go of Rose's hand. In fact, she couldn't. "It's okay," Lily said, but she was nearly whispering. "Rose is the captain of her own ship. She knows what's going on. You can tell me here."

Bonnie didn't really seem surprised. Mothers of cardiac peds patients were a tough bunch—but only half as tough as the patients themselves. Still, she pivoted away, and so did Lily, still holding Rose's hand.

"There's a note in her chart, that she's going to Boston for VSD surgery."

"Yes, she's scheduled for next week. The old patch is weakening."

"It is. We ran tests as soon as she arrived, of course. Her heart is enlarged, and her lungs are under pressure, which is why she's been cyanotic. She was able to tell us she's had some blue spells lately, and this is why."

Just then, two doctors walked over to say hello. Paul Colvin, whom Lily knew, and John Cyr, whom she didn't, explained that they were just doing rounds, and would Lily mind stepping outside the curtain.

"I'd like to stay," Lily said.

"I appreciate that," said Paul Colvin, the older doctor, a cardiac surgeon who had built a very respectable department here at Melbourne. "But we really need to ask you to step aside. Just for a few minutes." With silver hair and a steady stare, he might have intimidated a different mother. Lily shook her head, unable to let go of Rose's hand.

"Please, Doctor," she said. She didn't want to fight, and she didn't have to. He had encountered Lily before; he knew what he was up against, and let her stay.

The doctors listened with stethoscopes, checked machines, read the chart. Lily was glad it was just the two of them, and that Melbourne wasn't a teaching hospital. She thought back to when Rose was ten months old and they were in the Boston hospital, waiting for decisions to be made about surgery. Students were constantly stopping by to examine her—prodding and poking her, listening to her heart, surrounding her in their green scrubs—making her cry. Which made her turn blue.

It didn't take long for Lily—inexperienced though she was in the ways of hospital procedure—to complain to the cardiologist and put a stop to the student visits. She had learned right at the beginning how to be a mama bear, and she'd only gotten fiercer over the years.

Now, holding Rose's hand, she watched her daughter wake up, gaze at the two doctors working on her, and then look over at Lily for support. Lily squeezed her hand. Rose pressed back.

They were getting their fill of each other. The simple things. Just knowing the other was there; holding hands; smiling at each other; Rose drifting off, then waking up to see her mom at her side; Lily brushing her hair off her forehead. Soon it would be time for sleep, and Lily planned to sit in a chair beside Rose's bed.

When the doctors were done, Bonnie returned to Rose's bedside. She had the tray of medications, ready to administer. Lily felt better about leaving Rose for one minute with Bonnie than with the two doctors. While Bonnie measured out dosages, Lily walked to the desk with Drs. Colvin and Cyr.

"She's been having cyanotic episodes with increasing regularity," Dr. Colvin said, reading the chart. "She told us she had one today."

"Yes," Lily said. "It's the main reason she has surgery scheduled in Boston. To replace the patch for her VSD"— ventricular septal defect—"that they first put in when she was ten months old. Have you called her surgeon down there? Dr. Kenney?"

"Yes, as soon as she was admitted. He's aware of everything that's going on, but he's practicing in Baltimore now. He's recommending a surgeon in Boston, though, and he'd like you to call him later, after we've had a chance to finish testing her."

"What have you found so far?"

"Well, she's in congestive heart failure. She's got pulmonary edema with a substantial amount of swelling. We have her on Captopril and Lasix. I'd like to do a cardiac catheterization, to get a better idea of how her heart is functioning."

Lily was nodding—numb, in shock, on autopilot. When had she gotten used to hearing that Rose was in heart failure? It no longer punched her quite as viciously as it once had. She knew there was a finish line—the ER in Boston, where they would replace the patch and make her well again, almost good as new. If they could just get her stabilized here—and they would—Lily and Rose could keep to their plan, and the next surgery would be her last.

"When did she have the Blaylock-Taussig shunt?" Dr. Cyr asked.

"Ten months," Lily answered.

"In Boston," Dr. Colvin said.

Lily nodded, inching away, eager to get back to Rose.

"She's a fighter," Dr. Cyr said.

Those words made Lily's lips tighten, but she vowed not to explode. She had that geyser feeling—a buildup of pressure inside—that she was going to have to release somehow. Hearing about procedures sometimes had an extreme effect on her, as if the cells in her body remembered that first time Rose had had to kiss her goodbye as they wheeled her into surgery. That moment had nearly killed her, and it still did, every time she remembered it—or thought about what they had faced, and still had to face.

The doctors gave her a form to sign, which she did with

a scrawl that would have done them proud. Sign fast, get back to Rose...

"Is that all?" she asked.

"Yes," Dr. Colvin said.

"I'd like to request that you stop the morphine," Lily said.

"She seemed rather upset when she arrived," Dr. Colvin said. "We need to keep her calm."

"Morphine makes her sick to her stomach. And she likes being more alert."

"Still, we don't want her agitated."

"I'm here with her now," Lily said. "I think that will do the trick."

The doctors both nodded, and Dr. Cyr shrugged. They didn't get it.

Lily didn't care whether they got it or not. As long as she and Rose did.

Chapter 12

Back in Cape Hawk, the party had broken up. The Nanouk Girls had loaded up their cars, driven home, fed their families, and were already on the phone or Internet, exchanging information. Plans were being made to box up Nanouk Girl care packages for both Lily and Rose—filled with yarn, canvas, books, CDs and DVDs, and photos taken at the birthday party, especially the many taken of Rose with Nanny frolicking in the background.

Anne Neill had placed Rose's birthday cake in the inn's freezer, as promised. She and Jude ate together in the dining room, amid all the hotel guests, barely able to talk or do more than pick at their food. Jude looked as if he had aged ten years since that morning.

"When Liam asked me to captain the cruise, I never expected this. Annie, have you ever seen Rose look so bad? So blue?"

"No, dear. I truly haven't."

"What does Lily say?"

"I haven't talked to her yet. Has Liam called you?"

"No, and he has his cell phone turned off. What did Lily say before the party?"

"Well, I knew that Rosie had been having some problems. But they seemed routine, given her condition, and they were going to get taken care of once and for all with the surgery she was scheduled to have in Boston."

"Is it worse than Lily thinks? You know we all love her, she's the greatest—and with such spirit, and positive attitude—but Annie... is she living in a dreamworld about Rose?"

"Jude, Lily once told me that she and Rose are just used to things that would scare other people. Being a cardiac patient means never knowing for sure, I guess."

"I think we should pray for them tonight," Jude said.

Anne smiled at him. She knew that he prayed for them every night already, as she did. He was her sea captain husband, straight from the wilds of maritime Canada, but he had a heart as big as the Gulf of St. Lawrence.

"All three of them," Jude continued.

"Three?"

"Yes, if you count Liam."

Anne nodded. How could they not count Liam? It was an unspoken fact that he was an intimate part of Lily's life. Probably Anne and Jude knew it better than Liam and Lily did. Probably Rose knew it better too. Never had two such guarded people come together, and with such frustrating results.

"You think they'll ever have a romance?" Jude asked. "Or

is that like asking if there'll ever be palm trees in Cape Hawk?"

"I used to think palm trees were more likely," Anne said.

"Used to?"

Anne just shrugged. "Hope springs eternal."

"What do you hope for, my love?" Jude asked. He reached across the table, with its uneaten food, and covered her hand with his.

Anne whispered, "For my best friend to have a little more happiness than she's had so far in her life." When the waitress came over to clear, asking if there was something wrong with their meals, Anne was quite unable to speak.

Jude answered for both of them, saying no, everything was great, they were just still full from the birthday party. Anne thought of the uneaten birthday cake and had to reach for the starched napkin to dab her eyes. Jude took the opportunity to try Liam's cell again, but there was still no answer.

Anne looked across the table at her husband and wondered what was happening down in Melbourne.

Two days passed without any word. That night, Marisa and Jessica sat on the back porch. Cape Hawk was so far north, it stayed light hours past sunset in New England. The tips of the pine needles looked painted gold, and crickets chirped in the woods. They sat on the top step, their sides touching. Jessica hadn't smiled or said very much since Rose flew away in the helicopter.

After Rose's party, something in Marisa had given way, and she'd known that she had to be true to herself and her daughter, had to celebrate Jess's real birthday—just the two of them. What would be the harm in that? She—they— had been on guard for so long. Stopping at the grocery store earlier, Marisa had sent Jessica into the bookstore next door to pick out her summer reading choices, so Marisa could buy a cake. Now, while Jessica sat watching the stars just starting to come out in the darkening sky, Marisa went inside the kitchen.

When she came out, she was holding a cake burning with nine candles. "Happy birthday to you," she sang, and by the end of the song, Jessica was almost smiling.

"Mom, I thought we weren't having my real birthday this year."

"Well, we are. Go ahead, honey—blow out your candles. Make a wish!"

Jessica took a big breath, then blew. The nine candles went out in a rush. After today, Marisa felt extra grateful for her daughter's health, for the simple things like being able to blow out her candles. She began to cut two slices as Jessica slid the plates over.

"Know what I wished, Mom?"

"What, honey?"

"That Rose would come home soon."

"That's a good wish." Even as she said it, Marisa stopped herself. What would a bad wish be? She thought of Ted, how he would judge every single thing according to his own standards. Good wish, bad wish.

"Will she come home soon?"

"I don't know," Marisa said. "We're going to hope and pray that she does."

Jessica nodded, and together they dug into their slices of cake. Marisa felt a pang, remembering how her mother had always baked birthday cakes for her and her sister Sam. She had always made beautiful pink roses out of buttercream frosting, and written her name in pink script with a special pastry bag. What was Jessica missing, without extended family in her life?

Rose's party had felt exactly like a big family—Lily and Rose and all those strangers who by the end of the day had felt like sisters. Standing on the dock, watching Rose being loaded into the rescue copter, a woman Marisa had just met took her hand. They had all stood there, watching Rose take off in silence. Marisa and Doreen had held hands on one side, and Marisa and Jessica on the other side, and Jessica and Allie, and on down the line.

A gust of strength had entered Marisa at that moment, inspiring her to buy her daughter this birthday cake. She squeezed Jessica's shoulders and kissed the top of her head.

"It's expensive to go to the hospital, isn't it?" Jessica asked.

"Yes," Marisa said. Especially, she thought, when you're on the run and you don't have health care. She was sure Jessica was remembering falling right after they'd left Weston and having to get stitches. Marisa had had to pay with cash—health insurance was too easy to trace.

"Heart operations are a lot more expensive than stitches, right?"

"Quite a bit."

Jessica nodded. She ate her cake as the sun went down all the way, turning the forest purple, with shadows cast by the rising moon. A night bird called from the trees, long, throaty sounds that preceded the hunt.

"Mom," Jessica said, her mouth full. She chewed, swallowed, wiped her mouth. "I want to do something for Rose."

"I'm not sure she can have visitors," Marisa said, remembering the Pediatric ICU at Johns Hopkins, when she had done a rotation there, seeing all those sick children, knowing that Jessica wouldn't be allowed inside. "But I'm sure you could make her a card, and her mother would give it to her."

"I want to do more than a card."

"Like what?"

"I want to raise money for her. So she can have her operations and her mother won't have to worry or work so hard. Rose says she works all the time."

"Oh, Jess!"

"I want to make it so the hospital cures her. Makes her all well! Mom—why does Rose have to have heart defects? Why did she turn so blue?" Jessica asked, starting to sob. "I don't want her to die!"

Marisa pulled her onto her lap, rocking her and trying to soothe her. Jessica cried with unbridled grief—the way she had when her father died, and when she saw her puppy killed. Marisa's own eyes filled. She thought of all the sick children she had worked with, of the pain she had felt seeing them suffer. She had worked on learning detachment—it was taught in nursing school, but she had had to get extra help from groups and friends. It was the hardest thing she'd ever done, and it escaped her right now.

Holding Jessica, she wished she could soothe the anguish of losing her father, seeing Rose so sick, watching Ted kill Tally. Marisa knew that she would do anything to protect her daughter, keep her from the harshest realities of life. She thought back to the nursery, nine years ago today, when she had held her daughter in her arms, wrapped in a pink blanket. The baby had been so tiny; the blanket so soft. Yet Marisa's memory of the moment was ferocious—she felt love so enormous, she knew she would do anything to protect her baby.

She had once wondered whether she could ever love anyone enough to die for them. Jump into freezing water to save them, step in front of a wild animal, give up her life. Holding her baby, all doubt had been removed. Sitting on the back porch now, she remembered the feeling of love that had come over her, all the promises she had made to protect her tiny daughter from anything or anyone who ever tried to harm her.

Yet she couldn't protect Jessica from this: the terrible hurt she felt to see her best friend suffering.

"Mom?" Jessica asked now, wiping her eyes. "Will Rose die?"

"Her mother is doing everything she can to make sure she doesn't. She has excellent care."

"But you don't know?"

Marisa shook her head. She stared into Jessica's brown eyes, smoothed the hair from her high forehead, thinking of Jessica's father. His death had hit them both so hard, and she could hardly bear that Jessica had to go through the same kind of worry about Rose. "No, honey. We don't know."

"So many bad things happen," Jessica whispered. "Like when Ted kicked Tally downstairs, just because she was barking."

"Good things too, Jess. I want you to think about the good things."

"I have to help Rose," Jessica said, jumping up from the step as if she couldn't bear to waste even one minute.

"Honey—we can pray for her. Make her cards . . ."

Jessica shook her head. "That's not enough. I want to raise money, so Rose can be cured. I don't want her to die, like Daddy did, or Tally. I'm going to start now." She had been powerless to save her puppy, but she wasn't going to turn her back on her friend.

Marisa nodded. The screen door shut behind Jessica, leaving Marisa alone on the porch. Her thoughts were racing. Maybe it was the big event of her daughter's birthday here in hiding, or maybe it was the shock of seeing Rose taken to the hospital. She knew, from her rotation on psychiatric units, that old trauma could be triggered by the oddest things. From experience, after living with Ted, she knew how easily she went numb, shut down, wanted to pull the covers over her head. Those had been her old ways.

But something new was happening. She felt a ripple run

through her body, like a river under her skin. She thought of Paul, Jessica's father, and suddenly shivered, feeling alive in the cool sea air. The bird called from the woods again, announcing itself to the night. As Marisa watched, it rose on wide, silent wings, beating high over the ground. She heard its wing beats as it flew up, and saw its yellow eyes: an owl.

For the months since April, when she and Jessica had left home, she had felt like a hunted creature. Change of name, change of home, change, even, of country. She had packed up her daughter and taken her away from every single thing that mattered to them. How many sleepless nights had she felt guilty for doing that to her daughter? Hugging her pillow every night, she had prayed for Paul to forgive her.

Tonight, it felt as if he had. Marisa felt her strength returning. Holding hands with the Nanouk Girls, seeing their love for Lily, and knowing that Lily understood, somehow, what Marisa and Jessica were going through—all those factors had changed Marisa today.

So when she saw that owl—with its hot gold eyes and killer talons—instead of feeling afraid, being reminded that she and Jessica were hunted by a man she still, crazily, wanted to understand—she felt thrilled and powerful. Ted had wormed his way into her life, pretending to help her invest the money Paul had left them. He had known Paul from business and golfing, and he had used that to win Marisa's trust. He had traded on Paul's friendship to work his way into Marisa and Jessica's life.

The problem was, Paul hadn't known Ted. Not really. Not like Marisa did. Life sometimes handed people strange, dangerous gifts. Ted had done terrible damage to the people Paul had loved most. She closed her eyes, listening for the owl, and she thought of herself and Jessica, Lily and Rose. She was beginning to see clearly now.

Jessica went into her bedroom and stared up at the crucifix. She made the sign of the cross. Then she went over to the statue of Mary—the one she loved the most, because she had several. This was Mary with her blue robe and crown of yellow stars, standing barefoot on a snake. Jessica stared down at the snake—which was very scary. Its mouth was unhinged and wide open, with yellow fangs and a pink throat. But Mary had killed it by stepping on it with her bare feet. Jessica had to check every time—that the snake was still dead. She kissed Mary's face.

Then she picked up *The Lion, the Witch, and the Wardrobe*. It was her and Rose's favorite book. She loved it for its magic, secrets, evil, and, especially, goodness. She thought probably Rose loved it for the same reasons, but in the way of newly nine-year-old girls, they had never talked about it.

Looking through the book—a hardcover edition her aunt Sam had bought her for Christmas two years ago— she found a picture of Aslan, the kind, wise lion. Jessica stared into his sad, knowing eyes and felt her heart tapping in her chest. She touched his picture and thought of Rose needing help and said, "Daddy."

In the book, Aslan let himself be attacked and killed, so the children and all the inhabitants of Narnia—the magical, secret world on the other side of the wardrobe door—could live free. When he rose from the stone table and came back to life, Jessica always felt chills and a little rush of tears—as if she couldn't believe that something so brave and true could happen.

Before Ted, Jessica had believed in brave and true. Her own father was like Aslan. He had died, and the last thing he said to Jessica was, "I'll be looking down from heaven, taking care of you and your mother. I'll never really be gone, sweetheart. I'll be looking over you. Call me when you need me." Jessica had held on to his hand as long as she could, till the doctor and her mother had pried her away. Then her mother had had some private time with him, and then he died.

Ted came along right after that. Well, maybe almost a year after that—but to Jessica, it had seemed fast. She could still smell her father in his closet, she knew that. She could stand in the dark, with her head in his suits, with her eyes closed, and bring him back. The smell of his sweat and cigarettes and just *him* was all around her. She would stand there and remember what he had told her: *I'll never really be gone.... I'll be looking over you and your mother....*

And Jessica would breathe in his scent and know that he had spoken the truth. He was right there with her, protecting her. She liked the door to be partly closed, so no one would see her in the closet; it was her time alone with him.

She would stand in a different spot each day. Although the closet was quite small, it seemed like a whole world—just like the wardrobe in the book.

Jessica would go through her father's pockets, one suit at a time. He had been a businessman who valued looking good. So he had seven suits and five sports coats, with lots of slacks. His pockets were like treasure to her. At first, before she had gone through them all, the things she found were thrilling and magical. A few coins, a business card, his tarnished silver Saint Christopher medal, a stray Rolaid, torn bits of foil from a pack of cigarettes, his mother's mass card.

After a time, some of the magic began to wear off. She would look in the left pocket of his glen plaid suit and know that she would find his money clip, matches, and appointment calendar. Or she would reach into the back pocket of his green golf pants and there would be a grass-stained tee and a short yellow pencil for keeping score. Standing on tiptoes to feel inside the breast pocket of his summer-weight blue blazer, she would find her kindergarten school picture and a pocket rosary.

Even without the excitement and anticipation of not knowing what she would find, spending time in her father's suits was the happiest Jessica felt during that time. She could smell her father's smell and know that he had been here, on this earth. That he wasn't just an angel or ghost looking down from heaven—but that he had walked and talked and saved her kindergarten picture and worn nice suits and sometimes forgotten to empty his pockets.

Sometimes she'd stand there in the crush of wool blend and summer cotton and tell him about her day, and she would hear him talk back.

Once her mother opened the closet door while Jessica was in there. Jessica had held her breath, so her mother wouldn't see her there. Not because she'd thought her mother would be mad, but because she thought she might be sad—even at seven, Jessica had known how bad her mother would feel to see her there among her father's suits. But she needn't have worried; her mother had just stood there for a few minutes, and then she'd closed the door and walked away.

Maybe her mother liked to do the same thing, Jessica had thought—go back in time and remember how happy they had all once been, when he was still alive to wear all those beautiful suits. Maybe being near his suits made her mother able to hear his voice, just like Jessica did.

Then Ted had come.

Her father had known him from golf. Ted became his stockbroker, and he did a good job investing some of her family's money. Jessica remembered hearing her parents talking about Ted so often—"We couldn't do it without Ted," her father had said again and again about his business expansion. "He's a godsend," her mother had said. Oh, Ted had sounded like the family miracle. He had helped her father afford a new office for his title search company in downtown Boston—instead of out of the way, in Dorchester. The money had helped buy a new computer system, hire more people, and provide health insurance.

Jessica remembered wondering about Ted, before she met him. How did stocks work? Why would the family pick someone they barely knew and give him their money to grow? It had seemed almost unbelievably wonderful and benevolent. Could someone's job really be to oversee a family's savings and help them earn more? She asked her father once, and he told her, "He's a smart man, honey. He went to the best schools to learn business, and he only chooses stocks that he thinks will make money."

"But he's nice, right?" she had asked, unable to conceive of Ted's role in their lives any other way.

Her father had laughed. "Yes, he's a great guy. Everyone likes Ted. He has a lot of friends, and he's the vice president of the Rotary Club in the town where he lives."

Jessica didn't know what the Rotary Club was, but she thought it sounded very exciting. Her father's words made sense to Jessica. Ted had to be a great guy. Money was hard to come by—her parents worried about things like their mortgage, and car bills, building the business, and a college education for her when the time came. If they trusted Ted with their savings, then Jessica trusted him too. Her father once said that he was "as generous as they come," because of his volunteer work with poor kids.

Now, staring at the lion's sad face in *The Lion, the Witch, and the Wardrobe,* Jessica took a deep breath. She wished Aslan could come out of the book and talk to her. She wished her father would come down from heaven and tell her what to do. If Ted was "as generous as they come," Jessica wasn't sure she should try to raise money for Rose. She didn't want to be anything like Ted.

The problem was, she knew her father couldn't talk to her anymore. Not since that day, right after Ted had moved in. Jessica had come home from school and gone to the closet—not because she was upset or anything about Ted. Maybe just a little upset—but mainly, she just wanted to talk to her father the way she always did. It was spring, and she had caught a fly ball in baseball.

She had the baseball with her. Her mother and Ted were in the kitchen. She could have showed it to them, but instead she ran by, up the stairs, to her father's closet. And she opened the door, and—

All his suits were gone.

Instead, Ted's clothes were in there. Suits and jackets and pants and coats and his robe. Even now, remembering that moment, Jessica felt her chest cave in. She touched her heart and sat down on the bed. Staring at Aslan's face, she sobbed silently. *Mary, Jesus, God...* Seeing Rose turn blue and fly away to the hospital had brought it all back. People she loved going away. Her father, Rose... Her father had never really gone away, not until the day Ted and her mother threw his suits out.

"Tell me what to do," she whispered now, getting onto her knees.

Outside, the owls were hunting and calling. She had heard them every night since the snow melted. Sometimes she listened extra hard—as if she might be able to understand what they were saying. She stared at the picture in her favorite book, and listened for the owls, and she was sort of praying, but she was really asking her father.

If ever there was a day for him to come back to her, it was now: her real birthday.

Ted had chased him away. And because of Ted, she now had a pretend name, a pretend birthday, and a pretend story. Only her father knew who she really was. Only he could handle her huge requests. Her mother had once been able to, but those days had ended. Her mother was just a ghost now—a skinny, scared, scarred ghost left behind by Ted. She and Jessica were just bones spit out by the wild animal they had let into their lives.

Ted had often seemed so angry. Then he had killed her puppy, Tally. Jessica had thought he wanted to kill her and her mother too. He wasn't generous at all. Her father hadn't been wrong about much, but he had been wrong about that. That was Jessica's first request tonight:

"Daddy, don't be mad, but you were wrong. Ted wasn't generous. He came to hurt us; that's all he wanted. He took everything we had. Well, almost."

An owl called out in the woods, and Jessica smiled—her father answering her.

"Help me to help Rose—please, Dad? I don't want her to go to heaven yet. Help me, Dad. I want to keep her with me. I want her to live." She pictured her father standing in heaven with Saint Agatha and Saint Agnes and Joan of Arc.

And the owl screeched again, and a branch crashed to the ground, and Jessica knew: she had her inspiration. When the sun came up, she would go into the woods. And she would come out with secret treasure, to earn money for Rose.

Chapter 13

Getting Rose stabilized enough to travel to Boston was the goal, so that was all Lily could think of. Liam had gotten them two rooms at the Holiday Inn on the harbor, just down the hill from the hospital. She told him he should go back home, and he said he would as soon as Rose was out of the ICU. Meanwhile, he had arranged with his friend to keep the car indefinitely. And he could do his monitoring work on his laptop.

Lily shrugged. She didn't know what he was hanging around for. She barely even saw him, and because he wasn't a relative, he wasn't allowed into the unit to see Rose. She knew she should be appreciative of his support, but honestly—she was so exhausted and ragged by the time she got to her room each night, she barely had the energy to order soup from room service and eat it in front of the TV.

The first four mornings, she found him in the hotel lobby, waiting to drive her up the hill to Melbourne General. The weather was cool and foggy, with morning mist hovering over the water and town. They took the five-minute ride in silence, with Lily staring over the silver-coated harbor, thinking of questions for Rose's medical team.

On the fifth morning, the fog had lifted, and the sun shone brightly. When Lily entered the hotel lobby, Liam rose to greet her. She held up her hand.

"Look, this is silly," she said. "It's nice out. No more fog. I'm going to walk up to the hospital, and I think you should go back to Cape Hawk."

"It is a nice morning for a walk," he agreed.

"I'm glad you see it my way."

"Good. I'll walk you," he said.

"No! Liam," she said. "You have work to do, back home. The commander needs his car back. Rose is improving."

"She's still in the ICU," he said.

"I think they might release her to a regular pediatric floor today," Lily said. "She's so much better—the fluid around her heart is almost gone, and her lungs are nearly back to normal size."

"The Lasix is working," he said.

"Yes," Lily said, a little surprised by the fact he knew the name of Rose's diuretic, or even that she was taking one. She hardly ever talked details with anyone not a doctor.

"So, they might move her to the floor today?" he asked.

"Yes," Lily said.

"Good," he said. He nodded, smiling. Lily thought she could see the relief in his eyes—his self-imposed burden, whatever it was, had been lifted, and he could go back to the sharks and whales of Cape Hawk. They grinned at each other easily, among the hustle and bustle of the busy hotel lobby. He touched her arm as they walked out into the sunlight.

"Okay then," she said. "Thank you—for everything. Will you thank Anne for sending me that bag of my clothes? Tell her the laundry delivery guy was a brilliant idea—he delivered it when he brought the tablecloths to the hotel."

"Maybe you should just call her yourself," Liam said.

Huh? Lily thought. Was it really too much trouble for him to give his sister-in-law Lily's message? "No problem," she said. "I just thought you'd probably see her at the inn."

"I will, when I get there. But not today..."

"But you're heading home."

Liam shook his head. "No," he said. "Not till Rose is okay."

"Liam!"

"Don't even argue with me, Lily," he said. "Like it or not, I'm staying. Come on—if you don't want a ride, I'll walk you up to the hospital. Let's go—I know you want to catch the doctors on their morning rounds."

Lily opened her mouth to speak, but instead she just started walking up the steep hill that led to Melbourne General. Liam walked silently by her side. Even in the city, there was no doubt that they were in Nova Scotia. The scent of pine filled the air, and the sound of ship traffic—bells, horns, engines—wafted up from the harbor. Seagulls cried overhead. She thought back nine years, to her first days in Nova Scotia. Liam had been with her then too.

"Why are you doing this?" she asked.

"You know why," he said.

"It doesn't make sense. Not after all this time."

"It does to me."

"Look—I know what you said. I think your words are engraved on my heart. I'll be forever grateful. But that was a long time ago."

"Do you think time invalidates promises?" Liam asked.

And Lily had no answer for that. At least, not one she felt like saying out loud. The truth was, she did think time— and other things—invalidated promises. The world was full of evidence supporting just that: broken marriages, broken vows, changes of mind, changes of heart. It was easier to break promises than keep them, that was for sure.

The hill became so steep, her calves began to ache. They passed people walking down the hill, to work. The city park crowned this crest, and they entered between two stone gates. Traffic flowed into Melbourne through the park, coming from points north. As they walked along, they passed a long row of cars. For years now, Lily had been free of the habit of scanning—looking at every face and license plate while trying to keep her own face hidden. She almost wished she'd be seen sometimes—during certain sleepless nights, she actually longed, ached, for a final confrontation.

They walked briskly along a lane that led through the park's rose gardens. The air smelled sweetly of flowers and freshly tended earth. Lily thought of her own garden, which was inspired by the roses of her childhood. Rose loved digging, planting, pruning—and sometimes, when Rose was sick, unable to do more than lie in a hospital bed,

Lily took comfort in thinking of rosebushes—how they had to stay dormant all winter, in order to bloom in summer. Rose would bloom again too.

Suddenly she realized that Liam wasn't walking beside her anymore. She stopped, turned, saw him standing still. Her first instinct was to be impatient—she literally didn't have time to stop and smell the roses. The doctors were making their rounds now, and she needed to catch them.

"What are you doing?" she asked, walking back.

But Liam didn't reply. He was just standing there, gazing over the roses and through the pine trees, to a pond in the woods. Lily tried to follow his gaze. She saw that the pond was ringed with tall, green marsh grass. The water was dark and appeared greenish-brown in the shadows of tall pines and oaks. At the other end of the pond was the World War I monument. In fact, Lily realized that its reflecting pool must be fed by this wilder, more rustic body of water.

"Liam, what are you looking at?" she asked.

"There," he said, pointing. "You have to look carefully. She's hiding in the shadows."

It was a blue heron, standing on the very edge of the pond. The bird was tall and almost unimaginably still—it might have been a statue. The morning sun shone through the trees and grass, silhouetting the long legs, long curved neck, sharp bill. The heron's posture was perfect and vigilant—as if waiting for something more important than anything in the world.

"She's so camouflaged," he said. "She wants to make sure no one sees her till she's ready."

"Why do you say 'she'?" Lily asked.

"I don't know," Liam said, looking her straight in the eye.

"It could be a male."

"I guess it could."

"Liam, there are plenty of herons back home. What's so special about this one?"

He gazed down at her. He had dark blue eyes with lines around them that made him look tired and worried. Yet the eyes themselves were bright as a young boy's, especially in this morning light. Lily blinked and frowned.

"She's in the middle of a city park," he said. "Don't you think that's amazing?"

"A city park in Nova Scotia," she said, "is not the same as a city park somewhere else. But you're a scientist," she continued, and shrugged. "I guess it's your job to catalogue natural phenomena."

"When you put it that way," he said, staring at her even more intently, "I suppose you're right."

"Come on," she said impatiently. "Can we hurry up, please?"

"Natural phenomenon," he said under his breath.

Lily felt a breeze swirl up the hill from the harbor. It came across the pond, through the trees, making the boughs and grasses rustle; it ruffled Lily's hair, and although it was warm, it made her shiver. The heron didn't stir, and neither did Liam. He was still staring at Lily, and he wouldn't look away.

"Come on," she said again. "I'm late."

"I know," he said.

And something about the way he said those words, "I know," made her shiver again. And she began to run, the rest of the way through the park, to the front steps of Melbourne General Hospital. She joined the flood of health care workers—doctors, nurses, aides, therapists—streaming through the double doors. There weren't many patients' parents in this flood—it was much too early for visiting hours.

The security guard noticed Lily, without an ID badge, and he signaled her to stop. She had wasted too much time already, so she just waved at him and jumped into the next elevator. Out of the corner of her eye, she caught sight of Liam—stopping to be grilled by the guard.

Oddly, as the doors closed, Lily felt a pang.

She was crushed in with twenty other people, and Liam wasn't one of them. He had walked her all the way up the steep hill, shown her the heron, accepted her slightly insulting comment about his cataloguing of natural phenomena. The funny thing was, she felt that he was the one making an inside joke. She didn't get it.

And she didn't get why she felt so sorry that she'd gotten on the elevator without him. He had come all this way with her. He was trying so hard to keep that stupid promise she'd never wanted him to make in the first place. Maybe this would give him the hint: he was off the hook. As far as she was concerned, she'd never wanted him on it.

So why did she feel so bad about the fact that he was no longer at her side? She shook the feeling and stepped off on Rose's floor, the Pediatric ICU.

Chapter 14

"Excuse me," the security guard said. "But may I see your ID?"

"ID?" Liam asked, watching the elevator doors close behind Lily.

"Your work badge, for here at the hospital."

"Oh," Liam said. "I don't work here."

"Well, sir, visiting hours don't begin until eleven. It's only eight forty-five now. Doctors have to make their rounds."

"I'm here to see someone in the Pediatric ICU," Liam said. "I think the visiting hours are more flexible up there."

"Yes, they are, sir. Family member?"

"Well, no. Close family friend."

"Sir, only family members are allowed in that unit. We have very strict rules about that. Very strict."

Liam nodded. He knew better than to argue with a security guard—he did. But he had to get up there, had to be with Lily and Rose. He nodded toward the elevator. "I'm with that woman, who just took that last car."

"The small dark-haired woman who ignored me? Shrugged me off?" the guard asked, raising his eyebrows.

"Uh, maybe."

"That one. That one ignores me every morning. It's like I'm not even here. That's right, I've seen you with her before. I took notice of you, on account of—" He stopped himself.

"My arm," Liam said. "Don't worry about it."

"Well, I caught you this morning. One of you, anyway."

Yeah, the one of us that's not a natural phenomenon, Liam thought, picturing Lily weaving through the crowded lobby like a waterspout. High velocity, with the speed of a tornado and even more force. Touching down just long enough to gain more strength from the water's surface, then whirling on her way to Rose.

"You're welcome to wait in the lobby for your friend," the guard said sternly. "But I can't allow you up on the unit without a special pass."

"How would I get one?"

"From a doctor. As well as permission from a parent of the patient. It's best you just wait here."

"Right," Liam said. "Thanks."

But instead, he walked back outside. He crossed the street, went over to the reflecting pool, looked up at the monument. He touched it with his good hand, thought of how strange it was that a big piece of stone would outlast so many of the people he loved: his parents, Connor. Now he gazed down the length of the pool, to the pond at the far end. He peered into the shadows, looking for the heron.

If she was there, she was too well hidden for him to see.

Lily hadn't wanted to pause long enough to look. Forces of nature were like that. They were too busy fulfilling their purpose. Hurricanes, waterspouts, heat waves, Lily Malone. Nothing was going to keep her from Rose for two seconds—not even the poetry of a blue heron, the same color as Lily's own eyes, in this city park.

Liam walked slowly along the west side of the long reflecting pool. He stayed in the shade—not because the sun was so hot, but because he wanted to stay hidden. He, his brother, and Jude had prided themselves on being able to sneak up on wildlife. They could swim silently into a pod of fin whales and not even disturb them. Connor had once swum up to a beluga and touched her dorsal ridge. And they had tracked a pair of snowy owls one winter solstice, crawling to within fifteen feet of them.

He had his cell phone on vibrate, and checked it to be sure: he hoped Lily would at least call him if there was some change.

The idea of Lily as a force of nature was not new to him. In fact, it had inspired their entire unbalanced, undefined, and completely confusing relationship. He thought back nine years, to the first time he'd ever seen her.

She had driven into town in a rusty old Volvo, with holes in the floor and the hood literally held down by baling wire. She had cut her hair very short, she wore glasses, then, that she hadn't really needed. Since his family basically ran Cape Hawk, her first encounter had been with Camille, his aunt, the family grande dame and owner of Neill Real Estate. Lily had been looking for a place to live. It had seemed odd enough to Camille—a pretty, young, and, oh yes, extremely pregnant woman, obviously American, looking for a house in Cape Hawk—to discuss at the family Friday night dinner. Although she was clearly trying to hide her pregnancy with bulky clothes, it was obvious to everyone.

"Cheap," Camille reported. "She actually said that was her main requirement."

"Where's her husband?" Jude, Camille's son, had asked.

"He's a fisherman," Camille said. "Gone for weeks at a time."

"What boat?"

"That's precisely what I asked. She was vague, to say the least. Do you think he's a drug smuggler?"

"Probably runs the maritime heroin trade," Liam said. He hadn't wanted to attend the dinner—he never did— but tonight his aunt had insisted. Sitting next to Anne, he felt her jab his side with her elbow. But she connected with his hard prothesis, so the whole table heard the crack.

"Don't be fresh, Liam," Camille said, giving her daughter-in-law an evil look. "As a matter of fact, this is why I wanted you to be here tonight."

"Because of my expertise with drug smugglers?"

"No. Because she is looking for something cheap, and I thought of that cabin on the back end of your property."

Liam's stomach churned. The building had started out

as a shack—it had been his and Connor's fort, when they were kids. Two rooms that, over the years, his parents had turned into a fairly decent guest cottage.

"I thought you might rent it to her. But first, I thought you should meet her. If you get a bad feeling, or sense that there is indeed something suspicious about her and her husband—well then, we'll find something else. Do you know what I think?"

"No," Anne said. "Please, tell us, Camille."

"I think there is no husband. I think she's an unwed mother!"

"How vile," Anne said.

Now it was Liam's turn to jab her. But Camille took her seriously and nodded gravely. "Precisely. I think she may have moved to Canada to take advantage of our health system. The States' is so abysmal. I don't like the idea of supporting anything like fraud. . . ."

"But it's better than a drug dealer husband," Liam said.

"So true, my dear. Well then—I leave it to you. She is staying right here at the inn. Room 220. Will you take her to see the property?"

"Don't forget your revolver," Jude said. "Just in case."

"Don't you be fresh," his mother said, then hailed the waitress to clear their dessert plates.

As Liam prepared to go to room 220, Anne stopped him.

"It was nice to have you at dinner tonight. Jude was just saying, you've been such a stranger."

"It's hard to resist a Friday night with Camille," Liam grinned.

"I know. I find it's the centerpiece of my week," Anne said. "I think her whole problem comes from the fact that when she married Frederic, her name became Camille Neill. That's quite a handle. It sounds a little like something out of a comedy skit."

They chuckled, glancing around to make sure Camille's spies—her favorite waitstaff and chambermaids—weren't listening.

"Seriously," Anne said. "Where have you been? Have you fallen madly in love with that girl shark researcher who came up last summer?"

Liam shook his head. "No. She was just a colleague from Halifax."

"She was pretty. And she liked you, Liam. Jude and I both noticed."

"Hmm," Liam said.

"Well, at least you're not growling at me, the way you usually do when I try to ask about your love life. I wish you had more of one. You're my favorite in-law."

"Same to you," he said. "Now, I'd better go do my duty."

"Oh, right. Vetting the mysterious unwed drug dealer."

Liam had gone down the hall, not knowing what to expect, just wanting to get the whole thing over with. The hotel was big, rambling, with two long wings. Room 220 was all the way at the end of one, on the second floor. It was on the side of the hotel that faced the employees' parking lot, instead of looking out at Cape Hawk bay.

He knocked—no answer. So he tried again. He checked his watch—it was eight-thirty. Could she already be asleep? There wasn't much to do after dinner in Cape Hawk. Perhaps she had taken a walk. He leaned closer to the door. Small sounds were coming from inside.

Holding his breath, he listened. At first he thought it was the TV. A high thin voice came through the door. It sounded unnatural for a human—more like the keening of a seabird. Or the singing of a whale, picked up on hydrophones. But the sound did something to Liam's heart that made him realize that the source was very human after all, that it was the woman crying.

Liam had heard crying like that only once before: his mother, the day Connor died. He raised his hand to knock again, but stopped himself. The stranger's grief was too terrible and private to disturb. So he backed away, deciding to return the next morning.

He didn't have to.

Camille left him a message at his office: *"Never mind about the rental. She has found lodging elsewhere."*

Liam felt relieved. Whatever had been going on inside that room was too much for him. He had spent the night wondering what was wrong—and he warned himself that he couldn't get involved. Not that that would be so hard; not getting involved was what Liam did best. Just ask the Halifax shark researcher Anne had mentioned. Julie Grant. She still sent him letters—or did, until the last one, where she'd said, "Call me when you realize that people are better to spend time with than sharks. I thought we had a chance, but now I know I'm wrong. Goodbye."

Liam had learned that it was easier on the heart to stay distant from people—even, or especially, the ones he cared most about. After Connor's death, his mother had disappeared. Not in body, but in spirit. She had gotten quieter, lonelier, more distant, until it was just her and the bottle. No matter how hard Liam had tried to bring her back to life, remind her she still had a son, she wouldn't listen. When he had gone for surgeries on his arm, his father had dropped him off. His mother couldn't even bear to visit the hospital where Connor had been pronounced dead.

Now, walking the length of the reflecting pool, Liam looked over his shoulder at that same hospital. Lily and Rose were in there now. Lily's way of being a mother was so different, outwardly at least, from his mother's. Inwardly, he suspected they were exactly the same. Two women who loved their ailing children so much, it controlled every aspect of their lives.

The heron was right there—where he had seen her with Lily. Walking quietly in the shadows, Liam took a few steps closer. The heron didn't move. She held her elegant pose, blue neck craned, yellow bill pointed downward. The pond seemed as still as glass, but the heron saw movement and in one swift shot lunged, stabbed, came up with a silver fish.

Liam watched her swallow; when she was finished, she resumed her pose. He felt the surge and amazement of watching nature at work—much the way he felt watching Lily the natural phenomenon.

He figured the security guard had to take a break at some point, and in any case, regular visiting hours would soon commence.

So he turned and headed back toward the hospital, to keep the promise Lily had never even wanted him to make, wished he wouldn't keep, just because he really didn't feel he had a choice.

Rose had defied plenty of odds in her day, and today was no exception. By the time her mother arrived, she had already been moved onto a pediatric surgical floor. She was breathing well, and she'd lost five pounds of fluid, and her heart and lungs and all her organs were going back to normal size. So why was it so hard for her to even smile? Even a little smile seemed almost impossible.

"What's wrong, honey?" her mother asked, standing beside her bed.

"Nothing."

"Are you sure? You look upset."

Rose tried to make her lips turn up. It wasn't a real smile—it didn't come from inside. But she didn't want her mother to be worried. The doctors and therapists were always telling her that her feelings were *fine,* and that she should *honor* them, even when the feelings were unwanted: unhappy, sad, angry, hurt, things like that. But the one thing Rose couldn't bear was seeing her mother with those worry lines in her forehead—so she faked a smile.

"Mom," she said. "Did you see Dr. Colvin?"

"Yes. He told me you're making great improvements. And I know he talked to Dr. Garibaldi in Boston, to discuss how soon you can go there."

"I don't want to go to Boston, Mom."

"But, honey—"

Rose clenched her fists. The tips of her fingers were numb; they were always numb because her heart didn't pump enough blood fast enough. She had funny-looking little fingertips, almost like tiny paddles. She tried to keep the pretend smile on her face, but inside, she was melting.

"It's summer," she said. "Jessica's first summer in Cape Hawk. I've already been to the hospital now. I knew I had to go, and I had it planned, but now this is it. This is my hospital time. I want to have fun, Mom. Fun with Jessica."

"I know, sweetheart. And you will. That's what the surgery is for—to replace the patch, so you'll be able to have all the fun in the world."

Rose just stared. She wanted to believe her mother. She had been in so many hospital beds over the years. She remembered a time when she was five, and she'd had a valve replacement, and developed endocarditis—a bacterial infection that attacks people with heart problems. She spent months in the hospital, taking in antibiotics through her veins, which practically ruined her kidneys and liver and made her hair dry out. She had looked like a straw doll.

"Jessica will make a different best friend," she said.

"No, she won't."

"How do you know?"

"Because who could be a better best friend than you?"

"Someone who isn't in the hospital."

"Honey, why are you so down?"

Rose took some deep breaths, but it was getting harder to keep the smile on her face. How could she not be down? Her birthday party had been so wonderful, magical—and then Rose's heart had given out. The drugs were stabilizing her now, but she felt groggy all the time. And instead of getting to spend the summer in Cape Hawk, now she was going to have to go to another hospital—the big one in Boston. Jessica would probably just forget about her.

"That was a pretty stupid question, right?" her mother asked.

"No," Rose said. "It wasn't stupid. I'm sorry."

"Rose, never be sorry. You've been through so much, and we just keep asking you to go through more and more. No wonder you're—"

Her mother's voice was shaking, and she sounded so down herself that Rose thought she was going to start to cry. But just then, looking over her mother's shoulder, she saw something framed in the doorway that brought a true smile to her face—the first one she'd had all day.

Dr. Neill stood in the doorway, holding a huge bunch of balloons. Every bright color, just like a rainbow.

"Dr. Neill!" she said.

"Hi, Rose," he said, walking straight over to her, bending down to stroke her forehead. "How's my girl?"

"I'm glad you're here," she said, almost unable to believe her eyes. Why hadn't her mother mentioned it?

"Of course I'm here. You're a wonder, Rose. I thought

you were still in the ICU, but when I asked at the desk, they told me you were here."

"You've been at the hospital since I got here?" Rose asked.

He nodded. Rose gave her mother a surprised look, and her mother just stood there trying to appear innocent.

"What about Nanny, and all the other whales and sharks? Aren't you supposed to be keeping watch over them?"

"Nanny told me this was more important."

"Whales don't talk!"

"Well, Nanny and I speak a certain language," he said. "It's hard to explain, to people who don't speak it. . . ."

Rose reached out. She touched his prothesis with one of her clubbed fingers. She felt a spark inside.

"I think I speak it too."

"So do I," he said.

"I'm feeling left out," her mother said. "Herons, whales. Could someone speak human to me?" Rose heard her, but this moment was completely between her and Dr. Neill. She knew that he understood being in the hospital, fearing that she might never get better, that she'd always be different. She held up her index finger. He stared at it, the way it broadened at the tip. She saw him look at the IV needle in the back of her hand. She even saw him look at the catheter that ran from her to the bag beside the bed, and she didn't feel embarrassed. She wanted him to pick her up, as if he were her father.

"I'm not happy today," she said.

"No," he said.

"I'm scared."

He nodded. He crouched down by the side of her bed and looked into her eyes. The balloons bobbed over his head. He tried to tie the strings to her bed rails, but he couldn't with one hand. Rose helped him out. Their fingers touched, and she smiled. She was still scared, but having him there made her feel like smiling anyway.

"You brought me balloons," she said.

"Yes, I did."

"I thought balloons were bad. Because if you let go of the string, they might float out over the ocean, and fall, and the sea turtles will think they're jellyfish, and eat them, and die."

"You're right, Rose. You make a very good oceanographer. That's why I knew it was safe to give the balloons to you."

"Because I care about the sea turtles?"

"Yes," he said, holding her hand. "Because of that."

Rose closed her eyes and felt her pulse beating fast and light. She thought of how everything had to be protected, in different ways. Her mother had to be protected from worry; the sea turtles had to be protected from balloons; Rose had to be protected from being so scared of what would happen next.

What did Dr. Neill have to be protected from? She didn't know. But she knew that there had to be something, and she squeezed his hand to let him know that she was there.

Chapter 15

The hot weather arrived in Cape Hawk, making it seem more like the summers Jessica knew. Every morning, haze clung to the cliffs and pines before burning off. Sunlight beat down, the breeze stopped blowing. Jessica wore shorts over her bathing suit, but instead of going to the swim cove, she was hard at work.

She held the burlap bag in one hand, picked up fallen pine needles with the other. This was messy work—her fingers were sticky with pitch, but she just pressed onward. Bent at the waist, she made her way through her backyard, covering every inch. She ignored fallen leaves or twigs, concentrating only on long needles fallen from white pines.

Sometimes she'd pass under a hemlock or spruce—trees with short needles. Those were fine too, as long as they were pine. She found many pinecones—tiny ones that looked like doll-size beehive ovens. The hemlock cones were perfect and compact, with their petals drawn in tight like rosebuds. When she found them, she slipped them into a different bag, slung over her shoulder. White-pine cones were longer, with their tips frosted with silvery pitch. She ignored those.

As she scoured her backyard and the lower fringe of the hilly woods behind her house, she thought of Rose. What was she doing now? Was she getting better? Last night one of the Nanouks had called her mother, and she'd heard them talking. The report had been the same: *Rose is holding her own*, which didn't sound bad but definitely didn't sound all that good, either. Then, afterwards, Jessica had watched her mother go online, to the Johns Hopkins site, and do some researchy thing with a worried crease in her brow.

Jess tried to tell herself that what the grownups thought didn't matter. She was working for Rose. Her back ached and fingers itched, but she didn't care. Back in Boston she had gone to Catholic school, and the nuns had told them about Saint Agnes and Saint Agatha, as well as Joan of Arc: all young girls, martyrs, who had suffered for the Lord. Tales of hair shirts and beds of nails and being beheaded. Jessica had thought it sounded pretty lame at first. Especially hair shirts. She couldn't quite imagine such a thing; was it like a fur coat, only a shirt?

But then she had started thinking: maybe martyrdom could be a way to go—not beheading, but the other things. A lot of the problems those old saints had had involved demons. One Irish nun that kind of scared her, Sister Ignatius, had loved to tell them stories about the devil. "Lucifer is incarnate on this earth," she would say in her squeaky Wicklow accent. "He exists as surely as you or I. We encounter him on a daily basis and must fight to banish him from our lives!" Jessica believed Sister, and she began to think—if she was willing to suffer, or sacrifice something, maybe she could drive Ted out of the house.

For the first week, she tried giving up cinnamon Pop-Tarts. But Ted stayed and showed no signs of budging. Jessica began doing other things: sacrificing pudding at school lunch. Wearing shoes she had outgrown, that hurt her toes. Kneeling on the bare wood floor until not only her knees ached, but also her hips and spine. She didn't have a bed of nails, but she tried sleeping in the bathtub one night.

Her mother found her and thought she had been sleep-walking. She took Jessica back to bed very quickly—before Ted saw. Ted didn't like anything unusual. He would have somehow made Jessica sleeping in the bathtub seem like a slap in his face. He might have yelled, or he might just have gone silent—with those cold, evil eyes. Jessica could almost hear him hissing, "Why are you trying to hurt me this way?"

So with the bathtub off-limits and no bed of nails, Jessica had just changed her sheets—from the soft pink ones with white lambs imprinted on the fabric to the hard scratchy ones that her mother had bought by accident, on sale at Max-Mart. They didn't feel at all good on her skin. She also scratched her legs with pins. It used to give her fierce pleasure to see little dots of blood on the cheap sheets. Her mother just thought she'd been at her mosquito bites.

Jessica would never know whether her martyrdom actually worked—it didn't drive Ted from their house. It didn't save Tally. That was the night her mother decided they'd had enough: when Ted kicked the little dog and killed her, her mother packed them up in the dark of night, bundled them into the car, and drove them away.

Now, picking up more pine needles, she paused in front of a flat rock where she had seen a garter snake sunning itself last week. The serpent had opened its pink mouth and hissed at her, and even though it was very small, its presence had reminded Jessica of Ted, and shaken her.

Jessica wished the snake would come now. She would step on it, barefoot, and kill it like Mary. She wanted to drive the serpents and demons and evil wizards and Teds out, so that Rose could get well. It was the only way. She walked slowly through the pine woods, picking up more pine needles—her hand hot and sticky, her back aching—and she saw a flash of blue in the trees.

At first she thought it was Mary, leading her deeper into the woods, but then she looked up in the branches of a spruce and saw that it was just a blue jay. A bright, beautiful crested jay. Not Mary at all.

When Jessica had filled three large sacks, Marisa knew it was time to take her to town. They drove down to the harbor, parked in front of In Stitches. Marisa was glad to see that the door was ajar, the shop was open. For a moment she felt excited—to think that Lily might be back, working. But when she and Jessica went inside, she saw that it was Marlena behind the counter, with Cindy restocking shelves.

"Hi, girls," Marlena called. "How are you?"

"We're fine," Marisa said. "Have you heard from Lily?"

"Anne did. She came down with coffee and muffins for us, and said that Rose is improving quickly. She's lost almost all the extra fluid, and they're talking about flying her down to Boston in a few days."

"That's a good sign," Marisa said.

"You're a nurse?" Cindy asked. "Anne was telling us. A woman of medicine in our ranks!"

"Yes, I am," Marisa said, and it felt good to think of the Nanouk Girls talking about her, including her "in their ranks."

"What do you think it all means—all these complications?" Marlena asked. "Poor Rosie, having to go through so much."

"Tetralogy of Fallot is very complicated," she said, "but it's treatable, especially when the patient is young."

"I've known Lily since the year Rose was born," Marlena said. "There hasn't been a stretch I can remember when she wasn't taking her to some different hospital or specialist."

"Boston, Melbourne, once out to Cincinnati," Cindy said.

"Cincinnati has the best pediatric heart center in the country," Marisa said.

"I remember that what they did there had to do with 'transposition of the great vessels.' My father was a boat captain, and I thought it had to do with shipping. But it means that both Rose's main arteries were on the left side of her heart, instead of on either side," Marlena said.

"That's right. Her aorta was misplaced," Cindy said.

"What's her aorta?" Jessica asked, standing there with one of the sacks of pine needles.

"It's the large artery that pumps blood from the heart's left ventricle and sends it out into the body," Marisa explained.

"And the hospital lost it?" Jessica asked.

"No, honey," Cindy said. "It happened at birth. Before birth, in the womb. No one knows why, but it was on the wrong side of her heart."

"You mean, God did that to her?" Jessica asked, sounding outraged.

Marisa felt an aura, almost as if she was going to have a migraine. Only it wasn't that—it was Jessica about to go into a full-blown religious tirade. She watched her daughter's face turn red with outrage, and it reminded her of when Jessica would react against Ted, against his control and anger. Instead of getting mad at her, or even Ted, Jessica would get furious at God.

"Well, I wouldn't say he did it *to* her," Marlena said. "It's more like in his infinite wisdom and design, he thought it made sense at the time. We don't understand why."

"What kind of wisdom and design gives a misplaced artery to a baby?" Jess asked.

"Jessica," Marisa said warningly.

"I'm serious. It doesn't make any sense."

"The Lord isn't supposed to make sense," Marlena said, a little nervously. Marisa could see that she was rethinking the two newest Nanouks.

"That's right," Cindy said. "It's one big mystery. One big freaking mystery. Marlena, you might as well say he did it to her," Cindy said. "You sound all confused, and to tell you the truth, I've been confused myself. Who can understand why this happened? To think of our Rosie suffering..."

"It does pain me," Marlena replied. "From the time she was a tiny blue baby..."

"Probably it's not the Lord who did it," Jessica said. "Probably it was the devil."

"Jess, stop," Marisa said, feeling the blood drain out of her face. When Jessica got going on God, the devil, and Ted, anything could happen.

"The Lord doesn't hurt people," Jessica said. "I refuse to believe that."

Marisa stared at her. She thought of all the sickness she'd seen in her day. The injuries, illnesses, diseases, acts of violence. Although she had raised Jessica in the Church, she had been on a long, slow decline in belief herself. It had reached its final depths during the end of her time with Ted. "I do believe, help my unbelief," had once been her prayer. Now she just believed in science.

"God moves in mysterious ways," Marlena said. "But I'm with Jessica on this. I don't think God wants Rose or any of us to suffer. I'm going to bring this up the next time the Nanouks are all in one place. I think we should put it in our charter."

"Good idea," Cindy said, laughing. "We, the Nanouk Girls of the Frozen North, hereby decree that the Lord is off the hook when it comes to pain and suffering."

"I wouldn't go that far," Marlena said defensively. "I just don't think he does it on purpose."

"What's that lovely aroma?" Cindy asked, raising her eyebrow and changing the subject. "It smells like the North Woods in here."

"Pine needles," Jessica said.

"What are they for?"

"Well, to raise money for Rose's medical care."

"Heaven knows Lily could use help with it," Marlena said, "but how will pine needles help?"

"I want to make Cape Hawk pine pillows and sell them."

Marisa stood back, watching Jessica explain herself. This had been all her idea, coming down to In Stitches, buying the materials from Lily's shop—they had known the Nanouk Girls were keeping it open, taking turns covering different days.

"Where will you sell them, dear?"

"To the tourists who go on the whale boats."

"Pine pillows," Cindy said.

Jessica nodded. "They'll smell just like Cape Hawk. All the things that make it so special here—the woods, pine, birds, whales . . . I thought I could embroider little pictures of Nanny, or the owls that live in the forest behind my house, or the hawks that live on the rock ledges—right into the fabric, along with the words 'Cape Hawk,' or maybe even 'Get Well Soon, Rose.' "

"Do you do a lot of embroidery, dear?" Marlena asked.

"I've never done it before," Jessica said proudly, chin jutting out. Clearly she didn't see this as a setback—just another feat to master. Marisa watched Marlena and Cindy for their reactions. They both kept straight faces. What they didn't know was how determined Jessica could be, or how huge her heart was.

"It might take you a while to learn," Cindy said.

"And then even longer to actually embroider the fabric. And then put the pillows together," Marlena said.

Marisa's eyes filled up. She saw Jessica clutching her big sack of sticky pine needles, her fingers black with tar. Marisa foresaw hours of diligent embroidery ahead for her darling daughter. Jessica stood perfectly straight, undeterred by Marlena and Cindy's reservations. Her love for Rose was too strong for that. Suddenly Marisa had a memory—after Paul died, she had opened his closet, looking for something—she couldn't even remember what.

She'd seen a bulge in the center of his suits. And there, down below, were Jessica's thin legs. She was just standing there among her father's suits. She'd loved her father so much, and that was the only way she could think to be with him. Marisa knew that the pillow project was very much like that—a way to stay close to Rose.

"I'll help her learn," Marisa said.

"Thank you, Mom," Jessica said.

"So will I," Marlena said. "In fact, I give needlework lessons at the high school. I'll teach you for free, sweetheart."

"I'll go you one better," Cindy said. "I'll embroider the pillows myself! And I bet the other Nanouks will too. I'll call Anne and Doreen, you call Suzanne and Alison."

"Fine, and in that case, maybe Jessica and I can concentrate on making the pillow squares—cutting them out, sewing them together."

"And stuffing them with pine needles when they're done!" Jessica said. "And, of course, selling them—"

"I'll bet Anne will let us put some up at the inn's gift shop."

"We'll have to get them by Camille."

"Who's Camille?" Marisa asked.

"Oooh, Camille Neill," Cindy said. "She's the matriarch of the family. Mother, grandmother, great-grandmother of four generations of Neills. Think Catherine the Great meets the Wicked Witch of the West, with a soupçon of Lauren Bacall in the Fancy Feast commercials. She is the official owner of the inn and the whale boats."

"Imposing," Marisa said.

"Yes. And she's none too crazy about Lily."

"How could someone not be crazy about Lily?" Marisa asked.

"Well, it dates back to the year she first got here. And it has something to do with Liam."

"Captain Hook?" Jessica asked.

"The kids call him that, but he's really very dear. He's down in Melbourne with Lily and Rose right now."

"Really?" Marisa asked. "Are they—"

"An item? No one really knows," Cindy said. "There has been much speculation. Normally they act as if they can't stand the sight of each other."

"But whenever Rose has a problem, Liam is right there to help," Marlena said.

"We're gossiping," Cindy said. "It's beneath us, as Nanouk Girls."

"It's not gossip," Marlena scoffed. "It's concern. We love Lily and want her to be happy."

"With Liam Neill?" Marisa asked.

"I think we've said enough," Cindy said somberly. "Let's get cracking on the pillows. Unbleached muslin or canvas, Jessica? This is your project. We're just your assistants."

"I just hope the Fancy Feast lady lets us sell them at the inn and on the boats," Jessica said.

"Now is a time for prayer," Marlena said. "Because that's what it will take to soften the heart of Camille Neill."

Chapter 16

Taking Exit 90 off I-95, Patrick Murphy turned into the most crowded parking lot he'd ever seen. There were cars from every state, tour buses, motor homes, and not a parking spot to be found within walking distance of the Mystic Aquarium. He finally parked on the other side of the little shopping village, after beating a lady in a minivan out for the spot.

Ten minutes later, he was standing in line with a hundred other people, waiting to get in. Sandwiched between a family of five from Hartford and a honeymooning couple from Philadelphia, he eavesdropped to pass the time. Solving crimes was still his favorite pastime, and he liked to figure out as much as he could about every person he encountered, without them knowing he was listening.

After a few minutes, the mom of five had to take the youngest to the bathroom, and the dad of five took the opportunity to whip out his cell phone and call someone he addressed as "sweet baby." Behind him, he heard the young husband tell his new bride that the stocks her father had given them for a wedding present had gone up the night before, and he thought they should consider buying instead of renting their house.

Both instances affirmed his long-held belief that the only thing necessary to good police work was a deep curiosity about human nature and behavior. But then he got inside the aquarium—the super-cool air-conditioning very welcome after standing in the blistering heat—and was faced with the humbling reason for his mission here.

He asked directions to the membership office, thinking that over nine years later, he was still hot on the trail of the coldest case he'd ever had. All that deep curiosity about human nature had gotten him exactly nothing when it came to finding out what had happened to Mara Jameson. He might as well just spend the rest of his life praying Hail Marys for a big fat clue to drop right in his lap.

Throngs of kids were racing around, giving him a headache. It was a beautiful sunny day outside. What were kids doing in here? When he was young, his parents would have handed him a bat and a ball, or a fishing rod, and told him to go out in the sunshine and not to come back till dinnertime. But as he followed the crowd, he found himself being mesmerized by the glowing tanks, the schools of fish, the eel weaving in and out of its green reef—he began to relax.

Patrick spoke the language of fish. He looked at these and thought of how great it would be to be in a boat on the open water, with all these fish swimming below. Sandra had never understood that. She had thought fishing was nothing more than sitting on deck with a beer and a pole. She hadn't understood that it was clouds in the sky, the water changing colors, schools of fish breaking the surface. It was one big mystery, but a beautiful mystery—not like the kinds that tore at Patrick's heart every day.

Not like Mara Jameson.

So the aquarium tanks gave him some insight into what went on below the surface, and when he'd had enough, he drifted out into the corridor, looking for the administrative offices. A receptionist asked if she could help him, and he said he hoped so, he needed to see someone in membership. A few minutes later, a pretty blond woman came out.

"Hello, I'm Viola de la Penne," she said. "I'm associate director of membership."

"Hi," he said. "I'm Patrick Murphy." He paused. This was where he wanted to whip out his old badge and show her that he was official. Instead, he said, "I'm a retired state police detective."

"Oh, and with all your free time you want to join the aquarium—or maybe even volunteer!" she said. The twinkle in her blue eyes let him think she was kidding. At least, he hoped so. He seriously hoped he looked too tough and seasoned to be giving seal tours to the kiddies.

"If only there was time for such things," he said, cracking a three-cornered smile.

"You mean, crimes still need to be solved, speeders still need to be stopped, stuff like that?"

"You got it, ma'am," he said.

"I'm only forty-two," she said. "Does that put me in the 'ma'am' category?"

"To retired cops, I'm afraid so."

"Hmm. That's a sobering thought. What can I do for you, Retired Officer Murphy?"

He grinned at her giving it back to him.

"I am here about a membership," he said. "You're right about that. Only, it's not for me. It was a gift to a friend of mine."

"What's the name?"

"Maeve Jameson."

"Was there a problem with the category of membership? Would she like to upgrade?"

"There's no problem. It's just that it was anonymous. Whoever gave it to her wanted to keep it secret. I was wondering whether you could help me figure it out. Maeve really wants to say thank you. That's just how she is."

"I can understand that. I obviously have to balance the wishes of the donor, but I don't think there's any harm in taking a look."

Patrick followed her into her office, which was filled with family photographs—a man on the deck of a sailboat, and a beautiful dark-haired daughter. Viola sat at her computer, looking through files. Patrick tried to lean around, to see her screen, but he couldn't do it discreetly enough, so he quit trying.

"Ah, here we go," Viola said.

"Do you have a name?"

"Actually I don't, which makes it easier for me to say no

to you. There's a note here saying that the gift was to be completely anonymous—just as you said."

"There must be some record of who made the gift, right? Even if you can't tell me?"

Viola shook her head, peering at the screen. "No. All I have is a note to myself, that the giver wanted to be sure we still had beluga whales here. Somehow that was important—I don't suppose there's any harm in telling you that."

"Beluga? Isn't that caviar?"

"Retired Detective, it's also a type of whale, one of the few that can live in captivity. We've had beluga whales here at the acquarium for many, many years. People who are adults now still remember the thrill of seeing a whale for the first time—right here in our tanks. There's a show, starring Snowblind and Snowflake, beginning in just about fifteen minutes. Perhaps you'd like to go. . . ."

"Snowblind and Snowflake?"

"Yes. Belugas are white whales."

"Huh."

Patrick considered. Maybe Maeve loved whales, loved belugas in particular. Or maybe she had taken Mara to watch whales when she was little. Or maybe one of her ex-students wanted to give her a gift. Or maybe it was just a mistake, the gift had been from her insurance agent or greengrocer or freaking car repairman.

"How'd the person pay? Got a credit card number on file?"

"The payment was in cash. I have a note to myself, that

the exchange rate was a little off. The payment was over—
too much—once I calculated the rate."

"What rate?"

"The exchange rate—Canadian to U.S.," Viola said.
"The currency was Canadian."

"Did you save the envelope?"

Viola shook her head, smiling. "Sorry. I didn't know we
were going to be investigated for processing a gift."

Patrick smiled back. He thought for a minute she was
flirting with him. But she had on a wedding ring, and there
were those family pictures everywhere. He was so out of
practice, he didn't know the difference between friendly
banter and flirting. As Sandra had told him often enough,
he was hopeless—in many areas.

"Look," Viola said. "Just to make it up to you, I'm going
to comp you for the dolphin show."

"Dolphins?"

"Well, Snowflake and Snowblind make an appearance.
That way, you can see the belugas for yourself, and hope-
fully report back to Mrs. Jameson that they're worth coming to see."

Patrick thanked her, shook her hand, and accepted the
ticket. Who had sent Maeve the membership, and what did
beluga whales have to do with anything?

He made his way up to the marine theater and took his
seat among a crowd of people from Brooklyn. They were
part of a bus tour, and by listening to the women beside
him, he realized that the tour included the Seaport, the
aquarium, and dinner and a show at the casino. One

woman was divorced, and the other was a widow. The widow was saying her grandchildren loved dolphin shows.

Patrick squinted at the pool. He thought of Maeve, how much she missed her granddaughter, how she had never known the great-grandchild Mara had been carrying. What was he even doing here? Most of the time, he was 95 percent sure that Edward Hunter had killed her, that he had hidden her body where it would never be found. But that other 5 percent was powerful enough to send Patrick following crazy leads, even to the marine theater.

Some marine biologist took his place up on a platform and began his spiel about bottlenose dolphins and Atlantic dolphins, and then some dolphins—Patrick didn't really notice which kind—came out and began leaping into the air like circus animals doing tricks. Blowing the horn, catching the rings, bumping the beach ball.

He remembered going to Sea World with Sandra. She had worn white shorts and a blue halter, and she'd had a sunburn. Patrick had spread sunscreen on her shoulders and wanted to forget about the dolphin show and go back to the hotel. Now, he forced himself to stay in the moment. Sugar, one of the dolphins, landed with a huge splash, and half the audience got soaked.

Then the dolphins went away, and the ringmaster guy made his voice very serious. Patrick thought it was sad that he was a scientist who spent his time making dolphins do tricks. It made Patrick feel depressed somehow. And then the water's surface broke, and this big white creature stuck its head up.

Patrick was shocked—it was huge. A whale, a real whale, right here in a tank in Mystic, Connecticut. "This is Snowflake, our oldest beluga whale," the ringmaster said. "Her sister, Snowblind, is on vacation today, and won't be performing. The sisters come from northern waters, up in Maritime Canada, and we..."

Some kids in the crowd sounded disappointed. Patrick found himself standing up, pushing past the women from Brooklyn, casting one last look back at the white whale. Her eyes looked bright and solemn. Patrick felt them following him out the door, watching him go. It was the oddest sensation, being watched by a whale.

The scientist had said the belugas came from Canada. Viola had said the membership money came from Canada. Patrick wondered—was there anything Canadian in Mara Jameson's file? He had to get back to the boat to dig up his old notes and find out.

Maeve wasn't feeling very well. The heat had closed in on Hubbard's Point, making everything—including the roses and her—wilt. She was standing in the backyard, filling the yellow watering can from the hose, when she heard a car door close. It was probably Clara's son stopping by with his kids to take a swim, she thought. She leaned against the weathered shingle house, splashing her feet with the hose.

The spigot was attached to a corner of the house, right next to a small cement circle. Mara had always loved to create pictures out of odd materials: she would sew little quilts, make small pillows, embroider wall hangings, needlepoint bookmarks. But this was really her pride and joy: Maeve had helped her mix up cement, they had poured it into a one-foot-diameter circle, and Mara had pressed shells, sea glass, and a large sand dollar into the wet concrete. It was still beautiful.

"Hello, Maeve," came the low, familiar voice that she had heard only on the phone these last many years.

Maeve jumped. It was Edward—holding a small glossy blue bag. She saw that he was still tall, broad-shouldered, confident. He wore a white shirt over pressed khakis. No belt, no socks. Polished brown loafers. Rolex watch—the same one Mara had bought him with some of her inheritance. The sight of that watch made her stomach turn, and she had to literally hold on to the side of the house. She raised her eyes to his—they were the same, cold black fire. Icy yet scorching at the same time—the damnedest eyes she'd ever seen. And dark hair combed back, and a tan—a golf tan, or maybe this year it was a tennis tan, or maybe he'd bought a yacht and now it was a yachting tan.

"Edward. What brings you here?" she asked with enough coolness to keep him from kissing her cheek.

"I was in the neighborhood on business," he said.

"Really. Hubbard's Point?" She glanced around—beach, rocks, salt water, roses, wishing well. "Not much business here."

"Not Hubbard's Point, exactly. Black Hall, Silver Bay, and Hawthorne. I have clients in all three towns."

"Aren't you successful. Three of the most affluent towns

on the Connecticut shoreline. You've always known where to find new prospects." She felt the words burning on her tongue. During the investigation, she had been quoted as saying he was a predator and Mara had been nothing more than a mark to him.

"Yes, I am successful," he said, staring at her, unable to keep himself from taking her on. Everything to Edward was a challenge. Maeve knew that she could push his buttons and have him slobbering with rage in ten seconds flat. Instead, she counted to ten and smiled.

"Your mother must be very proud," she said. "That you made something of yourself."

His jaw rippled. My, but he was transparent. Maeve could almost see the wheels turning. Should he put her through the plate glass window, or just continue his Ivy League act? Maeve would refrain from pointing out that it *was*, in fact, an act. That Mara had discovered his lies about Harvard and Columbia Business School. Sadly, in his profession of stock brokerage, they didn't matter. Too bad they couldn't disbar him or revoke privileges or something.

"She *is* proud," he said.

"Of course she is. And so must your new wife be." Maeve thought of what Patrick had told her about the marriage falling apart. Edward flinched.

"How have you been?" he asked, not taking the bait.

Maeve smiled gently and didn't reply.

He waited for a few seconds. When he realized that she wasn't going to answer, he nodded briskly, as if he hadn't really asked the question. They stood there, facing off. Did he really have the nerve to show his face here? The last place on earth Mara had been seen alive? Maeve found her attention drifting across the yard, to the only flat section big enough to hold a tent.

It had actually straddled the property line between her and Clara's houses. For Mara and Edward's wedding, eleven years ago this month, they had put up a pretty yellow-and-white-striped tent in that very spot. There had been tables with pale yellow tablecloths, white wooden chairs, vases of roses and wildflowers picked from Maeve and Clara's gardens, and a string quartet.

Everyone from Hubbard's Point had attended. All of Mara's childhood friends: Bay McCabe, Tara O'Toole, Dana and Lily Underhill, and all the other now grown-up Point kids. Maeve had invited people from school—other retired teachers, as well as some still at Black Hall High, her old principal—and her roommate from Connecticut College, who had flown out from Chicago, and some of her son and daughter-in-law's friends. Aida Von Lichen, Johnny Moore's sister, had come, and his daughter Stevie—from whom Mara had once taken art lessons—had read a love poem of Johnny's.

Edward's side of the aisle had been less populated. That should have been a red flag, she knew now. But at the time, it had been just another reason to feel sorry for him. His sister hadn't been able to get time off; his mother had come down with pneumonia; his father had spent the airfare Edward had sent him on booze. It was all so sad; so Mara had worked overtime, extra hard, to make sure every one of her and Maeve's friends gave him extra love and attention.

Those thoughts were crackling in Maeve's mind as she stared at Edward now. Her fingers literally twitched—she wanted that badly to rip his eyes out. She had never known that she was capable of true, passionate, unadulterated hatred until after Mara disappeared. Eight and a half months pregnant, her darling, beloved Mara had just fallen off the face of the earth. . . .

"Let's forget the pleasantries, shall we?" she asked now. "What brings you here?"

"I found some things of Mara's I thought you should have," he said, now clutching the bag to his chest. "The police had them for a while, but they returned them to me. They've been in my trunk, waiting for a chance to bring them to you."

"I don't want them," she said.

His eyes widened with surprise. Maeve's lips trembled. She half-turned away, began to train the hose on the roots of the rosebushes climbing up the side of the house. They were thick, hardy bushes of white and yellow roses—and they were in full, delicious bloom right now. She couldn't bring herself to look up, to where the roses were most lush. The trellis stopped just short of a bedroom window— Mara's childhood bedroom, and the one they had decided would be the nursery when the baby visited.

"I'm sure you do want them," he pressed.

"Hmm," she said, feigning indifference. Her hands shook, she wanted so badly to look inside that bag. But

Maeve had learned something about Edward, through Mara. She remembered one of Mara's visits, early in her pregnancy. Some of the truth about Edward had started leaking out—and Mara was fighting awareness with every inch of her body. She wanted to stay in the denial of a "happy" marriage, part of a couple expecting a much-wanted—by Mara, at least—child.

"I don't get it, Granny," she said. "As soon as I let him know I'm happy about something, or excited, it's as if he wants to take it away from me. Like last night. He's told me all spring that he wanted to take me to dinner at the Hawthorne Inn. But at first I was sick, and then I was so tired, and I've had lots of work—so last night was the first time I really wanted to go. We were all dressed and ready—out the door—when he changed his mind. He just looked at me and said he didn't feel like it. That now *he* was too tired to go."

"Maybe he was," Maeve had said. She kicked herself now, but back then, she had tried to help Mara give him the benefit of the doubt.

"No," Mara had said, starting to cry. "He left me home, and went to hit golf balls at One Hundred Acres."

Maeve remembered Mara's tears. She stared at the spray coming from the hose and thought of all the tears Mara must have cried—that she didn't let her grandmother see. She could almost feel Edward twitching with frustration.

"These are things of Mara's," he repeated. "I thought you'd want—"

"Leave them by the door," she said.

"You're her grandmother," he said. "I thought you'd care—"

Maeve glared down at the roots of the rosebushes. A cool breeze blew off Long Island Sound. Did Edward remember the times he and Mara had gone sailing? The times they had rinsed off in this exact spot, using this exact hose? Maeve heard a screen door slam, and not thirty seconds later, a breathless Clara appeared.

"Hello, Edward."

"Hi, Mrs. Littlefield. Wow, you look great. I haven't seen you in so long!"

"It has been a long time," Clara said, her tone slightly more friendly than Maeve wanted it to be.

"I came to give these things of Mara's to Maeve, but it seems she doesn't want them."

"I'll take them," Clara said, and the instant Maeve heard the bag passed from Edward's hand to Clara's, she felt something relax inside—as if the wire holding her stiff and brittle had been cut, and she was suddenly a rag doll.

"It's been a long time," Edward said. "I thought by now there'd be water under the bridge. Every June and July, just past the time of year Mara disappeared, I miss her so much. I swear, I've never gotten over it. I just thought that we could maybe talk—"

"Nine years," Maeve said. "Three weeks, six days..."

"But if we could just talk—"

"I don't think that's such a good idea," Clara said. "Why don't you leave now, Edward?"

"I'm staying at the Hawthorne Inn," he said. "For the

next three days. I live near Boston now, but I have business in the area . . . in case you change your mind, Maeve."

"Thank you for dropping Mara's things off," Clara said as coolly as she—the warmest person in the world—was able. Just then a noise clanked—the hot-water heater under the cottage, trying to restart itself. Odd, Maeve thought—she hadn't been running the hot water.

"What's that sound?" Edward asked.

"None of your concern," she said.

"Better get it looked at," he said, but Maeve ignored him. She looked away until she heard Edward's car start up. Then she did look—it was a big black Mercedes with low-number Massachusetts plates. She watched him put on dark aviator glasses, check his face in the mirror. He backed out into the dead-end turnaround, drove away.

"He still looks at himself in the mirror every chance he gets," Clara said. "I remember you saying you didn't trust him, the very first time Mara brought him home, because he couldn't take his eyes off himself."

"She loved him."

"And you accepted that. Why wouldn't you take the bag from him?"

Maeve wiped tears from her eyes. "Because I was afraid that if he knew how badly I wanted it, he'd change his mind."

"But he'd brought it all this way—to give you."

"You don't know Edward the way I do," Maeve said. "No one does."

"He's always seemed so charming," Clara confessed.

"And vulnerable. Even today...In spite of what we know about him."

Maeve nodded. Her stomach flipped. Edward's charm and friendly manner had gotten him far in this world. He still fooled people like Clara. Only Patrick Murphy had really seen through him. Even with a murder accusation hanging over his head, Edward had been able to get clients. People had short memories, especially when dealing with charmers like Edward.

"Let's go inside," Maeve said. She heard that clanking again—the hot-water heater making noise. She'd have to remember to call the plumber to come look at it. "I can hardly stand to wait another second. Clara, hold my hand."

"Are you okay?"

"I just have to see what's in that bag," Maeve said, feeling as if she might faint, her eyes glittering with tears as she realized she was about to see and touch items that had once belonged to Mara.

Chapter 17

Liam had driven home to Cape Hawk, to give the commander his car back, check the mail, make a few changes to a program he had running along the beaches east of Halifax—where the great white attack had been last month—and pick up clothes and other things for Lily.

He stopped at the inn to see Anne, who had been to Lily's house. She took the laundry bag of old clothes from Liam, handed him back a bag of clean ones. They stood by the front desk, and Anne wanted to know everything. There was a Ceili band playing that night, and their Celtic music filled the lobby.

"Rose has been doing better and better, every day," he said. "She'll be moving to Boston tomorrow. The doctors say she's ready."

"Thank God," Anne said. "How is Lily holding up?"

"She's fine," Liam said, holding the truth inside. His eyes must have told more than his words, because Anne came around the counter to give him a hug.

"You give her this from me," she said, holding him hard.

He nodded, thinking that would be the day. He'd have to get through about six inches of body armor as well as a Kevlar force field before that happened. The hide of a bull shark was less rugged than Lily's. But he told Anne he would deliver her good wishes. Just then he happened to notice the display set up at the front desk.

"What's that?" he asked, pointing to the placard saying "Help Our Rose Grow." There were pictures of Rose—in her school class, at her birthday party, and standing with Lily.

"Oh!" Anne said. "I almost forgot. Rose's best friend, Jessica Taylor, came up with it three days ago, and the Nanouks immediately got on board. We're selling these pine pillows, raising money for Rose. You know—pine is such a Nova Scotia thing, the visitors love it. The girls have been staying up all night to make them."

Liam picked one up—it had a picture of Nanny embroidered in green thread, with the words "Bring Rose Home" underneath. It smelled unmistakably of pine. Anne showed him the cash box, with twenty dollars inside. "We've sold four already. People checking out of the hotel have been snapping them up."

"I'll take one," he said.

"We'll give it to you," she said. "You're doing plenty for the cause."

"Let me pay," he said. "I want to."

Almost reluctantly, she took his money. She handed him change, along with a small bag. Looking inside, he saw jewelry made of tiny pinecones spray-painted gold. Several pairs of earrings, a couple of necklaces, and a ring.

"Jessica made them for the nurses," Anne said. "She wanted to be sure they treat Rose right."

"She's a good best friend," Liam said, feeling proud of Rose for instilling that sort of love and loyalty. He wasn't surprised. She'd been special since the day she'd been born.

Just then Camille came around the corner. She had had a small stroke last year, and she walked with a cane. But her expression was just as dour, and her white hair was tinted just as blue as ever. Liam knew that she hadn't had a happy life—ever since her husband had drowned in Ireland.

"Liam, dear," she said, coming over to kiss him. "Where have you been?"

"In Melbourne," he said.

"Melbourne? Courting someone new in town?" she smiled.

"No," he said, and gestured at the poster emblazoned with Rose's picture. "I'm down there with Lily and Rose."

Camille's smile dissolved. "You know, I've never felt the front desk is quite the place to raise money. Our guests pay quite enough to stay here, without guilting them into giving to our local charities."

"It's Rose," Liam said, staring her down. "Not a local charity."

She laughed nervously. He was very tall, and he had just used his shark researcher voice on his own aunt, but she was so imposing on her own, he didn't feel bad.

"Dear. You'd almost think she was *your* daughter, the

way you act. If I didn't know for sure that her mother was pregnant on arrival, I might have my suspicions."

"Pregnant on arrival," Anne said dryly. "POA."

"She's not my daughter," Liam said quietly.

"But you care about her. It's touching, it really is. Only you know—I'm going out on a limb to say this, and I'm sure I'll get my head bitten off—as the stand-in for your dear parents, and the last of their generation alive, I have to state the facts as I see them. It just seems to me that this attention you pay to the Malones has kept you from meeting women of your station. Intelligent, educated women who would be just dying to marry such a fine young man!"

"Women of my station?" he asked, feeling—as he often did when talking to his aunt—as if he had wandered into a Victorian novel. He also knew, complicated woman that she was, that she had contributed money to the trust he had established for Rose years ago, once her problems had become obvious.

"Yes. I'm sure you know what I mean. You have a *doctorate.*"

"Look," Liam said, shaking his head, "I've got to head back to Melbourne. Thank Jessica for trying to raise money."

Anne's eyes twinkled. "We all know who takes care of Rose."

"Sssh," Liam said.

"The pine pillows can stay," Camille interjected. "They're charming, in a rustic way. No one will say that Camille Neill is so hard-hearted as to banish the pine pillows!"

"Thank you, Camille," Anne said, winking behind her back at Liam. "Ever the humanitarian."

"She's right, Aunt Camille," he said, giving her a hug.

"Let's not get carried away," Camille said, resting her head against his shoulder before limping off.

" 'Women of your station,' " Anne said, smiling. "Sounds like the strangest combination between Jane Austen and *Debbie Does Dallas*."

Liam chuckled, trying to gather everything together with his good arm. Anne helped load him up, but suddenly she stopped, reaching up to pat his cheek.

"You're a really good man, Liam Neill. Right up there with your cousin Jude."

"Thanks," he said.

"My friend Lily is a hard case, but don't give up on her."

"It's not like that between us," Liam said. "I just care about Rose."

"Uh-huh," Anne said. "Just remember what I say—don't give up. She needs you, Liam. She always has."

Liam shook his head, trying to hide how her words made him feel. He was very good at that—shoving his emotions out of sight—so he scowled and hoisted the bag over his shoulder.

"She has," Anne said, giving him one last pat on the cheek. "Ever since she arrived in town POA. Give her my love, will you?"

"Sure," Liam said, somehow unable to laugh, even though the twinkle in Anne's eye was asking him to. He started to stick the pine pillow in the bag.

Anne glanced down, pointed at the embroidered image. "You know, no one has seen Nanny since Rose's birthday," she said. "Jude says the whale boats are all watching for her, but she's just not there."

"Really? Once she comes for the summer, she usually stays till the snow falls."

"I know. Jude says it's strange."

They said goodbye, and Liam left. He walked out of the inn, through the parking lot to his truck, having dropped his friend's car off at the Coast Guard dock and hitched a ride from the lighthouse keeper. Climbing in, heading south on the rocky road, he looked out at the bay. He saw the black backs of several fin whales, on their way to the feeding grounds. Glossy black cresting the surface, disappearing underneath.

He had his laptop beside him, and he pulled over to the roadside to tap in data. The screen began blinking with dots of green and purple. Lots of sharks in the Halifax area—more than usual. The purple dots, indicating great whites, were especially thick down there. Liam typed in "MM122," waiting for Nanny's green dot to start blinking on the LED, but it didn't.

Liam typed it in again—still no sign. Could her transmitter have failed? The battery pack was a few months old; he had been planning to replace it, if Jude could get him close enough this summer. His stomach fell, thinking of predators. Sharks were everywhere in this bay—he didn't even need the purple dots to tell him that. Suddenly he remembered how avidly Gerard Lafarge had watched Nanny with binoculars the day of Rose's party. Predators came in all species. He felt sick to think of it.

He dialed Jude's cell number.

"Hey, where the hell have you been?" Jude asked, answering instantly upon seeing Liam's number on caller ID.

"At the hospital."

"How are they?"

"Strong as ever. Listen—Anne tells me none of the boats have seen Nanny."

"That's right," he said. "She's disappeared."

"You know what? I saw Lafarge watching her. He hates me, and he knows how I feel about belugas, her in particular."

"More like he knows how you feel about Rose, and he saw Rose and her friends going crazy for Nanny that day of her party. That scum of the earth."

"Do you think..."

"Fuck. I wouldn't put anything past him. I'll ask around. Some of his crew hang out at the inn bar. Maybe I can get something out of them."

Liam thanked his cousin and hung up. He had to get on the road, get down to Melbourne. He kept his laptop on, and he keyed "MM122" to beep if it showed up. Every mile seemed longer and longer as the computer stayed silent.

Losing Nanny—he couldn't even think of it. Thoughts of Connor filled his head, but even more so, of Rose. How could he tell Rose, if something had happened to Nanny?

He couldn't. That was one thing even the rough, tough shark researcher wasn't brave enough to do.

Lily sat beside Rose as she slept. Sunlight streamed through the window. She hadn't been outside all day; it was easy to forget what summer was like. She had pulled out her needlework—she always stitched in the hospital; it was one of the reasons she finished so many things—and was finding comfort in pulling and pushing the needle in and out of the canvas, just repeating the motion over and over, just like breathing, or the beating of a heart. After a few minutes, she closed her eyes, and the images that filled her mind were from summers long ago—those of her childhood.

A garden full of red roses, orange day lilies, honeysuckle, their sweet fragrance mingled with the tang of salt air ... So different from the salt air of rocky Cape Hawk, the scent of her childhood sea mist mingled with the tide lines of a sandy beach and the sweet decay of marsh flats. Not that there weren't rocks ... there were. Long granite ledges sloping down to the water, in front of the cottage, the place she had called home for as long as she could remember. And the woman who loved her, had raised her—

Lily opened her eyes. Don't think of that, she told herself. It was too hard, too painful. Staring at Rose, all hooked up with wires and machines, she knew that if she started remembering that other time of her life, she would not be able to get through this next part. She would cave in. Her hands began to move, soothing her as she started stitching again.

She had made the decisions she had out of love. People's

lives had been at stake: it was nothing less than that. Lily had grown up reading Nancy Drew mysteries. She had heard stories about people who disappeared, assumed other identities. There was so much loss—the sacrifice of family, relationships, endless love between the generations. But look at what was saved—people's actual lives. There was evil in the world, and Lily had encountered it. No one would have believed her, because his mask was so effective. He was so good at hiding who he really was.

She thought of Scott Peterson, the case that had so recently dominated the news, of how even Laci's family had supported him at first. Lily believed that even Laci didn't know she was going to be murdered until she looked up and saw her husband with his hands around her neck. How could Lily make everyone understand that she would have done anything, anything, to protect herself and Rose from becoming like Laci and her baby, Conner?

Shaking those feelings away, she gazed down at her half-finished canvas and thought of Liam, wondered where he was, why he hadn't gotten back yet. He was picking up all the stuff she'd need for Boston—she couldn't leave without it. She told herself that's all it was; she wasn't missing him, didn't need his or anyone's support. The Nanouk Girls were there for her, and Liam had certainly pitched in more than his share. But other than that, it was just Lily and Rose, the way it had always been.

With Rose fast asleep, Lily put her needlework down and reached over to touch her chest. Light fingertips, wanting to feel the heartbeat. She remembered when Rose was just a few days old. The birth had gone so smoothly; Lily had had her at home. All had been fine. She was overjoyed, relieved that they were safe, but so sad to know her grandmother couldn't meet the baby, not yet, and she didn't know when she would.

Rose's first bath...

Lily had filled the sink, tested the water with her elbow, just as her grandmother had told her in the early months of her pregnancy, when everything was a lesson, when the idea of having a baby was so incredible and new. It was as if her grandmother were right there with her, telling her she was doing a good job.

Holding Rose, regarding her with total love, she had touched her tiny chest. What was that feeling beneath her fingertips? Not just the reassuring thump, thump of the heart, but more like a trembling, like the purring of a cat. But the timing felt different; while cats purr along with their breath, this sensation seemed to follow each heartbeat. Rose gazed up at Lily, immersed in the warm water, seeming to love her first bath, so Lily tried to dismiss it. But it bothered her, and she kept checking.

Rose's first blue spell didn't occur till a few days later.

Liam had come back—as he had every day since Rose's birth. Lily had felt shy with him, knowing what he'd seen and heard that night, but she secretly welcomed his visits.

The days were long, so it was still light when he arrived after his day's work on the research vessel. He was administering shark studies down on the surfing beaches east of

Halifax, but he'd rush back to Cape Hawk to check on Rose and Lily.

The sun was setting behind the pines, and the cottage was filled with long shadows and golden light. Lily was too content to turn on a lamp; she rocked Rose, breastfeeding her in the dim light. When Liam's truck rattled down the stony drive, she wrapped Rose in a blanket and waited for his footsteps on the porch.

Liam came in, bearing groceries. Lily felt uncomfortable—he refused to take money for them, and she really wasn't sure what he wanted from her. After she had moved out of the inn, they had met in town—when he saw her, a pregnant stranger, he'd realized instantly she was the woman he'd heard crying in the inn room. He told her that she had left some of her books there, and asked if he could bring them to her new place. It had been a complete accident that he'd stopped by to drop them off the night Rose was born—and discovered her in labor.

He never really left after that. He came by every day. He told Lily she could have the lease on the store beside his office, for any kind of shop she wanted. And he brought food and diapers—told her she could start paying him after she got her feet on the ground.

While Lily was putting away the groceries, she handed Rose to Liam to hold. It seemed like the least she could do—he cared about this baby he'd helped bring into the world. But when she glanced over, saw him holding her against his chest with his one arm, her eyes had filled with tears. That kind of tenderness should be reserved for a baby's father—but Rose's father would never know her, never see her, never even learn of her existence if Lily had anything to do with it.

"Lily?" Liam called.

His voice was calm, but there was something that made Lily drop the bag on the floor and walk right over.

"What's wrong?" she asked.

Rose's expression was anxious; she was breathing at twice her normal rate. The shadows falling through the window, from the pines, had masked it at first—the room was violet, slate, purple—but when Lily flipped on the lamp, and the room was light, she saw that Rose was blue.

"What should I do?" Lily asked, panicked.

"Stay calm," Liam said. "She's breathing... she's not choking or anything. Let's call the pediatrician."

Lily's hands were shaking, so he found the number of the doctor in Port Blaise—recommended by Anne. Lily had taken Rose in for her checkup, and everything had been fine. But now, on the phone, Dr. Durance was asking questions that made Lily worry.

"Is Rose anxious? Has she been fussing? Does she feed eagerly? Does she sweat during or after feeding? Skin is bluish?"

"Yes," Lily answered to all the questions, denial falling away, everything suddenly pointing back to that strange feeling under her fingertips. Yes, yes, yes... She told the doctor about that sensation, and he said, "Sounds like a heart murmur."

Were heart murmurs serious? No, they weren't—were

they? Lily remembered a girl from school who had one. She had used it to get excused from gym—that was all. Didn't kids outgrow them? She asked Dr. Durance, and he said, "Usually."

They called, and were told to bring Rose in. That was the first time Liam insisted on going along—and Lily was too worried to decline. He drove, and Lily held Rose in her lap.

Dr. Durance did a standard exam, found a heart murmur, and immediately referred Rose for further tests at the regional medical center. There, they did a Doppler echocardiogram. Several views were obtained: Rose's heart was observed beating in her tiny chest, the thickness of the heart wall was measured, and the valves were counted.

Lily knew the test was similar to the many ultrasounds she had had during her pregnancy, home in New England. She knew the doctor would hold a transducer against Rose's chest wall, and Lily hoped he would remember to warm it. She knew that high-frequency sound waves sent into the chest would return with images of the heart and other structures.

Now, nine years later, she kept her hand on Rose's chest while her daughter slept. She thought of how intrigued Rose had become with ultrasound—she loved to collect the pictures the doctors printed out for her, and she had done a school project on how ultrasound works the same way bats see in the dark—through sound waves bouncing off objects. At night in Cape Hawk, when Lily and Rose heard bats screeching through the woods, they felt comforted by the tiny creatures, instead of scared.

Still touching Rose, Lily thought of how those first ultrasounds had led to the diagnosis of Tetralogy of Fallot: four complex heart defects. She learned that Rose's bluish skin tone was due to cyanosis—reduced blood flow to the lungs. It was called Blue Baby Syndrome. But that was just a symptom—the Tetralogy of Fallot was the cause. It sounded like a monster to her, and was one: a four-headed creature, brutally dangerous, fatal if ignored. It required open-heart surgery, so Lily had flown her infant daughter to Boston, one of the best heart centers in the country. And Liam had paid.

"I can't accept," Lily had said, panicked.

"You will," Liam had said. "It's not for you. It's for Rose."

And he had surprised her, showing up at the hospital just before Rose went under sedation. "I have to see my girl," he said.

Lily tried to hold it together. *My girl…* That's what Rose's father should be saying; emotions seething just below the surface began to pour out. Lily had to run out of the room, sobbing.

"What's wrong, what did I say?" Liam asked, coming to find her.

"You're not her father," she sobbed. "What do you care, why are you here?"

"Of course I care, Lily. I helped deliver her."

"It never should have happened," Lily wept, standing in

a corner of the hospital corridor, people rushing by without paying any attention—it was the pediatric cardiac care unit, and mothers losing it were a common sight.

"What never should have? My being there?"

Lily sobbed, thinking she might break apart. When she went into labor, the night Rose was born, Liam had been like an angel sent by God. Lily was all alone, in the rocky wilds of the northernmost part of Nova Scotia, on the run from a man who wanted to kill her, the father of her baby. She was lying on the kitchen floor, wracked by hard labor, screaming out loud because she knew she was safe enough—for no one to hear her.

And Liam had walked in, dropped the books he'd been carrying on the floor, come to her, crouched by her side—a total stranger, at her greatest hour of need.

"What does it mean, that I felt safer having my baby alone than asking anyone for help?" she said.

"You had no one to trust," he said.

"I didn't know anyone; I didn't know whether he might have been looking for me, asking around. . . . I was afraid someone would tell him."

"You were all alone, Lily."

Lily had looked up into his eyes—no one but Liam knew how alone she really was. He knew, because he was too.

She couldn't tell him about the dreams she had about him—beautiful dreams of a one-armed man leaning over her with tears rolling down his cheeks, holding her, supporting her as she gave birth on her kitchen floor, as he caught Rose as she came out, nestling her and handing her to Lily with his good hand.

Since leaving her husband just weeks earlier, Lily had had dreams of monsters. Frightening, shape-shifting monsters that wanted to eat her alive. Lily had married a handsome, charming man. He could sell anybody anything. His smile was perfect—his teeth so white and straight. But in her dreams, he used those perfect teeth to bite her flesh, drain her blood—just as he'd drained her bank accounts in real life.

He had broken Lily's heart. She thought of all the lies he'd told her. All the ways he had made her feel their problems were all her fault. She was too demanding, possessive, questioning, he had told her. Any time she suspected him of cheating on her, or being somewhere other than where he said he was, he turned it on her. By the time she found out the truth, her heart was shattered.

In Lily's dreams, her handsome husband was grotesque, and the shark-ravaged Liam was gentle, beautiful. Life painted such pictures of confusion.

That day in the hospital, Lily had cried in the corner, feeling Liam's breath warm on the back of her neck.

"Don't cry, Lily," he whispered. "The doctors here are the best. She's in good hands. . . ."

"I think I brought her heart condition on," she whispered.

"How? That's not possible."

"You don't know," she said, pacing. "I was so anxious, all the time I was with him, Rose's father. I felt such tightness in my chest—I used to think I was having a heart attack. I was afraid, and I felt turned inside out. The baby was inside me all that time, being affected."

"By your emotions? No."

"I should have left him sooner," Lily cried.

"Lily—I don't know what happened, why you left. I wish you would tell me."

"I can't," she said, upset she'd said as much as she had. Her husband had always been so careful to do everything in secret. He had never hit her—not once. He'd never left even one bruise. She had never called the police—because the things he did weren't illegal. They were murderous, but not illegal. No one would believe Lily, that her husband was a killer.

"You can," Liam pressed. "I'll do anything I can to help you. . . . You already got away from him. I'll help make sure he never hurts you again."

"You don't understand," Lily said. "The law isn't on my side. If you're not a victim of domestic violence, you don't understand. He was a predator."

"I believe you."

"And do you also believe that Rose is here because of what happened to us before she was born? Because it's true. We both have broken hearts."

"If you say so," Liam said solemnly, touching her face. "I do believe you."

"Thank you."

"Then listen to me, Lily. Whatever he did to you, I want you to know this. You and Rose can count on me—forever. No matter what you need, I'll give it to you."

"I can't—"

"If you can't for yourself, do it for Rose," he said. "I'm a biologist, not a doctor. But I know this—the two of you were imprinted on my heart the minute I helped bring Rose into this world. I never thought I'd say this, Lily—I've never been married, never been engaged, never been a father. I'm none of those things to you and Rose, but I'm yours for life. It's just the way it is."

"Liam—"

"It's just the way it is," he repeated, his blue eyes serious and steady. "Like it or not."

And then the doctor had called them in. It was time for Rose to be wheeled away for open-heart surgery. Standing there as they took her daughter away, Lily thought her own heart would explode—but Liam held her hand. He held it the whole time Rose was in surgery. The team performed a double bypass on her baby daughter, using the Blaylock-Taussig shunt.

When the doctors emerged, Lily let go of Liam's hand. What he had said was nice—very noble. But Rose had survived the surgery, and now Liam could go back to his own life and they'd continue on with theirs. The surgeons explained to her and Liam that the procedure was merely palliative, until Rose grew big enough for more-extensive surgery.

"More?" Lily asked, feeling her knees go weak.

"Ms. Malone, Tetralogy of Fallot means that there are four different defects. Rose will need extensive, complex open-heart surgery to reconstruct her heart. A hard road lies ahead. But Rose is amazing—strong, a fighter." They kept talking, but Lily stopped listening. She just shut down, unable to take it all in.

"We can't go through all this," Lily said to Liam, sobbing again when the doctors left.

"Yes, you can. You have to."

"I can't," she cried. "I can't watch her suffer!"

"Lily, my mother couldn't stand to see me suffer after we lost my brother. I had a lot of surgeries too. But she just . . . went away. I needed her, just like Rose needs you. I promised you, and I'll never break it—I'm going to help you. Anytime you need to be strong, call me and I'll help. The doctor is right: Rose *is* a fighter. You'll see. She's a miracle girl."

"A miracle girl," Lily murmured, grasping the phrase, looking up with red, swollen eyes.

"She is," Liam said. "I knew it from the minute she was born."

"How?" Lily asked.

"Well," he said. "I'll tell you sometime."

Now, nine years later, they were all still on that same hard road. Lily sat by Rose's bed. The balloons Liam had brought were still tied to the rail. They had fizzled out some, but Rose refused to let them be taken away. Lily looked at her watch—Liam still wasn't back. She tried to needlepoint again, but her heart wasn't in it—she couldn't concentrate on the canvas.

She constantly told him she didn't want him there, but the truth was, when he wasn't, she felt empty. During the nine years since leaving Rose's father, she had become very strong and sure of herself. She had done a lot of research on domestic violence, realized the danger she'd been in. She had dealt with her guilt over staying as long as she had, and her grief over having to leave behind everything she'd left. She was a fighter, like Rose.

But at moments like this, she realized how much Liam's promise had meant to her. Being so strong and tough, she didn't want to rely on anyone else. Liam was in a category all his own—he wasn't "anyone else." She told herself that the promise was for Rose. Rose loved him—that was for sure.

So, on Rose's account, Lily stood up from her chair and went to the window. The World War I monument shimmered in the reflecting pool. A few doctors and hospital visitors had pulled park chairs into the shade and were reading beneath the trees. Lily pressed her forehead against the glass, trying to see the heron. She couldn't—the bird wasn't visible from here.

And neither was Liam. Maybe he had finally gotten tired of strong-arming her into letting him keep his promise. She could hardly blame him.

The thing was, she realized she'd never gotten him to tell her why he'd first called Rose "the miracle girl." Maybe she hadn't wanted to hear, was afraid to believe. But knowing the difficult surgery that lay ahead for Rose, the one that might finally fix her heart, Lily thought that now would be a really good time for her to hear that story. She found herself hoping Liam would come back soon.

Chapter 18

Liam pulled into the hospital parking lot just before eight—he wanted a chance to see Rose before visiting hours ended, and he was elated by what he had just seen on his computer screen—MM122 blinking away, safe and alive, but in a spot so completely unexpected, he had failed to plug the GPS coordinates into the program—because it had been too unlikely.

Walking into the lobby, climbing into the elevator, he was struck by the juxtaposition—from the wild, fresh air of Cape Hawk to the hermetically sealed atmosphere of the hospital. When would Rose be well enough to stay out of places like this? Liam's excitement over finding Nanny disappeared, replaced by a physical aching for Rose's confinement—the nine-year-old girl he loved, having to spend so many summer days imprisoned in here, in her body.

But by the time he got to the floor, he'd calmed himself down, set the expression on his face. He paused at the door to her room.

Lily had pulled the chair next to the bed, and was needlepointing while Rose read. Liam saw the way Lily's dark hair fell across her face, sharply angled and neatly cut, a raven's wing. It blocked her vision, but Rose looked up from the book, over her mother's head, and saw Liam standing there. He put on his biggest smile for Rose.

"You're here," Rose said.

"Wild horses couldn't keep me away."

"Are there wild horses in Nova Scotia?"

He looked deep in thought. "Wild eagles, I should have said."

"Or wild whales."

Lily smiled, but she seemed to be looking everywhere but at Liam. He couldn't quite figure it out—usually she had no problem just gazing at him head-on, with that inscrutable look in her eyes. There was most often a challenge in Lily's gaze—her chin tilted slightly up, as if saying "Bring it on." But right now, she looked almost fragile, as if the fight had gone out of her, her hands trembling as they held the canvas.

He wanted to ask, but he knew he had to wait until they were out of earshot. So instead, he unpacked the bag Anne had sent.

"Anne wanted me to give you these things," he said. "Your friend Jessica made this pillow—"

"My best friend!"

"Well, that's obviously how she feels too."

"It's Nanny," Rose said, touching the embroidered whale. "It smells like home."

"Filled with Cape Hawk pine needles," Liam said.

"Why does it say 'Bring Rose Home'?" she asked.

"She misses you," Lily said as she gave Rose a secret look of pleasure and triumph.

"She does," Liam said. "The Nanouk Girls are helping her make more of these, and they're selling them at the inn, to raise money to get you well as soon as possible. Nanny wants it too. Rose, she's telling you in as strong a way as possible."

"I want to get well," Rose said with a tiny voice.

"You will," Lily said. "You are getting well. It's happening right now, every minute."

"Jessica also made these," Liam said. "For you to give the nurses."

He watched Lily and Rose look through the plastic bag of pinecone jewelry, and suddenly Lily excused herself, dropped her needlework, and walked out into the hallway. Liam wanted to follow her, but Rose was watching her mother anxiously, so he stayed.

"Why did she go out?" Rose asked.

"Maybe she went to get the nurses," he said.

"We're going to Boston tomorrow," Rose said.

"I know."

"Did you see Jessica? I thought maybe she wanted a new best friend. I wouldn't blame her—I'm not there anymore."

"You'll be home soon," Liam said. "And it seems to me that she has only one best friend—you. That's why she wants to 'bring Rose home.'"

"She and Nanny are waiting for me?"

"Rose," Liam began, not even knowing how to tell her. It seemed so scientifically impossible—he hesitated to mention it, until he was able to tell for sure.

"Are you coming to Boston with us?" Rose asked, interrupting his thoughts.

"I wouldn't miss it," he said.

"Sometimes I wonder..." she said, stopping herself. Liam didn't push, or try to urge the words out of her. He just waited. She cleared her throat. He saw all the tubes and wires going in and out of her body, listened to the machines whirring and clicking around her. He wanted to pick her up and hold her, tell her that everything would be all right. But Rose knew too much for such platitudes. Her nine-year-old eyes were wiser than those of most of the professors he'd had in college.

"What do you wonder, Rose?"

"I wonder what Mom would do without me. I'm all she has."

Liam saw her reaching across the bed to hold his hand. He started to squeeze her fingers, but she reached past his good hand and held his prosthesis instead. Her tiny hand, tinged blue, with those clubbed fingers, grasping his big, fake, clunky hand. The gesture touched and shocked him, and he had to fight from showing it. Rose stared into his eyes.

"Maybe I'm not all she has," Rose said.

Liam felt his pulse racing. She wouldn't look away.

"Maybe not, Rose," he said.

They gazed at each other for a long time, and Liam felt himself making a new promise, too deep for words.

By the time Lily walked back into the room, everything was clear. Outside, the sun had set, and the footlights had come up on the tall monument. Liam saw it glowing out the window. He thought back many years, to the day his brother was born. He thought of how much love there was in the world, of how impossible it seems that it will ever be taken away.

Gazing down at Rose Malone, watching her mother brush her hair and get her ready for bed, her last night in this hospital, he realized something he'd never known before: it had to do with Connor, and his parents, and Lily, and Rose, and Liam himself. He had never realized it before, but now he knew he'd never forget it. He had to tell Lily, and he had to tell her tonight. And he had something to show her, that not even he could believe.

After Rose gave the nurses their pinecone earrings, and the doctor came for one last visit, and the night nurse gave Rose her sedative, and Rose fell asleep, Lily gathered up her things. She kept looking around the room, thinking she'd forgotten something. But she had her bag, her needle-pointing stuff, her hotel key, the pine pillow Liam had brought. Liam waited at the door, watching her—with anticipation, but as if he wanted to give her all the time in the world.

They walked outside, and the night air felt so hot

compared to the air-conditioned hospital chill. Lily felt nervous and keyed up about tomorrow, but also exhausted. She headed for his truck, when she felt him grab her arm.

"What?" she asked.

"Come with me," he said.

Lily gave him a puzzled look, but he didn't explain. He led her in the opposite direction, toward the city park. Kids were hanging out at the band shell, laughing and playing music on a radio. Liam steered her around the public garden, straight to the reflecting pool. The monument, lit by bright halogen lamps, rose into the hazy sky. Lily saw its image shimmering in the long pool of water, and she felt a pang of homesickness for the sea.

"I miss..." she began.

"What do you miss, Lily?"

"Salt water," she said.

"It's right down the hill," he said. "Melbourne Harbor..."

"I know," she said. "But I miss Cape Hawk. And even more than that, I miss my home."

"I thought Cape Hawk was your home."

"Before Cape Hawk," Lily said. Her throat was tight, memories flooding in of warm sand, silver-green marshes, and a beloved rose garden tended by a woman she had loved her whole life. What did it mean? Lily usually held herself together so well, especially gearing up for one of Rose's procedures. But right now, she felt as if she might die of old sorrow and longing.

"The night Rose was born," Liam said, "you were crying for home."

"I knew I'd never see it again," she said.

"And you cried out 'I need you, I need you...'"

Lily nodded, staring up at the granite column. He was waiting for an explanation, but Lily couldn't trust herself to give it. She felt as if an earthquake was just starting deep inside. She needed to contain it—hold back the emotions, try to keep the plates from shifting. She felt the waves beginning, rising, and she didn't want to test their power.

"Who did you need, Lily?"

"I want to tell you, Liam," she said. "But I can't."

"Don't you know you're safe? I'd protect you from anything."

"You can't protect me from my own heart. It breaks when I think of her—I can't talk about her."

He was so silent for so long; crickets sang in the bushes, and animals rustled in the woods. Lily's heart ached—for love so deeply buried, she had almost forgotten it was there. She saw flashes of an old smile she knew so well, blue eyes, silver hair, gnarled fingers closed around the wooden handle of a garden trowel.

"I wish I could introduce you to her," she said, letting her gaze move upward, to Liam's deeply set blue eyes. "She's someone who was very important to me—the most important person, until Rose. Liam, I don't seem very grateful to you, I know. But that's changed this time. I know what you've done for me, for Rose. Thank you for staying with us. The waiting has been so hard...I'm so scared, Liam."

"About the surgery?"

Lily nodded, hugging herself. The crickets sounded so loud. She looked up, saw bats circling the monument in the orange light. Her heart split, to think of Rose's school report, the one she had done on echocardiograms and the sonar of bats.

"I've never been like this before. Rose is just—well, you know. Everyone says she's 'such a fighter,' and she is. She is! She's had this condition since she was born. You were there—you know. We've just lived with it, never questioned it. I've followed her lead, and she's always been so brave. But this time—Liam, the waiting is so much harder. What if something terrible happens? Or what if the surgery doesn't work?"

"It will work," Liam said, standing very close. She couldn't stop looking into his eyes—he sounded so sure.

"I just can't stand waiting," she whispered.

"You told me you had someone you wished I could meet," he said. "It's the same with me," he said. "I wish I could introduce you to my family."

"I know Jude," she said, puzzled at the change of subject. "And Anne, and all the other Neills. Camille—"

Liam shook his head. "Others, who aren't here anymore. It's why I wanted to walk you over here, to the monument. I stood here with my father the day my brother was born."

"Connor," she said. The little boy who had been killed by a shark...

"Yes," he said. "The day he was born, my father and I were standing out here. I was just three, and I was really worried about my mother. She was in the hospital, and I didn't understand. My father pointed up at the monument, and he told me a family story. My great-grandfather had fought in the war."

"Your father's grandfather?"

"Yes. Tecumseh Neill—the son of the sea captain that founded Cape Hawk, the one we named the boats after. He was over in France, and letters were very scarce. Even his father, the fearsome whale captain, was terrified that his son would never come home."

"What happened?"

"My father told me that his grandfather had been wounded on the battlefront and was last seen lying in a muddy trench. His squadron had retreated—and when they got back to camp, he was gone. The word came that he was missing in action. The whole family waited for word, but thought he must have been killed. Time went past— weeks and then months."

"How awful," Lily said.

"Everyone gave up hope except his sweetheart—my great-grandmother," Liam said. "She just knew."

Lily nodded eagerly—she understood that. The connection that was there, even when you couldn't see the other person. She had never lost it, for the woman in the garden that she loved so much. It glimmered, alive in her now. And she had it for Rose, always.

"She knew that he was alive?" Lily asked.

"Yes. She was positive. But every day that went by without word was like torture. She knew he was there, but she couldn't get to him. She knew that he needed her—just as she needed him."

"Your father told you, because you needed your mother," Lily said.

"I did. And I believed, in that three-year-old-boy way, that she needed me."

"I'm sure she did," Lily said, thinking of Rose at three, of the hospitalization here, and of how every second without her had been excruciating and almost impossible to bear. "What happened to your great-grandfather?"

"He had been badly injured behind enemy lines. He was taken to a field hospital, and it took months for the word to get out. At first, it was just a rumor. Just a hint, that maybe he was alive after all. My great-grandmother didn't care about the rumors—because she had something better. She knew for sure—in her heart—that he was coming home. And he did, Lily. He spent time as a prisoner of war, but eventually he came home to her."

"She knew."

"Yes, she did. All that time."

"She waited for him."

"It's what I want to say to you right now, Lily Malone," Liam said. "People say Rose is a fighter, and she is. Just like my great-grandfather. But as much as anyone, my great-grandmother is the hero of the story."

"She never gave up on him."

"No, she didn't. Some things are worth fighting for, Lily. And some things are worth waiting for."

Lily stared up at him, the monument silhouetted behind his head, her heart pounding in her chest. He was talking about his great-grandmother, so in love with her husband, their connection so mysterious it didn't need letters or telephone calls or spoken words. And he was talking about three-year-old Liam Neill, waiting for his brother to be born—so he could meet him for the first time, and see his mother again. And he was talking about Rose, just about to have the final, and most important, surgery of her life, replacing the old VSD patch once and for all. But he hovered over Lily, his face just inches away, and she knew—he was talking about something else too.

"You told me once," she whispered. "That Rose was a miracle girl. You told me you'd tell me what that means. Will you tell me now?"

He nodded. He put his arms around her—both arms, and the left one felt just as tender as his right. She had the feeling her legs were dissolving; she leaned into him, hoping her heart wouldn't fly out of her chest.

"The night I helped deliver Rose," he said, "and watched you give birth . . . she brought me back to life."

Lily couldn't speak. She thought back, remembered the crashing pain—she had been traumatized by what had driven her to Cape Hawk, so much so that she was in hiding like a wild animal in a cave, not even daring to go to the hospital—for fear that her husband would be looking, or that the news accounts would cause doctors and nurses to recognize her, to call the police.

Liam had been the only person she dared trust—and only by necessity. Because he was *there*.

"Brought you back to life?" she asked finally.

He nodded, brushed the hair from her eyes, and caressed the side of her face.

"The shark that killed my brother," he said, "killed my whole family as well."

"He took your arm," Lily said.

"He took my heart," Liam said. "And you and Rose gave it back to me."

"You hardly knew us—"

"I know," Liam said. "I guess that's what made it a miracle. A stranger I'd never even met—you. In a cabin, in the middle of the woods. Giving birth to this beautiful, tiny little girl. And trusting me enough to bring her into the world."

"I did trust you," Lily whispered. And she knew that—given what she was running from—that in itself was a miracle.

"There's something else I want to show you tonight," Liam said. "If you wouldn't mind taking a ride with me."

"Anywhere," she whispered.

The passenger seat of his truck was cluttered, so when Lily climbed in, she had to push his laptop aside. He drove through the park, through the stone gates, and down the hill toward town. Melbourne Harbor twinkled with lights—the business district and hotels, restaurants and houses. Liam drove past the citadel—the old battlements that had once guarded the harbor, dating back to when the land was known to the French as Acadia.

They headed southwest, along the south shore. Lily felt the tug of home—whenever she was in a vehicle pointing toward New England, it overcame her. She wedged herself lower in the seat, feeling the sea breeze through the open windows. She felt a special tingle tonight, almost as if her grandmother was calling her name.

The sky was filled with stars. They swung low on the horizon. The rock scree slanted down to the Atlantic, and the constellations seemed to spring straight out of the ocean.

They rounded a bend, came upon the lighthouse at the outer edge of Melbourne Harbor. Its beam flashed across the sky. Liam turned left, taking an unpaved road out to the farthest reaches of the lighthouse's promontory. Now he reached across for his laptop; he balanced it on his knee, turned it on. Lily saw the screen light up with green and purple dots of light.

"What are they?" she asked.

"Sharks and whales," he said.

"How can you see them?" she asked, fascinated.

"I run a catch-and-release program," he said. "To research migratory and predatory patterns."

Predatory. The word had old associations, and made Lily shiver.

"Which ones are sharks?" she asked.

"The purple ones," he said.

"Where are they?"

"This screen represents this coastline right here," he said. "See the darkest section? That is the landmass—southern Nova Scotia, from Melbourne to Halifax."

"I never really noticed before how Nova Scotia is shaped like a lobster," Lily said, staring at the computer screen and the island's silhouette against the lighter, slate-colored sea—filled, alarmingly, with purple dots.

She glanced up at Liam's face. He looked so content and gentle—how was it possible, considering that the sea was filled with sharks just like the one that had killed Connor?

"Why do you do it?" she asked. "Dedicate your life to studying something so evil?"

"Sharks?"

"Yes."

"They're not evil, Lily. They're dangerous, though. There's a difference."

"What is it?" she asked, thinking of another predator.

"Sharks don't kill to inflict pain or suffering. They kill to eat. It's just their instinct—the way they stay alive. I had to learn that about them, so I could stop hating them."

Lily thought of her broken heart, and Rose's. She knew that a human shark had caused the hurt and stress that had nearly ripped her apart, driven her from her home, caused Rose to be born with four heart defects. "How can you stop hating something that did such damage?"

"You have to," Liam said. "Or it will kill you too."

Lily stared at the purple lights on the screen. Then she looked out the truck window. They were facing south. A few hundred miles away, straight across the water, was Boston; beyond that was her old home. She wondered how many sharks were swimming between her and the place she loved so much.

"I know about hatred," she said.

"I know you do," Liam said. "It's one of the reasons I wanted to bring you here tonight."

"How do you know? Does it show?"

He paused, staring out at the dark sea. The lighthouse swung its beam across the smooth water, illuminating it in four-second flashes. Then he turned to her. "It does show," he said. "You let some of your friends in—Anne, the Nanouk Girls. But you've kept yourself and Rose hidden from everyone else."

"You should talk," Lily said, smiling.

"I know—that's why I recognize it in you. I've got this computer program, to help me learn about the thing I hated most."

"I've done my best to study him," Lily said. "But he's not like a shark—he inflicts hurt on purpose. I know a little about the dynamic."

"You can get lost in it," Liam said, turning the computer screen to face Lily. "If you're not careful, all you see are the purple lights. You forget to look for the green ones."

"The green ones?"

"Whales," he said. "The most gentle animals in the ocean."

Lily studied the screen. "There aren't many whales on

here," she said. "Look at all those purple lights—and only three green ones."

"Whales are harder to tag," he said. "We don't like to crowd them."

"So you're saying there might be lots of undercover whales?" She smiled.

"Yes," he said. "Along with one very visible one." He tapped the screen with his finger. "This one right here." He hit a few keys, and the whale's ID showed up in a window. Lily read out loud.

"MM122," she said.

"That whale was in Cape Hawk just a week ago," he said. "She disappeared for a few days, but that was only because I had narrowed the program to track her in familiar waters—the area I always expect to find her in the summer months."

"The whale swam down to the southern shore?" Lily asked, feeling a shiver run down her spine. She knew but didn't know.

"Specifically, to Melbourne," Liam said. "The waters closest to Melbourne."

"Is that surprising? Unusual?"

"Very."

"Why?"

"She's a beluga," Liam said. "Belugas rarely travel south of Cape Hawk. They are northern whales."

"But why would this one be here?" Lily whispered. Liam lowered the laptop and reached across the console between them. He held her hand. She felt a new shiver go down the backs of her legs. Liam held her hand only rarely. His palm and fingertips were rough, from all the work he did on boats. Lily felt a chill, and she was afraid he had taken her hand because he was about to tell her something that was going to scare her.

"To be near Rose, I think," he said.

"What do you mean?"

"It's Nanny," he said.

Lily stared at the blinking green light marked "MM122." Then she lifted her eyes to look out at the endless black sea. The lighthouse beam spread across the water, highlighting whitecaps of small waves. Liam took a pair of binoculars from his door pocket. He scanned the surface, then stopped.

"It's too dark to see," he said, "but she's there."

"She can't possibly be here because of Rose," Lily said.

"Why not?" Liam asked. "Why isn't it possible?"

"Because she's a whale—she can't feel emotion. She can't know how much Rose needs her and loves her."

"Why can't she?" Liam whispered, touching Lily's face. His hand was warm, and she leaned into it.

"Could it be like a bat, sending out signals, just like in Rose's report? Or like sound waves, in her echocardiograms?" Lily asked. "Could Nanny feel how much Rose loves her? No . . ."

Liam didn't reply—at least not with words. He pulled Lily tenderly close, leaning across the console, to kiss her. His mouth was hot, and she melted into him. Waves beat against the rocky shore, wearing it down, smoothing the edges. Lily heard the waves, and she felt the earthquake. It trembled inside her chest, and she reached up to caress Liam's cheek.

Lily heard her own question, reverberating in her ears. And she knew—yes, Nanny could feel Rose's love. Lily had been frozen solid for so long, she had forgotten that love came in waves—mysterious, long-reaching, never-ending waves. If you waited long enough, they eventually touched the distant shore. The waves never gave up.

She reached up both arms, put them around Liam's neck, and kissed him with nine years' worth of passion. He wrapped his good arm around her waist. Outside the truck, the sea splashed against the granite. One wave flew up, and the fine spray misted their faces. Lily tasted salt water, blinked it away.

"What does it mean?" she asked.

"Whatever we want it to, Lily Malone," he said.

The lighthouse beam clicked on again, lighting up the bay. She stared up at Liam, and she knew—if she turned her head right that instant, that very second, she would see Nanny. She would see the white whale, the mystical beluga who had followed Rose south. But Lily couldn't look away. She was lost in Liam's eyes, which were filled with mystery and miracles of their own.

 *Chapter 19*

Patrick Murphy sat in the main salon of the *Probable Cause*, Flora at his feet, looking up whales online. Specifically, beluga whales. It was all very strange, all the websites devoted to marine mammals. There were boat tours on the east coast, west coast, Mexico, and Canada. But very few places boasted the presence of the elusive white beluga.

Angelo sat up on deck, smoking a cigar, listening to the Yankees.

"Hey. Bases are loaded. Will you get up here?"

"In a minute."

"You invite me over for beer and baseball, and you ignore me. What've you got down there? A sweetheart in a chat room?"

"I'm doing police work."

"You're freaking retired."

"Shut up for a minute, will you?" Patrick asked, making a list of places that ran tours to see beluga whales. He was drinking Coke, because he had sworn off beer and stronger things eight years earlier, but he was getting a caffeine buzz. Or maybe it was just the thrill of knowing he was close to something.

"You tell me 'shut up'? I'm your best friend, I brought nachos, and you tell me 'shut up'?"

"You're right—I'm sorry. I'm looking up beluga whales."

"Beluga? Like the caviar?"

"That's what I thought, but no. They're white whales."

"Like Moby Dick?"

"Huh. Maybe. I'll have to ask Maeve. She was a teacher—she'll know."

"Fuck—is this about Mara Jameson? Tell me it's not. Whatever else you're doing down there, tell me you're not wasting another night of your life on the case that went nowhere, is going nowhere, and will always go nowhere."

"I can't tell you that," Patrick said. He had a list, and started studying it: beluga whales could be viewed during summer months at several places in Canada's Gulf of St. Lawrence—Newfoundland, New Brunswick, Nova Scotia, and even Quebec Province. Whale-watch tours were offered by companies leaving from Tadoussac, St. John, Gaspé, Cape Hawk, and Chéticamp.

"Martinez just homered," Angelo called down. "Grand slam. You missed it."

"Hang on. I'll be right up," Patrick said, trying to find the names of all the tour operators. What was he going to do—call each one and ask them if they'd ever had a passenger on any of their whale-watch boats that looked like Mara Jameson?

"Yankees are up 6–1."

"Go Yanks," Patrick said, typing "Mara Jameson, beluga whales," into the search engine. Nothing. He tried "Mara Jameson, Tadoussac," then "Mara Jameson, St. John," and so on. Police work was still often a thankless job. Only, now he wasn't getting paid for it.

His cell phone didn't work in the cabin, so he climbed up on deck. Angelo gave him a reproachful glance, reminding him of how Sandra used to look at him, back when he was ruining their marriage by dogging the Jameson case every minute of the day.

"Hang on," Patrick said, walking up to the bow for privacy.

"The nachos are getting cold!" Angelo called. "And my beer's getting warm!"

Patrick put one hand over his ear to block out all the boatyard noise—including his friend's voice—and dialed Maeve's number.

"Hello?" she answered.

"Maeve," he said. "I've got to ask you something. Did Mara ever say much to you about whales?"

"Whales?"

"Beluga whales, white ones, like the kind they have at Mystic Aquarium?"

She was silent, thinking. "Not that I can remember," she said.

"Huh."

"Ask her about Moby Dick," Angelo called from up front.

"Will you shut up a minute?" Patrick called back.

"Shut—?" Maeve began, shocked.

"Not you, Maeve," Patrick said hurriedly. "Did she, Mara, ever mention places up north? Spots she wanted to visit, maybe? In Canada, is what I'm getting at."

"Canada?" Maeve asked, sounding interested.

"Specifically, places on the Gulf of St. Lawrence?"

"How funny you should ask," Maeve said. "Because Edward stopped by with a bag of Mara's things—"

"Edward Hunter? He stopped by to see *you*?"

"Mmm," Maeve said, coughing. It went on for a moment, until she composed herself.

"And he gave you a bag of Mara's things?"

"Yes. That's what I'm trying to tell you. I didn't think much of it," she said. "But there was something very odd, having to do with Canada. Nothing to do with whales, though..."

"What was it?"

"Just something to do with her parents' deaths. It surprised me."

"Can you stay right where you are, Maeve? I want to see it."

"Where would I go?" she said, chuckling.

"I'll be right over," he said, watching Angelo smack his head with frustration and stuff his face with the last nachos.

Maeve and Clara were sitting in the living room, playing setback and listening to the Red Sox game on WTIC.

The cards were very old, somewhat waterlogged, from so many years in the salt air. Maeve wondered how many games of setback she and Clara had played, dating all the way back to their girlhoods. Candles blazed inside tall hurricane lamps so that they wouldn't be blown out by the sea breeze. The windows were open, and the smell of salt and honeysuckle filled the room. Maeve felt a bit dizzy, feverish, as if she were coming down with something.

"What time will he be here?" Clara asked.

"Well, he said he'd be right over. As long as it takes to drive from Silver Bay."

"Twenty minutes, at the most. Now that he's retired, I wonder whether he ever misses using lights and sirens."

"I wonder," Maeve said, swallowing hard. She had a touch of indigestion. Perhaps she had eaten something that didn't agree with her. Or maybe it was just a little stress—waiting for Patrick, after the excitement she'd heard in his voice. Reaching for her old needleworked eyeglass case, she tapped her bifocals out and put them on.

"Do you have Mara's things all ready to show him?" Clara asked.

Maeve gave her a deadpan look: *What do you think?*

"Well, excuse me! I just wonder what he'll find that no one else has found before. It seems like a wasted trip."

Maeve's mouth dropped open, shocked at her best friend's words.

"How can you say that?"

"I just . . . I just don't want you getting your hopes up."

Maeve closed her eyes. She wrapped her Irish linen

shawl more tightly around her shoulders. Her stomach was bothering her, and it wasn't helping her mood. Clara, of all people, should know that her hopes would stay up until she had one breath of life left in her body. She hoped she was doing the right thing. She shivered; it had been chilly the last two nights, and she had turned on the heat. Getting old was no fun, she thought.

"So much time has passed," she murmured.

"Exactly," Clara said, taking it the wrong way. "That's what I'm concerned about. That so much time has passed, yet still you keep the home fires burning. My darling, what if this is just another false lead?"

Maeve nodded, seeming to agree. She had hoped never to see Edward Hunter again for as long as she ever lived. But he had given her a great gift, bringing the bag over. And Patrick Murphy—dedicated police detective, superior investigator that he was—had followed every clue, more diligently than any grandmother could ever hope or expect. He had never stopped looking for Mara, never for one day.

"He's here," Clara said, spotting Patrick's headlights.

Maeve rose, walked through the kitchen to the front door. Moths swirled around the outside lights, and the yellow watering can stood illuminated by the rose arbor. Opening the screen door, she let Patrick inside.

"Hi, Maeve. Thanks for letting me come over so late."

"Hello, Patrick. Clara and I are just having some tea, playing cards."

"Sorry to intrude. Hi, Clara," he said.

Clara had already poured him a cup of tea, and now

handed it to him as he entered the living room. Maeve felt herself weave slightly. She steadied herself without the others seeing. On nights like this, when the summer stars rose out of Long Island Sound and an unexpected visitor came to the door, Maeve never quite got over wishing it was Mara. She saw Patrick waiting expectantly, and went to get the bag.

"This is it?" he asked.

She handed him the glossy bag and nodded.

"He brought it down last week!" Clara said. "The nerve of him, showing up in Maeve's garden."

"Edward Hunter has never lacked nerve," Patrick said. "May I look?"

"Certainly," Maeve said. She cleared off the card table, and Patrick spread the bag's contents on the surface. She had already gone through everything piece by piece, as had the police before her. She suspected that Patrick himself had already seen everything.

"Yep," he said. "Her phone book, her car keys, her silver pen, a little leather sewing kit . . . we've seen all this before. He gave it back to you—why?"

"I think he wanted to see me," Maeve said. "For another reason. This was just his excuse."

"What other reason?"

"To see whether I hate him or not. Edward could never stand to be hated. That is his entire reason for living—to be liked by everyone on earth. Even if it is just to get over on them."

"But he's such a slimy salesman," Clara said. "I never saw

it myself, at the time. But now I do. And I can't understand why darling Mara fell in love with him."

"She fell in love with him because she thought she could help him," Maeve said. "She had the biggest heart in the world, and Edward has a very sad hard-luck story."

"But that was so long ago," Clara said, not getting it. "When he was a child. What does that have to do with Mara? Or the kind of man Edward became, for that matter?"

Patrick seemed not to be listening as he went through the rest of the items in the bag: a book of poetry by Yeats, one by Johnny Moore, and a collection of newspaper clippings about Mara's parents' deaths.

"It shouldn't have anything to do with it," Patrick said. "But guys like Edward use their childhoods as their bread and butter. It's currency, and they use it to gain sympathy."

"Mara's only mistake," Maeve said, "was in finally seeing through it."

"You think that's why Edward came back to see you? To see if you see through him?"

"I'm sure of it. He was bragging about his success as a broker. It's subtle—he taunts me. Knows that I'm onto him, but can't do anything about it."

"Where's the part about Canada?" Patrick said. "I don't see it."

"In this article," Maeve said, separating one yellowed clipping from the rest. Feeling queasy, she watched Patrick read.

Mara's parents had been killed in a famous ferry accident in Ireland. As a teenager, she had written to several local Irish papers and asked them to send her the clippings. Maeve's pulse quickened as she watched Patrick's face. She wondered what he would make of the mention—how would he put it together with the other clues?

" 'Residents of Ard na Mara,' " Patrick read. "What's Ard na Mara?"

"The town in the west of Ireland where her parents were killed."

"What does it mean?"

"In Gaelic, *Ard* means 'peak,' and *Mara* means 'sea.' "

"I never knew Mara was named for the sea!" Clara said.

Maeve nodded. "And for that town. It's where her mother was born. Keep reading, Patrick."

" 'Residents of Ard na Mara have set up a memorial for the victims of the ferry disaster. A brass plaque containing the names of each person aboard the fated vessel will be mounted on a slab of granite, donated by a family from Nova Scotia, Canada. Frederic Neill had come to Ard na Mara to meet with Aran Shipbuilders, to commission the third and largest vessel in his family's tour boat fleet. Camille Neill, his widow, was reached at her innkeeping office in Cape Hawk, Nova Scotia. "The family wishes to keep Frederic's memory alive," she said of the monument. She had no further comment.' "

"Wasn't that a lovely thing to do?" Clara asked.

"I wonder whether the family tour boat fleet includes whale-watching boats," Patrick said, staring into Maeve's eyes.

Her hands were shaking, so she held them quietly in her lap.

"What do you think, Maeve?" he asked.

"I really haven't any idea."

"Cape Hawk," he said. "That's one of the places people can go to see beluga whales."

Clara smiled. "Well, they have belugas right at the aquarium in Mystic. And Maeve, you have a membership!"

"Yes, you do," Patrick said. "Don't you?"

"Mmm," Maeve said, holding her shawl tighter. It wasn't a cold night by any means—the fireflies were dancing in the side yard, and the air smelled of summer flowers. But she felt something like an arctic chill blow through the open window. Perhaps her stomachache wasn't indigestion at all, but the beginning of the flu. She had had a terrible case last winter. It had nearly landed her in the hospital. Maybe she'd put the heat on again tonight.

"You look pale, Maeve," Patrick said.

"It's just the candlelight," she said.

"So, that's why it was so hard to read the stories," Patrick said, but he didn't smile. He seemed fixed on his plans, whatever they were. Maeve was sure he was just being polite, sipping his tea. She wished he'd hurry up, get started on the next phase of his investigation. Or did she? Her stomach churned at the thought. There had been so much hurt, danger, disappointment.

"Did you find the articles helpful?" Clara asked.

"I don't know yet," Patrick said. "There's at least a coincidence. . . ."

"What would that be?" Maeve asked.

"The mention of Cape Hawk in the story about the

ferry memorial, and the fact that it came up in my research earlier tonight."

"Regarding whales," Maeve said.

"Isn't that an odd coincidence?" Patrick asked.

"I don't believe in coincidences, myself," Maeve said. Patrick was staring at her. She held his gaze for a few seconds, then saw his eyes flicker down to her eyeglass case. It was old and well worn, some of the needlepoint stitches worn off after so many years. He stared at it for a moment, as if trying to decipher the word and discern the shape. Could he make out the tail?

"You're saying you think there's a connection?" he asked, steering himself back to the matter at hand.

"No."

"You sure?"

"Quite."

She took off her bifocals and put them back into the case. Her hands were shaking, and she felt a sheen of sweat on her brow.

"You know, dear," Maeve said. "I'm not feeling well. I have quite a case of indigestion, and I might be coming down with a summer flu. I'm chilled to the bone. Why don't you take the articles with you?"

"I'll do that, Maeve," he said, not looking away.

And Maeve shivered—not because the room had gotten any colder, but because for the first time, Patrick Murphy had looked at her as if she were the enemy. And he had every reason to.

Chapter 20

Marisa's fingers ached from pushing the needle in and out, embroidering the words "Bring Rose Home" on pillow after pillow. Lily's shop was quiet, except for the Spirit CD playing on the stereo. Marisa had put in *Aurora*, and Jessica kept playing the title song over and over. The sounds of boats and seagulls drifted in from the harbor. As she sewed, Marisa's mind wandered back to her childhood, when she had sat at her mother's knee, learning how to mend her clothes.

"That's it, sweetheart," her mother had said, praising her for the worst, biggest stitches anyone had ever made. "You're really getting the hang of it!"

Marisa had loved all the time she'd spent with her mother. Sewing, cooking, gardening—it didn't matter. Even driving—her mother had let Marisa sit behind the wheel of her bright orange Volvo, driving it in and out of their cul-de-sac, when Marisa was only twelve years old. She'd been the envy of all her friends.

Her mother had taught Marisa and her sister how to drive a stick shift, how to prune roses just below the new growth, how to look for three- and five-leaf sets on old rosebushes, how to transplant orange day lilies, how to take ivy cuttings, where to look for wild blackberries, how they should never approach swans—because swans, although beautiful and graceful, were very aggressive, and would attack humans.

She had taught Marisa to protect herself from swans, but not from sweet-talking men. Not from Ted. Glancing up, Marisa looked at Jessica across the shop. It was their turn, among all the Nanouks, to work in Lily's store. They wanted to keep it open—keep Lily's business going strong—so that when Lily and Rose returned from the hospital, they wouldn't have to worry about an income.

Lily had told Anne, who was serving as the In Stitches bookkeeper until Lily's return, that she should pay everyone a salary for their work. Many of the Nanouks refused—donating their proceeds straight back into the "Bring Rose Home" account—but Marisa didn't have that luxury.

Their exodus had been a financial hardship. As carefully as she had planned the escape, she hadn't counted on such difficulties. She had followed instructions from a couple of different domestic violence websites: stayed as even-tempered as possible, so Ted wouldn't suspect her intentions, hidden money in a fake frozen orange juice can in the freezer, started emptying accounts, taken proceeds from the house sale.

He had charmed her into putting his name on so many of her investments, including her main account at the brokerage where he worked—United Bankers' Trust. All of her first husband's pension had been there, as well as her inheritance from her father. Ted had made such a show of caring, of wanting to help her invest wisely—"so you will never have to worry."

"You" meaning Marisa and Jessica. How benevolent he had sounded—when, in fact, he had been using them the whole time. The longer Marisa stayed away, the more she was beginning to see. Was it possible that just a few months ago—right after leaving him—she had had some doubts, had actually felt some longing for him? Had been missing the feeling of his arms around her shoulders?

He had been like Dr. Jekyll and Mr. Hyde. He could be so funny and sweet, but his mood could change in a flash—just like a storm whipping up on a summer day. His moods had kept both her and Jessica so off-balance.

Now, listening to Spirit sing "Lonesome Daughter," Marisa looked over at Jessica and wondered how long they would have to keep up the charade. Knowing that Lily was down in Boston, in New England, made Marisa homesick. She missed her sister Sam and the music they had played together. What had she been thinking, hauling her daughter way up here, to this far-north outpost? "White Dawn" came on, haunting and powerful.

"Mom?" Jessica asked.

"Yes, honey?"

"When is Rose coming back?"

"After she has surgery, it should take about two weeks before they let her leave the hospital."

"I want to talk to her."

"I know. You will, soon."

"She'll be happy to get home, won't she?"

Marisa nodded, looking over with curiosity. It seemed funny to hear Jessica refer to this place as "home."

"We're so lucky to have such a cool place to live," Jessica said. "With so many whales and hawks and owls, and friends. I never thought I'd be a member of a secret society."

"The Nanouk Girls?"

Jessica nodded. "They didn't even know us, but they took us right in and let us be members. And now look at us, raising all this money for Rose."

Marisa swallowed hard. Hearing her daughter sound so happy and grateful was worth almost everything—all the pain that had led up to her decision to do this, to drop out and abandon everything at home, even their real names and identities. It reminded her a little bit of the Internet— message boards, where everyone took on a phony name and tried on different personas. Discouraging, to say the least. Yet she did it too. Marisa had logged in her share of time chatting online, at times when she couldn't sleep or didn't want to feel.

Footsteps sounded on the porch, and then the bell above the door rang. Marisa looked up to see Anne, Marlena, Cindy, and two of Cindy's daughters walking in with sandwiches from the inn.

"Lunchtime," Anne announced.

"I'm almost finished with another pillow!" Jessica announced to Allie.

"We made two last night," Allie said.

"They're selling out, as fast as we can put them at the inn desk," Anne said as everyone pitched in. Thermoses of iced tea and lemonade, plastic cups, slices of lemon and orange, turkey sandwiches, chocolate chip cookies, paper plates, napkins, all came out. Marisa cleared off the counter; women friends amazed her. Although they hadn't known each other for very long, they had bonded completely over concern for Rose Malone.

Marisa watched Jessica, carefully passing out paper plates. Her heart swelled, thinking of how it was Jessica who had made this happen. While Marisa hid inside, afraid to trust anyone or show her real self, her daughter had reached out to Rose—and beyond that, to Lily and the Nanouks.

Now, looking around the circle, Marisa desperately wanted to tell them all the truth. It killed her, to hold so much back from these women who had given her—and continued to give her—so much. She thought back to nursing school, when she had first realized how generous and healing women were by nature. She thought of Sam. The Nanouk Girls of the Frozen North were further proof.

"I have to tell you all something," she said out loud, her mouth dry.

They looked at her, smiling, ready for anything.

"Jessica and I..."

Anne paused, thermos poised over the empty glasses.

"We're not who we seem to be," she whispered.

"Mommy?" Jessica asked—and there was warning, even panic, in her eyes.

"What do you mean?" Cindy asked.

"We're on the run . . ."

"You told us," Marlena said. "On the boat, the day of Rose's birthday party. We understand, honey. You're escaping a bad marriage. It happens."

"But we're using false names."

"Mommy!"

The women stared at her. Marisa was shaking, thinking that they would feel so betrayed, they'd just walk out the front door. They wouldn't speak to her again; they'd kick her and Jess out of the Nanouks. Anne's eyes were bruised, as if she was terribly hurt. Marlena's eyes widened, and Cindy hung her head. Cindy's two daughters just stared at Jessica, and Jessica turned bright red.

Suddenly Anne stood up, came around the circle, put her arms around Marisa. She hugged her so hard, Marisa felt it in every bone in her body.

"I'm so sorry," Anne said. "For whatever you went through that made it necessary for you to do that."

"We know something about it," Cindy said. "Because one of our other members had to do it too."

Anne and Marlena nodded, exchanging glances with Cindy. Marisa knew, without them telling her, that they were talking about Lily.

"Did you ever go to a safe house?" Cindy asked. "Were you able to get a restraining order against him?"

"You don't have to tell us," Marlena said gently.

"Yes, I did try," Marisa said. "But the kinds of things he did were too subtle. The judge, when I went to court begging for an order of protection, told me that if Ted hadn't literally tried to kill me within the last twenty-four hours, he wouldn't issue one."

"Fucking idiot," Marlena said. "It's just what Lily told us. The courts don't understand domestic violence."

"You can say that again," Cindy said.

"How can it happen to such strong women?" Marisa asked, not understanding, thinking of Lily, with her clear eyes, with the fortitude she had to get through Rose's illness. "How did we attract them?"

"First of all, you can't blame yourself. That's what we told Lily," Marlena said. "You were both vulnerable. You'd lost your husband, and Lily had never really gotten over losing her parents. Her husband saw that she made good money—from her needlework design business—and he went after it."

"Mine did the same," Marisa said. "He came after my first husband's pension."

"The point is, you're both wonderful. We all have different sorts of issues and problems—that's life. Thank God we came together—to keep each other safe and warm. We have a lot to talk about, and a lot of strength and spirit to offer each other."

"It's not all about escaping rotten husbands," Cindy said. "In fact, they are completely beside the point. It's about being friends and having fun."

"We have plenty of other things in common," Anne said. "Beyond our problems and worries."

Marisa smiled, remembering how Lily had said, "Welcome to the thaw."

"See?" Marlena asked. "We don't care what your real names are. We love you for who you are inside."

"Sometimes I don't even know who that is," Marisa whispered. "I feel as if I left her someplace far away...."

"Well, we know who you are," Anne said. "Someone loving, kind, caring, and open. A woman who'd give up her summer afternoons to look after Lily's store, and make pine pillows to raise money for Rose."

"Thank you," Marisa said.

"The pine pillows were my idea," Jessica reminded everyone, and they all laughed.

"That's right, they were," Cindy said.

"I still want to tell you our real names," Marisa said. "I trust you all, so much. And he—Ted—lives hundreds of miles away. He has no idea where we are—none at all. Cape Hawk is a mystery to him. He'd never suspect that we'd come here."

"He wouldn't," Jessica said, her eyes brightening at the idea of revealing the truth.

"Well," Anne said. "We can promise you that nothing you say will leave this room. We won't even tell the other Nanouks, unless and until you say it's okay."

"I believe you," Marisa said.

"So do I," Jessica said, smiling.

"Okay then," Cindy said.

"Who are you really?" Marlena asked, with a big grin.

And Marisa told them their real names.

The Florida disaster, Hurricane Catherina, had brought out the best in people—especially in Spirit fans. Secret Agent had filled his coffers the last few weeks, with contributions sent in by all his friends on the SpiritTown message board. He had woven a story that just kept getting better and better. His sister and her husband had lost everything—everything. The 150-mile-per-hour winds had blown the roof off their house in Homestead and destroyed everything inside. His poor little nephew Jake had needed stitches from all his cuts caused by flying glass. Now he needed plastic surgery.

Secret Agent started a new topic: "Jake Update." Then he typed in his message: "Hey you guys. Here's the latest on my nephew, Jake. Thanks to all of you, my sister was able to take him to the best plastic surgeon in Miami. And you *know* they've got great plastic surgeons in Miami. (We know all about face-lifts and boob jobs.) Anyway, now they're talking about a few operations."

He paused, wondering how far he could go with this. He had learned, over time, to set the hook and then be patient—let the people on the board reach into their hearts and pocketbooks and offer. He rarely had to actually ask. Rereading his writing, he deleted the part about face-lifts and boob jobs—it struck a wrong chord. Then he hit "Send."

Didn't have to wait too long, either. It was late night, past midnight, and there were plenty of Spirit fans camped out by their computers, chatting with each other.

"So sorry, man. That family's been through too much," came the reply from Spiritfan1955.

"What kind of surgery? How extensive?" came the question from SpiritGirl—who posted a signature picture that showed she was hot, blonde, and, interestingly enough, surgically enhanced.

"Pretty extensive," Secret Agent typed back. "His face is very scarred. He's only 13, so he's pretty devastated." Here came the bait: "The worst part is, my sister has used nearly all the money you folks have been so great to send—trying to fix up the house. It's a disaster."

Now he waited again. He was itching to get out of here. He had a porn site open at the same time, and he was really dying to get back to his hot, horny, barely legal honeys. But he couldn't resist making a little money tonight—not that he needed the funds. He had plenty from the bitch. But Secret Agent's theory was, if people wanted to give it, well then, it was his job to take it. He stared at his "Jake Update" heading, and opened the single new reply.

"Like you said: it's a disaster. That means it's a disaster area, and your sister is getting money from the government."

Whoa! Who the fuck was this? Secret Agent looked at the signature: White Dawn. Had to be a woman—no guy would sign on with a name like that. On the other hand, it was the title of a Spirit song, and these Spirit fans—men or women—were freakily obsessed. Then Secret Agent noticed the number positioned right next to the screen name: 1. It was this person's first post on the message board.

"Nice first post, White Dawn," Spiritfan1955 wrote back sarcastically. "You don't know the whole story."

"Exactly," wrote PeaceBabe. "Welcome to the board, White Dawn. Secret Agent's sister and her family were affected by Hurricane Catherina, and we've been pitching in to help. Disaster aid goes only so far—and it takes a long time to sort out the bureaucracy. We've just given the family a little boost."

That was Secret Agent's cue. He typed: "Thanks everyone. I'm sure White Dawn didn't mean any harm. It's just, we're like a family here, White Dawn. These guys have been a lifeline to my sister." Should he remind everyone about little Jake and his cut face, the reason for starting this topic in the first place? Money for young Jake's reconstructive surgery? People, get ready, there's a train a-comin'... He'd give it a couple of minutes. But he didn't have to: *bingo*.

"Hey White Dawn," Spiritfan1955 wrote. "Here's how the SpiritTown board works. This thread started out with a story about Jake. Thirteen y/o boy, needs plastic surgery? I'm in—Secret Agent, PM me your PayRight info, and I'll make a contribution."

Secret Agent didn't waste a second: he sent Spiritfan1955 a private message, containing his account information, along with the requisite "thanks, man."

"I'm in," wrote PeaceBabe. "I have a thirteen-year-old daughter."

"Dude, so sorry about Jake," wrote OneThinDime. "I'll help out as much as I can. My wife was in a car accident last year, and I know how bad it can be. Plastic surgery isn't cheap, and those bills mount up. She went through a lot—we all did. We listened to the box set *Spirit Days and Spirit Nights* for about a month straight—got us through. My prayers are with you."

"Thank you," Secret Agent wrote back. "I'm humbled by your generosity. Truly. And I think I'll get my sister that box set—great idea. Her spirits are very low right now, needless to say."

"We're with you, man," Spiritguy1974 wrote.

"Totally with you," LastCall25 chimed in.

The PayRight account was filling up—a good night's work, Secret Agent thought, just getting ready to say good night to his fabulous friends, his SpiritTown family. He had been slipping back and forth between websites, tuned in to a webcam focused on the nether regions of some horny housewife in the Badlands somewhere—but now the time had come to give Ms. Housewife his full attention.

Just then, White Dawn's screen name appeared in the "Jake Update" thread. Secret Agent chuckled. Another convert to the world of give-me-your-money. He'd had just about enough of this, and was really ready to click onto his porno screen. He'd just see what White Dawn had to offer, so he scrolled down to her post.

"Beware."

Secret Agent's blood turned ice cold. He couldn't believe it. Just one word there on the SpiritTown screen, for all to see: Beware. White Dawn's second post—warning the world. Secret Agent felt as if he had a new enemy—as if he had just turned over a rock and found a rattlesnake coiled and ready to attack him.

He couldn't believe his eyes. Another post had popped up, and he read it:

"Hurricane Catherina didn't hit Homestead. It tracked north, dude. You can do a better job conning people if you first check out the storm track on the NOAA website."

"You fucking bitch!" he yelled. But he didn't even know whether it was a man or woman—he knew nothing about White Dawn at all. He looked for the profile and found none. He was going to find out—that was for sure. He would learn this person's identity and make White Dawn sorry for shaming him on the board.

"Fuck you!" he said out loud, totally losing his erection.

Chapter 21

Boston was filled with kids. Lily saw them everywhere: with their families, with groups, on camp outings. Heading to the Public Gardens, the science museum, the Freedom Trail, Faneuil Hall, the aquarium. Kids having fun, too excited to walk slowly or in single file. They tried to outrun the rain. They tried to outshout the city noises. They tried to have more fun today than they'd had yesterday.

Lily hoped they would all succeed. Even more, she hoped that Rose would one day be able to join them. She turned away from the wide plate-glass window overlooking the playground on the banks of the Charles River. Then she sat in one of the orange chairs of the hospital waiting room, Liam by her side, while Rose was being prepped for surgery.

She glanced over at him. She felt she was in a dream, where everything was both normal and bizarre at the same time. Here she was, sitting with Liam Neill, as if they were a longtime couple. They were waiting for Rose to have open-heart surgery. Two nights ago he had kissed her.

That was the part that made life feel like a dream. Lily couldn't understand how she could be feeling so secretly happy and tender while her daughter was in the fight of her life. Liam touched the back of her hand, and Lily turned liquid inside. He asked if she would like a cup of tea, and she was so befuddled, she couldn't quite stop looking at his eyes.

But there had been no chance to talk about what had happened—or even to repeat it. Since getting to Boston, every minute had been focused on being with Rose and talking to the doctors. Lily knew that was for the best: she didn't want to be distracted. Rose was her full-time job, and more: she was Lily's life. And Lily didn't want to jeopardize anything by messing up her priorities.

At least, that's what she told herself about the fact that Liam hadn't kissed her again.

"Are you okay?" Liam asked now, sitting in the waiting room.

"I'm fine. Are you?"

"Yes," he said. But the way he said it, "yes," with his blue eyes glowing and fixed on Lily's—well, it confused her, made her blush.

"Um, good," she said.

"Something has changed," he said. "And you don't have to be afraid of it, Lily."

"About Rose? About her tests?"

Rose had had another echo test; she was so tired now

from the cumulative effect of not getting enough oxygen, she slept while the technician rubbed cold jelly on her chest. She seemed oblivious to the loud sound made by the Doppler. But the test had revealed no surprises—Rose had been stabilized by her time in Melbourne, and she was now ready for surgery.

"No," Liam said, smiling. "Not about Rose."

"She's all I can think about right now, Liam."

"I know. We're almost there," he said.

"We've been here so many times before," Lily said—and as she looked up into Liam's weathered face, she felt her stomach flip. They had both said "we," and the word was apt. Liam had been with her and Rose every time. Why had Lily never let that sink in before?

"This time is different," Liam said.

"How do you know?" Lily asked.

Liam reached for her hand. She shivered, wanting him to hold her—she felt like a tornado of emotion. She wanted him to hold her together, keep her from flying apart. She felt her skin tingling—and the length of her spine, and the backs of her legs—all from some fantastic longing that confused and shocked her and seemed like the worst timing possible. All he had done was hold her hand.

"This time is different," he said, "because the procedure is straightforward. All they're doing is replacing an old patch. The hole in her heart hasn't torn or grown or widened. The only problem is the patch, and this surgery will be definitive."

"She's not getting worse," Lily said.

"No. She's not. Her symptoms are all related to the patch, and to the stenosis."

"I can't take it," she whispered.

"Yes, you can," he said, giving her hand a firm shake. "Just think it through, Lily. You know it's going to go well."

She watched Liam, who was watching the door through which the doctors would walk—to tell them Rose was ready. Her mind clicked through everything she knew about Rose, a laundry list of what would happen today. Although Tetralogy of Fallot included four defects, only two were of supreme importance today. Pulmonary stenosis—the outflow passage, where Rose's right ventricle and pulmonary artery connected, was narrow and blocked; and the large ventricular septal defect—the patch had become brittle, allowing blood to freely mix between the two ventricles.

Rose's severe stenosis meant that less blood reached the lungs with each heartbeat, causing her to turn blue. Her surgery today would involve removing the thickened muscle beneath the pulmonary valve and replacing the old worn-out patch with some brand-new felt Gortex. It all sounded so simple—yet Lily felt that she herself might not survive another minute of stress.

Now the doctors came out, wheeling Rose alongside. Prepped for surgery—groggy, hair held back by a paper cap, hooked up to monitors and an IV—she managed to lift her head slightly, searching for Lily. Only, the person she called for was Liam.

"Dr. Neill," she said.

"I'm here, Rose."

"Remember what I said."

"I do remember. I never forget."

Lily saw the looks pass between them, and felt that mysterious stomach drop—not knowing what they meant, but realizing it was important.

"Did you find her again? Nanny?"

"Yes," Liam said, crouching down, face-to-face with Rose. "I did. It's so unbelievable, but you know where she is?"

Rose shook her head, eyes rolling back as she tried to stay awake. Lily touched Liam's back—partly for support, and partly because they were all together in this.

"Tell Rose, Lily—"

"Honey," Lily said, hardly able to believe it herself. "Nanny is swimming south from Nova Scotia. While all the other whales are migrating north, we think she's coming to Boston, to find you—"

"Will she be okay?" Rose asked, looking worried.

Lily nodded. "Yes." The moment shimmered between them. "Nanny will be fine," she said. "And so will you, my darling girl."

"You will," Liam said.

"It's time to go now," Dr. Garibaldi said. "When you see Rose again, she'll be as good as new. She's told me all about this Nanny character—and she'll be back in Nova Scotia before the week's out, and by August, she'll be swimming with all the whales she wants. We're going to put on the best, strongest patch in the world, and this will be Miss Rose Malone's last surgery for a long, long time. Now come on—let's go."

Lily and Liam bent down to kiss Rose, and that was that—they wheeled her away. Lily's own heart nearly gave out, watching her go into the elevator. She felt Liam's arm come around her, she let him lead her to the chairs in the waiting room. There was a television on—there was always a television on—and a pile of magazines, and that morning's papers. But Lily just put her head in her hands and tried to hold herself together.

"You heard the doctor," Liam said. "He sounded so positive—he said Rose will be home by the end of the week. Lily—that's six days."

"I know," she said.

"Six days, Lily. We'll be back in Cape Hawk. Rose can have her summer."

Lily let him hold her. There were times when she couldn't talk, couldn't even really think. There were aspects to life nine years ago that were so traumatic, she had developed a fight-or-flight response. Her body would flood with adrenaline, and she would go totally numb. She was right there, right now.

Rose's father had created so much terror back then. He had been so angry about the pregnancy—and his behavior had gotten so much worse. Lily, not getting it, had tried every way possible to reassure him that she would love him as much—or even more—after the baby was born. But he was unmoved by her promises.

"Promises," she said now.

"Which promises?" Liam asked.

Lily was almost in a trance—her baby was about to be

hooked up to the heart-lung machine. The idea was so terrifying, all Lily's old trauma was being reactivated. She started to tremble, and couldn't stop.

"I made promises to Rose's father," she said to Liam now. "I promised that we would stay together, that I would love him as much or more after the baby was born. I promised that she wouldn't take up all my time—that I'd still have plenty of time for him. More, I said. Because I was going to stop work and stay home..."

"Lily, what are you thinking of him for?" Liam asked. "You know he doesn't deserve your words or thoughts."

That's right, Lily thought. She had told Liam about him that very first night—when she was nearly crazed with pain—both physical, from giving birth, and emotional, from having run for her life from Rose's father. She gulped back a sob.

"And he doesn't deserve your tears," Liam said, leaning over to kiss her forehead, her cheek, the corner of her mouth.

"I used to drive myself mad," Lily said. "Wondering *why.*"

"Why?"

"Why Rose? Why did she have to have these problems? We don't have heart disease in our family—the only person who ever had a heart attack was my great-grandfather, and he was ninety-one. I ate a healthy diet during pregnancy—gave up caffeine. I'd given up wine even before I got pregnant.... I didn't smoke. I exercised, but not too much. Why?"

"I don't know, Lily," Liam said, kissing her hands, looking into her eyes.

"The doctors didn't know either. They say Tetralogy of Fallot isn't hereditary. It just happens—and it's random. There's no knowing who gets it."

"Lily, don't do this—"

"It should be so simple—it is for other children. Air and blood meet in the lungs, and then the heart pumps the blood through the body. Why can't it work for Rose? It's so simple...."

"But it does work for Rose," Liam said gently. "She's had some challenges, that's true. But I believe the doctors. They say that this will be her last surgery for a long time."

"A long, *long* time," Lily corrected.

"Right. A long, long time. And we're going to hold them to that."

We. That word again.

"There are mysteries about Rose, it's true," Liam said. "We don't know why. We might never know why. But there are other whys we might never know either. Such as why I went to your house that night, the night Rose was born. Why I had to take the books back to you that exact night. And why, once I walked through that door, I never wanted to walk out again."

"Liam," she whispered, remembering the promises he'd made that night, and for the first time, wanting him to keep them.

"Why," he began, but stopped himself. His lips moved against her skin, and she felt rather than heard him say

"Why I love you both so much." But then she realized that he had just kissed her neck—he hadn't said anything at all. Of course he hadn't—they were in the middle of the waiting room—with nurses and doctors and other parents walking in and out.

She held his hand tighter, listening to him—feeling herself materialize more in her own body, no longer numb and floating up in the air, a traumatized ghost.

"We love you too," she wanted to say, but didn't. She wanted to tell him that, because it was finally washing over her—the reality, that this man had been with her and Rose, right by their side, since the very first day. He was like Rose's father. Rose's real father was nothing to them—nothing at all. Liam was one reason why Rose felt so loved, one of the reasons why she thrived.

"You're right," she said. "There are a lot of whys."

"And they're not all bad," he said.

"I know," Lily said, just smiling. But she looked up at the clock and saw that it was ten o'clock—the time that surgery was going to start. Open-heart surgery never took long. Generally sixty minutes at the most. So much could happen during that single hour. A life and death could pass before a family's eyes.... *Oh God*, Lily prayed, closing her eyes. *Help her through this hour....*

Liam opened his laptop, hoping Lily would take pleasure and comfort in watching the green light that represented MM122 tracking ever closer to Boston Harbor. But Lily seemed unable to watch anything but the clock and the door through which the doctors would emerge post-surgery.

It was ten-fifteen. Liam tried to hide his own nervousness. He had sat beside Lily through Rose's other open-heart surgeries. Because of Rose's aortic valve stenosis and her ventricular defect, the very wall of the heart had to be opened.

To keep the blood flowing to other vital organs, Rose had to be hooked up to a heart-lung machine. Liam had studied up on it, spoken to a friend from McGill who'd gone into cardiac surgery in Vancouver. He knew that Rose was under deep anesthesia. Dr. Garibaldi would have gone in through her breastbone.

Catheters were draining blood from the veins in the right side of her heart into the heart-lung machine—which, in a pumping rhythm, was passing the blood over a special oxygen-containing filter, sending the oxygenated blood back into Rose's body through a catheter in her aorta.

Her heart itself was now without blood—and the doctors were working fast. The operating room was very cold, so Rose's heart and brain would require less oxygen. Liam tried to imagine what was going on, but he—like Lily—was now watching the clock. Ten thirty-five.

"Her last operation took forty minutes," Lily said. "The doctor will be out anytime."

"Yep," Liam said. "Any minute now."

"They're just going to remove the blockage and replace the patch."

"Right," Liam said. "Dr. Garibaldi has done this exact surgery hundreds of times."

"But not on Rose," Lily said. "He's never operated on her before. It was Dr. Kenney before. And then he took that position in Baltimore, at Johns Hopkins. We could have gone to Johns Hopkins."

"Boston is fine, Lily. It's the best. Dr. Garibaldi is the best."

"But we could have gone to Baltimore...."

"I know. But Boston is closer to home. You like this hospital, and Rose feels comfortable here."

"That's right," Lily said, staring at him earnestly, as if he were telling her something she'd never heard before. "You're right. That's why we chose Boston—because it's so good, and because Rose feels comfortable here."

Ten-forty.

"She's been under for forty minutes," Lily murmured. "I think that's as long as she's ever been on the machine before. I'm not sure, but I think so."

"It's not too long, Lily. The doctor will be out in a minute."

"It's just..." Lily said. "They have to make sure the blood and oxygen mix properly. I never understand how a machine can do that. But it's been done before—lots of times before. Rose has always been fine afterwards. Except that time she got the bacterial infection—"

"She won't get one this time," Liam said, reaching for

Lily's hand. But she wouldn't let him hold it. As if remembering that terrible time when Rose had contracted a virulent staph infection—she had survived the surgery but nearly died from the infection—Lily jumped out of her seat and began to pace. She went to the window, rested her forehead against the glass.

Liam ached with helplessness, so he forced himself to focus on science. He turned up the brightness of his computer screen—it wasn't like sitting in the dark with Lily, in his truck by the lighthouse, with the night so black, and the screen showing every dot, with his arm around Lily, and her skin soft against his. It wasn't like that here.

He peered at the screen. There she was—Nanny, MM122—blinking off Gloucester. She had swum her amazing journey in one and a half days—from Melbourne, slanting across the Atlantic to the Gulf of Maine, passing Matinicus and Monhegan, Christmas Cove, Boothbay Harbor, Yarmouth, Portland, swinging past the Isle of Shoals, down the coast of Massachusetts.

Here she was, right on Boston's North Shore, speeding south. Liam wanted to call Lily over, to show her, but something in Lily's posture told him that she couldn't take hearing about Nanny just now. Liam's own stomach dropped a little.

MM122 was way out of her range, out of the normal geographic areas where beluga whales were found in July. What if Nanny did have some mystical connection to Rose? What if her coming here was some sort of harbinger—living in Cape Hawk, the whale could certainly say hello to

Rose any time she wanted to. What if Nanny was coming to Boston to say goodbye?

Liam refused to think that. Gazing at Lily across the room, he pushed himself up. The clock now read ten fifty-five. Rose had been under for five minutes shy of an hour. Liam tried to think of the things he could say to Lily: maybe the doctors got started late, maybe the operating room wasn't ready, maybe...

This wasn't the time for speculation. Liam was an oceanographer, and he knew: it was a time for science. He walked across the big space to Lily—a distance that seemed interminable. He was reminded of the first time he saw his mother, after Connor had died, and after Liam had had what was left of his arm amputated. His mother had been looking out a window then. Liam had called her name, and she didn't turn around.

"Lily?" he said.

When she wheeled at the sound of his voice, he felt so much relief, he felt his eyes fill.

"What?" Lily asked.

"I wanted to tell you something," he said, blinking back the tears. He wanted to come up with something factual, scientific, indisputable, and wise. But the thing was, he really had nothing to say. All he could think of was Rose.

"You were talking about the mix before," he said. "Blood and oxygen."

"Yes..."

"I was thinking back to grad school," he said, struggling for something that would comfort her. "We learned a lot about that in a marine biology class. Whales are mammals, as you know, and our professor was teaching us about the cetacean circulatory system."

Lily nodded, listening. She seemed to notice that his brow was sweating—she reached up and brushed his damp hair back from his forehead. Her smile was very gentle, as if encouraging him to go on.

"In the earliest days of medicine," Liam said, "dating back to the sixth century B.C., on the Greek island of Ionia, doctors had the idea that when air and blood mingled in the lungs, the blood gained a 'vital essence.' But it took many centuries until they realized that the vital essence was—"

"Oxygen," Lily said, and Liam smiled, knowing she probably knew more about the process than most scientists.

"Right," he said. "I still remember reading William Harvey's famous treatise—I think it's from 1628—on blood flow and circulation. Of course, my class was on whales, not humans."

"Hearts are hearts," Lily whispered, watching the time click to eleven o'clock.

Liam watched the blood drain from her face. She began to tremble, and he knew she was losing it. He put his arm around her, tried to hold her tight. She was shaking so hard, grabbing his arm, burying her face in his chest.

"Where are the doctors?" she asked.

"They're coming," he said.

And before they could look up, they heard Dr. Garibaldi's voice. "Lily, Liam?" he asked.

"How's Rose?" Lily asked. She lurched toward the doctor. Liam looked around—as if it was possible Dr. Garibaldi could have rolled Rose out with him, into the waiting room. Then Liam looked at the doctor's pale, deep-set eyes, and he knew what he was about to say, before he even spoke.

"She's fine," the doctor said. "Went through the surgery with no problems whatever. We removed the obstruction and replaced the patch. Gortex, this time—it should last her the rest of her life. She's in recovery now, but she's already out of the anesthesia, and they'll be bringing her up here to the ICU in just a few minutes."

"Thank you," Liam said. "Thank you, Doctor."

Lily shook Dr. Garibaldi's hand, touched her own heart, and thanked him. After the doctor left, she turned to Liam.

"You thanked him even before I did," she said.

"Oh," he said, suddenly embarrassed. "I did. I'm sorry— I just—"

"No, it's good," she said, turning bright pink. "It's just . . . it's just something a father would do."

Liam stood straight, couldn't quite speak. If only Lily knew what was going on inside his chest, how he had felt about Rose since the instant he'd brought her into this world.

"I was thinking," Lily said. "About what you were saying just before the doctor came up. About the Greeks, and the vital essence."

"Oxygen," he said. As she herself had said. . . .

"I was thinking it must be something else too," she said, staring at the elevator doors, hearing the lift coming closer. The doctor had said that Rose would be up in just a few minutes, and Lily was ready. She turned her gaze from the elevator to Liam.

"What else?" he asked.

"Well," she said, stopping herself.

Liam wanted to tell her what he thought, but he couldn't say the word out loud: *Love.* The most vital essence of all.

And just then the door opened, and an orderly wheeled Rose out—there on the bed, attached to monitors, but with her eyes open. She was strapped down—the sight of those straps tore Liam's heart. They had to keep her from moving, at least overnight. She looked from Lily to Liam, and then back to Lily.

"Hi, sweetheart," Lily said.

"It hurts," Rose said.

"I know, honey. But it won't for long."

"It won't, Rose," Liam said, hardly able to bear seeing her in pain, knowing that the nurses would give her pain meds in a second, and knowing that she would heal fast from the surgery. "It won't hurt for long."

"Promise?" Rose whispered hoarsely.

"Yes," Liam said, touching her head—as his own father had done when he'd made a similar promise after Liam's arm surgery—knowing that that was just what a father would say and do.

Chapter 22

Rose was awake, opening her eyes as soon as they wheeled her out of the operating room. The medicine they gave her made her groggy, but she kept trying to tear the straps off her chest anyway. She wanted to move, run, hug her mother, go home.

She slept a lot.

Her mother and Dr. Neill took turns sitting by her bed. Sometimes they were there together, sitting so close they looked like one person. Their voices threaded in and out of her dreams, joining her waking and sleeping hours. When she cried, she wasn't sure who hugged her. Her chest hurt.

And then it didn't. The next day, when Rose woke up, the sun was shining, and her chest didn't hurt at all. Well, maybe a little—the nurse helped her sit up, and then she washed her, and then the doctor came to look at her stitches.

Her mother and Liam stood back while the nurses got

her ready to take her first walk. She knew that it was less than a day since her surgery, but she was used to being the wonder girl when it came to getting out of bed fast. She knew that walking and pooping were the big events. They were like getting an A+ on a book report or math test. Once you had them, you were on your way home.

Or at least out of ICU, to the normal floor.

"How's the pain, Rose?" the nurse asked.

"Not so bad. Mom, did you tell Jessica I'm coming home in a week?"

"Yes, honey."

"Dr. Neill, what's wrong?" She looked up, and he had a funny look on his face—as if he was frozen between wanting to stand back and trying to catch her. The nurse gave him a teacherly smile, as if he had a lot to learn.

"Children heal much faster than adults from open-heart surgery," the nurse said. "They experience much less pain in the chest wall. We're going to get Rose up and walking, so we can move her down to the pediatric floor."

"Okay," Dr. Neill said, holding his arms out, the way Rose remembered him doing when she was really tiny, learning to walk. The sight of him doing that made her laugh, which made her chest hurt. "Rose? What?" he asked.

"I can do it," she told him. "Watch."

"Ready when you are, honey," her mother said.

All the adults stood close by her side, and Rose inched to the edge of the bed. She reached her toes down to the floor, in her fuzzy slippers. The ground felt so solid. Rose hadn't wanted to tell her mother, but it had felt tippy for a long while, almost like the deck of the *Tecumseh II* at her birthday party. A boat, tilting fore and aft, sideways, all around. Rose had felt dizzy, and she knew it was because she hadn't been getting enough oxygen.

But that had changed. Already, just half a day after her operation, she felt ten, a hundred, a thousand times better than she had. She breathed in—and she actually felt her lungs expand and her strength return.

"I feel *good*," she said.

Everyone smiled, and her mother held out her hand.

"Walk with me?" her mother asked.

Rose nodded, but she didn't move her feet. She just kept waiting, staring up.

"Rose?" Dr. Neill asked.

She just reached out her hand, waiting for him to take it. He slid his fingers into hers, and then Rose was ready. She, her mother, and Dr. Neill took their first steps together. Through the ICU, around the nurses' station. She realized that in all the ICUs she had been in before, Dr. Neill had been there too.

Only family were allowed in ICU. Rose grinned, keeping her head down, afraid to let everyone know how happy that made her feel. Because she didn't know what it meant, and over the last nine years she had learned that she needed to take care of her heart, keep it from getting broken. But he squeezed her hand, and she decided to allow herself to hope.

Lily and Liam had started going down to Boston Harbor after leaving the hospital. They would cut through Faneuil Hall and end up on Long Wharf. People enjoying the summer night strolled by, but for Lily and Liam it was much more urgent: they were both sustained by the sea, and they needed to see it and feel the salt air of home.

Liam brought binoculars so they could scan the blue water, searching for Nanny. But she never came close enough to the shore, seeming to stay out beyond the harbor islands, just hovering in the area.

That night, when they'd had their fill of sea breezes, they walked back toward the hotel. Lily stared down at the cobblestones, tension building inside. There was so much she wanted to say to him, but she felt shy and tongue-tied, as if all the words were bound in thick rope. He hadn't taken her hand once tonight—not once on their whole walk.

"Life is funny," he said as they walked along.

"In what way?"

"You can think you know what's best, what's right for you, and then all of a sudden something happens and turns your plans upside down."

"What do you mean?" she asked. Was he thinking of his summer? He had given up so much of it to be with Lily and Rose; perhaps he was starting to resent the time, and the loss of research time.

"Just, bad things happen, but they sometimes turn out to be . . . good."

She tilted her head, curious about what he meant, but he just walked in silence. The space between them seemed so great, but Lily was afraid to close it; he seemed to need some distance.

"I was thinking of the shark," he said after a few minutes.

"Nothing good came of the shark, I know," she said. "You lost Connor, and a part of yourself. Liam, you don't have to pretend anything about that is okay." He didn't reply.

She glanced over. His brown hair was wavy, with strands of silver in the streetlights. His blue eyes looked sad. They got to the Charles River Hotel, just behind the hospital, and went to the elevator. As it clicked up to their floors, Lily wished she knew what to say. She was on the fourteenth floor, and Liam was on the sixteenth. When the door opened at 14, he looked at her.

"Good night," she said.

"Good night, Lily," he said.

She walked to her room, feeling upset and churned up. Not just because he hadn't touched her at all, not once, on their walk—but because he had looked so troubled, and made that comment about the shark, and she hadn't comforted him.

Lily felt torment inside. She paced her hotel room. She had been so hurt by her husband, her trust had been shattered. She had sacrificed everything leaving him. She had swallowed an iceberg. It had frozen her, cell by cell, until she was brittle and hard; she had learned, over time, how to guard herself—be tough, never let any man get close to her. The Nanouks had been her only friends. But Liam...

Over these last weeks, she had felt herself melting.

"Welcome to the thaw," she had said to Marisa, at Rose's birthday party. What Marisa couldn't know was that Lily had never really believed those words for herself. She had thought she was too glacial, too long frozen, too trapped by winter, to ever really experience anything like internal springtime.

She thought of Liam—the look in his eyes when he'd mentioned the shark. After all he'd done for her these years—and, especially, this summer—why couldn't she have reached up, put her arms around him? Why couldn't she have told him she was there to listen if he felt like talking?

Lily was shaking inside. She grabbed her key and left the room. Not wanting to wait for the elevator, she took the stairs. With every step, she felt more and more afraid. What if she was making a mistake? She hadn't reached out to a man in so long—she had stopped believing that she ever would again. Liam's kindness, the way Rose adored him, Lily's own growing feelings for him all seemed insignificant in the face of her old, terrible, very real fears. But she pushed through them and just kept going.

She found his room, 1625. Took a deep breath and knocked.

Liam opened the door. He stood there, surprise in his blue eyes. He was wearing jeans and a blue oxford shirt. His left sleeve hung there, empty. Lily had never seen him that way before. She gasped.

"I'm sorry," he said, glancing down, patting his empty sleeve as if he could will his arm to appear there. "I should have—"

"No—don't be sorry," she said. "I'm the one—I'm sorry, Liam."

"If it makes you uncomfortable, I can put my prosthesis back on."

Lily smiled and shook her head. "Uncomfortable? No. Liam, you just spent two days sitting in the ICU with Rose. You saw her stitches, her incision.... I'm not uncomfortable with anything like that."

"Most people are."

"I'm not most people," she said.

They walked over to the small table with two chairs, right by the window. The room lights were dim, so they could see the river, dancing with city lights. It was such a different water view than the one they loved in Cape Hawk. But it was still water, and Lily felt things starting to flow.

"When you said that about the shark," she said, "I wanted to hear more."

"Really? It was nothing—just some philosophizing."

"So, philosophize," she said, leaning back in her chair.

"I guess, what I was thinking was, sometimes it seems that my life ended with that shark," he said. "Other times, it seems it began."

"How?"

"You don't know how close I was to Connor," he said.

"We were inseparable. Even though he was three years younger, there was no one I'd rather hang around with. He was so funny. He'd swim up to whales while they were sleeping, and climb up on their backs. We used to dare him all the time."

"Is that what he was doing that day?"

"Yes," he said. "He was trying to get close to this one beluga. The whale was there, feeding on krill and herring. We didn't see the shark, until it was pulling Connor down."

"You saw?"

Liam nodded. "I did. Connor reached out both arms for me. I swam as fast as I could—I was pulling him, trying to get him away from the shark. And then he just...wasn't there anymore. I was there in my brother's blood, diving and diving for him. And the shark got me too."

Lily was silent, listening.

"He just—he grabbed my arm. It didn't hurt—I couldn't feel his teeth or anything. Later I learned they're so sharp, like razors, they just slice through skin and bone. It felt more like the most violent tug I'd ever felt. All I could think of was Connor—I tried to beat the shark with my other arm, pounding him, gouging his eyes. I dug my fingers into his eye socket—and that's what got him to let go."

Lily was so clenched, she felt like a closed fist. She knew what it was like to fight for her life. Liam's description of the teeth going in—so sharp and smooth, you almost don't know you're being eaten alive. She thought of the last day, pregnant with Rose, when her husband had knocked her to the ground—and pretended it was an accident.

"You got away," she whispered.

"I did," he said. "I was swimming on pure adrenaline—still diving for Connor, even though my arm was gone. I don't think I even knew. Jude was screaming—he had climbed up on the shore. He got someone's attention, and a boat came over. They had to haul me out—everyone was surprised I survived. The shark had severed an artery—I was bleeding out, right there in the spot where Connor went down."

"Oh, Liam." She jumped up, unable to withstand what he was telling her. Liam stood beside her; she was shaking so hard, she backed into the desk. Liam reached out to steady her—he surprised her, looking so calm. Beyond him, in the corner of the room, his artificial arm leaned against the wall.

"How do you do it?" she asked. "How do you go on, having lived through that?"

"How do you, Lily Malone?" he asked. "You encountered a shark too."

"Sometimes I wonder," she said.

"Good comes from bad," he said. "That's how. You got Rose out of it."

"That's true," she said. "But what about you?"

"Here I am with you," he said.

"That's . . ." she began.

"Something brought us together," he said. "To me, that's the good that came from bad."

Lily stood on tiptoes to reach up and slide her arms around his neck. She caressed the back of his head, looking into his eyes. She felt so much emotion, all of it just swirling around. She wanted to comfort him, but even more, she wanted to kiss him.

Liam took care of it. He held her tight, she tipped her head, and they kissed. It was so long and tender, as if the feelings had been building up forever, just like the last one. His touch was gentle, but so strong. Lily had come up to comfort him, but he was bringing tears to her eyes. She grabbed him, holding on, and with one arm he picked her up and carried her to the bed.

"I wanted to tell you," she said, lying beside him, eye to eye. "I think you're wonderful. You've been wonderful to me and Rose, and I'm sorry I didn't ask you before, when you—"

He put his finger to her lips.

"You don't have to be sorry for anything," he said.

And then it seemed that words were beside the point. They had nine years to make up for. Lily lay back, her hand on Liam's chest. He rolled over, on top of her, hiked up on his elbow, kissing her cheek, lips, the whole length of her neck, making her squirm and ache. She kept that arm between them, hand on his chest, and they both knew she was ready to push him away—she was always ready to push someone away.

It was now or never—she was sweating for his kisses, she needed them, but she was ready to fight. Tension coiled in her spine like a spring. Liam's eyes were bluer than any sea. They looked at her with such openness, all the while he was kissing her, slowly, one kiss at a time, and she felt the fight just go out of her.

She must have sighed, and Liam took it as a sign. He lay on his left side and, with his right arm, reached around her, stroking her back as he kissed her long and hard. His tongue was so hot, and she bit it—just lightly, but the unexpectedness of it just sent them both over the edge.

Their clothes came off. Lily wasn't sure who unbuttoned or unzipped what—but their shirts, and his pants, and then her pants, and all that underwear, all got thrown on the floor, and then they were on the bed again. The only light came from the small table lamp, warm and dim. Lily had never seen Liam with his shirt off. She wanted to look but was afraid.

Liam lay on his back, staring up at her. She let her eyes travel from his strong, broad chest to his left shoulder. It looked powerful, and extended down to his upper arm, which ended about six inches below the shoulder bone.

She saw his left side—it looked raw and scraped, crisscrossed with scars and old stitches. His arm looked healed, but his side was a reminder of the shark's ravages, of old surgery. Lily leaned over and gently kissed the side of his body.

They held each other, kissing. Liam ran his fingers the length of her torso, making her arch her back. He kissed her harder, and she got lost in the moment. She lifted her hips, wanting him inside her more than she'd ever wanted anything.

His kiss held her steady, but his touch made her lose her mind. Lily shivered, and felt everything about his body: the curve of his spine, the narrowness of his hips, his broad shoulders, his strong legs. He held her and rocked her, even when she cried out, letting go of everything old and cold and frozen, and even when she trembled and cried again, afterwards, because she hadn't realized that she could still feel and still love.

They fell asleep together, holding each other tight. Lily woke up a few times, but she didn't want to move—she never wanted to let go of Liam. Lying beside him, she felt reckless joy. He had shifted in his sleep; his right arm grazed her chest. They embraced, as if it was the most normal and familiar thing in the world. As if they had loved each other for years, and had been just waiting for the perfect time for their lives together to start.

Lily held on, feeling her eyes flicker as sleep overtook her again, wanting to stay awake just a minute more, knowing she was with Liam, knowing Rose was safe.

From the time Rose moved down to the pediatric floor, her healing really did begin to seem miraculous. Lily's own heart soared—because of Rose's fast recovery, and because of Liam.

Rose was unhooked from all the tubes, wires, and machines within twenty-four hours of the surgery, and by the time she reached her new room, she was moving unrestricted. She wanted to take lots of walks so that the doctors would let her out soon. Lily had never seen Rose so eager to leave. And Lily had never felt so eager about life—as if she had finally found the magical key that other people had, the one that made every day worth living.

Usually after surgery Rose was a bit hesitant, very protective—keeping her left hand at her shoulder, hunching her back to protect the heart area. Lily understood such maneuvers very well. But this time, Lily watched her trying to walk free, to stand up straight, remembering many of the exercises she had been taught after other procedures—because she really disliked going to physical therapy. Lily had never been sure why—of all the hard things Rose went through, why did something so ostensibly benign seem so threatening?

Now that the surgery was over, Liam returned home to catch up on work. His leaving had been wrenching for both him and Lily—she had felt herself cave in, just knowing he was going. But he called every morning and every night, and on the third day, as if the distance was too great, he drove back down—and Lily was overjoyed.

So was Rose. She was blooming like her namesake flower, getting pinker and more healthy by the minute. Lily stood back, watching her and Liam laugh and talk, watching Liam show Rose his laptop with Nanny's light blinking just outside Boston Harbor.

"Why is she there?" Rose asked—although she had asked it before, she liked to hear the answer again and again.

"We have no way of knowing," Liam said, glancing at Lily. "But we think it's because she wants to be near you."

"But she doesn't even know me!"

"I think she knows you," Liam said.

"But I'm a girl and she's a whale. We've never talked or played or swum together. Mommy made me all those needlepoint pictures of her, and I have them hanging on my wall, but she doesn't *know* me."

"I want to tell you a story about that," Liam said. "About how Nanny just might know you. It's about a sea hawk and a black cat."

"But—" Rose began.

Rose's green eyes were wide, and she had a big smile on her face. But just then the physical therapist stopped by, to let Rose know what to expect when she went home. She showed her how to keep her left hand down, keep her spine straight, and checked with Lily to make sure they had the name of a PT office near Cape Hawk. Lily assured her they did.

When the therapist left, Rose was clearly drooping. She glanced over at Liam, as if waiting for him to cheer her up with the tale of the fish hawk and black cat.

Lily wanted to hear too. She had thought Liam would jump right in, tell Rose the story to take her mind off the fact that the physical therapist had just outlined a fairly arduous program. And although the program didn't seem bad—and even seemed *fun*—to Lily, clearly it was upsetting Rose. But Liam looked unsettled, disturbed himself.

"It's not fun, is it, Rose?" he asked.

She cocked her head, as if to ask what he meant. But she must have read something in his eyes—a kindred spirit who knew how she felt. Because she just shook her head, and then bowed it so low, her chin drooped to her chest. When she looked up, her face was wet with tears.

"I remember how hard it was," Liam said.

"What do you mean?" Rose asked. "You've had PT too?"

"Yes," Liam said. "About six months' worth at first—and then another year."

"For your arm?"

Liam nodded. "I had to learn how to do everything all over again. And how not to do things."

"Like what?"

"Well, when I first lost my arm, I thought it was still there. I would wake up at night and reach for a glass of water with my left arm. Only it wouldn't be there. So I'd get all confused and upset. If I felt it, it had to be real, right? But it wasn't. So I got . . . kind of angry."

"I get that way," Rose said in a low voice.

"I'll bet you do," he said.

"What else happened?"

"Well, I began to do everything with my right arm. Things my left arm used to do. So I'd always be reaching across my body. That ended up hurting my right shoulder. And also my left shoulder—because even though I no longer had a left arm, I still had muscles in my shoulder that were starting to shrink and contract—I had to make sure to use them."

"I reach across my body," Rose said. "Only it's with my left arm. I do it because I don't want anyone to bump my heart."

"That makes sense to me," Liam said.

"I know, but then it twists me all up and ruins my posture! But I don't even care about my posture!" Rose said.

"I didn't care about mine, either, Rose," Liam said. "I just cared about doing twice as much with one arm. But you want to have good posture, you know? Even if you think you don't. You want to have a healthy spine, right? Let's see—we have to make a list of things to do. 'Protect heart, protect spine—' Anything else?"

"Use both arms!" Rose said, and giggled.

"Oh, yes. How could we forget?" Liam asked, pretending to write on a pretend pad. Seeing him hold the pad with his prosthesis, writing with his real hand, captivated Rose. Lily saw her staring intently, and she felt a spill of gratitude inside. Looking at Liam, her own heart melted a little more, and she just faded back, watching the two of them.

"What was it like?" Rose asked quietly after a moment.

"When I got my prosthesis? Well, that was the reason I had to go back to PT for a year. To learn how to use it right."

"And the whole time, you must have been so sad," Rose said.

"I was," Liam said, looking up. "How did you know?"

"Because I'm sad sometimes," she said. "Because I lost someone too. You lost your brother, but Mommy and I lost someone."

"Rose?" Lily asked, having no idea what she meant.

"My father," Rose said. "I've never had a father. The one that was there didn't want me."

"Rose, it wasn't you," Lily said. She had purposely never discussed him with her. "You weren't the reason he's not in our lives!"

"No matter what the reason, that's what she feels," Liam said, holding Rose's hand—and for the first time in a long time, Lily felt impatient with him. He was supposed to go along with Lily on this—reassure Rose that nothing she did had driven her father away!

"It is," Rose whispered. "It's why my heart doesn't work right."

"I felt the same way," Liam said. "I was with my brother when he died. I was his older brother, Rose. And I thought—if only I had protected him more. Swum faster, rescued him—it should have been me, not him." Lily steeled herself, remembering what he had told her the other night.

"And you thought the reason the shark took your arm was because you were bad?" Rose asked.

"Yes," Liam said. "For a long time I thought that."

"Just like me. Thinking I must have been bad, to have no father with me."

"Sweetheart—" Lily began, and stopped, searching for the right words.

"But you know it's not true," Liam said, stepping in. "You know that, don't you, Rose? You're the most wonderful girl there is. Sometimes things just happen. You were born with heart defects—but it wasn't because of who you are, the kind of girl you are. If that were true, you would have the healthiest, most beautiful heart in the world."

"And the shark didn't bite your arm because you're bad, right?"

"Right," Liam said, looking up at Lily. "I finally figured out that that wasn't true."

"When did you figure that out?"

"The night you were born, Rose."

"Really?" Rose asked.

Liam nodded. "Really."

Glad for something to do with her hands, Lily continued her needlepoint, watching them. She had heard Liam's story their last night in Melbourne, but she watched Rose's eyes widen as she took it in. What a gift for Liam to give a fatherless girl, Lily thought. Rose thinking herself so bad, she drove her father away—yet here was Liam, telling her the opposite, that she had given him back a sense of worth the night she came into the world.

Sitting back, Lily just kept needlepointing. She let her fatherless daughter and this daughterless man continue their conversation, and she tried to imagine what would happen next.

Anne Neill stood in the garden between the inn and the parking lot, clipping flowers to put on the dining room tables. She wore a wide straw hat and carried a flat basket, which she was filling with freshly cut zinnias, snapdragons, larkspur, and cosmos. She was well aware that Camille was stationed on a porch rocker, watching every move; these gardens were showpieces because of Camille's many years creating and tending them. As impatient as Anne sometimes felt with her mother-in-law, she never had any doubt about whose domain the flowers were.

Glancing up, she saw a hotel guest heading down the brick path. He had unruly red hair, glinting in the sun—it was curly and wild hair, the kind that must have driven his mother crazy when he was a kid. Anne smiled as he approached.

"Whew," he said, before she had a chance to speak. "I drove all night, and thought I'd never get here."

"Hello," she said. "Welcome."

"Thanks," he said. "So—this is the Cape Hawk Inn?"

"Yes, it is."

"Huh," he said, swiveling his head to look around. A slice of the harbor was visible between the trees. "So, that's where all the whale boats are?" he asked.

"Yes," she said. "Did you book a whale-watch package? Because I'll be happy to go inside with you and schedule you on a cruise." She slipped off her garden gloves, aware of Camille watching every move—at least Camille had stopped, after all these years, suspecting Anne of flirting with every unattached male guest. Her own marital tragedy had colored the way she looked at everyone else's marriage—including Anne's very happy one to Jude. Anne hitched the basket over her arm and began to walk with him up the front steps.

"Um, I didn't book a package," he said. "In fact, I don't have a reservation."

Anne grimaced. "Oh dear," she said. "We're completely booked."

"Really?" he asked, his blue eyes sharp with surprise. "You're so far away from civilization, I didn't think I'd have a problem."

"Well, many people come here for that exact reason," she said. "Especially during the summer. If you'd come in December, you could have had the place to yourself. I'm so sorry."

He sighed, leaning against the doorjamb and looking around the lobby. Because the day was so clear and fine, hardly anyone was around. An older couple sat on the sofa, gazing out at the blue bay. Chambermaids crisscrossed the wide space, on their way to clean rooms. The huge fire-places at either end of the lobby were swept clean, stacked with fresh wood. Bouquets of flowers graced nearly every table.

"Would you like to have lunch in our dining room?" Anne said. "That might be a good idea, if you really drove all night."

"I did," he said, but he didn't look a bit tired. He had fire in his eyes, as if resting or eating was the last thing on his mind.

"Well, if you came up for whale-watching, I might be able to get you onto the afternoon boat. I actually have quite a bit of pull—my husband is the captain."

The man chuckled, his freckled face creasing into a

wonderful smile. Anne found herself checking his left hand—wedding ring alert for her Nanouk friends. Not married, she noticed.

"Do you see any beluga whales around here?" he asked.

"Absolutely," she said.

"The same belugas that sometimes wind up in aquariums? Like the one in Mystic, Connecticut?"

"Yes," Anne said. "Although we think they belong in the wild."

"Right," the man said.

"I might be able to help you find a different place to stay," Anne said. "Some locals take boarders—and there's a motel a few miles up the road that might have a vacancy. It has a good view too."

"I might not stay," he said. "I've just come for some information." He seemed to be studying her face—as if trying to see if he knew her, or maybe she just reminded him of someone. "Are you from here? Cape Hawk, I mean? Have you lived here long?"

"My whole life," she said.

"So you know the people who come and go, I imagine."

"Yes," she said cautiously. "I married into the Neill family, which owns the inn and whale-watch boats. We sort of keep an eye on things."

"The Neill family?" he asked, reaching into his pocket, patting it madly, searching for something. "Are you related to Camille Neill?"

"Yes," Anne said. She glanced out the screen door, but

Camille had left her porch rocking chair—probably to lie down for her nap.

"Holy shit," the man said.

"Excuse me?"

"I'd like to talk to her," he said. "If she's still here. Is she still . . . alive?"

"Very much so," Anne said, chuckling. "I think she's just resting right now. I can check on that, if you'll wait for just a minute,"

Anne straightened out the display of "Bring Rose Home" pillows and began to lift the phone, when the man took a picture out of his pocket. He cleared his throat and showed Anne a badge.

"I'm Detective Patrick Murphy," he said. "Actually, retired detective, from the Connecticut State Police. Major Crime Squad. I've just recently gotten a lead on an old case, and it's led me here—to Cape Hawk. I'm looking for a woman who disappeared nine years ago. Mara Jameson, from Black Hall, Connecticut. She was pregnant at the time, so she would have a nine-year-old child. I'm going to show you her picture—"

Anne took the photo from his hand, and her heart stopped. There was her friend, eyes bright and shining, beaming for the camera as if she were the happiest woman on earth.

"Where did you get this?" she asked.

"You know her?" Patrick Murphy asked.

"I didn't say that," Anne said. She tried to keep anything from showing on her face. She swallowed hard, buying time. The picture itself might have been taken just yesterday—not nine years ago. Her fellow Nanouk Girl had hardly changed at all. . . .

Just then, she happened to look out the window and saw Marisa and Jessica Taylor walking up the hill from the harbor. Jessica was laden down with a big bag—obviously more pine pillows. Anne tried to catch Marisa's eye, to steer her around back—but she couldn't. Marisa was beaming—all those dark fears she'd arrived with seemed to have evaporated during the last weeks.

Very casually, Anne came around the desk, took the retired detective by the arm, and led him back onto the garden porch—opposite the entrance Marisa was about to use. Her heart was racing. She knew she had to check with her fellow Nanouk before deciding to tell the detective anything.

"I can help you," she said. "You say you want to talk to Camille? Well, that can definitely be arranged."

"But the picture," he pressed. "Have you seen Mara Jameson?"

"She looked a little familiar at first," Anne said. "But I really don't think I've seen her."

"I could have sworn . . ." the retired cop said, suddenly crestfallen. He looked pale, every freckle standing out.

Anne patted his arm. She had to get him out of here— now—to a place where he couldn't ask any questions that mattered.

"Look," she said. "You're tired—you've driven all this way. I know just the perfect spot for you to go and rest and wait for me to get hold of Camille." As she talked, she started walking him to the car. Not a moment too soon—because there was Camille, not napping at all, but right back on the porch, settling into her rocking chair with a cup of tea, this time with the old suspicion back in her eyes as she watched Anne walking this stranger to his car.

"Maybe I'll try your restaurant," he said. "For lunch."

"Of course," Anne said, cursing inwardly. "But why don't you drop your bag at the guesthouse first? It's absolutely lovely—just up the road, half a mile. It's called Rose Gables. It's run by a friend of mine, Marlena Talbot, and I know she would love to have you. Perhaps you can show her the picture—she might have seen this Mara Jameson."

Jessica opened the inn door and yelled out, "Hi, Anne! We brought more pillows for Rose!"

"Lovely, dear," Anne called back, flashing a smile at the detective, heart tumbling as she prayed he wouldn't turn around to see the nine-year-old girl standing there. He didn't. "Pillows," she said. "I really must go attend to the pillows. But you go to Marlena's and check in, and we'll see you back here for lunch in a short time. I'll round up Camille for you."

"Hey, thanks," Patrick Murphy said, stifling a yawn. "That drive really did me in. I drove straight through—it's a long way from the Connecticut shoreline."

"Yes, no wonder you're tired. By the way," Anne said, hoping she sounded cool. "What did this Mara Jameson do?"

"She disappeared," Patrick said. "At the very least, she

married the wrong guy, and he beat her up. At the very worst, he killed her. But lately something happened, to make me think she might have come up here, to hide out."

"Hide out? Is she in trouble?"

"No. Hide out from her husband. She was afraid for her life."

"The poor woman," Anne murmured. Then she gave Patrick directions to Marlena's, pointed him on the way, and ran back into the inn. Camille tried to call her over as she rushed by, but Anne didn't even stop or say a word. She just tore into the lobby.

Jessica and Marisa had piled the pine pillows behind the front desk. Anne's pulse was speeding as she picked up the phone, looking left and right for Marisa. Where had she gone? Anne had to find her. But first, she dialed Marlena's number and prayed she would be home.

"Hello?" Marlena said.

"Thank God you're there!" Anne said. "I've just sent a guest over, to stay at your house."

"A guest? What are you talking about? I don't take guests!"

"You do now. It's a Nanouk imperative—it's for the sisterhood. Listen, Mar, you have to give him a room, and then force him to stay for lunch. I don't care what you give him, but don't let him come back to the inn until I tell you it's okay."

"Who is he?"

"A retired cop. Working on an old case—a missing-persons case, Marlena. He's going to show you a picture, and just try not to drop your teeth when you look at it. Just tell him she looks vaguely familiar—keep him interested enough talking to you, so he doesn't come back here till I've had the chance to talk to our girl. Marisa, where are you? She was just here, two seconds ago—"

"How should I keep him occupied? Should I bed him?"

"If you have to."

"Mata Hari used to do that for the cause," Marlena said. And then she gasped, and through the phone wire came the sound of a car door slamming. "He's here," she said. "And he's a redhead. *Very* cute—although I was only joking about bedding him. I think."

"Just give him something good for lunch," Anne said, trying to get her breath. "Remember now—for the Nanouks."

"For the Nanouks," Marlena said, and hung up.

Chapter 23

When the time came for Rose to be discharged from the hospital, all the nurses lined up, wearing the gold-and-silver-painted hemlock pinecone earrings Jessica had made for them, her second batch, after Melbourne. They all wished Rose a good summer, telling her they would miss her, but not to hurry back too soon.

Rose thanked them all for everything, and so did Liam and Lily, and they climbed into the taxi for the airport. Rose kept wanting to reach up with her left hand—trying to keep her heart safe—but Dr. Neill kept gently touching her hand to remind her not to. She thought of his arm, knew that if he had gotten used to something so foreign to his body, she could get used to new habits too.

On the way to the airport, she couldn't help noticing that her mother and Dr. Neill kept looking at each other. Rose had seen Anne and Jude doing that before. It made her happy, but at the same time, scared. What if Dr. Neill was just being nice because Rose had been so sick? What if now that she was getting well, he went back to hiding out in his boat and office and house on the hill, far from everyone, including Rose?

And what if Rose's mother got busy at her shop again, frowning at everyone except Rose and the Nanouk Girls of the Frozen North? Sometimes Rose wanted to remind her mother that the club was supposed to be for escaping the Frozen North—*not* for building up icebergs, snow walls, and igloos as a fortress all around them.

So this new way of looking at each other—Rose's mother and Dr. Neill—was making her very nervous. Suddenly, she remembered something.

"Is Nanny going home too?" she asked.

"I don't know," Dr. Neill said. "It will be really interesting to observe, after you head back to Cape Hawk."

"Have you checked her on the computer today?" Rose asked.

"No, not yet," he said. "We can do that now...."

As he was opening his computer case, trying not to jostle Rose, Rose held her breath. She didn't know why, but she felt scared and worried. What if Dr. Neill couldn't locate Nanny on the screen? What if she didn't return home? Rose thought of all the dangers in Boston Harbor—all those ships with their big propellers.

"Hmm," Dr. Neill said after a minute.

"What's wrong?" Rose asked, feeling cold inside.

"I don't see her," he said.

"Liam?" her mother asked.

He was silent a few more seconds, tapping keys. Rose

gazed at the screen, and she saw all the purple lights. Suddenly she felt terrified, as if she knew for sure that Nanny had been eaten by a shark.

"Maybe expand the field?" her mother asked, leaning over Rose, as if she cared just as much as Rose did about Nanny—and *no one* cared as much as Rose did about Nanny.

"That's it," he said, sounding excited at first. "There she is—" He touched her green dot with his finger. "But . . . she's going in the wrong direction."

"What do you mean?" Rose asked, still unable to make sense of all the blinking lights, the curvy shape of the shoreline.

"She's going south," Liam said. "She's already far from Boston—see? She's rounded Cape Cod, and she's swimming toward Martha's Vineyard."

"But belugas need cold water," Rose said, remembering from her birthday cruise. "They live in the Arctic, and never go past Cape Hawk in the summer!"

"It's very rare," Liam said.

"I thought she came to Boston for me," Rose said, her eyes filling. Suddenly her heart ached—but not her real heart, the one that was just operated on, but the other heart, the one inside, the one no one could ever really see.

"She did," Liam said. "I'm so sure of it, Rose, I'd bet anything."

"Then why is she going the other way, away from home? Away from us?"

"I don't know," he said, hugging her. "Maybe she's confused. Sometimes a change in temperature can cause disorientation. We'll watch her for the rest of the day—I'll bet she turns herself around."

"She has to," Rose said, hot tears running down her cheeks. "If she gets lost because she came to find me, I don't know what I'll do."

"Honey," her mother said. "Haven't we convinced you to stop blaming yourself about such big things? Please, Rose—"

"I think it's time," Dr. Neill said, "to tell you that story."

"The story," she said out loud. When her mother looked confused, she said, "The sea hawk and the black cat! You were going to tell me that story," she said. "Two days ago, when the PT lady walked in."

"Yes, you were," her mother said, remembering.

"It was after you asked me how such different creatures can be friends. A little girl and a white whale. Or a sea hawk and a black cat."

"Tell us," Rose said.

"In the world of biology," he said. "Some animals are compatible, and others are natural enemies. Others might just be neutral—living in close proximity, with basic respect. Which, in the animal world, means that they don't eat or attack each other."

"Easier said than done," her mother murmured, staring out the window.

"Well, there was this sea hawk. He was an old guy, with tattered old feathers, and a fishhook caught in his left wing. He had once flown into a school of herring, and one of the fishermen accidentally caught him. The line was so taut and hard, and the tug broke the hawk's wing.

"All the young hawks used to laugh at him. They ignored him, didn't make him a part of their crowd. So he flew away, all by himself, up to the low, dark cliffs—you know, the ones at the top of the fjord, where the trees grow so thick, the light hardly ever shines.

"He was a pretty good sea hawk, though. He figured out how to fish, even with his broken wing. He let things heal—his bones and tendons, his feathers. And he'd sit on the banks of the fjord, and his timing got so good, he could just grab silver herring and salmon out of the water without even having to spread his wings.

"None of the other hawks ever went up there. The fjord was terrible and beautiful, but it was his alone. He had no competition for the fish that swam by. Until one day he noticed a black cat, sitting on the opposite bank.

"She was so glossy—at first he thought she was a seal. Her fur was black and smooth, and she had green eyes brighter than any star. But they weren't happy eyes. They were eyes that had seen danger—cruelty and brutality and starvation. She was a skinny cat, but she caught enough fish to feed an army of cats.

"So one day, the sea hawk watched her. Sea hawks have good eyes, even when they have broken wings. He saw her stalk through the brush, carrying a huge fish. When foxes and badgers tried to take it from her, she would fight them off. No animal was going to get her fish—and the sea hawk discovered why."

"Why?" Rose asked. The cab went into the tunnel beneath Boston Harbor.

"Because she had a kitten. This tiny, skinny black kitten with green eyes just as bright as her mother's." Dr. Neill looked across Rose's head at her mother, and Rose could see him swallow before continuing his story. "The sea hawk wasn't used to seeing any other animal fish his stretch of the fjord. He had gotten used to his independence, and to being on his own.

"But something about her made him glad she was there. He began to look forward to seeing her fish the water, on the other side. He found himself feeling lonely on the days she didn't show up. And when her kitten got big enough and began coming to the water to fish, well, it made him very happy."

"The kitten fished?"

"Yes. Because the mother taught her so well."

"Is this a story about animals who think they shouldn't be friends being friends?" Rose asked.

"Yes," he said. "Like you and Nanny."

"It's not about me and Nanny," Rose said, looking at Dr. Neill very hard.

"No?"

Rose shook her head.

"I think it is, Rose," her mother said.

"No," she said stubbornly. "The hawk had a broken wing, right?"

"Right," Dr. Neill said.

"Did the kitten have funny, flattened paws?" Rose asked, holding up her hands, wiggling her clubbed fingers.

"As a matter of fact, she did."

Rose nodded. She glanced up at her mother.

"Black cat," Rose said, reaching up to touch her mother's glossy black hair. Then she turned to Dr. Neill and touched his prosthesis. She didn't even bother to say, "Broken wing."

Instead, as the cab pulled up at Logan Airport, Rose just sighed. Dr. Neill had told a nice story, but it wasn't going to turn Nanny around. Rose felt so glad to be feeling better— that the operation was a success, and she was on her way home to spend the summer. But what did it matter, if Nanny was lost, swimming south? Couldn't everything work out, just for once?

Gone were the days of his youth, Patrick thought. All-night police work, when his mind stayed alert, and his body stayed strong, and his vision was sharp and didn't miss a thing. He remembered twenty-four-hour stakeouts, and long-distance chases, and investigations that meant visiting jurisdictions in twelve states and Canada. But last night's run—from Silver Bay, up I-95 to the Maine Turnpike, and straight on to Cape Hawk—forget it. He was only forty-six, but he felt like an old man.

After "checking in" to Marlena Talbot's "guesthouse"— Patrick was pretty sure that paying guests weren't a regular thing here—he followed Marlena upstairs to a very nice bedroom, thanked her, and lay down for a quick nap.

Three hours later, after sleeping through lunch and most of the afternoon, Patrick found himself in Marlena's dining room. He rubbed his eyes, reached for the glass of

Coke she'd poured, sipped and looked around. Driving all night had completely done him in, and now he felt jet-lagged, paying the price.

"Seriously," he said. "I can just head down to the inn for dinner."

"I wouldn't hear of it!" she said. "It's part of the charm of my establishment—you get a home-cooked meal. Can the inn provide that? I think not!"

"Your establishment," he said, taking a bigger slug of Coke, looking around. Never had he seen a homier place. She had knickknacks everywhere—personal things, like clay paperweights obviously made by children or grandchildren, needlepoint covers on every chair seat, samplers on the wall, and a pile of square pillows that all smelled of pine and said "Bring Rose Home."

"Yes," she said. "My establishment. It's not easy, working in the shadow of the Cape Hawk Inn. With all their central booking equipment and the whale-watch boats, it's not easy to compete with them. All I have is my home cooking to attract my share of the tourist dollar."

"I'm sure," he said, checking his watch. Why hadn't that woman from the inn called about Camille Neill?

Marlena was in the kitchen, bustling around. Patrick pulled out the newspaper article and Mara's picture. Marlena gazed at it, stone-faced. She read the story, took in the dark hair, the bright smile, the fact that she'd been pregnant when she went missing. No, she said: she couldn't recall seeing her here in Cape Hawk.

"Look," Patrick said, "I'm sure your cooking is delicious,

but I'd better get over to the inn. It's dinnertime there, and I have to ask some questions. I hope Camille Neill hasn't left—"

"Left? She never leaves. She owns the place, and runs it with an iron glove. Please don't go, Detective Murphy. What will Camille think, if you tell her you were staying at Rose Gables and I didn't feed you? Speaking of Rose Gables, would you like to know how my house got its name? Did you notice those white roses growing over the trellis as you came in? Well, I planted and trained them. Now, I know that this is a modest, humble little abode..."

"Marlena," he said.

"Not at all grand, not what you would expect of a house called Rose Gables, but it was the first home of my own. The very first place I ever bought on my own. And I did it, after the divorce."

"That's a good story, but—"

"And I got so much support from all my friends, my darling friends the Nanouks."

"The what?" he asked, wondering why that name sounded so familiar.

Marlena opened and closed the oven door. He heard the air escaping as she opened a bag of chips. The lid of a jar was unscrewed. A moment later, she entered the dining room bearing a tray. On it was an embroidered cloth, a vase holding a single white rose, and a plate covered by a second embroidered cloth.

Whipping off the cloth, Marlena said, "Voilà!"

Patrick stared down at his dinner: a grilled cheese sandwich, pickles, and some barbecue potato chips.

"Wow," he said. Was she kidding? For the first time, he
wondered whether he had wandered into the Nova Scotia
version of the Bates Motel. Or maybe she was like the crazy
lady in *Misery*. The sandwich looked good, so he ate it—
quickly. Maybe she really was proud of her grilled cheese
sandwiches . . . but he thought the protestations about her
food versus the inn's were a little odd.

"Very good," he said. "Thank you. Okay, I'm going to
head over to the inn now—"

"Would you like to listen to the baseball game?" she
asked, sounding manic and a little desperate. "Or would
you like me to play the recorder? I like it very much—I
played it as a child and have been practicing ever since my
divorce. Oh—or I could show you my needlework! I know
most men don't care about—"

Before he could stop her, she had whipped out a bag of
sewing, or something. He looked at the mesh, the yarn, the
whatever. Marlena's needlework reminded him of something, but he didn't know what. Even less, he wasn't sure
why he opened his mouth and said, "What did you say earlier? The Nanouks? What are they?"

"A tribe of ancient warrior women," she said, her face
ashen. "From right here in Nova Scotia. They dressed in the
aurora borealis, seaweed, and mother-of-pearl, and they
hunted the cliffs and bays, and they survived every ice age
that came their way."

"And they've helped you recover from your divorce?" he

asked, staring at her needlework, suddenly getting a very clear picture as the music played.

"Yes," she said defiantly.

"You're lying to me, aren't you, Marlena?"

"I am not lying. They helped me."

"You know Mara Jameson, don't you?" he asked.

Marlena Talbot didn't reply, but her reddening face and the angry tears in her eyes told him all he needed to know. Patrick Murphy grabbed the picture and his car keys, and he stalked out of Rose Gables.

When he got to his car, he grabbed for his cell phone. There was one person he had to call—to tell her how close he was to tracking down Mara. Someone who had known where she was all along—he was now sure of it. Hearing the word "Nanouk" made it all so clear. He dialed the number he knew by heart, ready to rip into her—but she didn't pick up, and he got the machine instead.

"Hello," said the woman's voice. "I'm not here right now, but if you'll leave your name and number, I'll call you back as soon as I can."

From the very first time he'd heard it, Patrick had told Maeve she should change her message. She should have a man's voice on the machine—or at least say "we" instead of "*I'm* not here right now." But just try getting Maeve to do anything.

"Maeve," he said. "It's Patrick Murphy. There's something I have to say to you. I'll call you later. But—I may have good news soon," he said. And he hung up, thinking that, of course, Maeve already knew that.

Chapter 24

Secret Agent had been checking every day, trying to beat back the tide of trouble caused by White Dawn. The whole message board was filled with threads titled "Secret Agent Stole My Money!" or things like that. Ever since White Dawn's post about checking the NOAA weather map, the whole SpiritTown message board had realized that Secret Agent's sister lived many miles south of the storm track and that her house couldn't possibly have been destroyed—or even badly damaged. And everyone wanted their money back.

Many thoughts ran through Secret Agent's mind. How could he have missed checking the path of Hurricane Catherina? He thought of all the people who were homeless, injured, just waiting for aid from the disaster relief fund. Why couldn't he have gotten better information?

The bitch had shamed him in the eyes of the message board. Whoever she was, she was as bad as his wife. Always blowing the whistle on him, spoiling his projects. No matter how hard he tried, it had never been good enough for her. Just like White Dawn—ruining his plans. And his reputation. He had carefully constructed the whole thing, and White Dawn had brought it down like a house of cards.

What if Secret Agent had really had a sister—and what if she had really lost her house in a severe hurricane? All it took was one vindictive bitch to take the candy cane away. Take the goodwill away. Take the money right out of homeless people's hands. All that money Secret Agent had collected—what if he had really sent it to his sister? These were the kinds of issues a vindictive bitch had no idea about.

White Dawn.

He signed onto the board, clicked onto her profile. What he saw gave him a start. Before, when he had looked, she had nothing listed there. Now he saw that she had filled in a name:

"Patty Nanouk." Patricia—that was his wife's real name. Could it really be her? Out there in cyberspace, bringing him down? And what did "Nanouk" mean?

He scrolled a few lines down, to the place where it said "occupation." Then he read what she—White Dawn, Patty Nanouk, whoever she was—had written:

"Crusader for justice against psychopathic con men."

It was her. It really was. How often had she called him a psychopath? And how often had he tried to soothe her, telling her that yes—he was one, it was true. But that was just because of his terrible, abusive childhood. No one had ever, ever loved him as she did, no one else was capable of healing him as she was.

He was getting therapy, he had told her. He was going to workshops. There was help available—he was trying to get better. Didn't she understand that? Was she willing to just walk away—throw it all away? Destroy him in the process? Because if she did, then she was no better than he was. In fact, she was worse.

He couldn't help who he was. Depression was an accepted illness, and so was what he had. He wanted to love her, and he was trying—but being a psychopath was hard. When they said he had no conscience or empathy, well, that just wasn't true. He did have empathy. He felt things. Deep in his soul, he felt the pain of being an abused child, and of what that made him. It kept him from all the pleasure he should have as an adult—as a husband or father. He grieved for himself!

How could they say he had no empathy?

Well, fuck White Dawn, Patty Nanouk, and his wife. He wondered whether they were all the same person. Honestly, he didn't really care. He had porn open at the same time, and he was in an incest survivor's chat room with a girl he'd met online last night, and he was totally over what had happened at SpiritTown.

Over it. There were plenty of other message boards out there, plenty of other bleeding hearts with too much money and a need to give it away—and Secret Agent had a PayRight account.

No more "Secret Agent" for him. That name was toast.

From now on, at least until he found an interesting prospect that required a more creative handle, he'd just go by "Edward."

Patrick finally made it back to the Cape Hawk Inn, just as the sun was setting over the harbor. The last of the whale boats was steaming back to the dock, leaving a wake of silver out behind. The big lightbulb going on about Maeve had thrown him into a dark sadness—he had thought they trusted each other.

He felt a tug to walk down to the water, get aboard a boat. He didn't like having ground beneath his feet for too long—he needed the feel of a deck, and the waves rocking. He hoped that Flora was okay without him, guarding the *Probable Cause* along with Angelo. More than anything, he hoped he would have this case solved for good by the end of the night.

Pushing those thoughts from his mind, he again climbed the porch steps to the inn. Inside, the lobby was lively. Strains of Celtic music wafted down the hall from the bar. People dressed for dinner walked in and out of the formal dining room. Waiters served drinks by the lobby fireplace, which was crackling with a fire. Even though it was July, the northern air had a slight chill.

The minute he stepped through the door, he noticed a semicircle of women looking over at him. The woman who had first greeted him—and sent him to Rose Gables—stood out front, and he made his way across the room to her. The women behind her were not smiling.

"Well, well," he said. "If it isn't the lady who told me there was no room at the inn. I really have to thank you—sending me along to Casa de Grilled Cheese. That was a clever diversion."

"Marlena sends her apologies. I really caught her up short. She's quite an excellent cook, but I didn't give her enough notice. I'm sorry."

He ignored the apology. "Is there really a Camille Neill?"

"There is. I'm her daughter-in-law, Anne Neill."

"So, that part's true."

"Yes. I'm sorry to say, though, that she really is asleep right now. She'll be up tomorrow morning. You can ask her anything you want then."

"Why are you stonewalling me," he asked, "when it's obvious that you know Mara Jameson?"

"How is it obvious?" Anne asked. She was tall and elegant, and she had a lot of practice dealing with people. Working at an inn, she probably had to handle lots of drunks and jerks. But Patrick's patience was pretty thin right now.

"Lady," Patrick said, trying to stay polite, "it's obvious because your eyes practically jumped out of your face when you saw her picture. And because you sent me on a wild-goose chase to poor Marlena's house—what the hell do you know about me? What if I were a serial killer? I'm a total stranger, and you sent me to your friend's house to take a freaking nap. Oh—and because she told me about the Nanouks."

"Excuse me?" Anne asked, and it was echoed by several of the women standing behind her, glaring at Patrick with daggers.

"The Nanouks. She said the Nanouks got her through her divorce, and then I knew."

"And just what do you think you know?" one of the other women asked.

"She told me they're a tribe of warrior women," he said. "Some ancient crew of women who wear the dawn and sunset or something like that."

"Ancient," one of the other women said, chuckling.

"The aurora borealis, not the dawn and sunset," someone else corrected.

"*We're* the Nanouks," Anne explained. "We're a club of friends."

"Friends?" he said, gazing across their heads at a poster advertising whale-watch cruises—with the outline of a whale's tail flaring out of the sea.

"Yes," she said. "We support each other."

Patrick frowned, puzzled. If that was true . . . he put it all together with the embroidered glasses case that he had seen at Maeve's. Just a small thing, always on her side table, with her stack of books—the eyeglass case had a cream background, with the word "Nanouk" done in block letters, in several different shades of blue yarn. And the very faint outline of a whale's tail, the stitches wearing out.

"If that's true," he said, "then I believe that Mara Jameson is a member of your club."

"We don't know any Mara Jameson," Anne said as Patrick began to pass her picture around the group.

"You may not know her by that name," he said. "But she's here, I know it. And she has a nine-year-old daughter."

Marisa and Jessica sat in Anne's office, off the lobby, watching everything through the glass door. Anne had warned Marisa about the detective's visit. She had intercepted Marisa and Jess earlier, when they had arrived with the latest batch of pine pillows. Because of the confusion—having a retired police officer here, looking for a woman who had disappeared nine years earlier—Anne had called a meeting of the Nanouks, to decide what to do.

Some of the women, having been victims of domestic violence, had had bad run-ins with the police and courts. The legal system didn't understand the problem. They would look at a handsome, well-spoken man like Ted, and at a shrieking, dissembling woman like Marisa, and more often than not, they would believe the man.

Once Marisa went to court to ask for a restraining order against him—but since she didn't have any physical evidence of beatings, and since his threats were over ten hours old, the judge had refused to grant an order. Marisa had left, trembling. How could she explain that she was in so much shock, she could hardly remember the details of what he had said, the terror of having him hold her by the hair and tell her that if she ever tried to run away from him, he'd track her down and make her daughter suffer?

Marisa knew that some of the Nanouks—older, wiser, and more recovered than Marisa—had had similar experiences with the police. Anne knew it too, and hadn't wanted to make any decisions without consulting with everyone. And Marisa had certainly needed her friends' advice, regarding the best tack to take.

"If you tell him, maybe Ted will go to jail," Jessica said, peeking out the window.

"Or maybe he won't," Marisa said.

"He killed Tally."

"I know, honey."

"And he said he'd hurt us."

"Exactly. That's why I want to be careful. Telling on Ted isn't necessarily safe."

"You mean people might not believe us?"

"Yes," Marisa said. But she couldn't look Jessica straight in the eye as she said it. She no longer felt sure about that. Back when she had first run away, she had been so afraid— a quivering wreck of her former self. But she had had the guts to pack up her daughter, take her to safety. Over the last month, she had made friends with these great women, and they had believed her—every single one of them. Making Marisa finally able to believe in herself.

"What would be so bad, telling?" Jessica asked. "We've already told the Nanouks our real names. We could go right out there and tell the policeman. And he could arrest Ted."

"Hmm."

"We could see our friends, back home. Aunt Sam...I wouldn't want to leave Cape Hawk for good—I'd miss Rose too much. But Mommy—don't you want to be able to go home again? If we want to?"

"Yes," Marisa said quietly, missing her old life so much she ached.

"So do I. Let's go out there, Mommy."

"Are you sure? Are we doing the right thing?"

Her daughter looked at her, long and hard. She tilted her head, touched Marisa's cheek. Her eyes were pleading with her, and Marisa could read the message even before Jessica said it out loud.

"You're the mother," she said. "You have to decide."

And Marisa knew she was right. She kissed the top of her daughter's head, took a deep breath, and because she was the mother, opened the office door.

The flight had been long, and the drive from the airport had taken forever, but to Lily's amazement, Rose was wide awake and feeling strong. The windows of Liam's truck were down, and cool, fresh Cape Hawk salt air blew through the cab. Lily had her arm around Rose's shoulders, and she breathed in the spruce and pine.

"Smells like my pillows," Rose said.

"It does," Lily said.

"Jess's card said they're selling them at the inn," Rose said. "Next to a picture of you and me."

"Wow," Lily said. "That's so nice."

"It's true," Liam said. "It's a big display, right in the lobby."

"Can we see it?" Rose asked. "On our way home?"

"Oh, sweetheart—it's so late. We have to get you to bed."

"But I'm excited," Rose said. "I want to see. And besides, don't you want to see Anne? And maybe some of the other Nanouks? And show them I'm okay?"

Lily's lips tightened. She had been longing so deeply to see her own most beloved relative—missing her so much during this last difficult time with Rose. Having Liam with her had been wonderful, but she had a primal need to connect with her grandmother, the closest person she had to a mother. Or in her place, the Nanouk Girls of the Frozen North.

Even if only one of them was at the inn—and she was sure that at least Anne would be there—she would so deeply love a hug, and the chance to celebrate with the friends who had been so supportive of her and Rose. She glanced over at Liam, concentrating on the road. It was as if her grandmother had tapped her shoulder, telling her to pull over.

"Would you mind if we stopped there?" she asked. "You must want to get home."

"Lily," he said, "if you and Rose want to go there, I'm going with you."

"So we can?" Rose asked, as the truck crossed the bridge over the fjord, and the lights of Cape Hawk—nestled in the valley between two formidable rock cliffs—came into view.

"We can," Lily said.

Anne was a nervous wreck. A total, complete basket case. Duplicity had never been her strong suit—she could barely even handle telling a white lie to Camille, telling her she looked pretty when in fact she looked very cranky and mean. But she had started lying almost from the minute Detective Murphy had arrived—and she hadn't stopped yet.

Getting poor Marlena to pretend she was running a bed-and-breakfast—and then practically mortifying her by getting her to serve a cheese sandwich with all the fanfare of a cordon bleu chef! God, the Nanouks would be teasing her about that forever.

Having the presence of mind to whisk Marisa aside, tell her to hide Jessica—and keep her hidden, until the coast was clear, and they were sure Murphy had departed— where had that come from? Anne was on top of her game, that was for sure—thinking fast, making sure *all* her friends were protected.

She had called in the Nanouks for reinforcements, and of course everyone who could get away had come—Cindy, Doreen, Alison, Suzanne, Kathy, Paula, Claire, and even Marlena, just behind Patrick Murphy. They all gathered around him, passing the very familiar photo—God, she had been so young, smiling and innocent—around the circle. Everyone had been coached to say the same thing: "She looks familiar."

A comment about her hair, her smile, her beautiful shining eyes. She had been so sweet, pregnant with the girl that they all loved so much. Just knowing that—and what she had run from—brought tears to Anne's eyes. She wiped them away, but they just kept coming.

"Mother in heaven," said Cindy, under her breath.

Anne looked up, and here came Camille, limping down the hall that led to the family's private quarters. Anne lurched, to try to stop her, but she knew she would look too obvious and forced herself to hold back.

"Good evening," Camille said, giving Anne a strange look. "Aren't you working tonight?"

"Genny is covering in the dining room," Anne said.

"I noticed this gentleman arriving earlier," Camille said, approaching Patrick. "Talking to you in the garden. Where ever is Jude? Still out on the boat?"

"Yes," Anne said.

"Hi, Camille," Marlena said from across the circle. She was trying to be helpful, but in that instant, Anne knew they were sunk.

"Camille Neill?" Patrick asked.

"Yes. And who might you be?"

"I am Patrick Murphy. Are you the same Camille Neill as mentioned in this article?"

Camille put on her reading glasses and looked at the yellowed newspaper clipping. She gasped, looking up at Patrick. "This is from the Ard na Mara paper—about Frederic's memorial. What are you doing with it? Did you know Frederic?"

"No, ma'am," he said. "I'm investigating the disappearance, nine years ago, of Mara Jameson." He took the photo back from Cindy, handed it to Camille. "Do you recognize her?"

Anne felt her pulse beating in her throat. It was just a matter of time now—before Camille blurted out the truth, and Patrick knew where to look. She glanced over at the office door—and froze. There were Marisa and Jessica, letting themselves out of the office, walking this way.

Camille cleared her throat, slid a glance at Anne. She shook her head. "No," she said firmly. "I don't recognize her."

But it was too late. Anne couldn't believe her eyes. She stared at Marisa, seeing steel in her posture she'd never seen before. Jessica skipped ahead, flinging herself into the circle, right in front of Patrick Murphy. And he turned—his long, lanky body just wheeling around, as if he had noticed the nine-year-old girl and wanted to see her mother—just as the front door of the inn opened.

Liam, Lily, and Rose stood there.

Everyone started shouting, shrieking, laughing, and crying. Every last Nanouk rushed across the lobby, arms open wide, to greet Lily and Rose. Marisa and Jessica were first in line, and the four of them hugged and kissed, and wept, jumbled in a pack by the other Nanouk Girls, all wanting to get close.

Anne held Camille's hand, walking a little behind the others, alongside Patrick Murphy. Camille squeezed Anne's hand, and Anne squeezed back.

"I've always felt bad, you know, Anne, dear," Camille whispered. "I've tried to help Rose in my own way, financially." She lifted her chin. "Even if I'm not a Nanouk."

Anne whirled to look at her mother-in-law with amazement, and to whisper back, "After what you just did, you're in, Camille."

The women were all clustered together, Liam off to the side, and as Anne got closer, she saw that everyone was hovering around Rose. They didn't want to get too close, to crush her—but they wanted to touch her, caress her, let her know how grateful they were that their girl had come home safely. The reunion was for everyone and Rose, and for Lily too. Anne watched as Marisa gave Lily a huge hug, then whispered something in her ear.

The room was buzzing so loudly—with everyone's laughter, tears, and talk, and with the Celtic music from down the hall, and from Anne's heartbeat thudding in her ears—she wondered whether anyone would hear him.

"Mara," Patrick Murphy called sharply.

And both Marisa and Lily looked up.

Chapter 25

"Yes?" Lily said.

The whole lobby went silent. Rose clung to her hand, looking up at the strange man approaching.

"I'm Marisa," Marisa said.

"I said *Mara*," the man said. Walking through the crowd, he stared at Lily as if he knew her. Not only that, but his eyes were filled with a mixture of victory and disbelief, as if he had come here to get her, but couldn't quite believe that his quest was over.

"Lily—don't say anything," Anne said, stepping forward. "Don't say one word. Liam, will you get Jude?"

But Liam just pressed closer to Lily; she felt his arm come around her shoulder. She had the vaguest of impressions of her friends not knowing whether to smile about Lily and Liam, or be afraid of what was happening.

"I have this picture," the man said, handing it to Lily. "And this news clipping."

She stared at them. They were artifacts from such a different time and place, but they made her eyes swim with tears. Not so much for the photo, or the content of the news story, but for seeing the date written in that fine handwriting on the upper right-hand corner.

"I'm Patrick Murphy," he said. "I'd say 'Detective Patrick Murphy,' but I'm actually retired. Your case was my swan song to a long career. Too bad I didn't manage to solve it."

Lily sensed Liam relax, just slightly. Until the man spoke, she realized that Liam might have taken him for the shark, her husband. Still staring at the handwriting, Lily wasn't quite ready to speak yet.

"Touché to your friends here," Patrick Murphy said dryly. "They all recognized you in the picture—how could they not? You haven't changed one bit. But they stayed cool, acted as if they'd never seen you. Of course, I only got here this afternoon. I'd have worn them down with my relentless questioning."

Someone, probably Marlena, snorted.

"I know about the Nanouks," he said.

"Is there a crime in belonging to a club?" Anne asked.

"No crime," he said. "No crime in that at all. The only crime that's been committed was long ago. And it was by someone who never answered for it."

Lily cringed. Was there some statute against running away? She knew there had been a huge investigation— many hours of police work, costing lots of money. Lily wondered what sort of penalties there were for disappearing.

"She didn't do anything wrong," Cindy growled. "I'll

kick your ass for saying so, even if you are a retired police-man. You don't know what she went through—"

"Cindy," Anne said evenly.

"The only crime was committed by the man who beat you up," Patrick said. He took a step closer. "Beat up his pregnant wife. That's right—after you disappeared, we treated your house as a crime scene, and we went over every inch with luminol. You should have seen the blood light up like a lightning storm. Everywhere in the kitchen. He must have hurt you, Mara. He must have."

"He did," Lily said. "But he never hit me."

"But the blood—"

"He sometimes knocked me down when he passed by," she said. "And he'd tell me it was because I was pregnant and clumsy, and he didn't have enough room. I hit my head, split it open. He said it was an accident." She paused, an old life coming back. "And I believed him for the longest time..."

"But not that night?"

"No," she said. "There was something different that night. His rage—" She stopped herself, looking down at Rose. "Excuse me, but I can't talk to you right now. I have to get my daughter to bed."

"She's beautiful," the red-haired cop said. For some reason, his eyes were glittering.

"Of course she is," Marlena said. "She looks just like Lily."

"I was going to say," Patrick Murphy said, "that she looks just like Maeve."

"Granny!" Lily gasped.

"She misses you, Mara. Whatever reasons you had for

leaving, she must believe in them mighty hard. Because I never saw such love, and I know that willingly letting you go had to be the hugest sacrifice any grandmother could ever make."

"She had nothing to do with it," Lily said, trembling, not wanting her grandmother to be in trouble.

"Be that as it may," the cop said. "She uses that Nanouk eyeglass case you made for her every day. And she finally got around to putting me onto the aquarium membership. You gave it to her—what was that, so she could visit with the beluga whales and imagine seeing you?"

"She told you?"

The cop nodded. "And she gave me that clipping—" He pointed to the one Lily held in her hand, the one about the ferry accident in Ard na Mara. "You know what I think?"

"What?" Lily asked, wrapping her arms around Rose, holding Liam's hand, knowing that she had to get out of there—out of the inn, away from the cop, away from all this talk about her grandmother. It was all too much—first Rose's surgery, then being with Liam, now this . . .

"That she needed me to find you. She sent me here, Mara."

"She wouldn't do that," Lily said. "She didn't even know where I went."

"Maybe not," he said. "But she knew I'd find you. I think she's done without you long enough. Something's changed, and she needs you to come home. Think about it, Mara."

"Mommy?" Rose asked, sounding distressed and tired.

Jessica stood beside her, as if standing guard. Allie, Cindy's daughter, was just a few feet away, looking equally fierce.

"My name is Lily," she said. "Mara fell off the face of the earth. Do you understand? I want it to stay that way. Right now, I have to get my daughter home."

"As long as you know I have some more questions for you."

Lily nodded, but didn't say another word. She just let Liam bundle both her and Rose out of the inn, into his truck, and they left the lights of Cape Hawk behind as they drove into the dark, secret cliffs and pines that Lily had for so long—and still—called home.

But just to be in the presence of a man who had recently seen her grandmother—that sent such a fierce tremble through Lily's body, she had to hold tight to Rose, just to keep herself together.

Marisa leaned on the desk, watching Jessica follow Rose out to the porch, to wave goodbye. As she did, all the Nanouks began buzzing.

"Did you know?"

"I knew that she had run away from something."

"Did you know what she was running from?"

"I guessed. She had such a hunted look, the minute she arrived in Cape Hawk."

"She stumbled the first time she said her name," Cindy said. "Alison and I talked about it right away. We figured

'Lily' was an alias. But it was so obvious she wanted to keep her identity secret, it was just an unspoken thing."

"We wouldn't have dreamed of questioning her about that," Doreen agreed.

"But you didn't even talk about it among yourselves?" Marisa asked.

Anne shook her head. "Not really. I didn't figure it out for a long time. She had her hair cut very short when she first got here—almost like a boy. She wore a pair of tortoiseshell glasses at first. She tried to hide her pregnancy with big shirts. But after a time, her hair grew in, and the glasses went. I guess she started feeling safer."

"She eventually began to talk about her abusive marriage," Cindy said to Marisa. "That's how she began to heal. Opening up to us. We didn't care about the details of where she was from. Where she came from didn't matter. We just cared about helping her realize she didn't deserve the way he'd treated her."

"I knew who she was," Marlena said quietly. "I have a satellite dish, so I got local news from the States. Her story had such power over me—even before she got here. A husband everyone liked, handsome and popular, a beautiful young wife, five feet tall and pregnant out to there, with the biggest smile you've ever seen."

"Why?" Marisa asked.

"Because I had to know—were they the perfect couple? Or was he her murderer? Had he pulled off the perfect crime?"

"Those are good questions," Detective Murphy said,

overhearing the conversation and walking over. "Very good questions."

"Were you the officer in charge?" Marisa asked.

"I was," he said. He had bright red hair with a little white around the temples, a freckled face, and a great grin—it surprised Marisa to see him using it. He didn't seem mad at all, and she had expected he would—having been fooled for so long.

"What did you think? Did you think the husband killed her?"

"I was sure of it," he said.

"Why?" Marisa asked. He was looking past everyone in the crowd, directly at her—as if they were all alone in the lobby.

"Because he's a bad guy."

"But how do you know that? Since you just found out that Mara—Lily—is alive, he obviously didn't kill her; so, how do you know he's a bad guy?"

Patrick Murphy just stared at her, as if trying to read her story in her eyes. If only he could, she thought—he'd think her husband was a bad guy too.

"Because I saw the blood in their kitchen."

"But she said he never hit her."

Patrick shrugged. "I saw the blood," he said. "It got there somehow. There was a lot of it, as if she had lain there bleeding for some time. He knocked her down, and if he made it seem accidental—so she would think she was crazy—then he's even worse. I interviewed a lot of people that first year.... Mara Jameson tried to protect her husband, weave a story about a happy marriage. But it wasn't happy. And he wasn't a good person."

"Is he—still out there?"

Patrick nodded. "Yes," he said.

Just then Anne began lugging things out from inside her office: the basket of pine pillows for Rose, and the easel holding the placard with Lily and Rose's pictures on it. She and Marlena set everything up by the desk again. Anne had taken everything down when Patrick had started asking questions, because she knew he'd recognize Lily's picture.

Marisa saw Patrick glance at the front desk, piled high with CDs, posters, and photographs of the Celtic bands competing in Cape Hawk's upcoming Ceili Festival. A small smile touched his lips.

"What?" Marisa asked.

"Just that," Patrick said, gesturing at the pile of CDs. "A world with music like that can't be all bad."

"I played the fiddle when I was young," Marisa said, staring at the picture of one band, but remembering another: four young women wearing white dresses, holding guitars and fiddles, under the banner *Fallen Angels*. "I put myself through nursing school playing at Irish bars on Friday nights."

"Maybe you'll find the music again," he said.

"Mommy," Jessica said, coming over. "Allie asked if I can sleep over."

"It's fine with me," Cindy said.

Shaken by the conversation, Marisa thanked Patrick Murphy, then walked over to Cindy and Allie to discuss details. Jessica would be welcome to borrow a nightgown—and Cindy would have her home tomorrow by noon. Marisa said yes; she was glad Allie had asked Jessica to spend the night—she wanted to be alone. To think, and to investigate something just a little further.

She kissed her daughter good night, said goodbye to her friends, and shook Patrick Murphy's hand. He held on for a fraction of a second too long; Marisa looked up into his eyes, blue eyes shadowed with worry, and she saw a question. He was asking her something she couldn't begin to answer: she could almost hear the words coming out of his mouth, *Is everything okay?*

He wasn't a cop anymore—he was retired. And this wasn't—had never been—his jurisdiction, anyway. Marisa opened her mouth, wishing she could ask him a question of her own. But it seemed too presumptuous. It wasn't his problem. And besides, Marisa had never been one to ask for help.

"Don't forget that music," he called after her.

So she walked out to her car, got in, and drove past the stone gates of the inn's parking lot. Starlight sparkled on the onyx bay. Through her open windows, she heard the night birds calling. She thought of their golden eyes, watching her as she drove home. They were like sentries, keeping watch, protecting her from harm. The pine woods closed in around the road, branches interlocking overhead.

Jessica was settling in to Cape Hawk. Marisa thought of all the good that had happened since they'd arrived here. Love for Rose had driven Jessica into such a frenzy, making the pine pillows and pinecone earrings. Marisa felt so proud to have raised a child capable of such industry, and for such a generous reason.

She turned on her car stereo. When she heard Spirit's "Aurora"—Jessica's favorite—playing, she quickly changed the CD. Another good thing ruined. Marisa drove along, reflecting on how many good things in her life had been spoiled by a person she had loved so much. In spite of Patrick's words about music, right now the notes filled her with pain.

Since Jessica wasn't in the car, Marisa felt freer to let the emotions come—they had been living inside, deep in her heart and bones. They had wakened her at night, shaking her like little earthquakes. Now she began to cry, softly at first, and then she wailed. The cliffs rose high, and the trees muffled her sobs, and she just drove along, letting it all out.

Seeing Lily with Liam and Rose, having her real name and story out in the open—Marisa longed for that. She missed her mother. There were so many things she had given up, running away from Ted. But right now, it all coalesced into one sweet wish: to see her mother.

She parked behind the house, opened the car door, and just sat there for a minute. The smell of the woods and sea, spicy with pine and wild berries, salt and verbena, was like summer wine—heady, intoxicating. Marisa breathed it in, knowing that she had come here for a reason. Meeting Lily and the Nanouks had made her stronger.

Was she strong enough for what she had to do next? She wasn't sure.

But she shut the car door behind her, senses alert for anyone who might be hiding in the bushes—no matter how far she went from Boston and Ted, she was still on high vigilance—and walked into her house, alone.

Once the truth was out, and she realized her friend was in no trouble or danger, Anne managed to find a room for Patrick at the inn. He told her there were no hard feelings, and he told Marlena he'd be sorry to miss whatever she would have made him for breakfast. A Celtic band was playing—the music beautiful and haunting, just the way Patrick liked it.

"Why don't you come in and listen for a while?" Anne asked. "You can help me and Jude practice judging the band. We're getting set for this summer's Ceili Festival— with a big competition for the best band. How about joining us?"

Patrick hesitated, but shook his head. He was too keyed up to sit still. Instead, he went to his room, at the far end of the first floor, and threw his bag on the bed. A shower really seemed like the thing to do, so he stood under the spray for a long time—until his nerve endings started returning to normal. He couldn't get over the fact that he had found Mara—or Lily—he wasn't sure what to call her now.

When he got out, he wrapped a towel around his waist and tried Maeve again. Once again, he got the machine. He had to hold himself back from blurting out any number of messages: "Guess what, Maeve—I found your grand-daughter. Too bad I was the only one who actually thought she was lost!" Or, "Hi, Maeve—Mara is alive and well.

Thanks for keeping it a big secret—at least I got my salary paid while I looked for her."

He hung up, threw the phone on the bed. It was hard to feel elated—which he did actually feel—while feeling bitter—which he also actually felt. It was a mixed blessing, to say the least.

Who could he call? Sandra—he could call her, tell her the crime was now officially solved and, by the way, wasn't a crime at all. Could he please come home now? He could just hear her laughing at him. A crime that wasn't even a crime had wrecked their marriage. The great detective had really been on top of his game, all the way.

He could call Angelo. Angelo, boat- and dog-sitting for the *Probable Cause* and Flora, would be sitting up on deck, listening to the Yanks, watching the moon rise over Silver Bay, and enjoying the company of a great, loyal, and loving dog. Angelo might not be the kind of friend to say "I told you so," but then again, he might. Patrick just didn't feel he could risk it. He was feeling, in the words of the marriage counselor he'd gone to for a few sessions with Sandra, the sessions during which she'd broken to him her plans to leave him, "fragile."

"Fuck fragile," he said out loud, and started pulling on his pants and shirt. So what if he had blown his marriage and screwed up his career, so what if he was a washed-up retiree who even got fooled—let's face it, the side trip to Rose Gables was just icing on the cake—by a club of menopausal and premenopausal psychos?

Patrick Murphy was going to take a walk down to the

dock. There would be men and fishing boats there. Probably some of them would have beer. Patrick had been sober for eight years now, but tonight might be a good time to go off the wagon. He could almost feel the liquid relief of alcohol burning down his throat, spreading like hot wire through his body.

One hand on the doorknob, the phone rang.

Not his cell—so it couldn't be Maeve calling back. No, it was the house phone. He picked up, and a woman's voice spoke.

"Detective Murphy?"

"Not officially," he said wryly. "I'm retired."

"Well, then, *retired* Detective Murphy?"

"Yes?"

"This is Marisa Taylor. I met you earlier tonight."

"Right—the fiddle player. You have a daughter. Is it a joke among all of you—that I saw your nine-year-old and thought she had to be Mara's?"

She didn't reply. Then, "No. It's not."

Patrick didn't speak for a minute, and in the silence, something clicked in his brain. This wasn't about him. Mara hadn't hidden to thwart him. He heard in Marisa's voice the same fear that he knew had driven Mara to leave home. His stomach tightened.

"What is it, Marisa?" he asked.

"There's something I'd like to show you. I know this isn't your job, but I'd really like to ask you about it. Would you come over?"

"Yes, I will," he said.

She gave him the directions—involving driving over a chain bridge, taking a left at the chasm, going past the sawmill—landmarks appropriate to the kind of place a woman would come to hide in. Patrick had been on a roller coaster since getting to Cape Hawk, and it showed no signs of stopping.

He buttoned his shirt, strapped on his ankle holster, and tried Maeve once more—if she didn't answer tomorrow, he'd start to worry. Then he was out the door. Whatever Marisa was calling for, Patrick felt glad to be solving crimes again.

The road seemed like something out of a fantasy saga— it wound high into the rocky cliffs and was lined with tall trees that formed a crazily primeval forest. Patrick saw a family of moose staring out from the side of the road. A little further along, a black bear lumbered across. Owls called, and something swooped in for a kill, and the screams were terrible and then stopped.

Patrick actually found it comforting. Having worked the Major Crime Squad for so many years, he knew that people were capable of much worse cruelty than the vilest predator in nature. He could understand why a battered woman would find this environment so soothing. It was far from civilization—better known in America as "suburbia"— where everyone dresses nice, talks nice, and acts upstanding. Patrick had seen what went on behind the closed doors of some of those "nice" houses, including Mara Jameson's.

He turned into Marisa's driveway, saw her standing in the doorway. Her body was silhouetted from behind, and her loose cotton blouse rippled in the summer breeze. Patrick reminded himself she had called him as a cop.

"Hi," she said as he approached.

"Hi," he said.

"I feel funny, for calling you," she said, hugging herself, seeming very nervous as she looked up at him.

"Why?" he asked. She had beautiful eyes, brown velvet, soft and intelligent. She stared up at him.

"Because I once asked for a restraining order. I wasn't believed, and my request was denied."

"I'm sorry about that," he said carefully. He'd never want to bash his fellow law-enforcement officials. But he knew about some domestic violence complaints—especially upscale people, with successful, well-spoken husbands. By the time the woman was ready to ask for help, she often felt and sounded crazy—because he had driven her there, and because she had protected him for so long.

"My daughter's not here tonight," Marisa said. "I thought maybe I could talk to you a little. And run something by you."

"Sure," Patrick said. She was tall and slender, and she moved with grace and hesitation—as if she had been unsure of herself for a long time. Patrick saw her glancing back at him, as if assessing his thoughts and moves.

They walked through the living room, and she gave him an apologetic glance. "My computer is in the bedroom," she said.

"That's fine," he said, knowing she needed reassurance that he didn't have the wrong idea.

Nodding, she led him across the room to the desk. Her computer was a workhorse. The keyboard looked ancient, and the monitor was enormous. A worn Johns Hopkins sticker was stuck to the side of the monitor.

"You went there for college?" he asked.

"Nursing school," she said. "I've had this computer since then. When I left home, in April, it was one of the only things I took. It was so important to me, so I could have the Internet and e-mail—a way to stay in touch with some people I loved. My mother..."

"Why did you leave home?"

"The same reason as Lily. Mara."

"I'm sorry," Patrick said.

"Thank you," she said, looking over, as if she knew he meant it. Should he tell her that she shouldn't feel bad or ashamed, that it wasn't her fault? Did she know that already? Did she know that men like that often targeted women in the healing professions? But then, Patrick didn't like statistics. That particular statistic left out people like Lily—if that's what she wanted to call herself, that's how he'd try to think of her. He gazed at Marisa, sitting down at her computer, her thin shoulders drawn up toward her ears, and wondered how long she'd been carrying this kind of stress.

"Do you go online?" she asked. "Are you used to the Internet?"

"I'm retired." He smiled. "It's one of the ways I make the days go by. Fishing, the Yankees, and research online."

"I do that too," she said. "Research. Like, when I found

out Rose had Tetralogy of Fallot, I spent days on the nursing school website."

"Tetralogy of what?"

"Fallot," Marisa said. "It's a complex heart defect."

Patrick nodded and felt a tug inside. He pictured Lily and her daughter standing there at the inn door—and then he remembered Anne putting back the signboard—looking just like one of those small-town fundraisers you saw at diners and dry cleaners everywhere, where some child in the community needed medical help. Something new for Maeve to deal with—her granddaughter had heart problems. That made Patrick think of Maeve again, but right now he was focused on Marisa.

"Anyway," Marisa said. "There's a band I like—Spirit."

"Everyone likes Spirit," Patrick said, and he hummed a few bars of "Lonesome Daughter."

"Not bad," Marisa said, giving him a real smile for the first time since he'd arrived.

"Do you play their music on your fiddle?"

"Every so often. But that's not what this is about...."

"What, then?"

Glancing toward the computer, her smile faded. "Well, there's a Spirit fan website. It's embarrassing to admit, but I go there sometimes—and have, for a few years. Spirit fans tend to be, well, kind of like the band itself. Smart, playful, but with social consciences. My kind of people."

Smart, playful, social conscience: Patrick checked them off, nodding. Well, maybe not so smart. He found himself wanting to be the kind of person this woman with the brown velvet eyes would like.

"Besides which, there's a fair amount of trading of CDs and live concert recordings not available anywhere else. I mean, well—I know you're a police officer, so this isn't anything I do, but it is sometimes done on the board—bootlegs."

Patrick nodded, trying not to look too stern.

"Well, recently I was reading the posts on the board, and I realized that someone has been committing fraud."

"Fraud? How?"

"By pretending his sister lost her home in a hurricane. He told everyone that Hurricane Catherina swept through, wrecking her house and injuring her son very badly. Spirit fans, well, they came out in droves. He calls himself Secret Agent. I've printed out a few of his posts—" She handed them to Patrick and he began to read through them.

He saw the setup instantly—bait and hook. He shook his head. Years ago he had worked with the FBI on a case of Internet fraud. Chat rooms and message boards were prime opportunities for con men and predators. They were the perfect places for the Dr. Jekylls of the world—no one could look through the screen and see that the person they were chatting with was really Mr. Hyde.

"You can see that many people responded. At one point, Secret Agent kept a running tally of what people had sent. Right here, it's up to seven thousand dollars. Just like one of those fundraiser signs that looks like a thermometer— 'Help us meet our goal.' In this case, he wanted to get to ten thousand."

"Look at all the people who wrote in," Patrick said, amazed at the goodwill and innocence of strangers. He thought back to the FBI case he'd worked on—he and Joe Holmes, an agent who had married a local Hubbard's Point woman, Tara O'Toole, had run down a couple who had gotten retirees to invest their life savings in penny stocks. The couple had lived in a huge house overlooking Silver Bay. The retirees had lost everything.

"We're a trusting bunch," Marisa said.

"Spirit fans?"

"People in general," she said. "I trusted this man myself."

"You sent in money for his sister?"

She shook her head, and angry tears appeared in her eyes. "I married him," she said.

"Secret Agent is your husband?" he asked.

"My ex-husband," she corrected. "I think so. I know he used to troll message boards—I used to go on his computer sometimes, to find out if he was having an affair. There's something about the style of his posts here—earnest, funny—that makes me think it's Ted."

"Why would he choose the Spirit board?"

"He knows I'm a fan. I think maybe he was hoping to find me online. 'Secret Agent' is the title of the only Spirit song he really likes. The thing is, I never posted here until very recently—so he couldn't find me."

"That's good," Patrick said. "That's good."

"Here are my only posts," she said. "My screen name is White Dawn."

Patrick read the first, about how the sister would be getting money from the government if she was in a disaster area. Then he read the second, "Beware," and smiled. Then he read the third: "Hurricane Catherina didn't hit Homestead. It tracked north, dude. You can do a better job conning people if you first check out the storm track on the NOAA website."

"You wrote that?" he asked, grinning.

"Yep."

"Whoa," he said, reading the flurry of angry replies from the board. "And a shitstorm ensued."

"Yes, it did. Did he commit fraud? Can you catch him for it?"

"Well," Patrick said, remembering back to the FBI investigation. "Whenever you go online, you leave a trail. There's always a signature left at the website, of your IP number—which is really like a fingerprint." He took out his cell phone—to see whether he still had Joe Holmes programmed in. "I think it's a good possibility we can nail him," he said.

"Who are you going to call?" she asked.

"FBI," he said. "But first, do you mind if I try someone else? Just to update her on a different case?"

"Lily's grandmother?" Mara asked, smiling. "Go ahead."

Patrick hit redial, and the number rang, but again there was no answer. His stomach knotted—it was now ten at night, and Maeve should definitely be there. Before gathering his thoughts on her whereabouts, he needed to stay focused on this Secret Agent guy. Scrolling through his stored phone numbers, he found Joe Holmes's. Just before dialing, he glanced over at Marisa. "What's your ex-husband's real name?" he asked.

"Ted," she said. "Ted Hunter."

Patrick nearly dropped the phone. "What did you say?"

"Ted Hunter."

"As in—" It couldn't be possible. "What's his whole name? The one on his driver's license."

"Edward Hunter," she said.

And then Patrick had to sit down.

Chapter 26

Liam had a family now. That was how it felt to him, taking care of Lily and Rose. After the situation at the inn, he had felt them too vulnerable to go back to their own house, so he had brought them up the hill, to his home. Lily seemed relieved, as if she'd been on the run, making decisions for so long, and tonight she just needed a rest.

Determined to give that to her, Liam drove through the stone posts at the bottom of his property and then up a long, curving drive. He lived in a spruce forest, in a large stone house that had once belonged to a quarry owner. Because the house wasn't visible from the road, he knew that the local kids had turned it into a mythological mansion—where Captain Hook lived. He glanced over at Rose and hoped she wouldn't be scared. But she was half-asleep, just smiling to be back in Cape Hawk.

Liam carried her, and together the three of them walked in his front door. Liam's heart was pounding with excitement and nervousness and pride. To have Rose and Lily here meant everything to him.

"It's been a long time," Lily said, smiling wearily.

"Do you remember the first time you came here?" he asked.

"When Rose was about three weeks old," she said. "She had a fever, and there'd been a bad storm, and the phones were out, and a big oak was blocking my road, so I couldn't get out. I hiked up here, to ask you to help."

"Did he help?" Rose asked.

"He always helped," Lily said softly.

Liam smiled gratefully. He turned on lights, hoping his bachelor style wouldn't turn them away. He had stacks of oceanographic journals everywhere, alongside piles of shark books, photos of shark attacks on marine mammals, tapes and videos of eyewitness accounts of shark attacks on humans. He had solid oak furniture and a bunch of red pillows, a big Tabriz rug Camille had given him from the family collection, a lot of bookcases without space for even one more book, and a TV in the corner, as if by afterthought.

"It's cozy here," Rose said.

"Do you think so?" he asked, crouching down beside her. "I'm glad."

"I don't understand why we came here," she said. "Instead of our regular house."

Liam exchanged a look with Lily, wanting her to answer.

"Is it because of that man at the inn?" Rose pressed.

"Yes, honey," Lily said. "He's someone . . . who knows a

person I knew long ago. It's not important tonight. The only thing we have to do is get you to bed."

Liam carried Rose upstairs, to one of the spare bedrooms. Lily checked out the hallway and saw a second empty bedroom next door. Liam pulled out clean sheets from the linen closet in the hall, put them on the twin bed. Rose seemed to be studying him more carefully than usual. Every time he glanced over, he saw her gazing at him with complete intensity. Lily set Rose's medication out on the bureau and went to get a glass of water.

"What is it, Rose?" he asked.

"This is what I wished for," she said. "On my birthday."

"Coming here?" he asked.

But Rose was either too tired to talk, or she had decided she'd said enough. Lily returned with the water, and they went through the long process of giving Rose all her medication. Then Liam and Lily tucked her into bed, and Lily told her she'd be sleeping in the spare room just next door.

"Where will Dr. Neill be?" Rose asked.

"My room's downstairs. But I'll hear you if either of you needs anything."

"Thank you," Rose said, putting her arms around his neck to kiss him good night. Having this child in his house, knowing what she had just gone through, moved Liam to the core.

After Rose was settled, he and Lily went back downstairs. He put a kettle on the stove and turned to look at her. She stood there, leaning on his kitchen counter. Her sable hair gleamed in the lamplight. He went to her, tilted her face up, kissed her the way he'd been wanting to kiss her all day.

They were hungry for each other—in a way Liam had never experienced before. It was as if they were separate from real life, completely swept up in whatever was happening between them. But the reality was so deep and great, Liam knew he had to pull away.

"Are you okay?" he asked.

"I think so. I'm just not sure which end is up. Rose's surgery went so miraculously well, and then to come home to—my past."

"How did he find you?" Liam asked.

Lily blinked and smiled, looking down at her feet. Liam had expected her to be upset, even frantic, but she didn't seem that way at all. "My grandmother," she said.

"She knew?"

Lily nodded. "She didn't know where I was going, but I couldn't just run away without telling her. I could never do that to her. You don't know her, Liam, but she is the smartest, most amazing woman in the world. She raised me to be so strong. I thought I could go through anything."

Liam listened and watched, seeing sparks in the blue eyes he loved so much.

"But I couldn't. Not Edward—not when I was about to have a baby. I knew he'd never let me get away, and there was no way I was ever going to subject my daughter to him."

"You knew the baby was a girl," Liam said. "I remember

that, the night she was born. You held out your arms and said, 'Give her to me,' even before I told you."

"Yes, I knew. I'd had a lot of ultrasounds. He used to knock me down—I told you. And pretend it was my fault, try to convince me I was the clumsiest person. A cow, he called me."

"I'll kill him," Liam said, and he meant it. He felt hatred and rage boiling inside—something he'd never felt before. Even for the shark—when he was young, before he'd understood shark behavior and predation, even then he'd never felt this level of cold burning hatred.

"I couldn't let him be part of Rose's life," Lily said. "If I'd waited till after she was born, there would have been custody issues. Not that he wanted her—he didn't. He made it really clear. But I just knew—he would have used her to get to me. He would have tortured us both, and I don't use that word by mistake. Edward lived to cause pain."

"What kind of person would do that?"

"One without conscience or empathy," Lily said quietly. "And there's more too. Edward is a killer."

"What do you mean?"

"I'll tell you sometime," she said. "Not tonight, but soon."

"And your grandmother knew it?"

Lily nodded. "Most of it. Enough so she wanted to help me get away."

"Did she help you find Cape Hawk? As a place to run to?"

"No," Lily said. "I found it on my own. It turns out that I

have a connection with Camille, and that she has a connection with Edward."

"My aunt? Camille Neill?"

"Yes," Lily said. "My parents died in the same ferry disaster as her husband, Frederic. I used to keep all the clippings
about it, and once I came upon something about how
Camille donated the memorial stone. I felt so grateful to
her for that."

"She'd be happy to know that," Liam said.

Lily smiled. "I'm glad. I know she's scarred, just as I am.
Losing someone that way is terrible. It makes you vulnerable . . . I think it made me an easier mark for Edward. I was
an orphan—it didn't matter that I was thirty years old. I
was still needy."

"How is Edward connected to Camille?" Liam asked,
confused.

"He had this old framed photograph hanging on the
wall. It showed an old whaling ship at the dock in winter.
So beautiful, haunting—all the spars and shrouds covered
in ice. He would tell people that his great-grandfather was
a whaling captain. It was just a lie, like his story about going
to Harvard, but he told it so often, I think he almost believed it himself."

"What was the ship's name?" Liam asked.

"The *Pinnacle*," Lily said, her eyes shining.

"My great-great-grandfather's ship," he said quietly.
"The first Tecumseh Neill."

"I know," Lily said. "I used to stare at the picture and feel
as if the ice in my heart was right there in the photo. My

frozen veins—all the cold I felt inside from living with Edward. All he cared about the picture was using it to convince people he came from a sea captain background. But I felt haunted by the scenery. The cliffs, the frozen fjord, and the depth of winter, were so austere. They matched how extreme I felt inside."

"How did you find where the picture had been taken?"

"The provenance was very easy to track. It was an original taken by a well-known photographer. Sepia-toned, silver gelatin print, fairly valuable. The gallery stamp was on the back, and I called to ask. You see, it had once been owned by Camille."

"She has a fairly substantial collection of local maritime art," Liam said, amazed by the coincidence.

"I remember seeing the receipt and being shocked, because that was the woman who had donated the ferry memorial. And I remember thinking she had an odd name. Camille Neill. I never thought I'd meet her."

"So that's why you came here?" Liam asked. "Those two reasons?"

"Partly," she said. "I liked the connection with my parents, and I thought I'd never seen anyplace as beautiful as Cape Hawk. I felt a tiny, secret revenge, coming to a place Edward actually looked at every day—the picture he used to support the lies he told about his illustrious ancestor. He would tell people it was Newfoundland, because he had no idea."

"Good one, Lily," Liam said, hugging her.

"And also because it was so very far away."

"From Edward."

Lily nodded. "Which was wonderful. But also terrible, because it was so far from my grandmother. She wanted me to run far and disappear—she gave me money and helped me cover my tracks, lied to the police, I'm sure."

"Patrick Murphy," Liam said. When everyone else was busy greeting Rose and rallying round Lily, Liam had noticed the cop's eyes—happy, to see the woman he called Mara, but also something else. Sad, betrayed. Liam had felt for him.

"Yes," Lily said. "Do you think it's true, what he said? That my grandmother wanted him to find me?"

"I thought she knew where you were. Why didn't she just call?"

"She didn't know where I ran to. We decided that was the only way to really protect me and Rose. I sent her small, secret things. The clipping, a glasses case—making her an honorary Nanouk—a membership to a local aquarium. I thought that if Nanny brought such happiness to me and Rose, then maybe her relatives could somehow connect us with Maeve."

"Why don't you call your grandmother?" Liam asked, reacting to Lily's mention of Nanny, but not wanting to show how worried he felt about her whereabouts and the tracking data—she continued swimming south, and when he'd last checked, seemed to be feeding in the waters off Block Island.

"I would," Lily said. "But I'm still not sure we're safe. If Edward finds out I'm alive, he'll come after Rose for sure.

And I may just have given him grounds for custody—by disappearing. Liam, what if he tries to get Rose?"

"I meant what I said before," Liam said steadily, more seriously than he'd ever said anything in his life. He knew for certain that if Edward Hunter—or anyone else—ever tried to harm Lily or Rose, he would kill them without looking back. After what the man had done to Lily, he would almost welcome the chance.

Lily leaned into him, standing on tiptoes to rise up and kiss him. Liam felt a rush of heat inside, flooding every part of his body. He had kept his feelings for Lily and Rose secret for so long—because he'd known that she was too closed off, that her defenses were too impenetrable. Maybe he knew that his had been as well.

But now, kissing in his kitchen while Rose slept upstairs, Liam felt all the walls breaking apart. They were inside each other's fortresses, together and standing strong. She held him tight with both her arms, and Liam held her right back—with everything he had, his entire heart. He wanted to touch every part of her, every inch of her skin, right now. This is how people know they're alive, he thought. Making each other feel joy, because what else is life for? Both he and Lily had missed out on so much for so long. But not tonight—and not ever again, he thought, kissing the woman he loved.

Joe Holmes was fast asleep at home in Hubbard's Point. The windows were open, and the breeze cooled his bare back. It carried scents of beach grass, tidal flats, and his wife Tara's garden. Joe had been working the night shift on a white-collar-crime case, listening in on a wiretap on a banker in Stamford. So when his cell phone rang, he slept right through it. Then it rang again, and he cursed the caller. Then the house phone rang, and Tara shook his shoulder.

"Honey," she said. "It's Patrick Murphy. That retired Statie? Worked on Mara's case?"

"Rrrrungh," Joe said, taking the phone. "Holmes," he said.

"Hey, Joe. It's Patrick Murphy. Sorry to wake you up, but I have something big."

"Is it information on a dickhead banker in Stamford, I hope?"

"No. It's on Edward Hunter."

"Mara Jameson's husband?"

"Yes."

"You have new information? About Mara?"

"Yes," Patrick said. "And I'll get to that, but first—you know about Internet fraud. Do you know anything about people who run cons on message boards? Get people to donate to phony charities?"

"Yeah. Hard to prove, hard to prosecute. Generally because the con artists are so slippery. They run the con, then disappear. They change screen names so fast, and if someone doesn't think to check out their IP address before they fade away, then it's almost impossible."

"What if someone managed to save printouts of the entire scam?"

Joe was awake now, hiked up on his elbow. He had to wake up in an hour anyway—he could already smell Tara brewing the coffee.

"I'd say we could look into it," he said. "If it's not too late, if the guy hasn't bolted, we might be able to nail down his IP link and then trace him to an actual street address in real time. You want to tell me what this has to do with Mara?"

"Just this for now, Joe—the guy might be Edward Hunter."

"I'd love to nail that fucking arrogant jerk," Joe said.

"You and me both," Patrick said. Joe heard him breathing hard, probably excited about the possibility of finally taking Edward to task for something—even if they couldn't get him on Mara's disappearance. Joe yawned, blinking his eyes.

"It's such a shame about Maeve," he said.

"Maeve?"

"Yeah," Joe said. "Tara said she saw the ambulance up there two days ago. Clara Littlefield told her Maeve had some sort of attack, got taken to Shoreline General. I hope she pulls through—I know she'd love to see the heat go up on Edward. That slimeball."

"Thanks, Joe," Patrick said.

"No problem," Joe said. "Listen—"

But Patrick had disconnected. The line was dead. Joe just stared at the phone, shook his head. People had said

Patrick wasn't the same—that he'd gotten too emotionally involved in the Jameson case. Joe knew better than to throw stones—people were human, even cops. He had a lot of respect for Pat Murphy, and he had felt very sorry to hear his marriage had fallen apart. Joe knew he never wanted that to happen—he had too much to lose with Tara.

Waking up fully, he smelled the coffee. Then got out of his bed, still naked, and went to kiss his wife.

It took some doing, but Patrick managed to convince Marisa to tell him where Lily lived. She was so elated by the fact that he had called his FBI friend and learned that there might be a possibility of getting Ted. And then she was so confused by the fact that Patrick seemed to be saying that "Edward Hunter"—Ted's legal name—was also the name of the man Lily had been married to.

"It's not possible," she said.

"Why?" he asked. "He just cast a wide net."

"But for Lily and me both to end up here, in the same place, so far away from our homes—"

"I'll bet that once you and Lily start talking, you'll realize that something sparked you to choose Cape Hawk. A very similar reason."

"For me, it was partly spite," Marisa said, remembering the photo of Ted's great-grandfather's whaling vessel, so majestic with its spars coated in ice, with the Cape Hawk cliffs rising in the background. "I will confess that with pride. To get back at him, just a little, for all the humiliation he put me through."

"I bet Mara—Lily—has something like that in her story too. Deep down, she chose this location as a big fuck-you to the bastard who chased her from her home. Excuse my language."

"I understand," Marisa said. "It's very late. We're tired. Listen—I know that something's happened to Lily's grandmother, and she needs to know. But she's just been through the wringer with Rose. Her daughter had open-heart surgery a week ago, and I just can't let you disturb them tonight. Come back here tomorrow morning, and I'll take you to them. I promise."

Patrick Murphy stood at her door. He looked down, as if trying to decide whether to trust her or not. Marisa knew that he had reasons to be suspicious. Women like Marisa and Lily had to become very smart and shrewd and wily about protecting themselves. They had learned, with their abusers, to pretend everything was fine—while secretly forming escape plans in their own minds.

To let him know that she was true to her word, Marisa reached for his hand. The corners of his eyes were deeply lined, and his palm felt callused. He held on tight; Marisa could feel him wanting to anchor himself, to know that he was in a safe port. She gazed back at him with gravity, without smiling at all.

"I want you to believe me," she said. "So I'm going to tell you something. Just so you trust me. And then I want you to forget it. Okay?"

"Okay," he said. His voice sounded ragged, as if he was an old, finished fighter.

"My real name is Patricia."

"Patricia," he said.

"And my daughter's real name is Grace."

"Patricia and Grace," he said.

"But you can never call us by those names," she said. "Ever."

"They're pretty names," he said.

"They're the names we had when we were with Ted," she said. "And no matter what happens, we are no longer those people. We're Marisa and Jessica now, forever. Okay?"

"Okay," he said. She squeezed his hand, and she saw light behind his tired eyes.

"Till tomorrow morning," she said. "Come back at nine, and I'll take you to see Lily."

"Till then," he said. And as he walked out to his car, Marisa watched his back and hoped he knew that he didn't have to worry. He could go to sleep knowing she wasn't going to run away on him.

Chapter 27

Waking up in Liam's house, at first Lily didn't know where she was. The sun shining through the trees, and the wide blue bay out his window, seemed almost like a dream. She had hardly slept all night—walking into Rose's room several times, to make sure she was breathing regularly and sleeping well. Midway through the night, she had felt Liam lie down beside her, on the twin bed in his spare room.

The rusty old springs creaking under his weight, he had curled up against her back. The night was warm, even up here where the wind blew steadily off the Gulf of St. Lawrence. Liam's steady heartbeat and his breath on the back of her neck finally soothed her into a fitful sleep. Troubled dreams came and went, but when the sun finally rose, she sat straight up and said, "Granny."

"Lily," Liam whispered.

She looked around, trying to get her bearings. The stone walls, the leaded windows, the dark green trim—this wasn't Hubbard's Point. The fog cleared from her brain, and she realized she had dreamed of the beach. Of walking into her grandmother's rose garden with sand on her feet, of her grandmother rinsing them off with the watering can. She could almost see the little circle of shells and a sand dollar embedded in the cement.

"Lie down a little longer," Liam urged. "You hardly got any rest at all. You might have a long day ahead of you."

Somehow Lily knew he meant answering the police officer's questions, and getting Rose reacclimated to life outside the hospital, but Lily just thought of her grandmother and felt a warm breeze blow through the window. She swore it smelled of Hubbard's Point roses. Climbing out of bed, Lily checked Rose again. Her sense of vigilance was on very high alert.

She cuddled back into Liam's embrace, trying to close her eyes and settle down. Her body was so tense, her spine arched. Liam stroked her shoulder, rubbed her back. Just knowing that he was there made it safe enough for her to let the thoughts come. The dream had shaken her. Lately she'd been feeling her grandmother's presence. Starting with that night before they went down to Boston, it was almost as if Maeve had been calling to her; she'd heard her voice in the summer air.

The pull to southern New England had been strong. But Lily had been so focused on Rose getting well, she had pushed it from her mind. But the dream was so powerful tonight, Lily couldn't ignore her feelings any longer. She stared into the darkness, thinking about everything.

Her greatest fears had always been regarding Edward, and what he would do to her, her grandmother, and, now, Rose. Nine years on this rocky, austere Canadian coast had toughened Lily some—but so had being a mother. Giving birth to Rose had changed Lily and the world. From the very instant Liam had placed Rose into Lily's arms, she had turned into a mother tiger. She would fight to the death to protect her baby.

Lying with Liam now, Lily thought about what to do. She saw it as a quest: nothing less than life and death, with her and Rose's freedom as the prize. If she was brave and true, followed her heart, she would win their freedom. They could go wherever and whenever they wanted, and they would never have to worry about Edward again.

All that had come before had brought them to this point. What if Lily just faced Edward down? No more hiding, no more missing Maeve. She could finally go home, and introduce Rose to her great-grandmother.

"Why can't you sleep?" Liam asked after a few more minutes.

"I'm thinking," she said. "Of my old home."

"You're leaving, aren't you?"

"Liam," she whispered.

He didn't reply, but just held her tighter. Lily didn't know what to do, so she didn't know what to say. She linked her fingers with his, leaned down to kiss the back of his hand.

She never did get back to sleep. When she heard Rose stirring, she got up and walked into the next room so Rose would see her when she wakened. Rose struggled to sit up—she had gotten stiff during the night. Her left hand instinctively rested at her neck, protecting her heart. Lily helped her out of bed, eased her feet into her slippers.

They went downstairs, where Liam was in the kitchen, making coffee and pouring orange juice.

"Good morning, Rose," he said. "How did you sleep?"

"It was the best sleep I ever had," she said, smiling.

They sat at the round oak table, and then Lily saw what it had been too dark to see last night: pictures on the wall and refrigerator. Rose's school pictures in frames on the wall, a couple of her old drawings—from kindergarten and first grade—on the refrigerator. Lily had only vague memories of Rose insisting that they cross the hallway to Liam's office, to give them to him.

"You saved them?" Rose asked.

"Of course," he said. "Did you think I wouldn't?"

"Yes," she said. "I thought you wouldn't."

Liam chuckled, although when Lily saw him logging on to his laptop, she knew he was checking on Nanny. She glanced at Rose, to see whether she had picked up on it, but Rose was busily looking down her nightgown to see her stitches.

"How do they look?" Lily asked.

"Good," Rose said.

Lily leaned over to check—everything looked as if it was healing fine, the edges of the long incision drawn perfectly together, no clear fluid, no sign of yellow fluid or infection of any kind.

"You're right," Lily said. "Good."

They poured bowls of cereal, and then Liam came over to eat with them. Whatever he had seen onscreen was a mystery, because he didn't mention it. Lily's heart sank— she had the feeling that meant that Nanny was wandering even farther south. If only joy could follow joy. If only people could have everything, everyone they loved—all at the same time.

She thought of the singular love she had felt just twenty-four hours ago—when they were still in Boston, when her entire world was made up of newly found love and a newly healthy daughter. She had made peace long ago with her decision to leave Hubbard's Point, leave that life behind. But now, a day later, her world had been rocked by the hint of her grandmother needing her.

Lily stared out Liam's kitchen window, at the wide, amazing, blue Gulf of St. Lawrence. When she turned from the window, she caught Liam watching her. His eyes were sad, as if he could read her mind.

But because Rose was right there, no words were possible. They all just ate breakfast—or, in the case of Lily and Liam, didn't eat, but just pushed their cereal around with their spoons.

A knock sounded at the door, and Liam went to answer. Lily took a deep breath. Even before he returned, she knew that Patrick Murphy would be with him. And he was; but Lily was surprised to see Marisa there too. The looks on their faces told Lily that she needed to move Rose into a room where she wouldn't hear.

She settled Rose on the sun porch—with a book and her bag of needlepoint. Rose had started doing a project at the end of school, and this was the first she'd felt well enough to continue. Kissing Rose on the top of her head, Lily returned to the kitchen. The expression in Patrick Murphy's eyes made her feel she was about to be arrested.

"What is it?" she asked. "Are you going to put me in handcuffs?"

"He wouldn't do that to you or me," Marisa said. "We've done nothing wrong. But Edward has."

"Edward?" Lily asked, feeling electricity racing down her neck.

"Ted," Marisa said.

"Ted—that's your husband."

Ted, Edward, she thought, suddenly seeing the dull hurt in Marisa's eyes. Don't let this be happening. "No," Lily said.

"What made you come to Cape Hawk?" Patrick asked.

"It's a long story," Lily said. "I think you already know most of it. You have the news article about the ferry memorial stone. The other part has to do with a lie my husband used to tell—to get people to think he was descended from a ship captain."

"The whaling ship," Marisa said. "With ice on the rigging. And the cliffs of the fjord in the background."

"Tell me this isn't happening," Lily said, feeling the blood drain from her face. "You were married to Edward Hunter?"

Marisa nodded.

"Didn't you know he was under suspicion for killing his wife?" Lily whispered.

"No," Marisa said. "I had no idea until last night. You've been missing for nine years. I must have missed the story when it all started, because I was pregnant with Jessica—she was born the week after Rose, but it was a difficult pregnancy, and I had to go into the hospital. I vaguely remember hearing about a pregnant woman missing in Connecticut—but Lily, I couldn't bear to hear about the case. I was just about to have my baby, and I couldn't stand to think about what you might have gone through."

"Jessica and Rose have almost the same birthday."

"I know. Exactly. When I think of it now," Marisa said, holding Lily's hands, "I wonder whether that was part of the allure. Ted, Edward, knew my husband from the golf club. He'd done some stock transactions for us—he had all our family information, including birthdays. My husband liked him. So when Paul died, I just continued using Ted. He managed the inheritance funds—and when I remember that first meeting, he commented on Jessica's birthday."

"He did?"

Marisa nodded. "He told me that someone he had cared about deeply had had a baby at that time—and it was very sacred for him."

"Sacred!" Lily exploded.

"That's what he said."

"He scammed you," Lily gasped, grabbing her, hugging her and feeling them both shaking so hard, the two wives of Edward Hunter. "Just the way he scammed me."

"We almost had him too," Marisa said. "Patrick called his friend in the FBI, and we were right on Ted's trail—with another scam, on the Internet. But the agent called Patrick this morning to say he'd erased his account, and the message board doesn't archive old messages."

"It's true," Patrick said. "We'll have to get him another way. But never mind that for now. Mara, Lily—"

"Lily," she said. "Please, Mara is from another time and place. I can't think of her now."

"You might have to," he said. "There's no good way to tell you this."

"What is it?" Liam asked, stepping closer to Lily, putting his arm around her for support.

"It's your grandmother," Patrick said. "I spoke with Clara Littlefield this morning, and Maeve had a seizure at home three days ago. The ambulance took her to Shoreline General, and she's in a coma."

"Oh, Granny," Lily said, tears flooding. "It can't be true!"

"I'm sorry," Patrick said.

Lily leaned against Liam's chest, weeping. If only she had listened to her heart on that trip to Boston. Something was telling her to go home, go to Hubbard's Point. She had dismissed it, thinking it was just her old homesickness, kicked by being in New England. But it had been Maeve, calling her. They had always been so connected; how could Lily have thought she would go on forever, just waiting for the time when Lily felt safe enough to return?

"Why did I wait so long?" Lily wept. "She needed me, and I wasn't there."

"You had to think of Rose," Liam said, kissing her hair. "You had good reason to stay hidden."

"Maeve loves you," Patrick said. "She must have felt good, knowing she helped you get away. She wouldn't have wanted you to walk into harm's way."

"Patrick told me that she always carries the needlepoint case you made her," Marisa said.

"I made her an honorary Nanouk," Lily said, sniffling.

"The Nanouks will be with you," Marisa said. "Wherever you go, whatever you do. You know that—"

"I do," Lily said, touching her cheek. "And the same is true of you. They saved my life when I first got here."

"And you've saved mine," Marisa said.

"What are you going to do?" Patrick asked.

"I could go there," Lily said. "And Edward wouldn't necessarily have to know."

"Or he could find out," Patrick said. "And we could help you fight him."

"He'd find out about Rose," Lily whispered, her blood running cold. She knew that if she returned to Connecticut, she would have to face hard truths about the man she had left. He was the father of her daughter. She had been afraid of him for so long, but suddenly she knew that some emotions were bigger than fear.

"Maeve needs you," Patrick said.

"You have to go to her," Liam said.

"Oh God," Lily whispered. She held his hand and looked deeply into his eyes. They were as grave and sad as she felt. Now that Rose's heart was mending, she felt hers was breaking. What if her grandmother was very sick? Lily would stay and take care of her. There was so much she wanted to make up to Maeve: all the lost years, the birthdays and holidays she had missed. Maeve had never even met Rose. As wonderful a grandmother as she had been to Lily, she'd be all that to Rose. Edward had deprived them all of each other for too long.

"Liam," she said, looking into his eyes. How could she leave him now, just as they had found each other? "I can't go away from you."

"Nanny's leading you there," he said. "You know that, don't you?"

"What do you mean?"

He held her hand, leading her to the computer, showed her MM122's latest position: swimming in Long Island Sound, right off the tip of Hubbard's Point. Lily could barely take in the information—evidence of another miracle. How could she doubt it?

"She's leading you back home," Liam said.

"Home is here," she said.

"Lily," Liam said. "I know you're scared. But look—look at what's happening. Do you know how amazing it is that a beluga whale would make her way down the eastern seaboard, all the way south to Hubbard's Point?"

"Is it possible?" Lily asked, her throat so tight.

"It's happening," he said. "That is evidence that goes beyond possible—straight to reality."

Lily closed her eyes. When she opened them again, she saw a picture hanging above Liam's desk: Tecumseh Neill, the family patriarch, standing with his whaling vessel, the *Pinnacle*. Beside it, the copy of a letter he had written to his wife, waiting at home in Cape Hawk:

"I have been in pursuit of a single whale," he wrote in fine, elegant script. "She sings by night, when there's not a sound to answer her but the wind in the rigging. When she breached at first light, she was the color of blood—a sight to strike fear into every heart and yet make every man aboard gaze upon her with awe and reverence—that such a creature could exist! I will follow her, my darling, but I made a promise to return home to you, and that I shall do...."

"Liam," Lily said, turning to look into his eyes. "Would you come to Connecticut with us? You made that promise to Rose...."

"I made it to you too," he said.

"Then is that a yes?" Lily asked. Her heart was beating in her throat. Her pulse, the rhythm of life. Blood, oxygen, and that other vital essence mixing together in her body. Her Rose, reading on the sun porch. Liam took her hand.

Behind him, the windows were wide open. From up here on the hill, you could see forever—or just about. Way out into the Gulf of St. Lawrence, Lily could see whales playing. They breached, shooting straight out of the icy blue water like silver missiles, landing with exuberant, sky-high splashes. The day was brilliant.

About the Author

LUANNE RICE is the author of *Summer's Child*, *Silver Bells*, *Beach Girls*, *Dance With Me*, *The Perfect Summer*, *The Secret Hour*, *True Blue*, *Safe Harbor*, *Summer Light*, *Firefly Beach*, *Dream Country*, *Follow the Stars Home*—a Hallmark Hall of Fame feature—*Cloud Nine*, *Home Fires*, *Secrets of Paris*, *Stone Heart*, *Angels All Over Town*, *Crazy in Love*, which was made into a TNT Network feature movie, and *Blue Moon*, which was made into a CBS television movie. She lives in New York City and Old Lyme, Connecticut.

LUANNE RICE

THE NEW YORK TIMES BESTSELLING AUTHOR OF
DANCE WITH ME

SUMMER
OF ROSES

Watch for

LUANNE RICE'S

*Summer
of Roses*

On sale in hardcover June 21st

New York Times bestselling author Luanne Rice
continues the story begun in *Summer's Child*
in an unforgettable novel destined to take its
place as one of her most beloved works.

Please turn the page
for a special advance preview of
Summer of Roses.

Summer of Roses

On Sale June 21st

My wedding was like a dream. It was almost everything a wedding should be, and when I think of it, even now, I see it unfolding like the kind of beautiful story that always has a happy ending.

I got married in my grandmother's garden, by the sea. A brilliant early July morning at Hubbard's Point, the daylilies were in bloom. That's what I remember, almost as much as the roses: orange, cream, lemon, golden daylilies on tall green stalks, tossed by the summer breeze, trumpeting exultation up to the wild blue sky. But the roses were my grandmother's specialty, her pride and joy, and that year, for my wedding, they were all blooming.

Scarlet Dublin Bay roses climbed the trellis beside the front door of the weathered shingle cottage, while Garnets-and-Golds and pale pink New Dawns meandered up the stone chimney. The beds by the iron bench bloomed with red, yellow, peach, and pink classic English varieties, while those along the stone wall, by the old wishing well and the steps up to the road, were low shrubs of white and cream roses. A six-foot hedge of Rosa Rugosa—white and pink beach roses—lined the sea wall, along with deep blue delphinium and hydrangeas.

It was a perfect setting for a perfect wedding—something that most people, including me, never imagined would happen. I guess I thought I wasn't the marrying kind. Let's just say that I was a little on the guarded side. I had lost my parents very young. As a child I had been in love with our family. I know how dramatic that sounds, but it's true. We were so happy, and my parents had loved each other with wild, reckless, ends-of-the-earth abandon. I had watched them together, and taken it in, and decided that nothing less would ever do for me. When they were killed in a ferry accident, on a trip to Ireland, although I wasn't there, but home in Connecticut with my grandmother, I think I died with them.

So my wedding—and everything that had led up to it—the miracle of meeting Edward Hunter, and falling so madly in love with him, and being swept off my feet in a way I'd never expected or believed could happen—was a resurrection of sorts. A rising from the dead, of a little girl who went down to the bottom of the Irish Sea with her parents, thirty-four years earlier.

Edward. He was every love song in the world. He was a hero—not just because I loved him, but because he really, truly was one. He had sacrificed so much for his family, and he had literally saved his mother's life. You can imagine how completely—uber-motherless child that I was—that fact endeared him to me. How *couldn't* I adore him?

He was just over five-eight, but since I'm just under five-two, he seemed so tall to me; I had to stand on tiptoes to kiss him. A rugby player at Harvard, he was broad-shouldered and muscular. His red Saab bore three stickers: Harvard University, Columbia Business School, and a bumper sticker that said *Rugby Players Eat Their Dead.* The joke was, Edward was so gentle, I couldn't even imagine him playing such a rough sport.

When I go back to our wedding day, I see his red car parked in the road up at the top of the stone steps, behind the rose-and-ivy-covered wishing well. I can see the graceful arch curving over the well—with *Sea Garden*—the name of my grandmother's cottage, forged in wrought iron back when my great-grandfather was still alive—the black letters rusting away in the salt air even back then, nine years ago. I remember the moment so well: standing there in my grandmother's yard, knowing that soon I would drive away with Edward in that red car—that I would be his wife, and we would be off on our honeymoon.

Can I say now, for certain, that I looked at that iron arch and saw the corroding letters as a reminder that even that which is most beautiful, intended to endure forever, can be corrupted or destroyed? No, I can't. But I do remember that the sight of it gave me my first cold feeling of the day.

My grandmother and Clara Littlefield—her next-door neighbor and best friend from childhood—had gone all-out to make my wedding a dream come true. The yellow-and-white-striped tent stood in the side yard between their houses, on the very point of Hubbard's Point, jutting proudly into Long Island Sound. Tables with long golden-cream tablecloths were scattered around, all decorated with flowers from the garden. A string quartet from Hartt School of Music, in Hartford, played Vivaldi. My friends were in their summer best— bright sundresses, straw hats, blue blazers.

Granny stood before me, looking into my eyes. We were the same height, and we laughed, because we were both so happy. I wore a white wedding gown; she wore a pale yellow chiffon dress. My veil blew in the sea breeze; my bouquet was white roses, off-white lace hydrangeas, and ivy from the wishing well. Granny wore a yellow straw hat with a band of blue flowers.

"I wish Edward's family had been able to come," she

said as we stood by the wishing well, ready to begin the procession.

"I know," I said. "He's trying to make the most of it."

"Well," she said. "Things happen . . . you'll see them soon, I'm sure. One thing I know, Mara—your parents are with you today."

"Granny—don't get me started."

"I won't," my grandmother said, wriggling her shoulders with resolve. "We're staying strong as I walk you down the aisle, or I'm not Maeve Jameson."

"My parents would be proud of you," I said, because I knew she was thinking of them every bit as much as I was trying not to—and I gave her a big smile, just to prove I wasn't going to cry.

"Of us both," she said, linking arms with mine as the quartet started playing Bach.

So much time has passed, but certain memories are still clear and sharp. The pressure of Granny's hand on mine, holding steady, as we walked across the grass; my beach friends Bay and Tara beaming at me; the smell of roses and salt air; Edward's short dark hair, his golden tan set off by a pale blue shirt and wheat linen blazer; his wide-eyed gaze.

I remember thinking his eyes looked like a little boy's. Hazel eyes. He had been so helpful all morning—taking charge of where the tables went, which direction the quartet should face. It was sort of odd, having a man "in charge," here on this point of land filled with strong women. Granny and I had exchanged an amused glance—letting him do his thing. But here he was, standing at our makeshift altar in the side yard, looking for all the world like a lost little boy as I approached him. But then I caught that blank stare—blank, yet somehow charged—and it made me hesitate, holding tight to my grandmother's hand.

Yes, I remember that stare, the look in his hazel eyes. It was fear—standing there under the striped tent, watching me approach, my betrothed was afraid of something. The years have gone by and told me all I need to know about his fear—but let's go back to my wedding day and pretend we don't have all this knowledge. Back then, in quick succession, I thought one thing and felt another. No—that's backward. I felt first, thought second.

I felt cold—the same chilly primal shiver I'd experienced looking up at his car, seeing that salt-pitted, rusty metal arch. But I chased the unwanted, ugly chill with this thought: Edward—hey, honey, Edward! Don't be afraid...please don't worry that it's too soon, or my grandmother doubts you, or that I care about the jacket. I love you...I love you.

I love you.

Words I had said so rarely up until that time—but since meeting Edward I had used almost constantly. The old Mara Jameson had been too closed off and guarded to let them slip off her tongue; but the new Mara Jameson couldn't say them enough.

This was my home, my side yard, my family and friends—Edward was far from everything comfortable and familiar to him. His family hadn't been able to make it. He felt really bad about the whole blazer debacle. These thoughts were flying through my mind as my grandmother passed my hand into his with the whispered words, "Take care of her, Edward." Edward nodded, but the expression in his eyes didn't ease.

Memo to self and brides everywhere: if you're standing in front of a justice of the peace, about to get married, and all you can think about is why your husband-to-be looks very uncomfortable, it's a red flag worth paying attention to.

The ceremony occurred. That's how I think of it now: words and music. What did they all mean? It's hard to say, harder still to not be cynical. The ceremony disguised one basic truth: marriage is a contract. Let's put romance aside. First and foremost, marriage is a legal, binding contract, where two people are joined in partnership, their assets merged, their fates legally entwined through powers vested by no less than the state.

When I think back to the look in Edward's eyes, I believe that he was afraid that I might not follow through on the deal, might not sign on the dotted line. What would have happened if I hadn't? If I had listened to that tiny voice inside, if I had felt the cold chill and known that it meant something worth paying attention to?

But I didn't listen. I pushed my feelings aside and pulled other things out of the summer air: love, hope, faith, resolve. I held Edward's hand. "I do," I said, "I do," he said. He kissed the bride. People cheered, and when I looked out at my friends, I saw more than one of them crying and grinning at the same time. They were so very happy for me.

We stood there, husband and wife. Our brilliant summer wedding day, blue sky and sparkles on the calm water, Mozart and the sound of leaves fluttering in the breeze—everything was so beautiful, so spectacular, it had to be a harbinger of a joyful life to come.

I turned to look at him. It's true, my own eyes were moist, and my voice was thin with wild and rising emotion. "Edward," I said, trailing off into all the hopes and dreams and possibilities of our future together. He stared at me—the fear gone from his eyes, replaced by something else. It was the first time I saw—well, you'll hear about what I saw as my story goes on. All I can say is, I felt the earth—the thin layer of grass on granite ledge—tilt beneath my feet.

He touched the flowers in my bouquet and said, "You're so delicate, Mara. Like a white rose. And white roses bruise so easily. Is that what your grandmother meant when she said I should take care of you?"

His words took my breath away. Don't they imply great tenderness? Show true depth of caring, of understanding? Of course they do. He could be so tender. I'll never deny that. But do you also see, as I do now, that his words implied a threat?

It was as if he'd been focused on Granny's gentle direction—just an offhand comment was how I'd taken it, a rather protective grandmother giving away the bride. Had Edward even heard the ceremony? Had he even *been* there? His hazel eyes flashed black as he mentioned Granny's words.

Just recently, I dreamed of a woman who lived under veils. Black, gray, white, silver, slate, dark blue—layers of veils covering her face. Take one off, there's another underneath. The woman lived in darkness, even when the sun was shining. She existed undercover. She could barely see out, and others could not see in. The question was: Who put those veils on her? Did she do it to herself? In the dream, she took them off one by one—and at the very bottom, the very last, or first, was a white wedding veil. In my life, I had them torn from me. I wanted to keep them on—you have no idea how much I needed those veils.

Women learn how to hide the worst. We love the best, and show it to all who want to see. Our accomplishments, our careers, our awards, our homes, our gardens, our happy marriages, our beautiful children. We learn, by tacit agreement, to look away from—and hide—the hurt, the blight, the dark, the monster in the closet, the darkness in our new husband's eyes.

But in some lives, there comes a time when the monster comes out of the closet and won't go back in. That happened to me. He began to show himself. My grandmother was the first to see. Only the wisest people can observe a woman in such a relationship and not sit in judgment. Judgment is easy: It is black and white, as brutal as a gavel strike. It keeps a person from having to ask the hard questions: What can I do to help? Could that be me?

My grandmother didn't judge. She tried to understand—and if anyone could understand it would be her, the woman who had raised me in her rose-covered cottage by Long Island Sound. A woman patient enough to coax red, pink, peach, yellow, and white roses from the stony Connecticut soil, to ease her brokenhearted orphan granddaughter back into life, could sit still long enough to see through the lies, see past the veils—and instead of judging, try to help, really help.

People said, "How could you have stayed with him so long?" The true answer, of course, is that I had the veils. But the answer I gave was, "I loved him." In its way, that answer was true, too. My grandmother understood that.

It wasn't real love. I didn't know that for a long time. Love is a boomerang—it comes back to you. With

Edward, it was a sinkhole. It nearly consumed me, taking every single thing I had, and then some—until I, and everything surrounding me, collapsed.

I have Liam now, so I have learned the difference. And I have my daughter, Rose. The day Rose was born, nine years ago, I was on the run. I had left my home, my grandmother, my beloved Connecticut shoreline where I had always lived, to escape Edward and try to save something of my life. The Connecticut motto is *Qui transtulit sustinet*—"He who transplants sustains."

Leave it to the founding fathers to say "he." Perhaps they knew that "she"—or at least "me"—"who transplants shatters." I left home, pregnant with Rose, and I fell apart. But Rose coaxed the love right from my bones. I built myself back, with the help of Rose and Liam. And, although she wasn't right there in person, my grandmother. She was with me, in my heart, guiding me, every single day while I lived in hiding, in another country, far from home.

You see, my grandmother let me go. She made the ultimate sacrifice for me—gave me and Rose, her great-granddaughter, the chance and means to get away from Edward. She was a one-woman underground railway for one emotionally battered woman. And it cost her so dearly, I don't know whether she will survive.

My name is Lily Malone now. It was my on-the-run name, and it has stuck. I have decided to keep it forever.

Lily, for the orange and yellow daylilies growing along the stone wall of my grandmother's sea garden, waving on long, slender green stalks in the salt breeze. *Malone,* for the song she used to sing me when I was little:

> *"In Dublin's fair city, where girls are so pretty,*
> *I once laid my eyes on sweet Molly Malone.*
> *She wheeled her wheelbarrow through streets broad*
>   *and narrow,*
> *Singing 'cockles and mussels alive, alive-oh.'"*

Those lyrics are so sweet; and because my grandmother sang them to me when I was little and couldn't sleep, they seemed full of life and romance and the promise of unexpected love. I took the name Malone to honor my grandmother's lullaby, but also for a darker reason. The name helps me stay on guard—reminds me that someone once laid eyes on me, too. And like Molly Malone, I was a hardworking woman; he liked that about me. He liked it very much.

I would like to explain my chosen name to my grandmother. I would like to see her again. To introduce her to Liam—and, especially, to Rose.

More than anything, I've come back from my nine-year exile to try to save my grandmother, as she once saved me. I am remembering all this for her. I want to recapture every detail, so I can appreciate exactly what she did for me—for the woman I was, and the woman I have become.

This story is a prayer for her, Maeve Jameson.

It begins thirteen years ago, four years before I left Hubbard's Point for the most remote place I could find—back when I was Mara. Back when I was a rose that bruised so easily.

LUANNE RICE

THE NEW YORK TIMES BESTSELLING AUTHOR OF
DANCE WITH ME

STONE HEART